Tattoo artist June Coffin has another, more hidden talent: she's a Siren who can influence people with the sound of her voice. But in the wake of a murder and shake-up at the Institute of Supernatural Research, her own powers are starting to kill her. The only chance she has of saving herself—as well as her kidnapped brother and best friend—is to become a vampire. But joining the ranks of the vengeful vamp, Occam Reed, is the last thing June wants to do.

Occam isn't the only danger June needs to worry about. Power hungry telepath Robbie Beecher will stop at nothing to gain control over Chicago. He'll destroy anyone who gets in his way—and June's lover, Sam, is high on the hit list since his bid for Mayor. With the city and June's heart being pulled in different directions, it's only a matter of time before the powder keg explodes…and time isn't something June has much of left. With a city on fire, can she rise from its ashes?

Books by Megan Morgan

The Siren Song Series
The Wicked City
The Bloody City
The Burning City

Published by Kensington Publishing Corporation

The Burning City

A Siren Song Novel

Megan Morgan

LYRICAL PRESS
Kensington Publishing Corp.
www.kensingtonbooks.com

First Electronic Edition: July 2016
eISBN-13: 978-1-61650-687-2
eISBN-10: 1-61650-687-3

First Print Edition: July 2016
ISBN-13: 978-1-61650-688-9
ISBN-10: 1-61650-688-1

Printed in the United States of America

For Belle Christian, who is not in fact a sex witch vampire, but my best friend and my forever Chicago companion.

Author's Foreword

This was supposed to be the final book in the Siren Song series, but once I wrote it, I realized June's story was not over and couldn't be wrapped up neatly in this, what was supposed to be the final volume. She's the one who gets what she wants, influential Siren that she is, even though her author wanted to make this a trilogy.

While in the middle of writing this book, I took another trip to Chicago and renewed my love of the city. I took a few pictures of places that show up in the books. I took a sort of virtual tour of June's life and got to know her and the people in her life even better. She's grown a great deal since the first book, increasing in maturity and her own sense of self. She's had to make some tough choices and I've put her through some awful things. I've had great fun developing her through these trials and I hope fans of the series can look back now and see just how much she's grown too.

This won't be the end, I promise. People would hate me if I left it forever dangling on the cliffhanger at the end of this book. I won't do that to you.

If you've been reading this entire series, I thank you deeply for sticking around and continuing with this book. I hope I've entertained you and I hope you've grown to love June and her cohorts as much as I have. I hope I can continue telling this story in a way that keeps readers engaged and makes them happy.

Thank you for reading.

Acknowledgements

To my family and friends who have supported me in every effort over the years. Thank you for listening to me, encouraging me, and believing in me. Also to my wonderful son Cain, who is by far my greatest piece of work.

Chapter 1

On June Coffin's first official day of liberation, the day she could finally show herself to the world without fear of repercussion, she stood in a cemetery under the blazing July sun sweating her ass off—literally. Sweat trickled down the crack of her ass, and she struggled not to squirm.

Despite the venue, the conservative black dress she wore wasn't for mourning but to cover the majority of her tattoos. God forbid she appear anything but vanilla and meek on this day when the Chicago public would turn out to pity her. She'd been shot, hunted, taken prisoner, and unfairly maligned during the past six months, but being digestible for the viewing public remained priority number one.

Maybe liberation wasn't the right word.

Sam Haain, her boyfriend—God, that was weird to say—stood a few yards away in front of a pillar gravestone. He had dressed up too, in a suit and tie. She'd never had a thing for men in suits, but the way he wore his changed her mind. Maybe he'd had it tailored, or maybe he just possessed a body made for a suit. He'd pulled his long dark hair back, because propriety, after all. Their handlers had warned them repeatedly they needed to be "professional and presentable."

"How much time do we have?" she asked Aaron Jenkins, who stood beside her.

Aaron also wore a suit, nearly the same shade of gray as his hair; however, she rarely saw him in less.

"Twenty minutes before we absolutely must be on our way." He squeezed her arm. "I'll wait in the car."

He walked back toward the black limousine parked on the pathway. He hadn't approached the pillar, despite the fact his daughter lay beneath it.

June fanned herself. Her tits were sweating too. Wearing a bra sucked.

She walked over to Sam. His hands were tucked in his pants pockets. He'd taken his sunglasses off, and they dangled out of one pocket, his thumb hooked around them.

"It's nice," June said softly.

The pillar was slender and tapered as it rose, with an ornamental orb on top. The white granite glittered in the sunlight. The words "Mary Ellen Jenkins" had been carved into the base of the stone. June had known her only as Muse, and only heard her real name for the first time after she died.

Muse had been born in 1986. Twenty-eight, a year younger than June.

"Yeah, it's nice." Sam pulled his hand out of his pocket and slipped his arm around her shoulders. "Simple and graceful. She'd like it."

June leaned against his side, her head barely reaching his shoulder. Tall men gave her a reason to like being short.

"And white," June said. "She loved white."

"She didn't, actually. She hated it. She said it made her look like a ghost."

June tilted her face up.

Sam squinted at her. He had a strong jaw and dark eyes, was clean-shaven, and had a copper tint to his skin. Over the past month, as her emotions had grown stronger, his features seemed to stand out clearer in her love-addled vision.

"It was her condition," he said. "Most dyes gave her a rash. Her autoimmune response was out of whack."

June struggled for something to say. So many revelations about Muse. But then, June hadn't really known her. She'd wanted to, more than ever now that she was gone. June regretted deeply she hadn't tried to get to know her better when she was alive.

"Wow." June focused on the pillar. "She suffered a lot, didn't she?"

"She did." Sam's voice was hushed, as hushed as the sprawling somber yard around them. "This is the first time I've gone out to meet the public without her." He wormed his fingers under the shoulder of June's dress. "She won't be there to watch my back. It makes me nervous."

Muse had kept Sam safe with her mindreading, and when necessary, her knives. Going out in public without her made June uneasy as well.

"I doubt anyone will try to hurt us," June said. "After all, we've gone from villains to heroes. The biggest challenge we'll face is resisting the urge to tell everyone to eat shit."

"You should probably let me do most of the talking." He tugged her bra strap.

She swatted his hand. "Stop it. And I plan to say as little as possible."

"I'm sure it's Aaron and me they'll want to talk to the most." He released the strap, making it snap her shoulder. "You look nice, by the way."

She yanked at the sides of her dress, wiggling it down over her hips. The fabric was form fitting and sheer, supposedly to make it cooler. False advertising.

"This is ridiculous," she complained. "I'm the victim. Why do I have to be presentable? I can't believe they told me to take out my piercings too. I didn't take my posts out, though. That's why I have to wear a bra. God forbid anyone sees my nipples."

"They should be honored to see your nipples." He glanced down. "What about the other one? Did you take that out?"

She pushed her sunglasses up her nose. "Of course, because I plan on flashing my vagina at the crowd."

"We'll definitely make front page then."

He pulled her against him and kissed the top of her head. She had her hair pulled up, and at least that looked cute. Her first indulgence once she got out of hiding had been to have her hair done. The light brown roots were gone, all of it a nice solid black again. She'd been tempted to add some unnatural color as well, a few streaks, but ultimately decided against it. After all she'd been through, she wasn't feeling the punk vibe. Her mother would be relieved.

"Are you ready for this?" he murmured against her hair. "It's going to be a circus, you realize."

"No, but it's too much to hope they'd let us get back to our lives in peace. Or, as much peace as possible. Just leave us alone and let us find Robbie and Occam."

Her stomach lurched at speaking the vampire's name. Her brother, Jason, and best friend, Diego, had been Occam's prisoners for over a month now—longer than her brother had been held captive at the Institute. She had to make a choice soon: let Occam turn her into a vampire, or let him end their lives. Not a choice she could even remotely come close to making.

She prayed every day that he held them prisoner as disinterestedly as he'd held Micha Bellevue before them. A dirty mattress and bags of chips for sustenance was better than the other possibilities.

"Of course they can't leave us be," Sam said. "They need to ask us what it was like to be hunted and lied about for months on end. That's the human interest part."

"I wouldn't call that human."

"You realize it will be a long time before our lives get back to normal. Even if we hunt Robbie and Occam down tomorrow. Even if I kill that monster and you get Jason and Diego back."

She looked down at her feet cushioned in the bright green grass, her bare toes peeking from her black flats. She wouldn't risk wobbling around on heels in front of a crowd. Her toenails were painted black, her one "screw you" to the polite world.

"I know," she said. "I don't know that we'll ever be normal again. But I've come to terms with that."

"After today, we'll at least be out of FBI custody."

She lifted her head and took in the graveyard. The world was a cemetery, and in the end, that was where they'd end up. She would make her own gravestone, though.

"We just have to get through this," she said. "So we can begin doing what needs to be done."

He rubbed her back. "Don't worry. I have a little surprise."

"I don't like surprises." She eyed him. "I've had my fill of them."

"You know if I have an audience, I'm going to talk." He slipped his sunglasses on and tugged at the lapels of his jacket. "They should know better than to put me on a stage."

"Sam. What are you planning?"

"Something I've been thinking about for a long time." He looked at the pillar. "Something I discussed with her. She'd be proud."

"Sam."

He smoothed his tie. "You'd better get used to this. They've kept me in the shadows way too long. I'm going to run my mouth all I want. They owe me that."

She put her hands on her hips.

"You should take advantage of it too," he said. "They're giving us a platform to air our grievances."

"Tell me what you're planning. I don't want to be caught off guard."

He smirked smugly. Once, she'd wanted to slap that smirk off his face. She still did, but she would do it lovingly. Despite all the crap he'd been through lately, his self-assured punchy attitude hadn't dulled.

"You should fix your lipstick," he said. "You want to look your best for the gawkers, don't you?"

She touched her lips. "What's wrong with my lipstick? I just put it on before we—"

He swept in and kissed her, hard. She made a sound between an angry yelp and a grunt into his mouth and pushed at his chest. When he stepped back, his lips were smeared with her bright red lipstick.

He wiped his mouth with the back of his hand. "Like I said, fix your lipstick."

She huffed. "Way to be disrespectful, you friggin' meathead. Right on top of her grave."

"She'd be happy for me." He slid his arm around her, and they turned toward the limo. "She got tired of my fuming and swaggering every time I saw you and Micha together. She'd get on me about acting like a man and telling you."

"She...knew?"

"She could read my mind."

Muse and Sam's relationship remained shrouded in mystery, and June couldn't bring herself to press for details. His wound was still raw, and she would not be jealous of a dead woman, especially one who had been so amazing in life.

"I'll come back and put flowers on her grave," he said, "now that I know where it is." He'd asked Aaron this morning, in their hotel room, to bring him before the ridiculous press conference they were about to attend. June suspected he needed a morale boost from "seeing" her.

"I was going to bring some white roses." June glanced over her shoulder. "But now I'll bring something more colorful."

* * * *

Two weeks prior, at Aaron's urging, they had turned themselves over to the FBI. The truth had been confirmed by that time. They were never taken into legal custody, but a protective one, where they were questioned relentlessly and helped the Feds put the final pieces together.

June's role in the investigation was small; still, she must have talked to sixty different people about the same things, answering the same questions over and over. At one point, she asked them why they didn't employ telepaths. The suggestion was met with frowns and blank stares.

A week ago, the whole mess had gone public and the pace of events turned breathtaking.

First, the FBI, in conjunction with the state of Illinois, shut down the Chicago Institute For Supernatural Research pending a thorough investigation of "unethical practices, felony conspiracy and cover up, and crimes against humanity." Researchers were questioned and the governing board—who had not yet appointed a new head to replace Eric

Greerson—faced a huge, nasty federal probe. Warrants were issued for the seizure of all Institute property.

Paranormal folks the city over rejoiced. The various bickering groups actually shook hands and celebrated together. The night it exploded all over the news, she and Sam sat in their hotel room where the FBI kept them and watched in silence. June was too hollow and exhausted to either cry or celebrate.

The end of the Institute was a victory they'd long desired, but it wasn't the only one, and it wasn't the biggest one.

Directly on the heels of this bombshell, the FBI announced Aaron and Sam had been framed for the murder of Eric Greerson. Though the agency didn't release the video of what happened that night—the grisly revelation of Eric's shenanigans, their narrow escape, all the horrible things Eric had used Micha for—someone leaked it on the Internet. This, more than the FBI's statement, quickly turned the public's opinion of Sam and Aaron from murderous demons to avenging angels.

The sudden swell of fame was frightening. Luckily, June remained as always little more than a footnote. Her part in the story, and Jason's part, was mentioned when only the rest of the tale had already been breathlessly passed along.

The Paranormal Alliance—members of which Robbie Beecher hadn't turned to his cause or killed for not joining him—had risen up in glorious, roaring triumph. Sam said he couldn't wait to stand before them again. He would pace the hotel room, telling her what he intended to say to them, how he'd reward them for their loyalty, the whole time gesturing and full of fire. She'd try to coax him into bed to take a little of that fire out on her.

No wonder she had so many feelings, godlike as he was lately.

The FBI placed Robbie at the top of their Most Wanted list. They promised he'd be brought swiftly to justice. They'd find him and make him pay for the massacre in the park as well as the supernatural people he'd killed so the Institute didn't get their hands on them.

June laughed at this. Robbie was not the kind of man to be caught "swiftly." He was not the kind of man to be easily brought to justice, either.

But one could always hope.

She sat in the back of the limo, reapplying her lipstick in a compact mirror. The car slid through the bustling downtown streets of Chicago, beneath the looming towers. For the first time in half a year, the throngs of people and the chugging hub of activity didn't frighten her. She could actually walk among them again, if she wanted to.

"Any leads on Occam?" Sam asked. He spoke to Aaron.

Aaron sat on the bench seat across from them. "No. The vampires are keeping their mouths shut, as usual."

Aaron had people crawling all over the Nocturnal District, but no one was giving up Occam's whereabouts. The house he'd been staying in when she met him sat abandoned. The periodic messages Occam sent her—all handwritten notes—included no clue where they originated. Sometimes they just appeared, which meant he definitely knew her whereabouts.

"I may have to take drastic measures if you want me to continue to press." Aaron drummed his fingers on the seat. "The vampires take exception to our intrusion and they're constantly menacing my operatives."

June snapped her compact shut. "I want you to continue to press. Take drastic measures. I want to find my brother and Diego."

"Sam might not want me to take drastic measures," Aaron said. "I could pull my monetary donations that are still keeping Kevin Kramer safe. Or at least threaten it."

Sam rubbed his fingers over his lips.

"Does Kevin Kramer really mean that much to you?" Aaron asked him.

"He did to my brother," Sam said.

Sam's brother, Thomas, had been Kevin's best friend. When Thomas was murdered, Kevin had enlisted vampires to hunt down and slaughter Thomas's murderers—which they had, apart from one killer who remained unknown. The vampires, callous and careless as they were, would have given away Kevin's involvement without a second thought. Sam asked Aaron to pay them off for their silence. In return, Sam took Muse into his safekeeping to protect her from Aaron's organization, the anti-paranormal Secular Normalists.

Obviously, Aaron didn't need that favor anymore.

Sam squeezed June's hand. "We'll find Occam. It'll be easier now that we can move in the open."

Aaron sighed. "I wish he'd give you more proof he still has them alive before I take drastic measures. Something other than a strand of hair and my watch."

June blinked at him.

"I recognized it. You got it from a box in the attic at the house in Hyde Park. I lived there for a time after my wife passed. All the junk in the attic is stuff I left there when I relocated downtown."

"I gave it to him to hide the scar on his wrist," June said. "It doesn't even work."

Aaron looked out the window. "Something from that time in my life might as well be useful again."

She said nothing, rubbing her stomach. As always, it ached, partly from hunger and partly with the usual burning pain gnawing at her guts.

"Did you eat something this morning?" Sam asked her.

"I managed to keep some applesauce down. And the vitamins."

Since discovering her power would eventually kill her, much the same as Muse's power had been killing her, June lived as if she'd been given a fatal cancer diagnosis. She'd been through every stage of grief multiple times but had yet to find acceptance. She'd spent most of her life battling nausea, pain, and food issues. The added anxiety and dread made it worse.

"I still feel gross every morning," she said. "Maybe it's progressing faster than Occam said it would."

Sam squeezed her hand again. "You've been under a lot of stress lately. It's bound to take a toll on you. Everything is going to work out."

She looked into his eyes. Those dark depths were intense, sincere. He believed that.

"Occam isn't going to win this game," he said softly. "And Robbie isn't going to win his game, either. We're going to be the winners."

"I think you're just feeling smug right now because we've finally got a few punches on our scorecard."

"Or maybe it's because I've finally got you, and you make me feel invincible."

"Ugh." She wrinkled her nose. "I thought I was gonna keep the applesauce down."

He kissed her but didn't try to smear her lipstick this time. A brief, comforting kiss.

They pulled up in front of Tribune Tower on Michigan Avenue. June's heart raced. The beat quickened even more when she took in the crowds gathered outside.

People packed the sidewalks around the building, stretching down the street and across the bridge spanning the Chicago River. One lane had been blocked off and filled with police cars. The police were positioned everywhere, along the barricades cordoning off the crowds, around the building's entrance, in the street itself.

"Oh my God." June stared wide-eyed. "Are they serious?"

Sam was practically vibrating. "Finally, the city is in our favor."

She had attended a press conference once before, when Jason was being held by the Institute, in a ploy to get him back. She was now filled with the same horrifying nervousness as back then, her chest tightening so much she could barely breathe. Attention from huge crowds was not something she craved, yet since coming to Chicago that was all she seemed to get.

"You're gonna do all the talking, right?" she asked in a small voice.

"Have you met me?"

Aaron got on his cell phone. "We've arrived. Pulling up now in the Aston Martin."

June took a deep bracing breath, trying to open her chest up. Her pounding heart rattled all the wind out of her.

Chapter 2

Celebrities must feel this way, only they actually want it. As June walked down the narrow aisle between barricades, plastered to Sam's side and tucked under his arm, she made a mental note: leave the glamorous life to Jason. *He wants to be an actor.* People around them were shouting, waving, taking pictures. Some had signs.

The thought of Jason made her aching stomach worsen.

Sam seemed to eat it up—grasping hands, waving, blowing kisses like a superstar. The police moved them along, hustling them through the commotion. If Sam stopped to sign autographs, she would punch him in the kidney.

They passed through revolving doors and into the building's lobby. Inside, the atmosphere was slightly more subdued.

She had been inside the Tribune Tower lobby once before, when she and Sam met with Chicago's second greatest monster—or monster apprentice—Ethan Roberts. She'd been in disguise that day, in contrast to how all eyes were on her now. Most people in the room were obviously reporters, armed with cameras, recorders, and notepads.

The reprieve from chaos was short-lived. Flashes went off. Shouts rose.

They were directed around the crowd and into a hallway. The hallway was full of people too. Several of the FBI agents they'd been dealing with were there, along with other official-looking people and more police officers.

"Was that really necessary?" she demanded of no one in particular as they were escorted down the hallway. "Why couldn't we be brought in some back way?"

Sam chuckled. "The city needs to see their heroes."

They were ushered into a long high-ceilinged room. More familiar faces appeared. This was where the FBI had set up. These agents had been spending a lot of time with them the past two weeks.

A man stepped up to them. "Right on time." His name was Daniel Morton, the lead investigator on their case. "Good to see you." He shook Sam's hand and then Aaron's. He nodded to her.

She was so insignificant she didn't even warrant a handshake.

"That's quite a crowd," Sam said. He loosened his grip on her, and she forced herself to let go of him as well. "I'm impressed."

"We expected nothing less." Daniel gestured to a blond woman. "This is Mary Rourke. She's the coordinator. She's going to walk you through what will happen today. Remember, you're not to speak about privileged information that might be detrimental to your case or to the investigation at the Institute. If you're pressed with any questions that might force you to reveal sensitive information, simply say you can't talk about it due to the ongoing investigation."

June's head hurt. Her stomach grew queasier by the moment.

"There they are!" a female voice squealed behind them.

June turned. Cindy rushed in, arms open and lifted. She wore a blue dress and gold heels, as if she were going to a nightclub. Her bright red hair hung in loose ringlets on her shoulders. As she hustled over to them, her enormous boobs bounced.

She flung her arms around June. Cindy's heavy flowery perfume didn't abate June's queasiness. Her embrace was soft and overwhelming and all tits.

"That crowd is nuts," Cindy said as she drew back. "And it's all for you." She gave June a once-over. "Damn girl, look at you. That dress fits just right."

"A stylist came by this morning and took care of us," June said. "They made me cover up my tattoos, said it would make me more 'palatable.'"

Cindy huffed. "I'd tell them to kiss my big fat ass. You can save the city, but a tattoo is gonna scare people?"

"I wish I had a big fat ass for them to kiss."

Cindy winked. "Direct them to mine." She turned to Sam and flung her arms open again. "Look at you!"

Sam hugged her. Cindy was as tall as Sam, especially in heels. They looked disturbingly sexy in their embrace. June liked Cindy. She would not stab her.

Cindy even hugged Aaron, though it was a much more delicate, restrained hug. Her perfume lingered in the air, and June tried to subtly inch away before her gag reflex was triggered.

"You okay?" Sam asked June softly. Apparently, she looked as disgusting as she felt.

"I think I need some water." She fanned her face. "And a wastebasket."

Sam swiftly left her side. June located an empty chair. She plopped down in it as Cindy chatted with Aaron and Mary Rourke, the poor unfortunate coordinator patiently waiting for their attention.

At great risk to herself, Cindy had revealed her involvement in their plight and told the FBI everything she knew. She was more acquainted with Robbie than any of them and was able to fill them in on some details. She wouldn't be part of the press conference, merely present for moral support. Sam intended to make her an officer in the Paranormal Alliance as soon as he retook the helm.

The glaring omissions to this celebration stood out in June's mind. Jason and Diego should have been there, but they weren't the only ones. Someone else should get to sit in front of the crowd of reporters and finally be avenged for the sins committed against him.

Micha had been hospitalized and was under guard at said hospital. No one clarified why he was there—hopefully for study and not because his health had deteriorated due to the serum; however, his absence today presented a worrying sign it was the latter.

He deserved this day, and he'd been robbed of that, too.

Sam returned. He held a water bottle in one hand and a small plastic wastebasket in the other. Her hero in a tailored suit.

He plunked the wastebasket on the floor next to her and twisted the lid off the bottle. A few people glanced their way. Just what she needed, more attention.

He handed her the bottle. "Take it slowly."

She took it, smiling weakly. How did she not realize he was such a kind, patient man? Maybe she'd always realized it, but she just didn't want to realize she realized it, because that would mean facing her conflicted emotions. Or maybe he was just nice to broads he dated.

Dating. Were they actually dating? They'd never gone out on a date. They'd never been able to.

"Thanks." She took a tiny drink.

He knelt in front of her. Mary had her hands on her hips, lips pursed, her patience seemingly starting to wane. Sam kept his back to her.

"It's all going to be okay." He touched June's knee. "We'll get through this day, and then we'll start dealing with all the other crap we have to deal with. Just smile for the cameras and look pretty. That won't be hard for you."

"Oh my God." She rubbed her forehead. "If I knew you were like this, I would have run the other way."

"Sorry, you old sea hag. Maybe we should put a sack over your head before we go out there, so you don't scare the small children."

"That's better." She took another sip.

"Mr. Haain?" Mary said. "You have to go out in fifteen minutes. I need to fill you in on what's going to happen."

Sam rose. June stayed in her chair, close to the trash can. At least the vitamins would have absorbed by now. She hoped.

Mary, Aaron, and Cindy walked over to join them, since Sam didn't move from his spot, standing before her like a guardian, or a shield. A puke shield.

Mary looked at Cindy, arching an eyebrow. Cindy didn't seem to notice, stroking her fingers through her curls.

"Cindy," Sam said.

Cindy blinked a few times and then snapped to attention. "Oh!" She squeezed Sam's arm. "I'll see you out there. Knock 'em dead." She made a pouty face at June and blew a kiss to her before hustling out of the room.

"Okay," Mary said. "The conference is being capped at an hour, with only forty-five minutes of questions. Everyone in the audience knows this. Mr. Morton has told me there are things you're not allowed to talk about, so it's better if we keep this short to avoid too much questioning and pressure. If you wish to speak to anyone on the way out, that's your prerogative."

"This is our show today," Sam said. "We get the upper hand, finally."

"I'll present a general overview of the panel, and then you can each have a few minutes to say what you like. After that, we'll open the floor to questions. We do have moderators to keep things running smoothly and weed out any inappropriate pressure."

Sam huffed. "Good luck."

"We don't want this to become a free-for-all. I realize emotions are running high, but try to put your best face forward and we'll try to control the media. After the questions, you may supply some additional closing statements, if you like."

"Who do you work for?" Sam asked her.

This was all about to roll down the proverbial hill and explode.

"I work for the Tribune." She frowned. "I'm the media relations director."

"Then you know who I am," Sam said.

"Of course."

"And you know how we've been treated. Mistreated, I should say. Hunted. Vilified. Maligned."

"Disenfranchised," June added.

"Mr. Haain—"

"This is our day to tell those who ground us under their heels they can go to hell."

"Mr. Haain." Mary glared at him. "While what you've been through is traumatic, I'm sure you know as a public figure there's a certain decorum you must—"

"Never." Sam made a chopping motion with his hand. "If you know me, you know I don't give a damn about decorum. My brand of decorum is to slap them in the mouth if they're running it too much. These folks are going to sit down and listen to me today."

Aaron adjusted his tie. "I think, Mrs. Rourke, you'll agree that holding this press conference was the most foolish thing you could have done. Giving a voice to the wrongfully accused is just throwing more fuel on an already raging fire. A fire we intend to stoke."

She turned her glare on Aaron. "If you turn this into a fiasco, it's on you. Today is about triumph. I would strongly advise you not to turn it into a circus. State your side of the story with dignity and gain their respect."

"I have plenty of dignity." Sam drew himself up. "You're about to see how much dignity I'm capable of."

June's head spun. Their words swirled around her like a tornado. She clutched the bottle. Her mouth watered.

"What's left of the Paranormal Alliance is here," Sam said. "They're here to rally to me, and I will not disappoint them."

Mary drew a breath through her nose. "As I said, we have moderation in place, and that goes both ways, Mr. Haain."

June lurched forward and grabbed the wastebasket. She heaved into it. She didn't have much to bring up except the water, and it sucked. In the midst of her retching, Sam's comforting hand touched her neck. He couldn't have asked for a more attractive girlfriend.

After the puking stopped, she felt immensely better. She remained bent over the wastebasket, though, just in case. She would have to fix her damn lipstick again. She mused she should invent a lipstick line for chronic pukers. The commercials would be awesome.

Sam caressed and squeezed her neck. "Well, that's what we think of your moderation, Mrs. Rourke."

Chapter 3

Sitting in front of the crowd, June vividly remembered the field house at Promontory Point, when she'd had to face the press about her and Jason. A million cameras were focused on them. Eager faces, blinding lights. A constant murmur filling the hush between questions.

Gratefully, most of the attention was directed at Sam. Probably because he wouldn't shut up.

"Mr. Haain," a blond man near the front called out. "What are your thoughts on the massacre that Robert Beecher perpetrated against your group in Jackson Park?"

June rubbed her stomach, avoiding eye contact with anyone in the crowd. She was glad she'd thrown up before she came out.

"What do I think?" Sam snorted. "I think if I get my hands on him, he's going to wish he were in prison instead."

Sam sat in the middle, June on his right, Aaron silent and stoic on his left. June declined to give an opening statement, allowing Sam more floor time. The back of the room was filled with Paranormal Alliance members, and they started clamoring every time he talked.

"I'm grateful for every person who survived him and is here today," Sam said. Shouts rose in the back. "I've vowed to all my people that Robbie will pay for what he did to their fellow members, their friends, their families. He's worse than the Institute. He's insidious, and he destroys his own kind. He doesn't need to be put in prison. He needs to be burned alive like he did to my friends."

June winced. The shouting in the back got louder, mixed with cheering and clapping.

Mary sat tight-lipped to June's right. Just offstage was their squadron of FBI babysitters.

"So what do I think?" Sam spoke over the continuing commotion. "I think I'll send him to Hell where he belongs."

The moderators had to wrangle the crowd back into order—not the first time in the past fifteen minutes. June was watching the time on the big clock on the wall.

The commotion died down, and a woman asked, "Is it true Micha Bellevue isn't here today because he's suffering ill effects from the administration of the serum?" The serum was originally supposed to be kept confidential, but due to the leaked video, that bombshell was impossible to withhold from the public.

Aaron sat forward. "Mr. Bellevue is currently under the care of the Greater Chicago FPS. They will be doing all they can to assist in his examination and study."

The FPS were the Freelance Paranormal Scientists—in other words, "not the Institute"—the organization that Trina worked for.

The reporter added to her question, "Is it true the serum worked, and Mr. Bellevue is a normal who is now exhibiting paranormal symptoms?"

Aaron spoke as they'd been taught to. "We are not at liberty to discuss that at this time."

"Symptoms?" Sam said. "Did you just say paranormal symptoms?"

Mary interrupted. "We should move on to the next question."

Hands shot up.

A reporter stood. "Is it true what Mr. Bellevue has told the press? That the research his wife conducted on vampires was entirely fabricated by her, and that she was working in collusion with the Institute to perpetuate lies about and toward the paranormal community?"

June glanced at Sam. They couldn't blow apart that story, not if they wanted to get Jason and Diego back in one piece.

"It's true," Sam said. "At least from what I understand and the things Mr. Bellevue told me while we were in seclusion. I'm sure we'll learn much more about all the Institute's lies in the coming months. I wouldn't put anything past them."

June looked down.

"Ms. Coffin."

She lifted her head and stared into the crowd. A man toward the front had addressed her.

"Your brother," the man said. "The case against the Institute states that he was held prisoner there, while you managed to escape. Why is he not here today to talk about his role in the crimes committed against you?"

She'd told the FBI Jason left Chicago a long time ago and she no longer had contact with him, nor knew his whereabouts. They wanted to question him. She and Sam had agreed setting the FBI on Occam would sign Jason and Diego's death sentences. Occam didn't seem the kind of vampire to react well if the Feds swooped down on him.

She cleared her throat. "He didn't want to speak today. He's suffered enough during this ordeal."

Sam reached under the table and squeezed her thigh. "June and her brother have both suffered enough. They were victims, as so many of us were. She was forced to lie in January, at the press conference with Eric Greerson, to save her brother." He looked over at their babysitters. "I trust the FBI will get justice for both of them and for every paranormal person wronged by that despicable place."

Several encouraging shouts sounded from the back. Sam kept his hand on her thigh.

"What about you, Ms. Coffin?" the man followed up. "What have these past six months been like for you?"

She boggled. Everything she wanted to say would get her in trouble. Suddenly, everyone in the room stared at her, every camera focused on her.

"Um...it was..."

"What do you think it was like?" Sam snapped. "We've been hunted, menaced, lied about, mistreated—"

"Mr. Haain," Mary said. "Please let Ms. Coffin answer the question, if she wants to."

Sam snapped his mouth shut. June took a deep breath. Her chest wouldn't expand far.

"I've been through a lot." She didn't make eye contact with anyone. "I've been taken prisoner. I've been shot. I watched people die. People I cared about." She swallowed. "It sucked." She focused on the man. "It really, really sucked, if you wanna know."

Sam removed his hand from her thigh and rubbed her shoulder.

"But I stayed when I could have left." She looked down. "Because we were fighting for something important. The truth."

Sam stilled his hand.

"And Sam and Aaron didn't deserve the lies that were told about them. I had to stick around and see their names cleared."

"We were struggling in solidarity," Sam said. "June was invaluable to our plight. She was invaluable to me. She still is."

A hushed murmur passed through the crowd. At least they had something new and less horrible to gossip about.

"My story isn't the important one," June said. "Robbie needs to pay. And so does the Institute."

The moderators returned to fielding questions. Sam continued dominating the panel. Aaron announced he was in the process of dismantling the SNC. His intention was to filter any willing members into the Paranormal Alliance, since for the first time Sam was opening the group to normals in the form of a "normal allies" branch.

This announcement met with some derision from the back of the room.

"It's in our best interests," Sam explained. "In fact, I'd like to announce that on Saturday, four days from now, we will be having a gathering at North Avenue Beach, starting at noon. I welcome all good-standing members of the Paranormal Alliance and our future allies from the Secular Normalists to attend and get to know each other."

June blinked. This was the first she'd heard about a beach party. Aaron stared at him too, gaping.

"We'll be having an overnight gathering," Sam said. "Food, friends, camping, unity. I want us to come together and see that to win our fight we need help and solidarity. The coming months are going to be trying as we search for Robbie and watch the Institute go up in flames."

Was this his big announcement? It certainly seemed to stir up the crowd.

June leaned toward him. "We're going camping on a beach?" she whispered.

"Hope you like that sort of thing."

"I don't."

The rest of the questions largely centered around what they'd been up to the past six months, where they'd been, and how they managed to prove their innocence. Many of these questions they weren't allowed to answer.

Mary kept to her word, and at forty-five minutes, questions were halted. June breathed a sigh of relief. She declined to give a closing statement, but Aaron spoke.

"I would like to thank those who supported us through this ordeal," he said. "Those who believed in us and would not accept the lies that were being told about us. We have sacrificed…so much, but it's good to see justice finally being served. I hope the Institute will pay for the crimes they've committed against the paranormal community, and that Robert Beecher will be quickly found and brought to justice. And I hope, in some small way, this cleanses some of the sins left over from my father's negative, oppressive legacy."

The crowd applauded. June sipped from the water bottle she'd been given.

Sam rose to his feet, arms spread wide. The applause died off.

"I would just like to say," he said loudly, the microphone on the table still picking him up, "that the members of the Paranormal Alliance who supported me through this and who saw so many of their friends and family suffer at the hands of that monster will be rewarded for their loyalty and pain. I will make sure you have bright and prosperous futures and that no one will ever put his foot on your neck again."

Wild applause and hollering erupted from the back of the room.

"There will be many programs put in place this year to help you. I plan to funnel more funding into our outreach and education programs and have more charity drives to help those who were affected in Jackson Park. Additionally, I plan to set up programs to help those who suffered at the hands of the Institute."

The entire room applauded this time. June clapped quietly as well.

"And"—he lifted a hand—"I have one more very big announcement that you might enjoy."

Every camera and gaze focused on him. He took a dramatic pause.

"I'm throwing my hat back in the political ring. This election season, I'm running for mayor."

June was taking a drink, and she choked. The crowd lost their collective shit, from the hyper-excited ones in the back to the gasping, baffled reporters. The entire room exploded in an uproar. Sam stood smug, jerking the lapels of his jacket.

"What?" June croaked at him.

They were ushered out in a flurry of shouted questions and taken back to the room where they'd been before the press conference.

A distinct squealing followed them in.

"You're running for mayor?" Cindy flung her arms around Sam's neck. "You've got my vote!"

"What the hell?" June goggled at him. "You haven't said anything about this."

"I've been mulling it over," Sam said. "I miss politics. The iron is hot right now. It's a good time to strike. Public opinion has never been more in my favor."

"Or in your favor at all," Aaron said dryly. "My God, Sam."

Cindy clasped her hands under her chin, beaming at June. "You could be the first lady of Chicago!"

June cringed.

Sam chuckled. "Now, there's no saying I'll win. But I've decided. Why not give it a shot?" He winked at June. "Wouldn't be the first Jew in charge."

"You're not a Jew, as you explained." June squeezed the bridge of her nose. "I don't— How are you even gonna run a campaign right now?"

"And what's this about the beach?" Aaron asked. "Can you just do that? Don't you need a permit to have something like that? I mean, I know we discussed a get-together, briefly."

Sam huffed. "I'm on the Metropolitan Pier and Exposition Authority. Pretty sure my seat is available and I'll come back to open arms."

"We didn't discuss this." Aaron glared at him.

"We'll discuss it tonight." Sam turned to June and offered his arm. "Don't you want to be seen on the arm of the most loved man in the city right now?"

"I don't know. Is there room for me next to your ego?" She took his arm. "Can't we wait to leave until everyone else does?"

"Oh, they're not going anywhere."

They were ushered out, surrounded by police officers. Cindy and Aaron followed June and Sam. As soon as they stepped into the outer room, the chaos renewed. Sam slipped his arm around her and waved to the crowd.

"We love you Sam!" a girl screamed. "You have our vote!" She wore a blue shirt.

Like every other cause on the planet, the city had adopted a color as a show of support—for some reason, blue. Blue like they were feeling all those months, June supposed.

Someone else yelled, a man's voice. "This is a cover-up! The CIA is turning Micha Bellevue into a weapon!"

June stopped short.

The man who yelled had glasses and a long ponytail. He widened his eyes as June focused on him.

"Are you the conspiracy blogger guy?" June hollered over. "I love your stuff! It kept me entertained all those months."

He gaped at her.

"You were wrong, though!"

Sam pulled her away.

Outside, the screams were deafening. Cops kept a clear aisle between the onlookers, the crowd barely being held back by the barricades. At the end of the aisle—what seemed like miles away—their car sat at the curb.

June feared one of Robbie's supporters would be lurking in the crowd. If Sam went up in a pillar of flame, she would cling to him, because she didn't want to live in a world where things like that became an everyday occurrence.

She held her breath as they were hustled down the aisle. People grabbed at them. Sam touched their hands. He kept one arm firmly around her, so she at least had a place to hide. Her heart raced and her mouth was dry. Hopefully, all the water she'd drunk wouldn't come back up in front of everyone.

That would be festive on the front page of the newspaper.

They had nearly reached the car when someone grabbed her hand, which she'd foolishly left dangling at her side. She panicked and tried to yank it away. Something was shoved into her palm, and the hand released her. She almost flung away whatever it was, but she glanced down at it.

A small folded piece of paper. Surely some schlub hadn't just given her his phone number.

She wrenched her head around, trying to see who it was, but so many faces swam in her vision.

They reached the open back door of the car. Sam took his arm from around her and gently nudged her inside. He didn't need to, though. She scrambled in.

Cindy climbed in next, followed by Sam, and then Aaron. June scooted over as far as she could on the seat. Cindy sat across from her, next to Aaron, and Sam at her side. When the door slammed shut, June sagged, the commotion outside muffled. People huddled around the car, but they were all cops and FBI.

"This is so exciting!" Cindy clutched her hands to her chest. "Oh my God, Sam, listen to them. You're gonna be mayor without question."

Sam gripped June's arm. "You okay?"

"I am now. I'm not cut out for the limelight."

"You guys sounded great up there, though." Cindy leaned over and squeezed June's knee. "You handled those questions like a pro."

"Some of us more than others." Aaron eyed Sam.

June plucked the paper out of her palm.

"What's that?" Sam asked.

"Someone shoved this in my hand when we were walking through the crowd." She unfolded it. "It's probably a love letter for you."

Cindy laughed. "Do you like me, future Mr. Mayor? Check yes or no."

It was a torn sheet of notebook paper. Her brain recognized the handwriting before she read the words.

Good job holding up Micha's end of the bargain. I'm going to be a very busy man for the next couple days. If you call out for me, I may be slow, but I'll come.

The note was signed "O."

June lurched forward and stared out the window. Her heart pounded against her ribs, her breath short, gunshot wound aching.

"What is it?" Sam grabbed the paper from her.

"Occam was here."

Chapter 4

June sat on the bed in their hotel room—home for the past two weeks—staring blankly out the window at the city. She held the note. Sam was in the other room of the suite with Aaron, receiving their final instructions from the FBI.

A hand squeezed her shoulder. "So they're finally cutting you loose."

Trina stood over her. Her dark hair was pulled back and she had glasses on, the whole effect very mom-like. She held a plastic bottle out to June. "I brought you some more vitamins. Have you been keeping them down?"

Since the FBI had sequestered them, June hadn't been able to go to Trina's facility for an extensive battery of tests—something she was apprehensive about, anyway, given her past with scientists. In the meantime, Trina had prescribed her an intense vitamin regimen to help with the malnutrition from not being able to put most food in her mouth.

June took the bottle. "Most of the time. They don't irritate my stomach too much. That has to be a miracle in itself."

Trina knelt in front of her. "We're going to find a way to fix you. I'm good at what I do. We'll figure this thing out and reverse it."

June didn't bother to argue that no paranormal person dying from their powers had ever been saved—at least, not according to the extensive research June had done on the Internet.

"I want to believe you." June spoke softly. "The alternative is much worse."

"So what's the plan? Where are you going? What are you going to do?"

"There are still rules we have to play by. We're not allowed to leave Chicago, which means I'm not going home."

"Where will you go?"

"Sam says his house is still his. They froze all his assets and took over his property when this all went down, but it's getting transferred back to him. I guess… We'll stay there." She looked up at Trina. "You haven't heard anything from Occam, have you?"

Trina shook her head. "No vampires around the clinic. I can't say I'm disappointed."

June held out the note. "Someone slipped this to me today, when we were leaving the press conference."

Trina took it, read it, and frowned. "It's from Occam?"

"That's his handwriting. Either he was there or one of his minions was. He's still watching me. Waiting for me to send a message that I'm ready to be his vampire bride."

Trina scowled. "I hate him. I hate his smug, stupid fanged face. I hate the way he controls our governing board."

"As long as I don't say no, he won't hurt them." She gazed out the window again. "As long as he thinks I'm still weighing my options, he'll keep them dangling on a hook. The second I say no, I'll probably find them dead on my doorstep."

Trina handed back the note. June tossed it on the bed, along with the vitamin bottle. She had no way of tracking him. Just another taunt. A reassurance his eyes were on her always, watching.

"I hate that Jason is being held prisoner again," June said. "I hate that this has been his life. That I have to play superhero and rescue him again."

Trina squeezed June's knee. "You'll get them back. And Occam's bullshit will catch up to him one day. You can't be a jerk for several lifetimes and not have it snap back on you eventually. Listen." She stood. "Take the weekend to settle in and acclimate yourself. Monday, come to the clinic. We'll start running tests."

June looked up at her. "How's Micha? Can you tell us why he's in the hospital now?" She kept her voice down.

"Being studied." Something about the tone of her voice whispered of a lie. "He's tired a lot. He's been through so many tests."

"Is he sick?"

"Not any more than usual."

She was certainly lying.

"Do you think…I could get in to see him?"

Trina hesitated. "Maybe. I could talk to some people, see if I can get you a visit. They probably won't let you stay long, though."

"That's okay. I just need to see him. See that he's okay."

"I'll see what I can do." She patted June's shoulder. "Please be careful out there. This city is still an ugly place."

"Believe me, I know."

Trina left. A short time later, Sam walked into the bedroom.

"So we're being released into the wild." He sat down beside her. "We're free to go. For the first time since January, we're normal everyday citizens. We can walk the streets again. Hallelujah."

The July sun seemed too bright. Snow had been falling when she arrived in Chicago, the air so icy she could barely breathe. Now it was too hot to breathe. She could never breathe.

This moment was epic. She should feel something profound and a vast overwhelming sense of relief. Trumpets should sound. Angels should descend and bestow orgasms upon her. The world should shift into focus.

Instead, she felt numb.

"I don't think we'll ever be normal everyday citizens," she said. "Especially not you, Mr. Politician."

"That *was* my normal everyday life." He squeezed her arm. "What about you?"

"I don't get to go back to mine, remember?"

They were silent.

"What if you could?" he asked softly. "What if your brother and friend weren't prisoners, and the FBI would let you leave the state. Would you go home?"

She didn't know the answer to that, and she hated not knowing the answer to that.

"You're always trying to get me out of your hair." She winked at him. "Haven't you learned by now that doesn't work?"

He leaned over and rested his chin on her shoulder. "Even if I win? You won't ditch me?"

She was surprised, deep down, he would want her to stay by his side if he became mayor. She didn't know why that surprised her. Feelings were complicated. They were more annoying than vampires.

"I don't know anything about politics." She frowned. "Or relationships. I'm just gonna put that out there right now, so you know what you're getting into."

"I know the politics part. Guess we'll have to learn the rest together."

The FBI granted them a private car to take them to Sam's house. Aaron would get his own, to take him elsewhere. June gathered up her things. She didn't have much, as months on the run had instilled a certain sense of minimalism in her. At least a private car would help them move discreetly and keep them away from reporters.

They left the hotel through a private exit, also good—not that anyone outside the FBI and their trusted friends knew where they were. Into another car, to take another ride. She still didn't feel free.

"It's good they gave your house back." She slumped against Sam's side in the backseat. This time it wasn't a limo, merely a big car with a driver. "And they're unfreezing your assets."

"They know what's good for them. I'm already going to file so many civil suits their heads will spin. I'm sure my lawyer is drooling right now, and I haven't even called him yet."

"Does it really matter? It's over. We're never going to make them pay for what was done to us. You might as well save the effort."

"It's the only way we can make them pay. We'll never be justly compensated, but goddamn it, we will be compensated."

She didn't care about money. All her "assets" were probably long gone: the shop, her place, her car. If her mother was still paying rent on the shop, she would strangle her as soon as she got her hands on her again. After she finished hugging her a lot.

They left the hotel parking lot. They weren't far from Tribune Tower, just a few blocks. She was paranoid someone might have followed them.

"What are we going to do first?" She had Occam's note in her bag. "Where do we even begin? We have to find two people who are very good at not being found."

"Don't worry, I have a few ideas."

They drove through the city and out into the suburbs, the residential areas blending together. Apart from asking a few directions, the driver didn't speak. She and Sam didn't say much, either. June was tired, hungry as always, and she'd had way too much excitement for one day—for one lifetime, really.

They ended up in a neighborhood full of huge fancy houses, definitely the rich section of town. The car slowed and turned onto a driveway with a gate blocking it and high white stone walls obscuring the property beyond. The gate was wrought iron, arched at the top, and peaked with spires, like something out of a movie.

Sam sat forward. "I don't have the remote for the gate, obviously. I'll have to get out and open it."

"I'll do it," the man said. "Sit tight."

He put the car in park and got out. He unlatched the gate and pushed one side, making it swing open.

"You live in, like, a mansion?" June asked.

"No." Sam had grown strangely still. "I wouldn't call it that."

The driver climbed back in, and they pulled up through the gate onto a concrete driveway.

The driveway stretched in front of them and curved to the left up ahead. All she could see at first were trees and hedges and flowers landscaped like a tailored forest; however, once they drove around the bend, the massive house in front of them made her gasp.

"This isn't a mansion?"

Sam squeezed her hand. "I can't believe I'm home." He gazed at the house, his face an unreadable mask, but his eyes shone.

She tried to imagine walking into her apartment again, into her shop. She tried to imagine even standing on the street outside. She would probably fall apart.

She nuzzled his shoulder. "I'm happy for you. I'm happy for both of us."

"I'd given up hope I'd ever come home. Or I'd even have one to come back to." He leaned over and kissed her. "Welcome to my life."

The implication overwhelmed her. They'd known each other for many months, they'd shared hardships, but they didn't know each other. She didn't know Sam's life—who he was outside the fight, the things that made him the person he was. She was afraid she might not like them. She might use this newfound knowledge as an excuse to run. Because really—a rich, charismatic politician, who wouldn't have looked twice at her in the real world? She'd gone insane, or he had.

The house had multiple stories, but the number was unclear because it was architecturally complex, as if someone had put a bunch of Lego blocks together haphazardly. Tall windows looked down from its white stone façade. The roof was brown slate. As they pulled up in front of a long garage with three doors, she caught a glimpse of glimmering blue through the trees, a swimming pool. A set of stone steps led from the driveway to the house.

"My cars better be in the garage," Sam said. "If I don't get all my property back, hell will be raised."

They climbed out, stepping into the summer heat slightly cooled by the canopy of leaves. The driver popped the trunk.

"I think you'll like it here." Sam pulled their bags out. "I don't know if the pool is useable. I'm sure it hasn't been cleaned and treated. But there's a Jacuzzi, a gym, and a patio on the back of the house. Nice sun back there."

"Great. So I can get on the treadmill and then get a tan." She took her duffel bag from him. "I'll be the picture of health in no time."

Sam swung his bag over his shoulder. "If I can get my staff back, I'll also have a cook who can probably make things you can actually eat." He slid an arm around her shoulders. "Not to mention I'm pretty sure the place needs a good cleaning."

"Heaven forbid you cook and clean. But now you got a woman to do that, right?"

Sam turned to the driver. "Thank you." He held out a hand. The driver shook it.

"Thanks," June said. Maybe they should tip him, but they didn't have any money. She'd forgotten what money even looked like.

They stood in the driveway as the car backed up and drove off. The FBI would be sending a security detail before nightfall to watch the house—to keep people out, and probably keep them in. Though they were free, they weren't completely free.

"This is so weird," June said. "We don't have to hide."

"Yet I still feel like hiding."

"So do I."

They climbed the stairs, Sam going first. June followed, admiring the view of the grounds—and his ass, which was nice. Must be that gym.

The front of the house had a wide wraparound porch, and they crossed this to a set of wooden double doors with stained glass panels. The glass was decorated with blooming flowers.

"This is nice," June said, while Sam dug into his pocket. She tilted her head. "This glass…"

"Tiffany." He pulled out a set of keys. "Like the glass in the gallery at the pier."

The glass he'd shown her. It seemed like ages ago now—the one with the angel guiding someone into death, the one that made him think of his brother.

He unlocked the door. "This is surreal for me."

It was for her, too.

Chapter 5

She expected the inside of the house to be as ridiculously overblown as the outside, and she wasn't disappointed. The rooms were huge, with high ceilings, gleaming dark woodwork, and arty, tasteful décor. If this wasn't a mansion, she wasn't a spindly ragged little dying girl.

Sam dropped his bag in a chair. "Home sweet home."

The place had an empty feel, the air stale and still.

"At least they didn't gut the place." He walked over to a wall of windows and pulled the curtains across to open them. Dust billowed and danced in the sunlight that streamed in.

The windows looked out on the pool. A layer of green slime ringed it, and leaves floated on the surface.

"Ugh." Sam grimaced. "It'll cost me a fortune to get that cleaned out." He turned in circles, seeming lost. "I don't know if the cable is still hooked up, but you can enjoy the outdoors, I guess. There are walking paths and gardens all over the property. I'm sure things are overgrown."

She wrapped her arms around his waist. "We'll get it fixed up. It's gonna take time."

"And money. I need to talk to my accountant and find out what I have access to."

"I'm not worried about cable or a sucky pool." She rubbed his lower back. "This is the Taj Mahal compared to how we've been living lately. At least here we can go outside, and we don't have to take turns doing guard duty."

"True enough."

They walked into an enormous kitchen done in blue and green, the appliances gleaming stainless steel. Most of the cupboards and drawers were open, things strewn all over the place and heaped on the counters. Boxes and bins sat on the floor.

Sam slumped. "They went through everything in the damn house and were nice enough to not put it back."

"At least it's still here." She was trying hard to be positive for him. Had they trashed her apartment too?

Sam flipped a switch next to the doorway. Nothing happened.

"Of course." He glared at the light fixture. "'You can have it all back, Sam, but we're not cleaning it up or turning your utilities back on.' I don't even want to look in the refrigerator right now."

"Listen, don't worry about this mess right now. Make a list of people you need to call and start calling them. We'll get this sorted." When the hell had she turned into a crisis management expert?

"That means the security system isn't working, either. That makes me nervous. Being free also means we're targets for Robbie and Occam."

"We still have our guns, right?"

"Yes, I stashed them while we were in the hotel room. I wasn't letting the FBI take them, registered or not."

While Sam made phone calls, she explored the house.

She climbed a wide staircase to a floor as big and fancy as the downstairs. The floor contained five bedrooms and two giant bathrooms, one at each end of the hallway. Who the hell needed five bedrooms and two bathrooms when he lived alone? Did he have tons of sleepovers?

She peeked inside each of the bedrooms. They were all in disarray, but not as much as downstairs, as they seemed to be guest rooms. Sam wouldn't keep anything personal in a guest room. One was bigger than the others, the size of two of her own bedrooms combined, with French doors leading to a balcony. The master suite. Sam obviously didn't sleep there, though she would have taken it for herself in a heartbeat. She discovered he slept in a room across the hallway, smaller and more humble, if any of the massive rooms could be considered humble.

A huge bed sat in the middle of the room, draped in cream and hunter green blankets. The rest of the space was occupied by a wardrobe, a vanity, desk, and several armchairs. The colors in the room matched the bed. An en suite was attached.

The room was a mess. More bins full of books and folders sat on the floor. The bins were marked with tabs, the word "Haain" and numbers written on them. The sight made her skin crawl, and it wasn't even her stuff.

His clothes appeared expensive, even in heaps on the floor. Inside a walk-in closet, some of his jackets and shirts were still hanging, and he had racks of shoes. The more she saw, the smaller she felt. What the hell was a guy like him doing with her?

She stood in the middle of the room, sunlight flooding in as the curtains were open. For the ransackers to see by, of course, since there was no electricity. The room didn't smell like Sam at all. Too many months had passed.

Several framed photographs sat on top of the dresser. June picked one up and wiped dust from the glass.

The picture was of a younger Sam, along with, she assumed, his parents. Sam wore a suit, his hair pulled back. His father looked like an older version of him, though he had short hair and darker skin. She could see the Israeli heritage in him. His mother was fair-skinned with long, dark hair. Sam stood between them, their arms around him. His father had his arm around another man on his opposite side. This man looked a lot like Sam too—his brother.

June had seen him before.

She stared at the picture. She had questions for Sam.

She set the picture down and looked at the other ones. A picture of his parents sitting on a bench on Navy Pier in front of Lake Michigan. Another picture of his brother—something official looking, a headshot.

A picture of Sam and Muse.

They seemed to be at a party. Sam wore a suit, and Muse looked shockingly different, her hair in a cute pixie bob, white as ever, and she wore a white evening gown. They were both holding glasses of champagne. Muse was smiling, hugely. June never saw her smile like that. They looked like a happy couple.

"I'm sorry," June whispered. "I'll try to do right by him."

Something shuffled outside the doorway, and she turned. Guilt washed over her for being in his room, snooping through his things.

"Sorry, just being a creeper. I—"

She fell silent. No one was there.

She walked over to the doorway and peeked out. Sam wasn't in the hallway.

"Sam?"

No reply.

For some reason, Rose swam into her head. The back of her neck prickled. She hadn't seen her since the night in Occam's attic, when Micha made June summon her. But then, Rose had a habit of disappearing for a long time and popping back up when June least expected her.

Rose wasn't lurking around, though. Not that she could see.

With the place sitting empty all those months, maybe mice had moved in. Sam needed to add an exterminator to his call list.

She walked back downstairs. Sam was talking on the phone in the kitchen, his voice carrying in the quiet house. They'd gotten new phones from the FBI, sort of a pity present. She hadn't even turned her phone on yet.

She found the Jacuzzi—empty, the tiled room around it smelling distinctly of mildew. The gym next to it was full of home equipment: a treadmill, stationary bike, weight bench, and elliptical. Two walls of the room were windows looking out on an overgrown garden. The other two were floor-to-ceiling mirrors.

She stood in front of one of the mirrored walls. She looked gaunt and pale in her black dress, like a TV vampire.

"What a catch," she murmured, wiggling her bra around under her dress.

She wandered back to the kitchen.

Sam had pulled a stool up to the counter next to the stove and was hunched over on the phone and writing things down. He'd taken off his jacket and shoes, his bare feet perched on the bottom rung of the stool, his shirt half unbuttoned. His hair was pulled back in a sloppy knot. His casual appearance struck her as sexy as hell.

Eventually, he dropped the phone on the counter and rubbed the bridge of his nose.

She walked over to him. "Getting anywhere?"

He sighed. "They're going to turn the electric and water on sometime today, hopefully. There's enough in my primary bank account. I can take care of that. Is the rest of the house trashed too?"

She nodded. She didn't want to bring up the pictures of his brother right now. He had enough on his mind.

"Also," he said, "my old assistant is coming over. She's thrilled to quit her new office job and come back to my employ. She's going to bring over a generator. Cindy will bring us some groceries and bottled water. I don't think we're ready to drive to the store and walk around out in public."

"I can just imagine the attention we'd get if we did. No thanks." She stepped closer to him. "How come all your helpers are women, huh?"

He grabbed her around the waist, spread his legs, and pulled her against him. "Is that jealousy I hear?"

She huffed, draping her arms over his shoulders.

"My personal trainer was a man. So is my accountant."

"Do you do anything for yourself, Daddy Warbucks?"

He titled his head. "Hmm…no. I mean, there was even that busty blond model who used to give me my baths."

She pinched a nipple through his shirt. "Your sense of humor is coming back. That's good." He hadn't been quite as snarky since Muse's death.

"I'm not really into busty blondes." He squeezed her ass. "I like tattooed, pierced, small-breasted women."

"Which reminds me." She bent her arms around behind her and struggled to undo the clasp on her bra. "I never wear these things. I don't know how they work. I'm a useless female."

"Allow me. I'm an expert." He tugged the shoulders of her dress down. Instead of undoing the bra through the dress or reaching under, he peeled the entire top of the dress down to her waist, revealing the black silk bra and all her ink, carefully hidden away lest it scandalize the public. He slid his arms around her and popped the clasp on the bra, his face close to hers, smiling.

"When is your assistant coming over?" she asked.

"Not for a few hours. She has to quit her job first."

He pulled the bra down her arms, and she breathed a sigh of relief. She didn't know how gals like Cindy did it.

Sam tossed the bra on the floor and cupped her boobs. He wiggled the posts through her nipples, making her bite her lip.

She glanced at his phone on the counter. "Should we be doing this right now?" Surely he had a million more calls to make.

"There's not a damn thing else to do in this house."

He wrapped his arms around her waist, and getting to his feet, lifted her. She locked her legs around his waist and her arms around his neck. This wasn't the first time he'd picked her up like this, and each time it was a little less cheesy and a lot more hot.

He carried her to an adjacent room, a sunroom with a slanting glass roof and three windowed walls looking out on thick foliage. Dappled sunlight filled the room. He walked her over to a wooden-framed couch with mint green cushions and deposited her on it. The cushions were soft, but a cloud of dust billowed up.

June coughed, waving her hand.

"How romantic." Sam waved his arm as well. "Am I impressing you yet?"

She didn't care about the house. She was more impressed with other things. "You better go grab your bag."

He left the room. While he was gone, she sat up and slapped the cushions, getting more dust out of them.

Sam returned with his duffel bag, dropped it next to the couch, and crawled on top of her. She undid the rest of the buttons on his shirt.

He wiggled the dress off over her hips. She was glad to get out of it too. She had black panties on underneath.

"Now you can get on birth control." He tossed the dress on the floor. "Make this much easier." He pressed his hand over the crotch of her panties.

She opened her thighs. "Probably could have before now, but I wasn't asking Aaron to send a gynecologist over."

He tugged her panties aside and stroked his fingers up her slit, watching her face. "My, aren't we excited?"

She was.

She popped the button on his pants and gripped his firm cock through them. "Likewise. Maybe I like you in your natural environment."

"I was hoping you would."

He pushed a finger into her, and she clenched around it with a soft gasp. He gently massaged her piercing with his thumb. He was getting good at manipulating that thing. She'd taught him well.

He kissed her, and then ducked his head, bit gently at a nipple, and flicked the post through it with his tongue. He was getting good with those too.

She stared through the ceiling at the leaves, the sunlight glittering between them. Everything was so quiet, and his finger made sloppy wet sounds inside her. They hadn't fooled around much lately, given the FBI were nearly constantly in the room with them.

Sam sat up and opened his pants, his cock pushing his underwear out. He then tugged her panties down and off.

"At last, I have you naked in my house." He tossed the panties over his shoulder.

"And look at you, just sitting there with your clothes still on like a chump."

He peeled his unbuttoned shirt off. She admired his broad chest, his thick biceps, the flat plane of his stomach, and that delicious hip V. He could get back to working out before he lost any of it.

He tossed his shirt aside but didn't finish undressing. Instead, he pushed her knees back and buried his face between her legs.

She gripped a handful of his hair and pushed her hips up to the heat of his mouth, to the soft, wet probing of his tongue. He pushed two fingers into her this time and worked them harder and deeper. She dug her heels into his back, curling her toes.

"Oh, shit." She gripped his hair tighter, pulling. "Sam, fuck."

She craved more than his fingers inside her. They were nice, but she wanted to be fucked. After a minute, she pushed at the top of his head, her feet on his shoulders.

He lifted his head, his fingers still inside her, chin glistening. "Want me to stop? We've actually got plenty of time for foreplay, for once."

"We do. But right now, all I want to do is bang. Grab a condom."

He slipped his fingers out of her. "As my lady commands." He practically fell off the couch reaching for his duffel bag.

"Not that I wasn't enjoying that. You're wonderful."

"I know."

He pulled a condom out of the duffel bag, stood, and worked his pants and underwear off. She admired the rest of his toned body, and of course, his magnificently thick, currently rock hard cock. She rolled over on her stomach.

"Oh, like that, huh?" The condom wrapper crinkled.

As Sam knelt behind her, she crawled forward and propped her arms on the wooden arm of the couch. She spread her legs, dipping her back, ass in the air. She looked over her shoulder, her hair coming out of the pins and sliding across her back.

"Yes," she said, "like this."

She caught the faint scent of latex. She'd had him bare a few times, at first, when they were too full of hormones and too dumb to wait for protection. She wanted to feel that again. Soon, their lives might be in some sort of order and she could.

He gripped her hips and she closed her eyes, tense with expectation.

"I like you like this," he murmured. "All turned on and dirty." He caressed her back. In his other hand, he gripped his cock and pressed it against her.

"Oh, yeah," she gasped. "Put it in."

He slid into her with one smooth stroke, filling her up, the pressure so good it bordered on pain. He settled in deep, bringing his hips flush against hers.

She moaned, loud and full-throated, dropping her head on her arms. She squeezed around his length, loving being crammed full of it.

"Better now?" He rubbed her quivering thigh.

"No." She pushed back against him. "Fuck me."

And bless his beautiful cock, he did. He thrust into her, rocking her on her knees and making her clutch the arm of the couch for support. She moaned—hell, she screamed. He smacked her ass, firm and stinging, and even though it was totally a porn move, she loved it.

He leaned over her back and tucked his hand beneath her. "That what you wanted?" His voice was husky and dark. He pressed his fingertips to her ring and rubbed.

"Oh my God, yes." She reached down, dropping her head against the cushion, and slid her hand over his. "Sam, Sam…"

He fucked her deep and slow now. She tangled her fingers with his, helping him rub. She tightened around him, on the brink.

He rolled his hips, his muscles trembling and skin slick. He was close too. She ached to feel his release, to experience again when he filled her with it and it trickled down her thighs. So dirty and scandalous.

"I want you to come," he said. "Right on my cock."

She clenched her teeth, whining through them, eyes squeezed shut.

"Come on," he urged. "You need to come. I can feel it."

She almost wanted to draw the pleasure out, make it go on forever. But she couldn't hold back, not with him thrusting so deep inside her, not with both their fingers working her. Not with those words rolling off his tongue.

She pressed her face into the cushion and shrieked as the orgasm rocked her. Her entire body convulsed. She clenched around him, nearly pushing him out with the force of her contractions.

"Jesus," he groaned. "There you go."

He thrust harder. She continued shuddering, still coming, his pistoning cock drawing it out. She clamped his hand against her, too sensitive for more rubbing. Their fingers were soaked.

He pounded faster. She screamed against the cushion. She couldn't take much more, but he didn't last long.

"Fuck!" He pulled his hand from between her legs and gripped her hips, his wet fingers slipping on her skin. He buried himself inside her and snarled.

His cock throbbed, jerking and twitching in her still-clenching passage. He massaged her hips and ass roughly, rocking against her as he emptied into the condom. Her head was spinning so much her ears rang. She bit the cushion.

She was sore and soaked and buzzing and wholly, wonderfully satisfied.

He pulled out of her, and for a few minutes they lay spooned, June facing the back of the couch. She couldn't find words. She couldn't even think words.

Eventually, she groaned and rolled her head back against his shoulder. "Oh, man. God. Thank you."

He chuckled and patted her hip.

"Fuck, I'm starving." She rubbed her face. "And dying of thirst."

"We can actually order out now, you realize. I could have something delivered. Cindy gave me some cash earlier until I could get access to my bank account."

June gripped his hand and pulled it to her mouth. She kissed his knuckles. His fingers tasted like her.

"Wonderful." Her thighs were slick. Her insides throbbed. "I guess if your assistant doesn't show up for a while, we'll have to continue finding ways to pass the time."

"Give me like a half hour," he murmured against her neck. "I'll keep you occupied."

Chapter 6

By late afternoon, the silence of the house was shattered. The FBI security detail showed up first. Supposedly, they would be there only a few weeks until everything calmed down. June couldn't imagine anything calming down ever, especially now that Sam had thrown his hat back in the political ring; indeed, when the detail arrived, they informed them reporters and onlookers were already out on the street.

"This is your fault," June told Sam. "Why on earth would you want more publicity?"

"Publicity is my lifeblood. You'd better get used to it."

"You're lucky you're good in bed."

Sam's assistant arrived next, a young, black woman named Natalie. She was beautiful and had long tightly wound braids. She clung to Sam, crying.

"I knew you were innocent," she sobbed against his shoulder. "I never gave up hope."

He patted her back. "I knew you wouldn't."

June sat at the counter, picking at the remnants of the salad she'd ordered, eyeing them.

Sam introduced them, but Natalie already knew who June was. She shook June's hand in both of hers.

"It's good to meet you," June said. "I think Sam needs all the help he can get right now."

"I'm so happy to be back," Natalie said. "God, I hated that office job. I love your ink, by the way." She rolled up the sleeve of her blouse to show off some intricate black artwork.

June had changed into a tank top and jeans. She held her arms out. "I think we'll get along just fine, Natalie."

Cindy arrived shortly after, while Sam and Natalie were sorting through bins.

"They took my gun at the gate, Sam!" She slammed grocery bags down on the counter. "I have a license for that. You go down there and tell them to give it back!"

Sam sighed. "I need to talk to them about who's allowed in and with what. It's on my to-do list, okay? Right after I get the fucking lights and water turned back on."

June walked over to Cindy. "Is there more in the car? I'll help you."

Cindy placed a hand in the middle of June's chest. "You stay here. I have a surprise for you." She turned, her stormy expression replaced with delight. "Natalie! Oh my God, I haven't seen you in forever."

They embraced while June worried about her "surprise."

Cindy returned to the car, and June waited in the living room on the couch. When Cindy came back, June gasped and jumped to her feet.

"Is that...who I think it is?"

Cindy plunked an animal carrier down on the floor. "You betcha!" She opened the door on it.

Dipity peeked out, wide-eyed.

June knelt and made grabby hands at her. "Dipster! It's me. It's June."

Dipity gazed at her, slinking back. Then, she seemed to recognize June, though it had been months. The tortoiseshell cat streaked out of the carrier and over to her.

June scooped her up in her arms. She petted her, and the cat purred voraciously. June toppled over onto the rug in glee, and Dipity climbed on top of her and began kneading her stomach, purring like a jet engine.

Cindy laughed. "She remembers you."

"She better remember me; she saved my life."

"Oh, God." Sam stood in the doorway. "You brought it over here."

Dipity climbed all over June.

"June." Cindy towered over her. "I know these past six months have been probably the hardest in your life. You deserve something good."

Dipity walked through June's hair, which was spread out on the carpet. Claiming every part of her.

"So"—Cindy took a deep breath—"as much as I'll miss her, I think you have a much deeper connection with her. I think she'd like to come live with you."

June gasped. "Really?"

"Whoa," Sam yelped. "Wait a minute!"

Dipity walked over June's chest and settled there in a vibrating loaf.

"You hear that, Dip?" June lifted her head. "You wanna come live with me?"

Dipity meowed.

"I brought all her stuff," Cindy said. "Her litter box, her food, her basket of toys. Mommy will miss her so much, but I think she really belongs with you, June."

"You can visit her." June dropped her head back on the carpet.

"This is my house," Sam said. "This place is not pet proof."

"Don't listen to the noisy man." June petted Dipity. "We'll just sleep outside if he doesn't want us here. Out in the cold and rain."

Sam groaned. "Oh my God."

June twisted her head around to look at him. "She saved my life, Sam."

"So did I."

"Yeah, and I'm keeping you, aren't I?"

He rolled his eyes and left the room. June looked back at Dipity. The cat's eyes were narrowed, her purr rumbling June's chest.

Cindy squatted beside them. She had a skirt on, giving June a front row seat to her panties peeking out between her thighs. They were neon pink.

"Have you heard anything from Occam?" Cindy lowered her voice. "Since you got that note?"

"No, but I'm pretty sure he's always watching."

"I hope Jason is all right." She folded her arms on her knees. "And your friend…Ortega?"

June scowled. "Diego."

"I hope they're both okay."

"I'm sure they are, as long as I don't say anything one way or another." She grimaced. "Now get your vag out of my face." She rolled away, taking Dipity with her.

Sam spent the rest of the afternoon in high Type-A personality mode. Natalie brought him a mobile hotspot so he could do things online. He was constantly on the phone, arguing either with the utility companies or with a bank. Cindy and Natalie sorted through bins and put stuff away.

Around five PM, the first triumph of the day occurred—the power company showed up, and shortly after, the lights came on.

"Hallelujah." Sam lifted his arms. "Now we're getting somewhere."

The water company showed up as well. They took a bit longer, as more was involved in getting the water running. June and Cindy sat on the porch. Sam followed the workers around outside the house, haranguing them.

"It's good to see him back in top form," Cindy said. "I can't wait for this party on the beach. I think it's good we're reaching across the aisle."

"He's insane." June sat slumped in a chair. "How can he jump out of what we've been through and back into his life like this?"

"That's how he is. He thrives on being busy, on being a powerhouse. All this time he's just…not been himself. Being in hiding sapped who he was."

Maybe Sam wasn't the man for her. Maybe, once he was in his full glory, they wouldn't be right for each other, the way she and Micha hadn't been right for each other. Was she making another stupid emotional mistake?

"You two seem cozy." Cindy seemed to be reading her mind. "I mean, you look happy together."

"I know how it seems, me being with Micha that whole time, and now I'm with Sam."

"Honey, I've been married four times. Trust me when I say things change."

June looked over at her. "I guess if you were with a man like Kevin, you have experience with difficult men."

"Kevin wasn't always like that, though." Cindy tucked an arm behind her head and looked up at the porch ceiling. "I knew him when he and Thomas were best friends. Back in the day. Kevin was supportive of the paranormal community then. His grandmother was a powerful telepath. She was heavily involved with vampires. I know that sounds crazy, and it was."

June recalled Occam telling her Kevin's grandmother had a vampire lover, and that was how she got the Oracle of the Dead.

"That's why when Thomas died, Kevin was able to go to the vampires and hire them to seek out Thomas's murderers. But vampires are unreliable. He would have gone down hard for that. They would have given him up to the first person who asked about it. He wasn't thinking straight."

"So Aaron paid them off," June said. "In exchange for Sam protecting Muse. And Kevin owed Sam a favor."

"I was married to my second husband at the time Thomas died," Cindy said. "But after we split up, Kevin and I got together. We'd known each other a long time. I think I was Kevin's way of trying to shake his fear, trying to get over the bigotry growing in him. But the whole time we were together, his hatred toward the paranormal just grew and grew. It tore us apart."

The sound of Sam griping drifted around the side of the house.

"So believe me," Cindy said. "I get it. I've been through a hundred men, looking for the right one. Being what I am doesn't help. Being what I am is probably the reason I've been through that many."

June thought of how Micha had always been so reasonable about how they probably weren't right for each other, how they were merely a comfort to each other.

"Sam and I are so different," June said. "Like Micha and I were. I'm not the type of girl I could see Sam being with."

Cindy lowered her arm. "Sam's an unconventional man. I don't see him being with a conventional woman. He needs someone like you. I don't know if you've noticed, but he's a little off the wall. A nonconformist is exactly his type."

June narrowed her eyes. "What are you saying? I'm some kind of gutter punk?"

Cindy hauled herself to her feet. "Yes, you tattooed whore."

June grinned.

The water was restored, and they turned on all the taps in the house to let the sludgy orange water run out of the unused pipes. Dipity ran as the house was filled with sputtering and popping.

Sam shook his head. "I can't believe we have a cat."

"*I* have a cat," June said. "You'd better stay on my good side, or I'll make her eat your face."

Natalie and Cindy stuck around until after dark, helping unpack bins and clean up. Sam raged every time he discovered they'd taken something from the house. At least his cars were still in the garage—albeit rifled through like everything else.

"I'm bringing a professional cleaning company in," he told them as Cindy and Natalie were getting ready to leave. "I'm not opening that fridge myself. And I don't even know how you get six months' worth of dust out of furniture."

"Rich boy's never had to clean," June said. "He only knows how to do this with his hands." She did a mocking Queen of England wave.

Sam jabbed her in the side, and she leaped away, grinning.

"I like her." Natalie smiled. "Are you coming to the beach party, June?"

"Do I look like the kind of gal who misses a beach party?"

Hugs and good-byes were exchanged, and Cindy cuddled Dipity one last time, whispering to her to be good and that she'd visit her soon. She left with tears in her eyes and the cat in June's arms.

"Why don't you go upstairs and get a shower?" Sam said. "My bathroom is wonderful. Then we can get some rest. I don't know about you, but I'm exhausted."

"Am I actually going to be allowed to rest?"

He waved. "It depends. Can I do anything else with my hands?"

Upstairs, she tried to pretend it was her first time seeing Sam's room. He pushed bins into corners, muttering. He told her he would change the bedclothes so they weren't sleeping in a tomb.

His bathroom was indeed nice: big, white tile, a huge mirror, two sinks, and a massive tub as well as a glass shower. The room didn't seem to have collected much grime during six months of disuse; that was the nice thing about smooth nonporous surfaces.

She didn't lock the door, and she expected him to come creeping in while she showered, but he didn't. She was disappointed. He didn't even need to get in the shower with her; he could perv at her through the glass.

After she got out, she took her time drying off, brushing her hair, and going through some semblance of a beauty routine. Sam had all sorts of lotions and potions in a cabinet next to the sinks. She rolled her eyes at his collection of cologne, taking up one entire shelf. Men.

She blow-dried her hair, something she hadn't done in a while. Now that she'd actually had it colored and cut, she could bring herself to style it again.

She pulled on an oversized black T-shirt from her bag and a pair of panties, and finally emerged into Sam's bedroom.

Sam sat on the bed, which now had different sheets and a red blanket on it. The scent of Febreeze hung on the air.

He had his laptop on the bed in front of him. He looked up at her. "You should put some pants on."

She padded across the room, stroking her fingers through her dried, silky hair. "Are you serious?"

"Yes."

She stopped next to the dresser and glanced at the pictures. "Why should I put pants on? Why don't you take yours off?"

He clicked around on the computer. "Please."

He was serious. She stood staring at him.

He nodded to the bathroom. "Go get a pair of pants out of your bag, put them on, and then come here. I have something to show you. Just do it."

She huffed and walked back to the bathroom. She didn't want to go outside. Or meet anybody. Those were the only two reasons she could imagine needing pants right now.

She pulled a pair of black yoga pants out of her bag, yanked them on, and returned to the room. They were a little too long and hung over her feet.

Sam patted the bed beside him. "Come here."

She walked over to the bed. "What, do you have bedbugs or something? You don't want my ass getting bitten?" She flopped down on the bed.

Sam picked up the laptop and turned to her. He plunked it in her lap.

She was confused for a moment, but then she saw the screen. She clamped her hands over her mouth, her vision blurring with tears.

"Oh my God." Her mother did the same thing on the screen, clamping her hands over her mouth. "June, baby!"

June wasn't the type to burst into tears, but they spilled over and she drew a deep, shaky breath. Sam squeezed her shoulder.

"Oh, God, it's so good to see you again." Her mother was crying too. "Are you all right?"

June lowered her trembling hands, struggling for words. Her chest tightened and ached on the right side, like it always did when she got stressed out or emotional.

"I'm okay," June choked out. "Are you okay, Mom?"

Her mother's long, honey blond hair was pulled back, her face clean of makeup. She looked like Jason, with her high cheekbones and pale eyes. Contrarily, everyone else said she looked like an older version of June, but June didn't see it. Right now, what she saw was the best thing she'd ever seen in her life.

"I'm fine now." Her mother wiped her eyes with a tissue. "I watched your press conference today. It was so good to see you up there, to see you alive. You're so thin, though."

June swallowed the lump in her throat. Tears were still falling. "My allergies are making it hard to eat. Where are you? Are you in California?"

She nodded. "I've been talking to the FBI. They said I couldn't talk to you until you were no longer sequestered. This year has been so awful." She touched the screen. "My baby. You're alive."

June wiped her eyes. Sam handed her a wad of tissues.

"Is your brother there with you? He wasn't at the press conference."

June froze, tissues pressed to her face. She hadn't prepared herself for this moment, hadn't thought up a story yet. She couldn't tell her Jason had been kidnapped by vampires. She'd already told the FBI he wasn't in Chicago, and she'd told the masses he didn't want to speak at the conference. She was going to get tangled up in her lies and hang herself.

"He's not here." She lowered the tissues, sniffing. "We…um…"

"The FBI kept them apart." Sam leaned over in front of the screen. "They're still questioning him, but they should be releasing him in a few days. All this red tape, it's ridiculous." He sat back.

June swallowed. "Yes, but… He's fine, Mom. We're both fine."

Her mother broke down, crying into her hands. June cried, too, positively wept, like she hadn't done in months. Sam slid an arm around her and rubbed her back.

After a few minutes, they both composed themselves. June's side hurt worse.

"I've been searching for you since you disappeared," her mother said. "I even sent Diego to find you last month, but I haven't heard from him. I can't get him on his phone. He's not e-mailing or texting me..."

June cleared her throat. "The FBI has him."

She blinked.

"He found us," June said. "But it was dangerous. We couldn't let him contact you. The FBI is still questioning him and Jason."

She heaved a deep sigh. "Oh, thank God." She pressed a hand to her chest. "I was so worried something happened to him. He was my rock through this, you know. I wanted to come to Chicago so many times, but he told me to be reasonable. He kept saying if you were on the run, you'd probably come home, and I needed to be here to help you. I kept praying, hoping... I would have hidden you until the end of time. I kept waiting for you to reach out to me."

"I'm sorry." Fresh tears formed in June's eyes. "I couldn't... I couldn't get out of the city."

"Oh, baby, it's not your fault." She touched the screen again. "I know you've been through hell. I'm just so happy to see your face."

"It has. It's been hell, but I'm here."

"Don't you worry. I'm getting on a plane to Chicago tomorrow."

June froze again, widening her eyes.

"They said you can't leave there yet," her mother said. "But they've got no restrictions on me, so I'm coming. I can't wait to hold my baby girl in my arms again."

Her mother couldn't come to Chicago. If Occam found out she was there, he'd snatch her too. She could envision Occam with a zoo full of her friends and family, taunting her, telling her the key to letting them out was saying yes.

June glanced at Sam, panicked.

He leaned over again. "Mrs. Coffin."

"Andrea."

"Andrea. I understand wanting to come, but you can't, not just yet."

"Why?" Her voice sharpened.

"Because we're not sequestered anymore, but they don't want us having too much contact with people outside the case. They don't want to take any risks."

"So you mean after all this time, all we've been through, I still can't come see my children?"

"It won't be that long, Mom." June touched the keyboard, as if she could reach through it. "Just a little while longer. I promise we're all going to be together soon. I'm coming home. Jason's coming home."

Sam drew back.

"Oh, this is hateful." Her mother slapped her forehead. "But tonight might be the first time since January I've had a full night's sleep."

"Me too," June said softly.

"Do you have a phone? Can I call you?"

June went to the bathroom and retrieved her phone from her bag. Her hands were still shaking, the rest of her numb. She returned to the bed, turned the phone on, and found the number.

"The idea you're just a phone call away now." Her mother's eyes welled up again. "Oh, God, please don't let this be a dream."

June wiped her eyes with the back of her hand. "Diego told me you've been paying rent on the shop. Mom, you don't have the money to do that. Why?"

Her mother had her own cell phone and punched June's number in. "I couldn't let you lose it. Letting it go would be like—like saying you were never coming home."

June shook her head and grabbed up the tissues again.

"I got a loan. And Diego and the other guys were helping pay for it too. They've still been working. You wouldn't believe all the reporters and looky-loos who come around that place. Always someone nosing around." She placed the phone to her ear.

"I would. It's a circus here too." June's phone trilled in her lap. She saved her mother's number.

"It's been worse lately," her mother said. "Now that everyone knows the truth. Thank you, Mr. Haain, for all you've done for my children. I'm sorry you were persecuted."

"Sam," Sam said. "And we've all helped each other, haven't we June?"

June nodded.

"And you're running for mayor, Sam?" Her mother's penchant for gossip was still intact. "How do you think that'll go? The whole city must be rooting for you."

June almost laughed. Chicago, root for a paranormal person?

"I'm a politician by trade," Sam said. "It's in my blood. I'm already entrenched in the politics of this city. I have no doubt I'll be welcomed back into that circle with open arms."

"If I were there I'd vote for you, based on the fact you saved my children alone. You're a good man, Sam."

"Mom," June said, "just stay put for right now, okay? Just until the FBI clears things. This is…a complicated situation."

Her mother sighed. "Knowing you're all right is enough for now." She peered closer at the screen. "But God, you're so thin. Was it hard to get food?"

"We had plenty of food. Like I said, my allergies are giving me a lot of trouble." She fidgeted with her phone. "I think they're getting worse. Maybe the stress."

"When you come home, I'm taking you back to that allergist. And to a nutritionist."

"There's a doctor here. She's got me on vitamins right now. I feel a little better." She did, sort of.

"Drink lots of water and get some protein in you. No salt. It's bad for your heart."

She couldn't have imagined she'd treasure the day her mother would be able to nag her again. "I will, Mom."

"Have Jason get in touch with me as soon as he's allowed. I can't wait to hear his voice too."

Though June wanted to stay on with her all night, Sam had limited data on the hotspot. They said good night and June promised to call first thing tomorrow.

After Sam closed the laptop lid, she slumped against him and cried on his shoulder.

"Thank you," she choked out. "I wasn't ready for that, but I needed it."

He stroked her hair. Dipity found them, thumping onto the bed next to June's leg. June reached out and petted her, sniffing.

"I thought you deserved more than one nice thing today," Sam said. "You're on your way to having a normal life again."

She wiped at her face. "I'll never be normal."

Sam reached out and petted Dipity as well. "Well, I guess it's not so bad being different."

She had to rescue Jason and Diego before her mother found out the truth. Lying to her, after all she'd been through, made June's stomach hurt worse than all the gluten in the universe.

Chapter 7

June awoke feeling sick, but that was nothing new. Usually, the queasiness subsided if she could get some food and water in her and keep it down. Every morning, she sank deeper into dread. How long until the debilitating pain? How long until she couldn't eat at all? How long until she began to rot from the inside out?

She tried to shake these thoughts as she stood over the bathroom sink, splashing water on her face and trying not to throw up the little bit of water she'd drunk.

Stepping back, she nearly tripped over her duffel bag on the floor. She kicked it in frustration. Things fell out. She sighed.

Cramming the items back in, she scowled at her box of tampons. She was due for that too. Soon she'd have cramps on top of everything else. Her morbid line of thinking helped her find the silver lining, though—if she dropped below a certain percentage of body fat, she wouldn't have a period at all, like those female athletes.

"Take that," she muttered. "Point for me, Mother Nature."

Too bad she was playing a losing game.

By noon, the house was full of people: cleaners, assistants, Sam's friends, and members of his group. June retreated to the back patio, sunglasses on, and sat in a lounge chair, nibbling on an apple. Gardeners were crawling all over the grounds, trimming, mowing, digging.

She'd already had a long phone conversation with her mother, carefully explaining the events of the past six months while omitting certain details. She hadn't yet told her she and Sam were together, either.

Sam eventually found her. "There you are. Hiding?"

"I'm working on my tan." She was well under the shade of the awning.

"You should get naked for that." He motioned in the house. "Come with me. There's someone I'd like you to meet."

"I'm not a people person."

"I know, but I think you'll find this person interesting."

She slipped her glasses down her nose. "Is it another cute assistant?"

"No. Remember, I said I have a plan to find Occam and Robbie?"

Now he had her attention. She got up and followed him inside.

Sam led her through the house, past people vacuuming and scrubbing and dusting. He led her out onto the front porch, which was empty save for one person.

A young man leaned against the porch railing. He had a heart-shaped face and collar length brown curls. As they walked over to him, something strange seemed to happen to his eyes, as though they caught the light and reflected it like a cat's eyes. Maybe June had imagined it.

"This is Anthony," Sam said. "He's been a member of my group for several years, but I hadn't met him until today. Anthony, this is my girlfriend, June. She's a Siren."

"June Coffin." Recognition lit up Anthony's features. "It's nice to meet you." His voice seemed strangely familiar and unaccountably unnerving.

"Anthony has been so kind as to offer me his services," Sam said. "He doesn't do that very often."

June eyed Anthony. "And what are those?"

"Anthony is a precognitive. Institute research claims he doesn't exist, by the way."

June blinked a few times. "A pre….what?"

"Precognitive," Anthony said. "In the very simplest colloquial phraseology, I can see the future."

The back of her neck prickled. Why did he sound so familiar?

"The Institute didn't believe such an ability could exist," Sam said. "But Anthony, I'm sure, can tell you otherwise. He's going to help us find the monsters we're looking for."

June perked. "Oh, so like—you know where they're gonna be at a certain time?"

Anthony shook his head. "It's not quite like that."

"Let's get something to drink," Sam said. "We can all sit down, and you can fill June in. Come inside."

They all went in and to the kitchen. Something else about Anthony made her wary, something about his overall demeanor and the way he carried himself. Alarm bells rang in her head.

Sam made himself and Anthony coffee, and June had water. They all sat down in the dining room at the table, which was freshly cleaned. The scent of oil soap hung in the air.

June sat across from Anthony, Sam at the head of the table between them.

Anthony smiled faintly. "Are you ready to have your mind blown, June Coffin?"

"What's left of it." June stared at him.

"Do you know the cosmological theory of parallel universes?"

She propped her elbow on the table and rubbed her forehead. "Is it vital that I do?"

"What cosmic theorists speculate, I know as fact, but in such a way they can't imagine, and it would be impossible for me to clearly describe it to them. All you need to know is that every possible outcome of every second—everything you think, do, and say—is played out in an infinite number of universes. Everything that can happen does happen. I shift among the universes, so to speak, so I see all possible outcomes."

June dropped her hand away from her face. "You shift among universes?"

"Well, my mind does. And that's a very crude way to describe it. It's much more complex."

June narrowed her eyes. "Saying, 'if you make a decision, anything can happen' isn't exactly telling the future."

Sam spoke up. "You'll have to excuse June, Anthony. She's a skeptic." He was nearly bouncing in his chair, seeming excited about whatever this power was that Anthony had.

Anthony smiled wider. "'Parallel' is a misnomer. What I experience is more like a gel flowing in all directions. Everyone shifts. I'm just cognitive of it. The reason I can know a certain future is because people are sort of like"—he looked upward thoughtfully—"pin balls." He looked back at her. "You get a swat with the paddles when you're born, and there's all sorts of chutes and holes and things for you to bump into. And every time you make a decision—when you drop back down to the paddles—you get thwacked in a certain direction. That's when I see where you're going in this universe, after that smack. People's wills keep them going in the direction they're sent. It would take a pretty hard shake of the machine to change it. But I can—usually—only see one smack at a time. A series of decisions becomes astoundingly convoluted."

Sam rubbed his chin. "And you have to be face-to-face with a person to know their future, right?"

"Yes, technically. I can also see a bit of the future of people that person has recently come in contact with. It's like a residue that gets caught in their head."

"You can do it at will?" June was barely following this.

"For me, it's as perennial as breathing. Just like I don't have to think about breathing, I don't have to think about my power." He paused. "I can hold my breath or focus on my breathing, though. So in the same sense, yes, I can control my power."

"How does it not drive you mad?" June shook her head.

"How does not being able to do it not drive you mad? I don't know what it's like to be normal." Anthony's eyes flashed. She definitely didn't imagine it this time.

June frowned. "What's going on with your eyes?"

"It happens when my ability happens—makes life a little awkward, especially since it happens reflexively more often when I'm tense or emotional. I'm seeing the light spectrum. You're seeing me shift."

"So why doesn't your whole body do it?"

"Our eyes are connected to our brains, and to our powers."

She knew that all too well from her own vibrant green, intense, freaky eyes.

"Okay…" June said. "So how is this going to help us find Robbie and Occam? You said you have to be in contact with a person to see their future. So that means you have to find them, like we do."

Anthony held up a finger. "Or someone who's recently been in contact with them, as I said."

June shook her head. "I'm sure Robbie is not going to be in contact with anybody we know."

Anthony's eyes flashed again and he looked away. "I know who Robbie's in contact with."

Sam drew himself up in his chair and cleared his throat. "June, Anthony is…Robbie's brother."

June stiffened. Her instincts weren't off. She had recognized something familiar in him.

"Are you kidding me?" She nearly shouted.

Anthony looked back at her. "I'm not my brother's keeper."

"Anthony is one of three known precognitives in the entire world," Sam said. "The Beecher bloodline is incredibly strong with paranormal powers."

"How can you let this man sit at your table?" June clenched her hands into fists. "After what his bloodline did to you and your friends?"

"Robbie is not my blood," Anthony said. "I'll gladly deliver him into Sam's hands."

"He's our only chance of finding Robbie," Sam said. "Robbie is not going to walk right up to us. If he does, we've got much bigger problems."

"Robbie has had people watching me," Anthony said, "ever since he made his grab for power back in January at the press conference. He's always tried to sell me on his dogma, but I was never keen on it. I'm sure he was hoping I'd be impressed."

June remained guarded. "He was hoping a lot of people would be impressed, including the vampires."

Anthony crinkled his forehead. "I'm not surprised he's trying to impress the vampires. Robbie hasn't been well for a long time."

June sat forward. "Could you imagine the monster he'll be if he gets a vampire to turn him? A man as powerful as he is who can't be affected by anything?"

Anthony sat forward too. "We've never seen eye-to-eye. I'm sure he's waiting to see what I do, see if I'll join him or oppose him. He can't read my mind. I at least have that advantage. But I know his mind well enough, and I don't like it."

"So you always knew what he was up to?" June glared at him. "Before he orchestrated a massacre?" She was not going to trust Anthony, not so easily. She didn't care if he claimed to hate his brother. She'd been told too many lies already.

"I didn't know the extent of his intentions. He's always been a bit of a fanatic. He liked to go off on these long rants about the Institute and about the Paranormal Alliance and how he'd run it differently—all the things he didn't like about Sam."

Sam huffed. "The feeling is entirely mutual, trust me."

"He was always cocky and grandiose," Anthony said. "I'd tune him out. We never got along very well. I think he resented the fact my power wasn't eating me away too."

"That's the thing with fanatics," June said. "No one takes them seriously until they finally kill a bunch of people."

"If I could have stopped that"—Anthony's voice dropped a notch—"I would have. I never dreamed he would go that far."

"You're not much of a fortune teller, then," June said dryly.

Sam shot her a wide-eyed look, the kind she got from her mother as a child when she was acting up in a public place.

"My power doesn't work like that, as I explained," Anthony said. "I don't blame you, June, for mistrusting me, when my brother has done such horrible things to you and your friends. For what it's worth, I'm sorry those things happened. I'm part of the Paranormal Alliance, too, even if I don't go to any meetings. Those were my friends he killed as well."

June clenched her jaw. She was trying to have faith Sam's trust was well placed, but he'd trusted Robbie once too. She wished more than ever that Muse were there.

"I don't get out much," Anthony said. "I'm a bit of a recluse. Socializing is…exhausting. It's hard to be around people when my power mostly behaves of its own will."

"We won't keep you long, then," Sam said. "I was just thinking you could explain this to her better than I could."

Anthony's eyes flashed. "Robbie has people watching my house. I see cars all the time. I don't know if he's planning a visit. I haven't seen or spoken to him since late last year."

"Did you join the Paranormal Alliance together?" June asked.

Anthony shook his head. "I wasn't part of it until a few years ago. Robbie joined around the time it was formed."

"What made you join it?" She couldn't read minds like Muse, but she could damn sure interrogate him.

"Sam is inspiring. He finally made me believe in something. He made me believe that no matter how hard things are, there's a place for people like me in the world."

Sam beamed.

"I was able to get involved in some of their programs. I branched out a little and made contact with other people. It was nice."

He spoke to part of her soul—being hidden away and feeling disconnected. Still, she couldn't bring herself to trust him wholly.

"So how are you going to find Robbie?" she asked.

"I'm going to suck it up and socialize. I'll talk to the people watching me in the hopes one of them has been in contact with him recent enough that I'll see where he is."

"And then we'll have some idea how to proceed," Sam said.

June narrowed her eyes. "So you're going to strike up a conversation with the people watching you?"

"I'll take a walk. Go by the car. I'll say, 'I know my brother sent you, and I'm tired of you watching me.' Something like that."

June folded her hands on the table. "Does your brother know how your power works?"

"Yes…"

"Then there's no way he's going to risk coming in contact with any of the spies he sends in the timeframe you'd be able to see him. He's really fucking clever."

"He doesn't know Anthony came here," Sam said. "He doesn't know he's going to assist me. So why would Robbie care if Anthony sees him? He might even want him to, to entice him."

"What about the spies?" June opened her hands. "If someone is spying on you, that means they know where you're going."

"I was careful." Anthony sat back. "I sneaked out. No one saw me."

"You're absolutely sure of that?"

Sam leaned over to her. "This is the best chance we have of finding Robbie. It's our only chance."

She looked him in the eye. "I know. But you can't just throw caution to the wind."

"No one saw me come here," Anthony said. "And I will find my brother, even if I have to talk to all of his spies." His eyes flashed. "However hard it is for me, I have to do this. I have to help Sam find him."

She didn't understand what the hell Sam planned to do once he did find him.

"What about Occam?" she asked. "You said this would help us find both of them."

Sam sighed. "That will be harder, but Anthony is willing to help us on that too. Even if it means we have to go into Old Town."

"Your power works on vampires?" June asked. "I thought nothing did. That's like, one of the perks of vampirism."

"My power is extremely unique. It's one of the very few things that does work on vampires."

"How do you know that?" June stared him down. "You don't like to socialize. How do you know it works on vampires?"

Anthony shifted. His shoulders were hunched. His anxiety was not her problem.

"I've spoken to vampires before." He sounded edgy. "Robbie made sure I was exposed to all sorts of supernatural people when I was younger. It was his favorite game. He said it was good for me to learn about my own kind. My power works on vampires. It works on everyone. Which is what makes it so…consuming, at times."

"So we can talk to the vampires," Sam said. "Until we find one that leads us to Occam."

"What's in it for you?" June asked Anthony.

Anthony focused on her, eyes wide and intense. He did remind her of Robbie, something about the narrowness of his face, his willowy limbs, his penetrating stare.

"I mean," June said, "nobody does a favor like this just because they admire someone. It sounds like it's a pretty big deal to you. What's your stake in this?"

"June," Sam said lowly. "There's no need for—"

She cut him off. "You trusted Ethan Roberts. You trusted your entire organization, half of which were actively working against you behind your back."

Sam's face hardened. His eyes glittered.

"They even got past your foolproof telepath," June said. "So forgive me if I don't trust anyone you bring in here to try to solve our problems for us."

Anthony pushed his chair back. "I think you two should discuss this on your own. I need to get some fresh air and clear my head." He stood.

"What's your stake in this?" June slapped her hand on the table. "Why do you want to do this for us? And don't say because you respect Sam. Lots of people respect Sam. I want a better answer."

Anthony stared at her. His eyes flashed once, and then again. His hands were clenched at his sides.

"I want my brother to pay." His voice was strained. "I want him to pay for what he's done."

"To us, or you?" June kept her gaze fixed on him.

Anthony walked swiftly out of the room.

Sam pushed his chair back sharply. "You're being rude and mistrustful." He stood.

She gaped at him. "After all we've been through, don't you think mistrust is common sense?"

"You can't mistrust everyone, not if we want to win this. We have to trust someone."

"That someone sure as hell isn't going to be Robbie's brother." She got up and stalked out of the room.

Back out on the patio, her phone rang. It was Trina.

"Hey, I've got news," Trina said.

June squinted into the sunlight, scanning the grounds. Anthony going to "get some air" could be his way of creeping around the property, spying.

"What's the news?" June asked.

"You still want to see Micha?"

Her heart jumped, her attention immediately shifting. "Yes."

"I pulled some strings, but it has to be today. You have to get over here as soon as you can. You need a ride?"

She looked into the house. "I think so."

"I can come pick you up. Tell me where you are. I'll be there soon."

Chapter 8

Driving out in Trina's car would probably prove less conspicuous than leaving in one of Sam's, who had been frosty and silent since June announced where she was off to, even more so than he already was about her fit over Anthony.

When Trina arrived, June stood in the driveway, waiting. Sam stood on the porch.

"Do you want to come?" she asked. "For moral support?"

He stared down at her. "Do you want me to?"

"You don't have to. But I need to see him, and he deserves this visit. He deserves to see us again. We can't just abandon him."

"I don't disagree."

"I don't know if they'll let you in, but you might as well come. I'll tell him you said hi."

He walked down the steps. "Fine."

Such a bratty child.

Trina pulled the car up next to her and parked.

"I don't want you going anywhere alone right now, anyway." Sam strode over to her. "It's not safe."

"You mean anywhere without you." She walked around Trina's car. "I'm not alone."

Two security guards flanked the gate. People stood across the street, holding cameras. Sam and June slumped down in the backseat until they passed by them.

"Jesus," Trina muttered. "What a circus."

June sat up. "Well, you know, if someone hadn't decided he was running for mayor…"

Sam sat up as well. "They'd be here even if I hadn't. Welcome to freedom."

June gazed out the window.

The hospital was near Trina's clinic, and it took them almost a half hour to get there. June's stomach knotted up as they pulled into the parking lot.

"I can't take you both in," Trina said. "Only June. I'm sorry, Sam. They have all these rules. You could wait in the waiting room, though."

"It's okay," Sam said. "I'll wait out here. I don't think he really wants to see me, anyway."

June looked down at her hands in her lap. Her palms were sweaty.

"We won't be long," Trina said. "They'll only allow a brief visit."

Sam's expression was blank, but his eyes were hard.

"You sure?" June asked Sam, trying to lighten the mood. "Sitting out in the car like a dog?"

He grunted. "Just crack a window for me."

Trina parked, and they got out of the car.

Walking up to the hospital, June tried to brace herself. "He's not okay, is he? You've been lying to me."

Trina glanced at her. "You've had enough on your plate."

"I hate when people lie to me."

"Is Sam angry you're doing this?"

"I don't care what Sam thinks. He makes a lot of choices I'm not happy with, either."

Trina guided her inside and into an elevator. June kept her head down and avoided eye contact with anyone. In the elevator, a man seemed to recognize her, or else was curious about her tattoos, as he kept sneaking glances at her. He didn't speak, though.

The process of being checked in was like visiting someone in prison. She had to sign a form stating she wouldn't take pictures, record their conversation, or disclose any information on his whereabouts or condition. She was also patted down and her phone was taken away. Finally, they stepped into a small prep room, where June pulled on a mask, gloves, and gown.

"Avoid extensive physical contact," the female nurse suiting her up said. "We're trying to eliminate as much outside contamination as possible. A brief hug is fine, or touching his hands, as long as you keep the gloves on."

June glanced over her mask at Trina, who stood in the corner of the room.

"You're only allotted ten minutes," the nurse said. "He has a full schedule today."

"Yeah." June huffed through the mask. "Places to go and people to see."

The nurse led her to a door. June held her breath as it opened.

The room beyond seemed to be a regular hospital room—no cages or shackles or nefarious scientists looking down from a ring of windows. The hospital had attempted to make his bed look like a real bed, with a wooden headboard and colorful blankets draped over it. Despite that, it was tucked into a bank of monitors.

Micha lay in the middle of it, shockingly haggard and startlingly thinner than he'd been just a month ago.

"June." He smiled faintly. "God, it's so good to see you."

He looked awful. Bony and ashen, slumped in the blankets, his eyes sunken, lips dark. He looked like a zombie.

June blinked a few times, fighting back tears. No extensive physical contact be damned. She wanted to fling her arms around his wasted frame and never let go.

The nurse left the room and closed the door behind June, leaving them alone. A camera looked down from the corner above the bed.

"You look good." Micha's voice was cracked and weak. "I saw you on TV yesterday."

June walked over to the bed, trembling, stomach aching. The tables around the bed were filled with flowers, cards, teddy bears, all sorts of gifts. Chicago still loved their favorite paranormal advocate, especially now that they knew he hadn't killed his wife.

Micha patted the bed. She sat down carefully, afraid to jar him.

She gripped his hand, next to his hip. "How are you?"

He shrugged, eyelids drooping. "I've been better. I got lots of nice presents, though."

"You look awful." June's voice shook. "You've lost weight."

"Can't really keep anything down. You know how that goes, huh?" He squeezed her hand weakly. "How's that going, by the way?"

Micha didn't know what Occam had told her, that horrifying revelation.

"Don't worry about me right now." She clamped her other hand over his. "What's wrong? What's happening to you?"

He let out a wheezy breath. "I suppose I'm dying. They don't know why. It's not like there's any precedent."

"You're not dying." She clutched his hand tighter. "If the serum was going to kill you, it would have done it by now, right?"

"I've been sick since the day they shot me up with it. I'm just in the final stages."

"No." She scrabbled at the mask over her mouth and nose and yanked it down. She couldn't breathe. "You're not going to die, Micha. Trina is working on this. She'll find a way to stabilize you."

The door opened. The nurse stood in the doorway, hand on her hip. "Miss Coffin, put the mask back on."

June scowled at the camera. "I'm not breathing on him."

"Miss Coffin, put the mask back on or leave. If you care about him, you won't endanger him."

June jerked the mask back up. "Fine."

The nurse left.

Micha huffed. "They're overreacting. I don't think there's anything I can catch that's going to hurt me worse than what I'm already suffering."

"Micha…"

"You're so pretty." He tilted his head on the pillow. "You've lost weight, too, but you're just as beautiful as ever."

"Micha"—she fought back tears—"I wanted to see how you were doing. I was hoping I'd feel better when I walked out."

"Yeah, well. Looks like I got a whole lot of bad luck."

She wanted to sob, to fling herself on top of him and cry against his chest. All those nights they'd spent together, holding each other for comfort and reassurance—she wanted those back. Maybe they weren't in love, but they were in something, something deeper and more profound and much needed. He'd been her rock, more than Sam, more than Jason. He'd seen her through the darkness.

But now, he was lost in the darkness, and she couldn't pull him out.

"Do they know anything?" She tried to force her voice steady. "Are they getting anywhere?"

"I'm not supposed to talk about it." He drew a deep breath, the air rattling in his chest. "I've signed confidentiality forms. The FBI doesn't want me to compromise their case."

She glanced at the camera and then whispered, "Squeeze once for yes and twice for no."

Micha held her in his gaze, those once vibrant blue eyes dull, like a summer sky gone dark with storm clouds.

"Do they know what the serum is doing to you?" she whispered.

He squeezed her hand once, and then twice, a weak but obvious grip.

"Do you still have powers?"

One squeeze.

"Are they getting stronger?"

Two squeezes.

"Are you able to control them better?"

Two squeezes.

None of this surprised her. If his abilities hadn't taken root in the six months he'd been exhibiting them, they probably wouldn't now.

She moved on to the hard questions. "Are they trying to fix the way it's making you sick?"

One squeeze.

"Have they done anything that makes you feel better?"

Two squeezes.

She looked down, her vision blurring. She'd never done so much crying as she had after coming to Chicago, not in all her years and all the bullshit she'd endured, watching her family break apart and hiding from herself. She'd always been stoic, always held her head high and soldiered on, until this city had broken her.

"Do they think you're going to survive?" She barely forced the whispered words out.

No response for a moment, and then he squeezed once.

And twice.

She put a hand over her eyes, a sob catching in her throat. She wouldn't cry in front of him. She wouldn't stress him out. He needed support right now. She couldn't pull him out of the dark, but she had to be strong for him.

"June," he said softly. "I knew from the moment I was injected I wouldn't survive this. I knew it was poison. I just didn't know how fast or slow it would be. Eric wanted to play God, but there's no good outcome for that. You can't create what doesn't exist."

"You did so much for so many people." She lowered her hand. "You don't deserve this."

"I'd say that's your argument for there not being a God, then." He dropped his other hand on his chest. "Eric couldn't accomplish the impossible, just like I couldn't."

"How can you be so calm about this?"

"Like I said, I knew the moment that needle went into me it was over. I've had time to get used to it."

"Well, I'm not used to it, and I refuse to accept it." She gripped his hand in both of hers again. "Trina will find a way to fix this."

"I'm an abomination. There's no fixing it."

"You're not an abomination. Remember what you told me in the hotel room, back in January? You said I wasn't a freak, that paranormal people were not monsters."

"You're not. But I'm not you. I'm neither this nor that, and I don't belong here."

"Stop saying that." She jerked his hand gently. "If I deserve to live, you deserve to live."

"It's not about what we deserve; it's what we're allowed." He let out another rattling breath. "All those times when I was a kid, wishing I were like my mother and sisters, being jealous of them for having powers. I guess this is why they say be careful what you ask for."

"You didn't ask for this."

"I guess my detractors can't say I don't understand their plight now. What ironic suffering for all my presumption. They must be smug, and I wouldn't blame them."

"Micha, you're a good man who wanted good things for us. No one wants to see you in this kind of pain."

"I don't think you understand the people in this city. There was a time I'm sure Sam would have been gloating."

She didn't want to believe that, but he was probably right.

"Sam wants you to get better too," she said. "He sends his condolences."

"Does he?" Micha arched an eyebrow. "It's funny how I haven't gotten any flowers from the Paranormal Alliance."

"We just got away from the FBI. I'll make him send flowers." She sniffed behind her mask, the cloth getting damp from her hitching breath. "I'll make him send the biggest, most ridiculous bouquet ever."

"I'm sure he'll put a nice big wreath on my casket."

"If you don't stop talking like that, I'm going to beat your ass." Her voice cracked. "And I can do it, because you're weak." She wiped her eyes.

Micha smiled. "Anyway, I was hoping our future mayor would have a few kind words for me."

"Oh, God." She sniffed again, hard. "I had no idea that was coming. I mean, I know he's a politician, but I didn't know he was going to jump back in that fast or hard."

"I'm not the least bit surprised. He'll probably get elected too. He'll milk the city's guilt for all it's worth."

She couldn't even imagine how she'd connect with Sam as mayor when she couldn't get comfortable in his big house and with his obviously hefty bank account.

"Why are you still here?" Micha asked. "Why haven't you taken Jason and gone back to California yet?"

Her throat tightened. So much he didn't know.

"I don't have Jason," she said. "That's why I haven't left Chicago."

Micha furrowed his brow.

She lowered her voice. "I told everybody he didn't want to talk to the public because I didn't want anybody to know what's really going on."

"What's going on?"

She glanced at the camera. She stroked the inside of his wrist. "Occam kidnapped Jason," she whispered. "And Diego. They never made it out of Chicago."

Micha's eyes widened fully, for the first time. His fingers twitched against her palm. "Oh my God."

"I don't believe Occam will hurt them. He's using them as leverage. If he hurts them, he won't get what he wants from me. I'm guessing he's holding them the way he held you prisoner, a scummy mattress and some junk food, but no real damage."

"What does he want from you?"

"He—" Telling him the truth meant telling the whole truth, and he didn't need to be worrying about her at a time like this. "He wants me to become a vampire."

He blinked.

"That's why he helped us," she said. "That's why he did everything— why he saved us from Robbie at the apartment building, why he showed up at the park to warn us, not hurting you, helping Sam—all of it. He did it hoping to win my favor."

"And when that didn't work…"

"He made another bargaining chip. We're trying to buy time until we can find a way to get them back. My mother wants to come here, but I lied to her and told her not to. I'm afraid Occam will take her too."

"Why?" Micha screwed up his face. "Why does Occam want you to be a vampire that badly?"

"My power is strong." She chose her words carefully. "You know vampires and powers. Occam says they want to get rid of all the weak vampires, something he calls a cleansing. A pride thing, I guess. Or maybe they're building an army."

"So he wants a vampire bride." Micha grimaced. "He's so horrible that he would do this to you, manipulate you like this. There has to be a way you can put an end to this, put an end to him." He shook his head on the pillow, tight-lipped. "I shouldn't have lied for him. That no good, conniving—"

"I'm sure we're all alive right now because you told that lie. Occam always gets what he wants, one way or another."

Micha squeezed her hand weakly. "Please be careful out there. I know you have to get your brother and friend back, and you will. You've got

Sam helping you, and my feelings about him aside, he's a smart man. He's got resources."

"I hope so. He's already...trying something. But I don't know if it will work."

Silence fell. The TV was on in the corner, turned down low. The sun shone bright through the window, bathing the room in gold. The air smelled like flowers. Everything was peaceful and beautiful, apart from the skeletal, suffering man in the bed.

"You and Sam look good together, by the way," Micha said. "You suit each other."

She stared at him, heart stilling.

"At the press conference," Micha said. "He seems protective of you. I'm glad to see that." He rubbed the back of her hand with his thumb.

"Micha..."

"Are you happy with him?"

"I don't... I don't know. I don't know which end is up right now. I'm only beginning to learn what his life is really like. We don't have a lot in common."

"Neither did we."

"Yeah..."

"Comfort is important in times like these." He continued rubbing the back of her hand. "But you need chemistry to keep it going. That's the thing we lacked, I suppose."

"I thought we had it."

"We had sex. There's a difference." He smiled faintly.

"I feel torn apart." She looked down at their locked hands. "This was never the right time to be in a relationship with anyone, at all. It isn't now. I wish I weren't like this. I wish I could just turn it off. I mean, what kind of bitch am I? Here you are, like this, and I've already moved on. What the hell is wrong with me?"

"June. We had this discussion. We knew we weren't a good fit. It just... worked, at the time. It felt good. We both needed to feel good."

"And you still do. It must be so horrible and lonely in here."

"Not like they would let me have company, anyway. Apart from the doctors, you're the first visitor I've had. I'm doomed to spend my final days as a science experiment, locked away."

"Don't say your final days." She clutched his hand. "You're going to get better and get out of here. True, you'll probably be an unwilling celebrity for a while, but you won't be dead. You'll get to go back to your work and life."

His eyelids drooped again. "I don't regret us," he said softly. "I never regretted us. It was beautiful."

"I don't regret us, either." She blinked back tears. "And Sam isn't—he's not better than you. He's not more suited for me. Don't think that way."

Micha was silent.

"Maybe your powers will flare up." She took a deep, shaky breath. "And you can blast your way out of here."

"And go back into hiding? On the run from the scientists? No, thank you."

"They can't treat you like a guinea pig forever. You're a human being."

"A human being who's an important component in a huge legal case against the Institute. I'm the straw that breaks their back. Kinda makes me feel special. In the end, I'm helping the paranormal community in the biggest way possible. A true martyr."

She didn't bother telling him to stop talking like that again. Clearly, he believed this was the end. She didn't, though. She wouldn't believe that. Couldn't.

"Have you seen Rose?" he asked.

"No. Maybe I'll never see her again, now that everything's over. If she's innocent, they'll uncover it. That's what she wants."

She still had so much to say, so much to tell him. But the door opened then, and the nurse stepped in.

"Time's up. Say your good-byes."

June gazed desperately at Micha, clutching his hand.

"I'll come visit you again," she said. "For fuck's sake, they should understand you need some companionship in here." She looked at the nurse. "Aren't you guys at all concerned about his mental health? Or is he just a rat to you?"

"Not my decision," the nurse said. "I just do what I'm told, and I'm supposed to get you out of here now."

June looked back at Micha. "I will come see you again."

He smiled. "Be careful out there. Watch your back. And good luck. Make that vampire dick pay."

"You be careful in here. Don't let them abuse you. Don't let them do anything undignified to you."

"Come on," the nurse said. "Time's up."

Not caring if she got yelled at, June leaned over and pressed her forehead to Micha's. He seemed too fragile to hug. She didn't want to jostle him, afraid he would break.

"I'm sorry about all this," she whispered. "We're both going to survive, the way we always have."

She kissed him through the mask. His lips were cold and unyielding, like he was already dead.

In the outer room, she yanked off the mask, gloves, and gown, her hands shaking. Trina still stood in the corner, silent, arms folded.

June thrust the items at the nurse.

The nurse took them. "I don't treat him like a rat, by the way. I do actually care about his mental health."

June could barely see for the tears in her eyes or think because her head was spinning. Her stomach hurt. "Really? Can't tell from where I'm standing."

"I should have yanked you out of there the second you violated the rules. Why do you think I didn't?" She tossed the used protective gear in a waste bin. "I'm also not going to report anything you said in there."

June blinked, trying to clear her vision. "Thanks," she whispered.

"Come on," Trina murmured, motioning to her. "Our dog is in the car."

Chapter 9

Trina led her back through the hospital. They didn't speak, and June moved in a haze, trembling, fighting tears. She kept seeing Micha's gaunt face, hearing the despair and doom in his voice.

Outside, under the blazing sun, June stopped on the steps leading up to the hospital. Instead of following Trina down to the parking lot, she sat, drew her knees up, and wrapped her arms around them.

Trina stopped a few steps down and looked back at her. She had sunglasses on. June had forgotten hers in the car. She wasn't used to having accessories again.

"You okay?" Trina asked.

"I just… I need a minute." She told herself she would not throw up. Keeping a meal down was a nice change of pace. "You should have told me."

"I didn't know how."

June rocked on the step. "I don't want Sam to see me like this."

"I think he would understand."

"Maybe I don't want him to."

Trina looked out at the parking lot. "I'll go wait in the car. Take a minute, whatever you need. I'll tell him you needed to clear your head."

Trina continued down the steps.

June was cold, though the air was hot. Her interior had frozen, deep down under her skin, where the sun couldn't reach. Freedom was not the glorious thing she'd hoped it would be. People she cared about were still suffering, some of them still trapped. She remained helpless and defenseless; two things she'd gotten used to but had sincerely hoped she would finally be able to shed.

She wiped at her leaking eyes, sniffing. People passed by and glanced at her, but no one stopped. Perhaps they were used to people crying in front of the hospital.

A few minutes later, Sam crossed the lot toward her.

She took a deep breath and steeled herself; still, when he sat down beside her and placed a hand on her shoulder, she fell apart.

She slumped against his side, sobs wrenching out of her, the ones that had been threatening to break free in Micha's room. She tucked her head against his shoulder, hands over her face, and he wrapped an arm around her. He was taking a risk, sitting with her out in public, and she was drawing even more attention to them.

He stroked her hair and didn't say a word until her sobs tapered off.

"I take it he's not doing well?" No sarcasm in his voice.

She wiped her face. Her cheeks were soaked with tears, her nose running. "He doesn't deserve this," she choked out.

"No, he doesn't."

Sam could predict the future, or else he knew what a crybaby she'd turned into. Like the night before when she saw her mother, he was ready with a wad of tissues. She took them and drew back, mopping her face.

Sam rubbed her shoulder.

"We shouldn't be sitting here," she said. "If someone realizes who we are, they might put two and two together and realize Micha is here."

"Wouldn't that be a shame? Then these doctors and scientists would have to put up with the press hounding them too."

She still felt queasy, but not like throwing up, thankfully.

"He looks awful." She propped her fists under her chin, hands full of tissues. "He looks like a corpse. He's lost so much weight."

"Eric's noble work."

"He keeps talking like he's going to die. He doesn't believe they'll be able to make him better. He's so pessimistic. All this talk about how he's making the ultimate sacrifice for us."

Sam huffed. "Quite full of himself, isn't he? He's starting to sound like me."

She stared dully across the lot. Sunlight glinted on the cars. Her eyes hurt. They were swollen, her nose burning.

"He thinks he deserved this," she said. "That all his presumptions led to this. I kept telling him it's not his fault. He was a lab rat, like so many of us were."

"What if he *is* dying? Will you be able to make peace with that?"

"Are you making peace with the fact I'm dying?"

Sam didn't reply.

"Trina is going to save us both." June rubbed the heels of her hands against her eyelids. "She's smart."

"It's very big of her to even try after what we did to her."

"We seem to make friends in the worst ways, don't we?"

They fell silent, June breathing slowly, eyes closed, hands cradling her head. In the darkness behind her eyelids, she saw Micha's gray face, his half-lidded dull gaze, all the blue gone from his eyes.

She lifted her head. "I'm sorry about Anthony. I know you're trying to find a way. It's probably the best chance we have, all things considered."

"No, you're right." He sounded grim. "Trusting him blindly is the dumbest thing I could do, considering who he is. Considering all the people I've trusted who stabbed me in the back."

"Maybe we could watch him. Make sure he's not reporting back to Robbie. Maybe we should dig deeper into his background."

"That's a good idea."

She squinted at him. Concern filled his eyes. Once upon a time, she'd enjoyed needling him. Now, she felt guilty for every shitty thing she'd ever said to him. She felt guilty for doubting him.

"We can trust very few people," he said. "I need you to be the voice of caution and reason in my life."

"I'm not very good at either of those things."

"If this whole mess has taught you anything, it's not to trust people. I've gotten much too lax about that."

"So this hardened me up but made you softer? I'm not sure what that says about either of us."

"It says nothing about us. It says the world is vicious and wants to eat us."

Her side ached—a reminder of the past that she would carry forever, even when she was long free of this.

If she was ever free of this.

"I told him what Occam's done," she said. "I didn't tell him what's going on with me, not completely. I didn't want him to worry. He needs to focus on getting better right now." She sniffed. "He says you and I look good together, that we make a cute couple."

Sam squinted.

She shrugged. "I think we're very different. I'm not sure where he sees us matching up exactly, but I guess we do. A politician and a tattooed punk girl? Yeah, that works." She tried to make it sound light and teasing, not like she was filled with teenage angst.

"Trust me, I couldn't date someone like me."

"I don't think I could date someone like me, either."

"Then he's right. We fit together."

He leaned over and kissed her temple. She was getting sweaty. Such a contrast from when she first got to Chicago and was freezing her ass off. She hadn't visited the lake since. Maybe it was nicer when it wasn't frozen over.

"Come on." He patted her back and got to his feet. "We should probably stop testing our luck out here. Someone is going to recognize us."

She got to her feet as well. She was unsteady, but he took her arm, holding her up like he had for months.

"I want to come visit him again, soon," she said as they walked to the car. "They're keeping him holed up in there with no company, being all anal about anyone touching him. It's not humane."

"Is he allowed to receive calls? Maybe they'd be more relaxed about that."

"I don't know. The FBI is uptight. We can't compromise the case and all that."

"I think it's prudent that we don't. The Institute might be closed, but they're not closed forever, not yet. And I very much want to see that happen."

He was right, but she hated to think of Micha wasting away in that bed without a friendly face or voice.

She glanced back at the hospital as they reached the car. Which window was Micha's? Could he even get out of bed and look out? She waved, just in case.

On the drive back, she sat slumped against Sam's side in the backseat. The air conditioning was blissful. No one spoke.

When they reached Sam's house, she and Sam ducked down again. At the gate, one of the guards approached Trina's open window.

"Let us in," Sam told the man. "Before they come swarming over here." He was referring to the onlookers across the street.

The gate opened immediately. They passed through.

"Eventually I'm going to have to go out and speak to the gawkers." Sam sat up. "Give them their sound bites. It'll be good for my campaign."

"When's the election?" June asked.

"February."

"This coming February?"

"Yes."

She frowned. "That's only, like, six months away. Can you even jump in this late in the game? Don't you have to get on the ballot with a petition?" Her high school government class had been a long time ago.

"I'd like to see them try to stop me, after all I've been through. It would be outrageous. And don't worry. I'll get on there."

They climbed out of the car, but Trina had to leave, so she remained inside. June leaned in the window.

"Thank you," June said softly. "It was good to see him, despite everything."

Trina smiled faintly. "I'm sorry I lied to you."

"It's okay; I forgive you."

"I'll try to arrange another visit sometime soon, if you want. I think he needs the company."

"I'd like that."

"I'll keep you updated. I'm sure there are things I won't be allowed to tell you, things we discover, but whatever I can tell you, I will."

"Please do." June paused. "I guess… I'll see you soon? I'm going to come in so you can examine me, and we can work out some way to stop this thing inside me."

"I already have some ideas." She squeezed June's hand on the door. "Come by after this weekend, after your little shindig at the beach. Just call to let me know when you're going to stop by and I'll clear my schedule. In the meantime, keep taking those vitamins. Are they helping at all?"

"I guess. I don't really know. I didn't throw up today, so that's a plus."

"Maybe it's a good sign." She put the car in gear. "I'll talk to you soon, June."

June stepped back. "Thanks again." She waved.

Sam was already in the house, laptop open, phone in hand.

"I'm going to see what public records I can find on Anthony." He kissed her forehead. "And find out when and why he joined the Paranormal Alliance. You should take a nap. You look tired."

She was indeed tired, all the energy sapped out of her from crying, the angst of the day hanging heavy on her shoulders, pulling her down.

"I think I will." She forced a little smile. "Thanks for coming along. And thanks for…being cool about it."

"I know you're not going back to him. You wouldn't give up this fine specimen of a man. You're a smart girl."

"I'd miss the sex." She drifted toward the stairs. "Not really the attitude."

"Which is bigger, my ego or my cock?"

She didn't answer that, waving to him over her shoulder as she climbed the stairs. Dipity followed her.

Chapter 10

June awoke to late afternoon sunlight filtering through the gauzy curtains over Sam's bedroom windows. She rolled onto her side, groggy and heavy. She wasn't nauseated for a change. She was actually hungry.

Were vitamins going to save her after all? Had they not had them back in Occam's day?

Waking up was painful for other reasons, though. Thoughts of everything wrong flooded in—Diego and Jason, worry for her mother, Micha. She'd been dreaming about Micha lying in that bed. She was anxious and unable to do anything for him, unable to get him out of the hospital, no matter how much she begged him to move. He kept saying it was the end, and it didn't matter because he was dying.

Dipity was curled in a fuzzy ball next to her. The cat opened her eyes and gazed at June.

"Sam is going to kill you," June whispered. "Sleeping in his bed."

Dipity closed her eyes again.

Voices drifted from downstairs. The house was probably full of people. She didn't want to face anybody.

She'd almost dozed off again when a rustling brought her back. She snapped her eyes open.

She swore it was the same sound she'd heard in Sam's bedroom the day before. Dipity's head shot up and she stared at the doorway. It wasn't June's imagination.

June propped herself up on her elbow. Dipity leaped to her feet. The fur on her back stood up, her tail puffed. The doorway was empty.

"I think it's just mice," June said. "Maybe you can take care of—"

The cat jumped off the bed and shot into the bathroom. June blinked.

Now June's hackles were raised as well. She looked at the doorway again, an uneasy sensation prickling across her skin.

"Rose?" she said warily. "Are you creeping around out there, you scary bitch?"

No response. Nothing moved. June sat up fully. Maybe Sam's house was haunted. Or maybe it was just a mouse, and Dipity was spooked being in a new, unfamiliar place.

June crawled out of bed and walked to the bathroom. Dipity cowered in the corner behind the toilet.

"You're a scaredy cat," June informed her. "You can stow away in a bag and save my life, but a sound spooks you?"

June was spooked, too, and once she had herself looking marginally decent for all the people who were probably downstairs, she left the room with haste. Dipity followed.

Indeed, Sam had visitors. Natalie and Cindy were there, and several men. They congregated in the dining room, laptops and papers scattered across the table.

Cindy joined June in the kitchen and picked up Dipity. "How's my little baby taking to her new home?" She spoke in baby talk. "Mommy misses her, yes she does!"

"She's sticking by my side," June said. "I think she's freaked out, being in a new place."

"Poor thing." Cindy scratched Dipity's head. "I'm glad she's with you, though." She glanced at June. "I heard you saw Micha today."

June opened the fridge. "Yeah. He's not doing so well. But Trina will figure something out. Hell, just giving me vitamins seems to be helping. She's smart."

"I feel really bad for him." Cindy placed Dipity on the floor. "He doesn't deserve this."

June pulled out ingredients to make a salad. "No, he doesn't. But at least what's been done to him will bring the Institute down, and I think that gives him some comfort. He feels like he's helping us."

"Is there anything I can do?"

"Yes. Tell Sam to send him flowers. Something big and obnoxious."

Cindy returned to the dining room, and June chopped vegetables for a salad. She might even try some meat on it, and the tiniest hint of dressing, something bland and easy to digest. Her stomach growled. Dipity wound around her ankles.

Sam walked into the kitchen, holding a newspaper.

"I have something cute to show you." He tossed the paper on the counter in front of her.

"Cute?" She peered at the paper. "Oh, Christ."

He'd brought her the front page of the Paranormal section of the *Tribune*. Now that Ethan Roberts wasn't the lead reporter, the stories were a lot less lurid, but they stuck close to his tabloid-like style.

The page had a picture of her and Sam outside Tribune Tower. Sam looked self-satisfied and was waving to the crowd. She was clinging to his arm, wide-eyed like a cornered animal.

Beneath the picture the headline said: SAM HAAIN EXONERATED: AND IN LOVE?

June picked up the paper. "Seriously?"

He chuckled. "They're very interested in our closeness. They feel we were hanging all over each other during the press conference."

"I was hanging on to you in sheer terror."

"Well, they're not wrong." He snatched up a piece of cucumber and munched on it while she read.

She only skimmed the article, cringing. "Sam Haain and June Coffin seem an unlikely pair," the article said. "Though if anyone can tempt the fiery leader of the Paranormal Alliance, it would be a Siren."

June rolled her eyes. "Did you read this?"

"Yep." He grinned.

"Ms. Coffin was seen clinging to Mr. Haain's arm both entering and leaving the conference, the two locked together in a bolstering embrace. During the conference, Mr. Haain was continuously distracted by the quiet, reticent woman at his side. His affection and support of her was clear—at one point reaching over to grip her hand. Mr. Haain, who has announced he will be running for mayor in next year's election, may have formed a bond with the dark and mysterious Siren. Will she be our city's new First Lady come February?"

June tossed the paper on the counter and glared at Sam.

"What?" He laughed. "I didn't write it."

"They called me 'reticent.'"

"Aren't you?" He patted her hip. "They just need something to jabber about. Kind of nice it's something good for a change, don't you think?"

She resumed chopping. "I'm tired of the limelight, to be perfectly honest."

"Then you'd better break up with me, because I live in it. I love it."

She grabbed the bottle of dressing, silent.

"I did a background check on Anthony." Sam leaned on the counter. "Had a friend downtown pull his public records. He's never so much as had a parking ticket. He was homeschooled, took classes online for college. He joined the Paranormal Alliance two years ago online. He's only logged as having gone to one public event, a rally shortly after he joined. Robbie was there too. Maybe Robbie was dogging him to come."

"So he bows to his brother's pressure." She drizzled dressing on the vegetables. "Not a good sign. Anything else?"

"I've got folks digging deeper, but it'll take a few days. I got a text from him. He said he made contact with his brother's spies. He's coming over this evening to talk to me. He's afraid someone might listen in if he talks on the phone." He smirked. "He asked that we speak alone, because you make him nervous."

She jammed a forkful of salad into her mouth.

"He's a delicate flower, June. And while I don't find that appealing, he's the only hope I have of finding Robbie and you finding Occam. We have to give him a little benefit of the doubt, but we won't trust him fully. I agree that's foolish."

She chewed and swallowed. "I still feel like he's doing this for himself, if he's not going to double cross us. This isn't about you or the Paranormal Alliance."

"Hating Robbie is a universal language. I don't mind."

"If he's just using you to punish his brother, that could be dangerous. He might be doing this without thinking it through."

"I know." Sam stood up straight and squeezed her shoulder. "I'll be careful. By the way, it's good to see you with an appetite. The vitamins are working?"

She shrugged. "I'm hungry. So yeah, maybe."

Sam returned to the dining room. She borrowed one of his laptops, as he had several. He'd gotten the Internet turned on. She sat on the patio and visited her favorite bloggers, the ones who had entertained her through her long months in hiding.

To her vast amusement and slight disappointment, the CIA conspiracy guy had taken down his past posts. He'd made a short post in which he explained he was abandoning the blog and wished her, Micha, Sam, and everyone else involved a safe and peaceful life and told them to "keep fighting the good fight."

She laughed heartily.

Checking more blogs, she discovered her romance with Sam was a hot topic online too. Like a celebrity's, her personal life was on everyone's lips. How was she going to stay with Sam if he was always in the limelight? How was she going to be Chicago's First Lady? Did she even want to be?

Blessedly, her food stayed down. She was even still hungry and had an apple. It stayed down too. She was so relieved she texted Trina to let her know.

More people showed up as evening fell. June stayed outside unless Sam beckoned her in to be introduced to someone. The people were all pleasant and kind—some were even excited to meet her—but they were all vastly different from her, professional and smart and enthusiastic, and she didn't fit in.

Before Cindy left, she joined June on the patio, and they entertained Dipity with a laser pointer.

"I don't really fit in this world," June said.

Dipity skittered in circles as Cindy swirled the red dot around.

"I mean this political world of Sam's. I don't know anything about politics."

"Me neither."

Dipity crashed into a chair, and Cindy lowered the pointer.

"But I know Sam. And I believe in Sam, if not as a politician, as a person. He wants good things for me and people like me, so I'll support him in whatever he does."

Dipity walked over to June, looking up at her eagerly, as if she were the commander of the red dot and could bring it back. June held her hand out for the laser pointer and Cindy handed it to her.

"You like Sam as a person, right?" Cindy said. "You must, if you're climbing that."

June turned on the laser and Dipity immediately sprang back into action. "Yes, but this is all so much bigger than me."

"You don't have to understand politics. You don't have to know the issues he's running on inside and out. You just have to trust him like you always have, support him emotionally. He chose you, and Sam doesn't choose things lightly. He doesn't fake things. If he picked you, he really cares about you. He doesn't care that you don't know anything about fiscal graphs and community outreach."

June continued swirling the laser. Dipity scampered across the patio floor between them.

"Let Sam chase the red dot," Cindy said. "That's what he's good at. You don't have to be a cat to love a cat."

June smiled. "Thanks, Cindy."

Cindy left, and Dipity stopped playing and took a nap.

Sam stepped outside. "Anthony is here," he said lowly.

She sighed. "I'll behave myself and stay away, so he doesn't get spooked."

"I'll be in the sunroom. There's too many people here, and he doesn't like crowds. I'll try to get a better read on him. Pry into his life a little."

"If you need me to hold him down and threaten to break his fingers, just holler."

He kissed the top of her head. "My bodyguard."

She was restless and bored. Freedom didn't feel like freedom. It felt like the past six months, trapped in some house or another, forced to entertain herself, unable to go out into the world.

Like a bored, despondent child, she dragged around the house, on the verge of throwing a tantrum because there was nothing to do. She walked out on the front porch. Night had fallen, the stars out. She trudged down the long set of stairs from the porch to the driveway. Dipity plunked down the steps after her.

"Don't run away," June told her as they reached the bottom. "I'm not digging through the bushes to find you. You'll be sleeping outside tonight."

June sat down on the bottom step. Dipity walked around the yard, sniffing things. Lightning bugs flickered in the darkness, little yellow pulses of light. The driveway was packed with cars.

She picked at her fingernails, trying to shake the looming sense of awkwardness hanging over her, the loneliness of being an outsider, of being that left-out kid she once was. She'd vowed she would never be that girl again, yet here she was.

A nearby sound startled her. She jerked her head up.

What she'd heard was strange and alarming—the sound of leaves rustling and a weird, heavy thump.

Dipity shot back over to the stairs and stopped next to June, tail in the air, staring across the yard.

June got to her feet. She squinted into the shadows under the line of trees across the yard. The trees weren't too far away, maybe fifty feet, but it was so dark now she couldn't make out anything.

"Hello?" she called. Maybe one of the guards was patrolling the grounds.

Silence.

She was tired of being spooked, of hearing bizarre sounds and not knowing their source. She crossed the yard toward the trees, the grass prickling her bare feet. Dipity sprinted back up the stairs to the porch.

"Hello?" she called again. "Is someone there?"

As she drew closer to the trees, the shadows lessened in density, and she could make out something—a shape—lying on the ground. She slowed, holding her breath. She didn't want to be attacked by a nervous possum or sprayed by a skunk.

However, the shape was much too big to be an animal. In fact, it looked like a person.

She stopped, about ten feet away, standing beneath the overhanging branches. She tried to convince herself she wasn't seeing clearly.

"Hello?" She considered using her power. "Hey, can you hear me?"

The shape didn't move. It couldn't be a person. What the hell would a person be doing lying underneath the trees in Sam's yard?

Unless he wasn't alive.

Then came the unmistakable soft swish of someone walking through the grass behind her. Before she could turn around, someone whispered close to her ear.

"For you, darling. Come home soon."

She spun around, a scream catching in her throat.

No one was there.

"Occam!"

No reply. No movement. She turned in a circle, scanning the yard, heart pounding.

"Where are you?" she demanded. "Come out!"

Nothing.

She looked at the house. He was probably already gone, but she had to find out where he was going.

She ran up the stairs, taking them two at a time. She burst into the house, breathing hard, her side aching. Sam's friends were still in the dining room. She ran to the sunroom.

Sam sat on the couch they'd had sex on yesterday. Anthony sat across from him in a chair, and he looked up at her, wide-eyed, blanched. He gripped the arms of his chair.

She bolted over to him and grabbed him by the shoulders, staring into his eyes.

"Where is he going?" she asked.

"June?" Sam got to his feet. "What are you doing?"

"Concentrate!" She shook Anthony. "Where is he going?"

Anthony shrank down in the chair, staring at her. His eyes flashed. He trembled.

"I don't...I can't..." he choked out.

"Can you see him?"

"Yes." His eyes flashed again. "He's... He's in a car, a black car. He's laughing."

"June?" Sam said again. "What the hell is going on?"

"Where is he going?" June asked.

Anthony's eyes flashed again, and then he closed them. "Someone's in the front seat, driving. A black man with dreadlocks."

June ground her teeth. "Zack. Where does the car go?"

"I don't know.... It's getting fuzzy. I see a house—a yellow house. I don't know where it is." He covered his face with his hands. "Let go of me. I can't see any further."

She released him and stood. Anthony curled up in the chair, hands still over his face.

"June." Sam gaped at her. "What are you doing?"

Her heart hammered. She felt sick.

"There's a dead body in your front yard. I hope it's not anyone we know."

Chapter 11

"It's not Jason or Diego."

Those words nearly made June crumple. Her knees were literally weak, her vision going gray for a moment. One of Sam's friends gripped her shoulder, bringing her back to reality. Everyone was outside.

Sam stood under the trees, a flashlight in hand. "I don't know who the hell it is. He's been worked over, though."

June steeled herself and walked toward Sam.

"Should we go get the guards, Sam?" a man asked.

They hadn't called the police or summoned the guards yet. They wouldn't be able to get near the body once the authorities were involved, and she and Sam needed to get near the body. Occam was clearly sending a message.

"Go ahead," Sam said. "Tell them to call the police."

Several people ran down the driveway. June stopped a few feet from Sam.

"How the hell did Occam get on my property?" he asked.

"He's Occam. And he's a shapeshifter."

"He can't make himself look like a tree."

"Can't he? He could disguise an entire van." She stepped closer. "You're sure it's not Jason or Diego?"

"I'm positive." He moved the flashlight beam off the body. "It's pretty grisly. I'm not sure you want to see this."

"I need to see it. There's a reason it's here." Never in her life had she been eager to get near a dead body, but right now, she had to know.

Sam shone the light on the figure.

A man, dressed in jeans and a white T-shirt, or at least it had once been white. His shirt was saturated with blood, dark red and thickly congealed. More was splattered up his neck, his head twisted to the side, his face turned away from her.

Sam circled him slowly, keeping the light on him. "What the hell did that monster do?"

She edged closer, tilting her head.

"Gah!" Sam lurched back, making her jump. "Holy shit. There's a hole in his chest." He directed the light away. "You shouldn't look at this."

"Put the light on his face." She circled around the body.

Sam focused the light on the man's head. The beam trembled.

As she stepped closer, she caught a coppery smell, the raw scent of his insides exposed to the air. Her revulsion and fear disappeared, replaced by curiosity.

"Holy shit," she whispered.

His eyes were half-lidded, the irises peeking out, dilated and dark. His mouth hung slack. Blood coated his face but didn't disguise him.

"What is it?" Sam asked.

"I know him." She stared at his bloody, sagging face. "I know who this guy is. Who this vampire is, I should say."

"What?"

For you, darling.

"This is the vampire who shot me. The one who shot Rose."

She motioned for Sam to give her the flashlight. She passed the light down his body. Blood, so much blood. A ragged hole in his chest, the edges pulpy and glistening. She stepped closer, and her toes squished in the bloody grass. She jerked back.

"Are you serious?" Sam said. "Is this supposed to be a dead bird on the doorstep to get your attention?"

"I'm guessing."

The vampire was clutching something in his left hand. A Polaroid picture.

Voices came from down the driveway. Footsteps.

She knelt and snatched the picture out of his bloody fingers. She stuffed it into her back pocket, and she and Sam moved away from the body, June still shining the light on him.

"Over here!" Sam yelled, waving.

"This was definitely a message," June said lowly.

"He knows where you are, and he isn't afraid to visit. Wonderful."

Two guards rushed over, one talking on a radio.

"It's a vampire," Sam said. "We're pretty sure, anyway."

"Do you know how he got on the property?" the other guard asked Sam.

"I was about to ask you the same thing." Sam glared.

Commotion ensued. Cop cars and an ambulance arrived in a short time, and everyone present was questioned. June watched as they removed the body. She didn't pull the picture out of her pocket, afraid someone might take it from her.

She didn't tell the police about Occam. She simply told them she'd been outside, heard a sound, went to investigate, and found the body. She couldn't say anything about the vampire, either, because it was part of the federal case and she wasn't allowed to talk about being shot or Rose's death.

"Are there any security cameras?" a tall black policeman asked them.

"They're not operational." Sam sighed. "I just got my house back. We're lucky to have electric. The security company is supposed to come out tomorrow."

"Do you have any idea who might have done this?" The cop wrote in a notepad. "Although, I'm sure you have plenty of enemies right now, Mr. Haain."

Sam stiffened. "Yes, I do. I wouldn't be the least bit surprised if this was the work of Robbie Beecher. Shouldn't you be out trying to find him?"

"He'd definitely rip a guy's heart out," June said. Attributing this to Robbie was probably a good idea. It would keep the police from sniffing around and finding out about the kidnapping.

"I would like a police detail here tonight," Sam said. "Since clearly government employees are useless."

"We'll be patrolling the neighborhood." The cop snapped the notebook shut. "But we're not private security, Mr. Haain. You have to pay for that."

Sam glowered. "Can I count on your vote, at least?"

The cop walked away.

"You better send them home." June indicated Sam's friends, huddled together in the driveway. "Is it possible you could get them to not tell everyone they know about what happened here tonight? At least not yet? Let's not give Occam an edge."

"I'll swear them to silence."

Sam talked to his friends. The police were making a sweep of the property.

She slipped inside.

She blinked in the light, her eyes adjusting. The house was quiet. She didn't know if Anthony had left. Maybe he was still curled up in a ball in the sunroom. She hurried to the kitchen where no one would see her and pulled the picture out of her pocket.

She drew a sharp breath, tears springing to her eyes.

Jason and Diego. Alive. Not looking happy, but alive.

They were disheveled, their clothes dirty, Jason's hair sticking up. Occam probably didn't remember what a shower was, as bad as he smelled. They were both glowering at the camera, but they didn't appear sickly or wounded, just unkempt.

She pressed the picture to her chest, her hands trembling. Tears spilled down her cheeks.

"Thank you," she whispered. "A really fucking dramatic way to deliver your message, but thanks."

Sam entered the kitchen behind her. She turned.

"What is it?" He stared wide-eyed at her.

She held the picture out to him in her shaking hand.

* * * *

Sam's friends left, and finally the police. Anthony, according to Sam, had slipped out the back before the police arrived. He was rattled by June's over-enthusiastic questioning and didn't like commotion.

She went up to Sam's room while he made sure all the doors and windows were locked. Dipity joined her in bed, crawling under the covers.

"We've both had a long day, huh?" June patted the lump beside her. "Lots of scary stuff."

Sam came up and got in bed, laptop in hand. She cuddled against him, the picture tucked inside her shirt against her heart. She'd promised her mother she would Skype with her, but she couldn't face her tonight. She wouldn't be able to lie or avoid the topic of Jason. Instead she texted her, explaining it had been a long, tiring day and she would call her in the morning.

"They're alive," she said softly.

"Do you think it's a recent picture?" Sam opened his laptop.

"They look dirty and pissed off. I'm guessing yes." She paused. "He's watching me. He was watching me at the press conference, and he's watching me now. Hell, maybe he's even still here."

"I doubt he's here right now, unless he's hiding up in a tree like a fucking animal."

She glanced at the windows. "I don't think we need to go looking for him. I just have to call out when I'm ready to give an answer. If he wanted to send me a picture, though, he could have done it without the body. His idea of reassurance is horrifying."

"You know Occam loves to horrify." Sam clicked around on the laptop. "Anthony had information on Robbie. Something small, but it's interesting."

"Did he see him?"

"No, but he heard him. He spoke to the spies. Took them off guard, which he was hoping for. Immediately after Anthony left them, one of them called Robbie."

"What did he say?"

"He seemed pleased Anthony was finally taking an interest in him. Then he told the guy on the phone to 'get back here' and said 'we bypassed the secondary security system so you don't have to sneak past the police.'"

June lifted her head. "What does that mean?"

"I don't know. But it seems like he's holed up somewhere that's being guarded."

"Why would he stay somewhere with police around? And that has a security system he needs to bypass?"

"Those are good questions. Hell, why would he even stay in Chicago? At this point, his safest bet would be to get the hell out of the city, get away from the legions of people searching for him."

She dropped her head back down. "If he did that, he'd have to abandon his insane plan, not to mention his vampire friends he's sure he can convince to give him eternal life."

"Chicago isn't the only place with vampires. I'm worried if he doesn't get what he's seeking here, he'll go somewhere else and find a vampire that will bend to his whims. And then he'll swoop back into Chicago, horrifying and invincible...." A hollow chill filled his voice as he trailed off.

She took her hand off the picture and slid her arm around his stomach. "Maybe he'll die," she said softly. "Maybe the thing inside him will kill him."

"What about his followers? They'll carry on his legacy. His evil won't die with him."

"Maybe they'd lose focus without him."

Sam didn't say anything. She narrowed her eyes at his laptop screen. "What are you looking at?" she asked.

"It's Anthony's blog. I'm seeing if anything sends up a red flag."

"What does he blog about?"

"Most of it seems to be about the paranormal. A lot of navel-gazing and opinion. He doesn't mention his own powers. He was probably afraid the Institute would throw a bag over his head and drag him back to their labs."

The blog posts Sam scrolled through were long and dense. "He sure spends a lot of time on there," she said.

"The Internet is his only friend, I'm sure. He's got a lot of comments, though."

"Maybe I should start reading his blog too. I bet he's not as fun as the CIA guy."

"I'll be very careful when communicating with him. And I'll keep doing my research." He huffed. "By the way, the bloggers are talking about our love affair as well."

"I know. We're the talk of the town."

"It's thrilling."

"It's horrible."

"You're no fun." He continued scrolling.

She looked across the room, toward the dresser. She tried not to think about the heartless vampire in the front yard, or anything else horrible, like her brother and Diego ending up heartless. Or Occam sitting on her chest in the middle of the night. Or Micha, dying in a hospital bed.

Micha.

"That's your brother in those pictures over there?" she asked.

Sam draped an arm around her. "Yes. Lots of parties and awards dinners."

"I've seen your brother before."

He stroked his fingers through her hair. "Oh?" He didn't sound surprised.

"Yes, the night we met Occam in the restaurant, when he took Micha to the clinic. You disguised Micha as your brother."

"Very observant."

She moved her head to his shoulder and looked up at him. He stared at the screen.

"Is it easier to disguise people by making them look like someone you know?"

He shrugged. "Sometimes. It requires the same amount of concentration and energy to maintain it."

"Did Micha know you were disguising him as your brother?"

"No, and you didn't, either, until now."

"Was it supposed to be a secret?"

He looked down at her, his face unreadable. "No."

"What was he like?" She plucked at Sam's shirt. "You said he was into politics too. I don't know anything else about him, except he was Kevin's best friend. Was he involved in the Paranormal Alliance?"

"No, not hardly."

"Why?"

"He didn't like that sort of thing. He thought I was being arrogant. He thought creating an organization like that and openly hating the Institute would bring more violence and discrimination to our kind. He thought I would do more harm than good."

She continued playing with his shirt, twisting and tugging at it. "Was he a shapeshifter too?"

"No, a telepath. But he tried to suppress it. It was never very strong, according to him."

"So he wanted to be normal? And he wanted you to sit down and shut up about it?"

"More or less."

"That must have made things difficult between you." She tried to imagine Jason loving what he was and embracing it and crusading. She'd probably recoil like Sam's brother and tell him to knock it off too.

"We had our differences," Sam said. "As we got older, we didn't see eye-to-eye on many things. He also hated that I was besmirching his good name in politics by using my own political clout to harp on paranormal issues. I think sometimes he wished he could disconnect from me altogether."

"That sucks," she said softly. "I mean, like it or not, you guys were still in the same boat."

"Maybe he was right. Look what happened to my people. Look how many of them were hurt and killed by Robbie. Look how many went to his side because I wasn't doing enough."

"Stop it." She pressed her hand to his chest. "We've been over this a million times. You're not responsible for what Robbie did."

"Yet, it happened, like Thomas predicted. I created the Paranormal Alliance. I was the impetus for all this. I brought unwanted attention and pain on our kind."

"No, that was the Institute."

"It's hard to stand up for something, even something you believe in, when people are shouting you down and threatening you. I wanted to be brave. I wanted to be some kind of hero. That was selfish of me. It never should have been about me and what I wanted."

She propped herself up on her elbow. "Sam. Everyone needs a hero. If you hadn't been brave these past few months, none of us would have survived."

He scoffed. "You're quite brave on your own."

"Yes, but being brave doesn't always mean you know what to do. You have guts and smarts."

He shook his head.

"Your brother was afraid. Like I was afraid. Remember when you first met me, how I wanted to deny what I was? To hide it? That's because I was afraid of it. I'm still afraid of it."

"I guess my brother had a good reason to be afraid. He certainly paid for my sins."

"You didn't kill your brother." She sat up.

He gazed at her. His eyes were dark and glittering.

She lifted her arm and bent it, showing him the tattoo of the little girl. "You know who this is? It's my little sister, Katie."

Sam narrowed his eyes at the portrait.

"Jason accidentally caused her death when we were kids, with his power. It was a dumb, childish accident."

Sam's face softened. "I didn't know that. I didn't know you had a sister."

She lowered her arm. "I don't tell a lot of people, because he still feels guilty about it and blames himself. He didn't know what he was doing. He was a kid, a kid who didn't understand what he was and what he was capable of. Jason didn't kill her. Circumstances beyond his control killed her."

Sam was silent.

"And circumstances beyond your control killed your brother. Terrible people killed your brother."

Dipity stirred under the covers. June tried to keep her voice down.

"Terrible people killed your friends in the park that day. I can say my choices led to my brother being held hostage, both at the Institute and by Occam. Micha can say his choices led to him being used as a guinea pig. None of that is true. Things happen, and they happen because of the two A's: accidents or assholes. We're the victims of our circumstances. You wouldn't let me blame myself for everything, so why should I let you?"

"No," he said. "And you're right. We can't blame ourselves. But that doesn't mean we don't regret the things we did that played a part in our circumstances."

"You once told me regret is a useless emotion. You can mourn, but don't regret. I'm sorry assholes took your brother from you. Even if you two didn't get along, maybe someday you could have, if they hadn't taken that opportunity away from you."

He blinked a few times, looking back at the screen. "I'm sorry too." His voice thickened. "And I'm sorry that assholes hurt your brother. And your brother hurt your sister with something he couldn't understand or control."

"Accidents—we can't stop them from happening. But there's a lot of assholes in the world. We need some brave people to hunt them down and make them pay." She lay back down, stretching out beside him. She reached under the covers and petted Dipity, her other hand over the picture. "But why the woman thing?" She turned her head toward him. "Why do you always disguise yourself as a woman? Are they women you know?"

The tension broke, and he chuckled. "No. It's just fun being a woman."

"Sure it is, because you can change back into a man anytime you want."

"I like women. They're my favorite people."

"Yeah, it's awesome being a girl. Being catcalled everywhere you go, that's a big perk."

"Hey, I get catcalled all the time."

"And you consider it an honor." She scratched Dipity's head. "It's an annoyance for me. You'd think I'm scary-looking enough dudes would leave me alone. They just see it as a challenge."

"If anyone catcalls you from now on, especially in my presence, I'll make them eat their tongue. Literally."

"My hero." She pulled her hand from under the covers and rolled toward him. "There's all these other perks, too, like periods. Whoo! That should be arriving soon, by the way."

"Mine too."

She pinched his side. "Jerk."

He reached down and gripped her wrist. "I don't know. Disguising myself as a woman is challenging, to get the glamour to stretch over my frame and make it look believable. I like flexing my paranormal muscle, making it stronger. Your abilities get stronger the more you use them." He eased his grip. "If they're not getting stronger naturally, that is."

"I guess you're lucky. You have to practice."

"I guess I am." He smoothed his hand over her hair.

"I remember something Occam told me about his power. How he was able to disguise the van. He said he's had more than one natural lifetime to learn how to use it. So like, if you lived as long as him, you could probably disguise objects. You could probably do all kinds of things. Like sneak murder victims into someone's yard."

He took his hand off her hair. "I'm sure if the old vampires ever allowed themselves to be subjected to study, we would have found out about the growth of our abilities over unnaturally long periods of time. It would have been fascinating."

"You sound regretful it never happened."

"Well, I certainly wouldn't want the Institute studying those things. But someone, perhaps."

"If the vampires are worried their mystique is ruined now, imagine if people found out about that. I guess they have a point."

"They have plenty of points. Unfortunately, they use them to draw blood." Sam stared across the room, hands on the keyboard. "Maybe Occam has gotten so good at it he can make himself invisible. Maybe he can use his power to hide himself. I can imagine the mechanics of it, though I couldn't do it myself, of course. It would take an obscene amount of energy and intense, nearly inhuman concentration."

"Imagine if you could do it. You could make yourself invisible and hunt down Robbie."

"Maybe I should strike a deal with Occam. Get him to help me and give your brother and friend back at the same time."

She pushed a hand into her shirt and pulled the picture out. "You would need insane leverage to strike a deal like that. The only thing he wants is me. And I know—or at least I hope—you wouldn't give me up."

"God, no." He placed the laptop aside. "But maybe I can come up with something. Money, maybe. That's how Aaron plies them."

"I don't think money is going to buy you Robbie's head, and also Jason and Diego. You want Occam's help—or any of the vampires—you're going to have to appeal, and I mean really, really appeal, to the only thing they care about, and that's themselves."

Sam scooted down beside her. "Maybe."

She held the picture in both hands. Would she give herself up if it meant Sam could have Robbie? Was eternal life such a terrible price to pay to destroy the worst, most dangerous madman ever to run roughshod over the paranormal world and Sam's sanity?

Did she love Sam that much?

She pressed the picture to her chest and stared at the ceiling.

"I'm good at hatching plots," Sam said.

She glanced at the doorway. Nothing rustling out there tonight. Had Occam been in the house, spying on her? Was he the one scampering around like a rat? The idea was nauseatingly creepy.

"If you come up with something," she said, "I'm sure you can just call out to Occam, let him know you want to negotiate. I have a feeling his eyes are all over us, all the time."

Chapter 12

June slept fitfully, her rest full of jarring dreams about finding Jason, Diego, and Sam with their hearts ripped out, scattered through Sam's yard. In another dream, her own heart had been ripped out, but she was alive, sitting in a chair, blood dripping into her lap. No pain, just emptiness in her chest, coldness in her limbs. Occam sat in a chair across from her, smiling, his fangs glinting.

"You were heartless, anyway," he mocked her. "No more than I, though." He opened his jacket to reveal his chest and a ragged, bloody hole in the center of it, oozing gore.

She jerked awake, to sunlight.

Sam had his arm draped over her, his body pressed against her back. Dipity was curled in a ball against her stomach.

The morning quickly went downhill. Her enthusiasm about the vitamins faded as she sat in front of the toilet, her forehead resting on the cool porcelain. Dipity sat at her side. Sam brought her a glass of water.

"I thought this was over." She didn't lift her head. "Kind of dumb, huh?"

Sam rubbed her back. "It's not dumb to hope."

Once she got the morning vomit over with, she felt better and actually wanted food. She took her vitamins, trying to restore hope, and worked on a bowl of fruit in the kitchen.

She called her mother.

"Anything new with your case?" her mother asked. "Do you know when I'll be able to come see you?"

June nibbled on a strawberry. "No, not yet."

"Have you heard from Jason?"

"They're not giving us a whole lot of opportunity to communicate. But hopefully they'll be done with him soon."

"I can't tell you how much lighter I've felt the past couple days, hearing your voice and seeing your face."

"Me too, Mom."

"Your friend Sam seems nice."

Sam had gone to the living room with his own breakfast and turned on the TV. She got the feeling he didn't like to eat in front of her, like it would be mocking her or something.

"Yeah." June picked at a grape in her bowl. "He's a great guy."

"You seem very close."

"We went through a lot together."

"He's handsome."

"Mom."

"I'm just saying. Nice, smart, handsome, and a politician. He has money, doesn't he?"

She popped the grape into her mouth. "Please," she said around it. "Me and a politician? That's crazy."

"Oh, I'm sorry. I forgot, you're going to marry a biker and smoke at the altar."

She rolled her eyes. "For your information, I quit smoking."

"You did?" Her voice brightened. "That's wonderful news."

June would probably never tell her mother she'd been shot. Hopefully, her mother didn't see the scar.

"It's kinda hard to smoke in hiding," June said. "I guess that's the silver lining."

"I worry so much about your health."

Sam appeared in the doorway, his phone clenched in his fist. June frowned. He pointed into the living room urgently.

"Hey, Mom," June said. "Can I call you back in a bit? I gotta do some things."

"Yes, I'm not working until this afternoon. I'll be waiting to hear back from you. I love you, darling."

"I love you too, Mom. I'll call you back soon."

June clicked off, tense. "What is it?"

"You better come see this."

"It's not another body, is it?"

"Not here, no."

She left her bowl of fruit and phone in the kitchen and followed Sam to the living room. On the TV, a woman reporter was talking. She stood in front of a white building. Sam grabbed the remote and turned it up.

"And here at the transfusion clinic," the woman said, "a grisly scene, as in other places around Chicago this morning. Destruction, as well as brutal multiple murders. Police are urging anyone with information to please come forward. While this latest act of deadly paranormal violence seems to be only targeting vampires, many more could be in danger."

"What's going on?" June asked.

"Dead vampires. Everywhere."

She stared at him.

"I wanted to see if they said anything about what happened here last night. Apparently, it's happening everywhere."

"What do you mean?"

"They've found dead vampires all over the city—parks, alleyways, in yards, on sidewalks. The transfusion clinics were trashed too."

June's blood ran cold. "The cleansing."

"It would seem so."

On TV they were showing the inside of the clinic, which had been ransacked. At the bottom of the screen it said, "Seventy-eight Confirmed Dead So Far."

"Jesus," June breathed out. "The note—the one someone gave me at the press conference. Occam said he'd be 'busy the next couple days.' This must be what he meant."

"They might kill even more."

June stared at the TV, her head buzzing.

"They're no better than Robbie," Sam said. "Mass murdering for their own agenda. As if this city hasn't suffered enough blood and destruction."

"Our blood," June said. "The normals don't care if we kill each other. It keeps them from having to do it."

"I see you've been swallowing my dogma quite nicely."

"You didn't have to make me swallow it. The world did that."

He slid an arm around her shoulders. They both watched the TV.

"Vampires have always been separate from the rest of us," Sam said. "But they don't deserve this, any more than my people did."

"Occam said they would get rid of the young and weak. He said they only want strong vampires." She scratched her nails across her chest and shuddered. "I think they mean to take over this city one day."

"Occam can't possibly believe this would charm you to his cause."

"It's not just him, I'm sure."

The reporters navigated through the destruction of the clinic. Blood was splashed on the white walls.

"Too many of them think the same," June said. "They'll kill who they want to. No one can stop them."

"This is why it's necessary we have this gathering at the beach." Sam rubbed her shoulder. "We have to show everyone—our people, the normals—that we can still come together in peace, that there's solidarity in those who won't stand for violence."

They watched the news through the morning. Sam made phone calls, asking for information, arranging things.

The death toll climbed. Most of the bodies seemed to have been dumped in public, though a few were found in their homes. All were slaughtered horribly and missing vital organs. No transfusion clinic—she learned there were six in the city—had been left unscathed. Most were merely trashed, but one close to Old Town had been burned down.

The Nocturnal District was on lockdown. No businesses were allowed to open that night, and police were patrolling the streets and questioning people. No bodies had been found there, though. June could guess the vampires were probably sanctifying the area, and only the old powerful ones would be allowed inside it from now on.

Sam's name came up over and over, some people citing how if he became mayor he could stop things like this from ever happening again. Of course, others felt the opposite, that Sam's renewed presence and the whole mess with the Institute had been the impetus for this.

The body found in Sam's yard went unmentioned, thankfully. Either the police didn't tell the press or it got lost in all the other news.

Her mother would find out from the national news sooner or later, so June called her back and filled her in, not wanting her to panic.

"Oh my God." She panicked, anyway. "June! You have to get out of that city. Who knows what's going to happen next?"

"I wish I could. It's just vampires."

"It's probably that horrible man who killed all those people in the park." Her voice grew shrill and tremulous. "June, he's going to kill all the paranormal people. I don't care what the FBI says. You have to get out of there. You have to come home!"

"I can't leave yet, Mom."

"You're going to get killed! I just got you back. If I lose you, I won't be able to go on."

June wished she could tell her everything, to ease her fears. The truth wouldn't do that, though. She'd be ten times more hysterical if she found out June was dying and she'd been offered vampirism, and that her son was currently a prisoner of said vampires. The vampires who were busy killing their own kind right now.

"I'll be careful, Mom. We're somewhere safe. Nothing is going to happen to us, I promise."

The news didn't get any better as the day wore on. The death toll rose to a hundred, and then a hundred and fifty. Bodies were everywhere. A visit online found plenty of people who were snapping pictures. It was a gruesome, grisly mess.

Cindy and Natalie arrived in the early afternoon, ahead of a group of Sam's friends. Cindy stood in front of the TV, her hands clasped beneath her chin.

"This is horrifying," she said. "I mean, vampires aren't my favorite people, but this is awful. Just like at the park."

"We knew this was coming." June kept her voice down. "I don't think Occam makes idle threats."

"I hope Jason and Diego are all right. He wouldn't do anything to them because of this, would he?"

June slipped the picture out of her pocket and held it out to Cindy. "They're fine."

Cindy gasped. She clamped a hand over her mouth, her eyes going bright. She took the picture.

"Occam dropped that off last night," June said. "I think that's when the cleansing began."

Cindy blinked. "What?"

June told her what happened the night before.

"Occam dumped a dead vampire in Sam's yard?" Cindy sat down in a chair, still holding the picture. "Just to send you a message?"

"And to woo me." June sat too. "I guess I'm supposed to swoon now that he's killed the vampire that shot me, and I'm supposed to be grateful to him because Jason and Diego are all right."

"He can't take no for an answer. Talk about a creep."

"The thing is, I've never said no. Except at first, before I knew he was holding anything over me. If I flat out tell him no now, I'm afraid he'll rip out Jason and Diego's organs and dump them on me. I have to get them back first before I deny him anything." She glanced over her shoulder. "I think he's been watching me. I think he's been creeping around here, keeping an eye on me."

Cindy shuddered. "This is horrific. I bet Robbie is taking notes. It's only going to give him ideas."

June recalled what Sam had said the night before, what Anthony had heard Robbie say on the phone.

"There's this guy helping Sam," June said. "Trying to help him find Robbie. I'm not sure I trust him."

"Robbie's brother," Cindy said. "Yeah, I know."

June was taken aback. "He told you?"

"He told us everything. I don't know the guy. I know *of* him. He joined the Paranormal Alliance a couple years ago, but he doesn't participate much. It's fascinating, the power he has. Still, I understand not trusting him, even if he claims he hates his brother."

"I've just seen too many people we trusted betray us." June glanced toward the kitchen, where Sam and Natalie were. "I've seen Sam trust too many people and get burned."

"And now with Muse gone…"

"Maybe I need to get him a new mind reader for Christmas."

"Can you get me one too? It would make dating easier."

June was too scared to go outside, even in broad daylight, so she stayed in, despite the house filling up with people. Sam seemed to be having a big meeting. She escaped upstairs and checked the Internet to see what the blogs were saying about her and Sam today.

They were more concerned with vampires.

Eventually, Sam came upstairs. She was stretched across the bed.

"Would you like to take a little trip with me?" He sat down next to her.

She looked up from the laptop in front of her. "Where to?"

"I need to get something from my storehouse. The place where I keep all the stuff we pilfered from the Institute. Thankfully, the FBI knows nothing about it, so it remains intact, at least according to my officers."

She recalled the ultraviolet light Sam procured from his storehouse to use against Occam.

"What are you going to get there?" she asked. "Do you have more of those lights? We might need them."

"No, but I have other things. I also want to do a general inventory. See if there's anything else we might make use of."

"Why do you want me to go with you?"

He patted her ass. "I thought you might find it interesting." He rested his hand there. "And I'd rather you not be alone here."

She rolled over and reached for him. He took her hand in both of his.

"Do you think this is ever going to end?" she asked softy. "That one day we'll all be safe?"

He leaned over, kissed her gently, and rested his forehead against hers. She closed her eyes. The subtle, musky scent of his cologne enveloped her.

"It feels like we've been this way forever, doesn't it?" he whispered. "The days, the weeks, the months. It feels like an eternity we've been enduring this. We've lost so much in such a short time."

He'd lost more than she had. She had been lucky to get back the things she lost, and would be double lucky if she got them back again.

"What doesn't kill us makes us stronger, right?" she murmured.

"Or makes us wish we were dead." He lifted his head and kissed her again. "It's not all bad. A few good things came out of it."

"Are you getting sappy again?"

He answered with a longer, deeper kiss. She liked the way he kissed—no hesitation, no doubt. She liked everything about the way he treated her, paid attention to her, wanted her. She liked it all way too much—so much she was afraid if he figured out they weren't compatible, she wouldn't be able to sever herself from him without a great deal of pain.

He rested his head on her shoulder, holding her hand against his chest. She stared at the ceiling, her lips tingling.

"When are we leaving?" she asked.

"In an hour or so. I'll bring Cindy and Natalie with us. The place isn't huge, but there's a lot of stuff there. I don't want to miss anything." He sat up and let go of her hand. "Are you feeling better?" He rubbed her stomach.

She nodded. "I kept some food down. I'm starting to get used to the taste of puke. Maybe I can jazz it up by eating different things. You know, add some variety?"

He grimaced and then smiled. "I'm glad to see you have a sense of humor still."

"It's that or sit around crying and shaking." She placed a hand over his on her stomach. "I have faith in Trina. Or I'm trying to, anyway."

"I'm glad I kidnapped her for you." He leaned over and placed another firm, quick kiss on her lips. "You know, I don't have to go directly back downstairs. I can tell them I was up here looking for something...."

She pinched his inner thigh. "Later. Go play with your friends."

He sighed dramatically and slid off the bed. "I'll come get you when it's time to go."

"I'll be here." She rolled back over and faced the laptop.

Chapter 13

Cindy drove, Natalie in the front with her. Sam and June sat in the back and ducked down as they pulled out. The street was empty, apart from a handful of FBI guards.

Sam sat up. "The vampires are more interesting right now. I'm almost insulted."

He gave Cindy directions. They got on a freeway.

"This is exciting." Cindy drummed her hands on the wheel. "I've always wanted to go to the storehouse. I feel like it's some kind of treasure trove."

"It's not that exciting," Sam said. "It's probably pretty dusty these days too."

June sat close to Sam's side. His amorousness from earlier hadn't worn off, as he slowly rubbed her thigh, dipping his fingers deeper between her legs with each pass. When those fingers inched dangerously close to her crotch, she eyed him.

He smiled deviously. She wouldn't mind a clandestine finger banging, but that would be rude to the others in the car. Not to mention Cindy's sex witchery might get stirred up.

They spent a long time on the freeway. They were traveling in the direction of Promontory Point, where they'd attended the first press conference back in January. They passed it, though.

Sam finally sat forward. As he did, he slipped his hand up her thigh and into her crotch. "Take the next exit and make a right," he told Cindy.

June locked her legs around his wrist. Undeterred, he rubbed firmly.

As he sat back, she smacked his arm. He pulled his hand out, not looking at her but grinning. Naughty smug jerk.

They exited the freeway near the lake and drove through an industrial area, past factories with huge smokestacks, vast yards filled with machinery and textiles, and fenced-in lots. Though the windows were up, a sulfur-y metallic smell seeped through the air vents.

"Just keep driving for a bit," Sam said. "I'll tell you when." He kept his hand on June's knee, like a good boy.

They ended up in an abandoned train yard, or so it appeared. Rusted train cars sat everywhere, most of them with panels and doors missing and covered in graffiti. A small brick building sat on one side of the dirt and gravel yard, the windows boarded up and covered with bars. Cindy pulled the car beneath a sagging awning on the side of it.

The building was dilapidated, the bricks cracked and some fallen out, more graffiti sprayed across them. The area was open and eerily empty. In the distance, factories chugged out smoke, and a thin blue slice of lake glimmered on the horizon.

"This feels like the middle of nowhere," June said.

"It is." Sam took his hand off her knee and opened his door. "The best place to keep things you don't want anyone to find."

They all got out. The day was hot and humid and the acrid smell on the air made June's nose burn. The wind rattled the tattered plastic awning above them and made loose bits of metal clink on the train cars. The sounds added to the eeriness.

"How did you get a place like this?" June asked as they walked around the building.

"I bought it." Sam had a ring of keys in his hand. "This used to be a train car repair depot. I was planning on scrapping all that metal." He gestured toward the train cars. "Make my money back and more, and then develop the land. But that was around the time I was making my treaty with Aaron, and I got distracted."

They stopped at a wooden door on the side of the building. Sam unlocked it.

"I eventually realized this was a good place to hide things. I transferred ownership of the land to one of Aaron's many partners, just in case anybody dug into my business." He pushed the door open. "I pay his partner a little fee each year to leave it sitting here unused."

"So in the end," Cindy said, "you lost more on this wasteland than you meant to gain." She squinted up at the building. "Not as impressive as I hoped."

"You haven't seen the inside yet," Sam said.

They all filed in. The interior was cool and musty like a basement, also pitch black, since all the windows were boarded up. Shockingly, the place had electricity, as Sam turned on a series of utility lights strung through the wooden ceiling beams. The lights created disjointed shadows in the rafters, cobwebs clinging to the fixtures and making them fuzzy.

Shelves lined the brick walls, crates and boxes stacked on the floor. Most everything was covered in a layer of dust. The concrete floor was also thick with it, so much they left footprints.

June turned in a circle. "There's a lot of stuff in here."

"Not all of it is pilfered from the Institute." Sam walked over to a tarp and dragged it down. "I have a lot of Paranormal Alliance junk in here too."

"Do people guard this place?" June asked. When Muse had brought Sam the ultraviolet light, she'd mentioned his storehouse was left unguarded.

"They used to." Sam flung the tarp on the floor, a cloud of dust swirling up. "I'd have people ride past here a couple times a day. They dropped off in my absence, though. I don't blame them. My officers had more important tasks, like proving my innocence."

Natalie had a stack of notebooks. She patted them. "We better get to work. We got a big list to go through."

"I used to take inventory every six months," Sam told June. "I want to be thorough with this, given I've had no access to it for a while."

They pulled tarps off other things. June did a lot of sneezing and trying to avoid spiders. Most of the shelves were crammed with boxes. Another room was connected to the main one, filled with more shelves.

The second room held mostly Paranormal Alliance paraphernalia: flyers, booklets, posters, signage, and décor from various events, and also stacks of paperwork. Sam was a pack rat. This character flaw was oddly endearing, since he was so efficient in all other aspects of his life.

June held up a dusty poster. "'The Paranormal Alliance Winter Fundraiser,'" she read. "'Raising awareness for paranormal violence and creating community support for victims.'" The date was in late December of the previous year, and it had been held in a hotel ballroom. A fancy affair, judging by the flourished script.

Sam dug through a tote full of books. "Yes, we have it every year. It's a big to-do; lots of rich important people are invited. Not just paranormal people."

"And do they become aware of paranormal violence?"

"They claim to. They write big checks for people who have been beaten up and kicked around."

"Will they be supporting us, specifically, this year? After what we've been through?"

His eyes glinted in the light. "I'm sure we'll be the hot topic of this year's banquet, yes. You'll have to wear a nice dress."

She rolled the poster up. "One dress a year, that's all I can manage."

Sam pulled a book out of the tote and blew dust off the cover. He held it out to her. "One of my books," he said. "That I wrote."

She took it. "*Paranormal Politics*," she read the title. "*Social Issues in a Magical World*." She eyed him. "Is this about how to become Chicago's first shapeshifter mayor?"

He chuckled. "Something like that. It's about being a paranormal politician in a normal politician's world, and how to make those two things work together so everyone benefits."

She opened the book and flipped through it. So many pages, so many words. "Does it take a long time to write a book like this?"

"As much as I like to express my opinion?" He stood. "A lot of it is modified entries from journals I kept. I never intended to make it into a book until some literary agent told me I should. I think I should convince them to do a re-issue, given my current ambitions. The city needs to read it, if they haven't already."

"Does that mean you'll autograph this for me?'

"Can I autograph your boob instead?"

"Please, I'll never wash it again."

Natalie and Cindy took inventory, starting with the shelves in the main room. Sam showed her things they'd taken from the Institute. Most of it was not as impressive as the ultraviolet light they'd tried to use on Occam—in fact, most of it was just folders of research. Sam explained his people would photocopy test results and smuggle them out. He also had pictures—odd and clinical—of the insides of vampire's mouths with their fitted fangs, pictures of substances on fire after being ignited by pyrokinetics, and pictures of people's eyes, intense and vivid like June's.

He had a pair of noise-cancelling headphones, like the ones the researchers used around her and Jason—they were more advanced than regular noise-cancelling headphones and injected white noise into the wearer's ears to block sound further. June wanted to fling them away.

"I'm guessing Occam still has the ultraviolet weapon," Sam said. "Due to some news I heard this morning."

June stood in front of a shelf. A small wooden rack sat on the shelf, holding three dusty, grimy tubes of dark red liquid.

"What news?" Cindy asked from across the room.

"Apparently," Sam's voice echoed in the rafters, "some of the dead vampires had burns on them. A few had their eyes burned out."

June shuddered.

"I'm sure that's Occam's way of sending me a message." Sam carefully lifted a small box off a shelf next to her. "He wants me to know he hasn't forgotten."

"I don't think you could actually kill a vampire with it," June said. "Burning a vampire's eyes out isn't going to kill him, right? You can live without eyes. They're not a vital organ."

Sam stepped over to her. "No, but he's having fun, or one of them is. A little added torture."

"Are these what I think they are?" June pointed at the tubes. "Oracles of the Dead? Or the base, at least? Vampire blood?"

Sam rubbed his thumb over one of the tubes, wiping dust from it. "The Oracle of the Dead isn't just vampire blood and the blood of a powerful paranormal human. The vampire blood has to be old and just as powerful. Only certain vampires can make them. The one involved with Kevin's grandmother was older than even Occam."

June grimaced. "So this is vampire blood."

"God, no." He withdrew his hand. "Old vampires didn't go anywhere near the Institute. This is Muse's blood."

June flinched.

"She gave it freely," Sam said. "It's not to make Oracles, though it can be used for that, I'm sure. She was well aware of her mortality. She left it behind for research purposes—by proper researchers, not the Institute. Maybe someday, someone will find a cure."

June's trepidation melted away. "And you keep it here?"

"Where else should I keep it? This is the safest place for it."

"Maybe I should give some of mine too."

He lowered his voice. "I'm hoping there won't be a need."

June looked back at the tubes. "She was brave. Inspiring, even. I wish I had known her better."

"Inspiring, yes, like a muse." Sam smiled faintly. "That's where she got her name. I gave it to her, sort of. Going on about how much of an inspiration she was to me and to our kind. She thought 'Muse' was fitting, and it was a good way to shed her old identity and become who she really was."

"She told me her choice of name was complicated and a long story."

"I'm sure to her it was. Changing your identity is a big deal, and a long, sometimes difficult process. Just saying 'I picked a new name' doesn't really encapsulate the struggle in a way that feels respectful of it."

June had changed since the beginning of the year as well, the struggles she'd been through, the things she'd faced. She'd become a new person, less afraid of her past, more concerned about her future. Maybe she needed to change her name too.

"Yeah," June said. "I totally get that."

Sam turned away, holding up the small box. "Come outside. I want to put this in the car and get some air."

She followed him out into the heat and sunlight, squinting against the brightness.

"What's in that?" she asked as he placed the box in the backseat, through the open window.

"Something important." He slid an arm around her shoulders.

They strolled beneath the awning, toward the back of the car. The wind tugged at her clothes and hair, gusting away some of the heat.

"It's awful lonely out here." She squinted across the yard. The train cars loomed amongst the weeds, hulking and ominous. "I get creeped out in wide open spaces."

"A lot of people do." They stopped at the edge of the awning's shade. His arm rested heavy across her shoulders. "There's a story someone told me. It explains why we feel that way. I'll tell you about it later."

"Why not tell me now?"

"Because." He took his arm off her shoulders and gripped her hip. "I'm interested in something else right now." He backed her up, toward the wall of the building.

"Oh, is that what this is?" she taunted as she was pressed against the rough warm brick. "Getting some air, huh?"

He tucked a hand into her crotch. "The girls are busy taking inventory."

"You're a tease, the way you were messing with me in the car."

"I'm not teasing now." He popped the button on her jeans.

She glanced in the direction of the door. Several barrels and stacks of sheet metal were piled next to the two of them, so even if Cindy or Natalie came outside they wouldn't immediately be caught.

"Since I dragged you out here to be bored half the day"—Sam eased her zipper down—"I might as well make it worth your while."

"It is pretty boring. I thought you were gonna have, like, death rays and stuff."

He pushed his hand down the front of her jeans, into her panties. "You overestimate me. That's comforting."

She was already wet from earlier. He stroked and rubbed. She jerked her hips. In reciprocation, she reached for the front of his pants.

He gently pushed her hand away. "We'll take care of that later. Just enjoy."

She wasn't going to argue.

He pushed two fingers into her. She gripped his arm, the thick muscles of his forearm flexing beneath his sweaty skin. She was sweating, too, the wetness slicking her lower back.

She bit her lip as he worked his fingers inside her, not fast, but deliciously deep. He rubbed his thumb over her ring in slow circles.

"See?" he whispered, close to her ear. "Not a tease."

She moved her hips faster, riding his fingers. Her jeans and panties slid low on her hips, giving him access, the wind drying the sweat across her lower back. She braced her feet wide apart and pushed her shoulders back against the bricks.

"Fuck," she gasped, her body tensing. The buildup of pleasure made her right side ache, but she fought to ignore it. "Oh, God…"

Sam breathed heavy and close to her ear. Heat radiated off his body, warmer than the day. Sweat trickled down his neck. She wanted to lick it away.

"Almost?" His fingers were relentless, pounding into her now.

"Yes." She clutched the sleeve of his T-shirt, near his shoulder. "Don't stop, Sam."

He didn't stop. She reached the point of no return, her insides tightening. The tension broke in a glorious rush, and she let out a half-stifled moan, shuddering against the wall, squeezing around his fingers.

He slowed his thrusts but continued rubbing. "There we go." He caressed his other hand over her bare hip. "I love to feel that."

She shivered, eyelids fluttering. Little tremors shuddered through her and slowly tapered off. The stitch in her side was worse, and she tried to draw in slow, even breaths to stop it.

She quit fighting the urge and licked up the side of his neck. Salt coated her tongue.

He chuckled. "You okay?" His fingers were still inside her.

"I'm great. Not so boring after all."

He pulled his fingers out. She kind of wished he would pick her up and fuck her against the wall now.

"Sure you don't want me to return the favor?" She gripped the firm bulge in the front of his jeans. "My mouth is magic, remember?"

"How could I forget?" He kissed her. "No. We'll have fun later. I'm afraid I actually do have work to do."

She looked down at herself. "I'm a sloppy mess. This is going to be an awkward day."

"I'm sorry."

She tugged her jeans and panties up. "I don't believe you are."

He sucked his wet fingers into his mouth and winked.

June took a hair tie off her wrist and started pulling her hair back. "So what's this about why people feel creeped out in wide open spaces?"

"Oh, it's something I heard when I was a teenager. There was this old guy. I'd always see him at the bus stop near my high school. I liked talking to people. My mom said I was the most outspoken kid she'd ever met."

June shook her head. "You? Really?"

Sam walked over to the car and reached in the front seat through the window. He pulled out two bottles of water. "He was...something." He walked back to her and held one out.

"Something?" She took it. "Thanks."

"Something paranormal, I think. But I don't know what." He untwisted the cap on his bottle. "He seemed to know things about people. He could read you. Not like a telepath, though. It seemed to go deeper than that."

She uncapped her own and took a drink. The water was warm, but refreshing.

"He'd talk about all the places he'd traveled. And we'd talk about me, what I was doing in school, what my life was like at home. He was just... nice to listen to. You know those kind of people?"

She nodded. "There was a guy who taught Jason and me about our powers when we were younger. He was like that too. Real soothing to listen to, no matter what he was talking about."

"I felt like I knew him forever, but it was only that one year, my sophomore year, and only in the spring, toward the end of the school year."

"The wise old man at the bus stop." She grinned. "How cliché."

He shook his open bottle at her, splashing water down the front of her shirt. She yelped and laughed.

"He told me that people, even normal people, have this power, this energy. When a lot of people get together and focus their energy, it creates things." He waved a hand. "I know it sounds hippie and existential. Maybe he was just a chatty, lonely old man who liked to tell stories, and I was an impressionable teenager doing a lot of soul searching at the time."

"Somehow even as a teenager I can't picture you buying into folklore. You're too practical."

"I wasn't always. Or maybe the way he said it, just...seemed practical."

"So, we create things?"

"He said we not only create things, we give them life. Our energy puts energy out into the world. He said cities, especially big cities, like this one"—he waved vaguely in the direction they'd come—"we build them, we pour our energy into them, and they become living things. They become entities."

June blinked. She recalled standing on the balcony of Sam's hotel room in the middle of freezing winter. Micha stood beside her, and he'd said the city was a living thing, he'd said "we as entities create other entities."

"We all thrive on that energy," Sam said. "But we also thrive on the energy of nature, because it's where we came from. When you get out to the border between those two things, like here, where human energy is fading and the energy of nature hasn't taken over yet, that's where you feel strange. You've lost touch with everything. It's nowhere. A margin between worlds."

Sam took a drink and lowered his bottle. "He could have just been an eccentric old man. Summer break came, and I didn't see him when school started again. Maybe he died. I didn't think much about him after that. I only think about him at times like this."

"I've heard those words before," June said. "We as entities create other entities."

Sam squinted at her.

"Micha said that to me. He said the city was a living thing."

Sam shrugged. "I don't know how Micha would know that, but hey, the old man did say it was all humans, not just paranormal ones. It's kind of comforting, when you think about it."

They strolled back around the building, toward the door. June gazed across the empty yard at the dirt being kicked up by the wind, the rattling train cars, the swaying weeds. "Is it?"

"Yes. It's nice to know there's a place you can go to escape humanity, get away from everyone else's crappy energy."

"Yeah, I guess it is...."

Chapter 14

Back at the house, June's wariness grew as night fell. She kept glancing out the windows into the gathering gloom, expecting to see Occam staring back at her.

The vampire death toll continued rising, and paranormal as well as regular humanitarian groups got involved. Businesses catering to vampires closed out of fear. Cops were on high alert. Politicians pontificated loudly.

"They stole our thunder." Sam stood in the kitchen, his laptop on the counter. "I can't help but feel like the timing is meant to be personal."

June leaned next to the sink. "I feel sorry for them. Yeah, there's a lot of dick vampires, but I'm betting those aren't the ones they're killing."

"I don't even know the true vampire population in the city. So many of the old ones live on the fringes. So yes, I'm guessing it's the non-dick vampires being killed. Although, I've never met a vampire I liked. You have to have a certain dickishness about you to even want to become one."

June shook her head. "Really, I doubt this was done to spite us. Occam doesn't work that way. If anything, it would be to take attention off me so he can spirit me away without anyone noticing."

Sam looked at her. "Come here, I want to show you something."

She walked over to him.

He picked up something next to the laptop—the little box from the storehouse. He took the lid off. "I had to get the software working first. I was afraid it might not."

He pulled a thin green bag out of the box, as thin as a slip of paper, one of those static-free bags for electronic equipment. Inside was a small transparent rectangle, like a piece of cellophane with tiny circuits etched into it.

"This," Sam said, "is something the Institute was working on and had the audacity to claim it was benign and helpful."

June peered at the bag. "What is it?"

"A tracking device." Sam held it up to the light. "It attaches to skin or clothing. You don't even know it's there. They developed it to keep track of research subjects."

June blinked. "Like tagging them?"

"Supposedly, it would only be used with permission from the subject and only in cases of long-term research, where the subject wasn't going to spend all his time at the Institute. It was supposed to give researchers information about the person's habits. Behavioral stuff."

"I'm sure. I bet it was never to be used without the person's permission." She had the sudden urge to check her body over.

"There was a lot of controversy over it. My group protested it and the project was shelved. However"—he tapped the bag—"who knows how many they actually sneaked out there. This was one of the more advanced ones created just before they shut the project down."

"Too bad you couldn't steal all of them."

"I downloaded the software from the Institute servers back when we first stole it. I have some very talented hackers in my group. We'd raid their databases all the time, before they caught on and locked us out. It seems the software is still working. Imagine that."

She grunted.

"So now I have this tiny inconspicuous device and the means to track it."

She tilted her head.

"I could put that to good use, don't you think?"

She squinted. "You think Anthony could put it on Robbie?"

"Anthony won't get that close to Robbie, trust me. Robbie isn't going to crawl out of hiding, even for his brother. Especially for his brother, if Anthony's stories are true."

"Put it on one of his henchmen, then. That would lead you to Robbie."

"I thought about it. But I'm also not sure handing over one of the most powerful devices I have to a man we're not sure we can trust is a good idea."

"So... How are you going to use it?"

"I'm going to put it on Anthony."

She blinked.

"At first," Sam said. "We find out where he's going, find out if he's the real deal. If he is, I'll ask him to put it on one of Robbie's people."

He was actually taking her advice. However...

"How are you going to put it on him? He can see the future. He'll see you putting it on him."

"He can only see the future; he can't see the past. If I can plant it somewhere so he sits on it, or it gets stuck to him, he won't be able to see that."

"Yeah, but people take their clothes off. You can't stick it to his clothes. All that's going to tell you is where his laundry is."

"On his shoe then. He'd have to put on shoes to leave the house. It's durable and waterproof. I doubt walking on it would damage it."

"No, it's gotta go on his skin. You have to get it on his person."

Sam slumped. "Any ideas, then? Because yes, if I stick it right to him, he's probably going to see that coming."

She considered the bag. "That thing sticks to your skin without being noticed? Not even a little?"

He opened the bag. "Yes, one of the reasons we didn't trust it. It was obviously created with subterfuge in mind."

He dipped a finger inside and slid the chip out on his fingertip. He motioned for her to stretch out her arm.

She did. He frowned.

"Do you have an inch of skin that isn't covered in tattoos? I need you to see what it looks like against your normal skin."

She rolled her eyes and tugged up the side of her shirt. "Here." She turned her bare side to him. Her ribs stuck out. "I thought you knew every inch of my body by now."

He smoothed it against her side, above her hip.

Truly, she couldn't feel it. She'd expected it to feel like a piece of tape stuck to her, but there was no sensation whatsoever. She stroked her finger across it. It didn't feel like anything, either.

"That's freaky," she said. "There's no way in hell this wasn't made to be stuck on people without them knowing." She picked at it. "Is it hard to pull off? Do you think people might be out there right now with one of these still stuck to them?"

She had to dig her fingernails under the edge to remove it—and it only peeled off reluctantly, like a fresh Band-Aid.

"I don't know," Sam said. "I can only access this one with the software because I have the serial number. I'd have to know the numbers of other ones to see if they're still functioning and where they are."

She stuck it to the back of her hand. The material didn't catch the light, and the circuits were so tiny she had to search for them. The damn thing was nearly invisible.

"I doubt he'll feel it being attached," Sam said. "But how do we get it on his skin?"

"He can only see the future of the person he's interacting with, right?" She peeled the chip off and held it out to Sam on her finger. "And he can only see what's about to happen, right? In the near future?"

Sam took the chip and slipped it back into the bag.

"What if someone put it on him before he knows that person is there?" she said. "It would happen before he began interacting with them, so it would already be in the past."

Sam narrowed his eyes. "How would we manage that?"

"I'll sneak up on him from behind."

"You?" He blinked.

"You'll be talking to him. Someone needs to, so he's distracted. You keep his attention. I'll creep up on him."

"You realize he'll go through the roof if you sneak up and touch him?"

"Yeah, probably. At least we'll get some entertainment out of it."

Sam placed the bag on the counter next to his laptop. "There's a lot of things he might see. We have to be careful. He can't read minds, but any point past you putting it on him, he'll see and hear what we do."

"Okay, then I have to sneak up on you, too, so you don't know I'm coming, so he doesn't see you seeing me." She paused, trying to untangle her brain. "And we have to make sure after that we don't talk about it for a while and you don't start tracking it, maybe not for a day or so. Remember he said things get too convoluted after a while?"

Sam slipped an arm around her waist. "You're brilliant." He kissed her cheek. "He'll be over later, since we were so rudely interrupted last night. We're going to discuss what the next move should be."

"Just tell me where you'll be, and you won't know I'm coming."

He swatted her ass. "Unlike earlier?"

She pinched his side.

The house filled up with people again. They seemed to be engaged in a mixture of planning for the beach party, assembling Sam's mayoral campaign, and discussing the vampire murders. June considered maybe she could help with drawing some posters or something, but they weren't in the creative stages yet. Everyone congregated in the living room this time, and June lurked on the edges of the group, waiting for her cue.

Eventually Sam got a text, nodded to her, and left the room. She slipped off in the opposite direction, toward the kitchen. He'd told her he'd meet with Anthony in his office.

As she was retrieving the bag from the drawer Sam had stashed it in, Cindy walked into the kitchen.

"I need more coffee." Cindy made a beeline for the coffee maker, which had been in a constant state of percolation for the past few hours. "And some whiskey. There's too many pretty boys here."

June pushed the bag into her hip pocket. "Sam's got some in the cabinet under the sink. I found it when we were cleaning up."

"Oh, I know where he hides his liquor." She opened the cabinet beneath the sink and whipped out a bottle of Jack Daniels. "It's his emergency stash, for people like me."

"I take it you've been here a lot? Sam often has house parties like this?"

Cindy huffed, pouring whiskey into her cup. "There's always something going on at Sam's house. The various chapters have their own headquarters, but this has always been *the* headquarters." She plunked the bottle down. "And now I get to be part of the team. I'll be over here all the time. We can hang out!"

"Yeah. Get our nails done together and everything."

"How long has it been since you had your nails done?"

June held her hand out. The paint job she currently had was self-done and a little wonky, painted for the press conference. "Way too long."

"We're gonna fix that."

"Sure thing."

Cindy dived into her spiked coffee, and June left the room.

She locked herself in the downstairs bathroom and removed the chip from the bag. She perched it delicately on her middle and index fingers, an ephemeral slip of nothingness. She was paranoid she would drop it before she got to the office.

She stared at her reflection in the mirror, working out in her head the steps she would take. Sam assured her Anthony would have his back to the door. She had to be stealthy and quick.

As she gazed at herself, something struck her. Her reflection was the same as always—her face too gaunt, her shoulders too sharp under her shirt. Her hair looked good now that she'd had it done, full and shiny and the black lustrously dark.

However, maybe it was the renewed color of her hair, but her eyes seemed different. She leaned closer to the mirror, peering into them.

She was used to how vibrant green they were, how radiant, almost luminescent in the right light. But now they seemed duller. The color wasn't as intense.

She blinked a few times. Maybe she was imagining it. Maybe it was the lighting.

Or maybe she was dying. Was this the first sign of dying? Did the color fade from her eyes? She was instantly nauseated at the thought, her stomach clenching.

She drew back. Surely, she was imagining things. She'd been "dying" for years, according to Occam. Why would her eyes start fading now? Why would that even happen?

A soft rustling drew her attention. She jerked her head around and stared at the tub in the corner of the room, where the sound had come from. Shower tubing was attached to the tub, and a white shower curtain hung from it.

She'd heard the curtain rustle.

Her senses sharpened. She walked cautiously toward the tub. The curtain was open across the front, and obviously no one was standing inside; however, between the back of the curtain and the wall there was a space.

She stopped a few feet from the tub, holding her breath, the chip still delicately resting on her fingertips.

"Is someone there?" she whispered.

She scanned the ceiling and walls for a vent air might have come through. None. Had Dipity sneaked in the bathroom to hide from all the people?

June peeked around the back of the tub. No one—not human, vampire, or cat.

She drew a sigh. She was getting way too paranoid.

She left the bathroom and crept down the hallway leading back to Sam's office. He'd left the light off in the hallway, and she slunk against the wall, toward the open door at the end. Light shone from the room. Sam's voice drifted out.

She positioned herself outside the doorway and peeked in.

Sam sat at a desk in front of a wall of windows. The room was full of bookcases and filing cabinets. FBI bins and boxes sat on the floor. The desk was situated across from the doorway and slightly to the left. Anthony sat with his back to her.

Anthony wore a T-shirt, so the back of his neck was exposed. The back of his arm was also visible, his elbow resting on the arm of the chair. Touching his neck would be over-intimate and creepy, not to mention suspicious.

She waited. Sam promised he would give her opportunities to come into the room. They were talking about Robbie. She strained to hear.

"My brother was always vicious," Anthony said. "Even when we were kids. He didn't have friends. I didn't, either. I found it hard to be around people. I was always hiding. But Robbie was just...mean. He drove people away."

Sam was doing something on the desktop computer in front of him. "They say most psychopaths are like that, even as children."

"He got really involved in the paranormal community as he grew up," Anthony said. "But even then, he treated people badly. He'd get in fights and use his powers on people. He was violent toward me too." Anthony's voice dropped lower, so she could barely hear it. "He took his anger out on me. He said I was weak and I deserved it."

If he was legit, he'd suffered a lot. He'd been Robbie's whipping boy most of his life. She'd feel sorry for him, if he wasn't a liar.

"I can't wait until he's dead." Anthony's voice rose. "I can't wait until he pays for all the things he's done. I wish I could see that far ahead. I wish I could see it happening."

Sam turned his attention to him. "You and me both. If you're not there when it happens, I'll film it for you."

June was starting to get impatient, but then Sam gave her an opening. He turned away from the desk and opened a drawer in the filing cabinet behind him.

Quick and silent, she dashed across the room. She gripped Anthony's bare upper arm.

"Anthony!"

Anthony recoiled and jerked out of her grip.

"Sorry, sorry." She held her hands up. "I just didn't realize you were here. I wanted to say hi."

Anthony stared up at her wide-eyed, cringing against the chair. His eyes flashed.

Sam turned from the filing cabinet, eyebrows raised. "June. What's up?"

"I didn't realize you were in here talking to Anthony." She took a step back from the chair. "Listen, dude... I'm really sorry about yesterday, how I jumped on you like that. I was in a panic. I didn't mean to scare you."

Anthony sagged a little, though he remained tilted away, staring warily at her.

"Really," June said. "I'm sorry. And thank you for helping me. As much as you could, anyway."

"It's okay." His eyes flashed again. "I wish I could have seen further."

"Anthony is going to try to talk to Robbie's goons again," Sam said. "See if he can get some information. Robbie actually sent him an e-mail."

"Did he?" June asked.

Anthony nodded. "It was short, but it seems he's well-aware I'm interested in speaking to him again."

Sam turned to his computer. "Anthony forwarded it to me." He read, "'I'm glad you're finally starting to crawl out of your shell. I'm sorry for having you watched, but I don't want to see anything happen to you. If you wish to speak directly to me, let me know.'"

"I haven't e-mailed him back." Anthony sat up. "I have a feeling if I said I wanted to talk to him, he wouldn't summon me to him. He'd come to me, and that wouldn't help you guys. Also, I don't want him in my house."

"Can you figure out where the e-mail came from?" June asked. "Like an IP address or something?"

Sam nodded. "Possibly. I'll get some of my computer people on it."

"It came to the e-mail address I use on my blog," Anthony said. "So it wasn't overly personal."

June fidgeted. "Well, I should let you guys get back to what you were doing. I just saw you in here and wanted to say I'm sorry, Anthony, and thank you."

Anthony nodded. "I hope we all get what we want out of this."

She waved at Sam. "I'll go hang out with your friends."

"Tell Cindy to break out the liquor. I think they could all use a drink. It's going to be a long night."

June left the room. She surreptitiously checked her hands to make sure the chip wasn't sticking to her fingers still.

June tried to hang out with Sam's friends and had a coffee and whiskey when Cindy got the bottles out. The whiskey made her queasy. She set the mug aside.

"Shit," she muttered. "*Et tu*, alcohol?"

Sam eventually joined them in the living room. She passed her drink off to him as he sat down beside her on the couch.

"We have a lot of planning to do still for the party," he said. "I'm going to be up late. You can go to bed whenever you feel like it."

She reached over and patted Dipity curled up beside her. The cat didn't seem to mind the visitors, and they all played with her. "I think I'll just curl up somewhere down here. I'm paranoid with Occam lurking in the shadows. I don't feel like giving him opportunities to catch me alone."

She wouldn't tell him about the strange sounds she'd been hearing. He had a lot of work to do, and he couldn't waste tonight tearing the house apart for vampires.

He kissed her and then stood. "Make sure that cat doesn't cover my upholstery in fur, all right?"

June gasped. "She's a lady. How dare you."

"I'm jealous. You touch her more than you do me."

"She's soft and doesn't smell. Go. Have fun planning your beach party."

He walked behind the couch, stopped, and leaned over to her. "You and Cindy should go shopping tomorrow. I'll give you one of my credit cards."

"Oh, Daddy Warbucks. Should I get myself a pretty new dress?"

"No, but you will need a bathing suit. Preferably a bikini."

She tilted her head back. "I know it's hard to tell under all this ink, but I'm actually whiter than a corpse. I sizzle in the sun."

"Get an umbrella." He kissed her forehead. "I want to show you off."

She rolled her eyes, but part of her, a tiny part, both celebrated and threw up from nerves at the same time. Show her off? Like a trophy? Like a real girlfriend?

She patted Dipity again. "I want to be a cat so they don't take me to the beach."

Dipity mewled sleepily.

"Screw you too."

Chapter 15

"All ready for some fun and sun?" Sam plunked his bag in the back of their rented van. "I, for one, am ready to spend a day having a good time and not worrying about anything."

Sam was up before sunrise, and people were over before she even crawled out of bed. She'd puked again this morning and was still a little queasy. Hopefully, her rotting guts wouldn't ruin the day—not that she was looking forward to spending the day in the great, hot, sandy outdoors.

"I think you might be overstating how much you're actually going to relax," June said. "I know you."

"This is a political and social event. I'm not going to deny that. I'll have to shake some hands and kiss some babies. Aaron and I have to put our best faces forward so our groups will mingle. But I fully intend to kick back and have a good time. I need it. So do you."

Sam wore a pair of knee-length swim trunks. They showed off his tanned, muscled calves quite nicely. He also wore a pair of flip-flops and a T-shirt. She had a weird thing about seeing him barefoot or nearly; it made him seem more vulnerable somehow.

"The city won't let you relax," she said. "They need a break from the vampires. They're going to be all up in your grill with cameras."

The vampire death toll had finally halted at around five hundred. A staggering number. Such a huge loss of life that she, like many others, wasn't sure she was supposed to grieve. Surely, some of those vampires were innocent and didn't deserve it. Occam and his kind were unrelenting monsters.

"You look nice." He eyed her up.

She'd gone shopping with Cindy and bought more than she expected—such a treat to have clothes again that were not only made for women but were her size. She could actually have some style.

She wore a black bikini with a loose cheetah print cover-up over it, cinched at her waist like a robe. That was her style. She also wore a pair of big round sunglasses, a floppy sun hat, and sandals.

She untied the cover-up and opened it. "I don't want to blind the entire city."

Sam whistled. "Damn, look at you."

She tried to close the wrap, but he snaked his hands underneath it and slid them up her sides.

"Stop." Her cheeks warmed. "I look like a skeleton."

"You do not. You've actually put on a few pounds, I think."

"The only time in the history of the world it's been a good thing for a man to say that to a woman."

He continued feeling her up. If he didn't stop, they would end up in the back of the van.

"I think you're beautiful," he murmured. "I always have."

"You don't look so bad yourself. I was hoping for a Speedo, though." She reached around and groped his ass.

"That'll have to wait until I'm drunk."

"Don't get too drunk. You're supposed to make a good impression, remember?" She let go of him and tied her cover-up.

"That'll make a hell of an impression."

She was trying to be a good sport. She had her hair pulled up so she wouldn't sweat to death, her various layers of protection on so she wouldn't bake, and Cindy had dragged her to the salon. She now had shiny black-lacquered nails. Cindy had also talked her into being waxed: legs, armpits, bikini line. She almost felt pretty.

Sam, June, Cindy, and Natalie all rode in the van. The interior already smelled like sunscreen. Cindy wore a bright red one-piece and a flowery sarong, her cleavage absolutely mesmerizing. June sat in the front seat with Cindy behind her and tried not to stare at her boobs in the side mirror.

"I'm working on my tan today," Cindy announced as they drove. "I've had so little time, since I've been helping you guys. I actually have free time again. I don't know what to do with it."

The day was sunny and hot and the sky clear. They'd brought two full cases of water with them, a cooler with food June could eat, and several battery-operated fans for their tents.

"I don't even know what people do on a beach," June said. "Make sandcastles? Bury each other?"

Sam was driving. She kept getting distracted by the muscles in his arms, all sleek and shiny with lotion.

"We can go swimming," Cindy said. "Or we can rent some skates. They have a path right by the water. There's this cool bridge too. It goes over the highway."

"Skates," June said. "Do I look like I'd function well with wheels on my feet?"

Sam chuckled. "Don't worry. You'll find something to do."

June was doubtful but tried not to be a wet blanket. After all, today they got to do something other than worrying, hiding, or plotting to take down a terrorist.

Jason would probably love the beach. Diego, too, maybe. He wasn't outdoorsy, either, but he took trips to the coast with his friends every summer. Her heart sank. Were they tucked away in some dark, windowless, reeking room somewhere? Were they being fed only potato chips and root beer? She'd brought the picture with her. She couldn't bear to leave it at the house, to not have it next to her while she slept.

They drove the freeway next to the lake, the sun glinting on the water, the road packed with cars. Hopefully they weren't all going to the beach.

"Your tent is set up for you, Sam," Natalie said from the backseat. "I just got a text."

"Good," Sam said. "I'm going to be a little too busy to take care of it."

"Aaron is just arriving," Natalie said. "He'll meet you at the beach house."

Sam had gotten a lot of concessions for their gathering. Part of it was his political smoothness and an exchange of promises and cash, and part of it was him bringing up over and over how the city had disparaged him, how he'd been slighted and maligned and they owed him this.

The beach was closed to the public today, and anyone attending the party was on a list and couldn't enter the area without being checked-in. The beach usually closed at seven PM, but they were given permission to camp overnight. Some caveats were involved, however: anyone leaving the beach after seven would not be allowed to return; no fires were allowed and only tents could be used; no vehicles were allowed on the beach; no alcohol or drugs were permitted; if things got rowdy, the police had the authority to shut the whole thing down. Additionally, in the morning, they had to clean the beach and return it to its pre-party state. Sam and Aaron already had a volunteer group prepared to do this.

When they arrived, June groaned inwardly. People were everywhere, teeming on the long wide stretch of golden sand. The lot was filled with cars, but Sam had a reserved spot close to the beach entrance.

Sam killed the engine. "We can drag all the stuff to our tent first. Then we can head to the bar and have a drink. What do you say?"

June perked. "They have a bar?"

"In the beach house, yes."

Maybe she could choke down a few drinks and loosen up a little, if her stomach didn't rebel.

"Just take the things we need right now," Sam said. "I'll send someone out to get the big cooler and the sleeping bags later."

"I'll make sure someone grabs it." Natalie opened her door.

June tried not to roll her eyes. *Yes, Jeeves, send the servants to fetch my things.*

As soon as they started pulling their bags out of the back, they had attention. People in the parking lot wandered over to greet Sam. She tugged the brim of her hat down over her glasses.

"It's gonna be like that all day," Cindy said. "Don't worry. We'll have fun together. I won't let you sit around alone."

Getting from the car to the beach proved a task. People kept stopping Sam. Natalie carried his things.

When they finally started across the beach, the progression got even slower. People swarmed around them. Sam needed bodyguards. Judging by his enthusiastic reaction, though, he ate it up.

"Can we just go to our tent?" June asked Cindy. "If he has to stop and say hello to everyone on this beach, it's going to be midnight before we get there."

"Good idea," Cindy said. "We're chopped liver, anyway."

Natalie stayed with Sam, as was her punishment for being his assistant, and June and Cindy walked off.

The beach was nice, actually—long and curving, with several piers jutting from one end and a big hook on the other, curling out into the lake. Out on the hook, a forest of volleyball nets were already strung up. The skating path Cindy mentioned snaked through the sand, an asphalt line following the water's edge out to the hook. The bridge arched over the highway that ran parallel to the beach.

The centerpiece was the beach house, blue-and-white, in the shape of a giant cruise ship. On the lower level were kiosks to rent bikes and skates. On top was a bar. The place was swarming with people.

Sam's tent had been erected out past the volleyball posts, near the hook. Cindy, Natalie, and a few others would be out there with them, a little city surrounding their emperor. Sam's tan-and-green dome tent was no bigger than the others.

"You can leave your bag." Cindy stepped over to another tent and began unzipping it. "No one's going to bother our stuff. Don't worry."

June unzipped Sam's tent and ducked inside. Since she was short, she could stand upright, though her head brushed the canvas ceiling. That was a new experience, being able to touch a ceiling. The tent was plenty big enough to hold both her and Sam and all their crap comfortably.

She set her bag and a small cooler with water in it on the floor. She knelt, took a bottle out, and unzipped her bag, though she wasn't sure what she was looking for. She rooted around inside. Clothes, sunscreen, tampons—because God knew her body would probably choose the beach to give her a surprise—and some bags of freeze dried fruit, in case she couldn't digest anything else. Her phone so she could call her mother. She pulled out the picture of Jason and Diego.

Their solemn expressions twisted her heart. Micha appeared in her mind, wasting away in his bed. What right did she have to be here? How could she have fun while they were all prisoners?

"Hey!" Cindy slapped the side of the tent. "You ready? Let's hit the beach house."

June tucked the picture back into her bag. "Yeah, coming."

Cindy had ditched her sarong, and June struggled even harder not to stare. Her booty was as big as her boobs. She wore a sun hat and sunglasses, and they covered more than her suit did. June remained huddled in her cover-up.

They got quite a few looks as they walked, but most of them were not for June. She should drag Cindy around with her like a busty shield from now on.

"I really need a drink," Cindy said as they trudged through the sand toward the beach house. "Like, really-really."

"So do I."

They ascended the stairs to the top. The bar was a concrete patio populated with tables and chairs, most of which were occupied. The scent of grilling food hung on the air, and for once, it made June's stomach growl instead of turn.

The patio looked out over the beach, giving them an idea of how many people were already there. How many were Paranormal Alliance members and how many were SNC members? June had never been in the same place with so many paranormal people before. She wanted to run screaming as she imagined how many were telepaths.

June hung back while Cindy fought her way up to the bar to get them drinks. She returned with two obnoxiously huge pink drinks in hurricane glasses with umbrellas and fruit spilling over the rims.

"That's not a drink," June said. "It's a dessert."

Cindy handed one over. "I got double shots of rum. And I asked—only natural fruit juices, so you can drink it."

June carried her ridiculous drink as she followed Cindy around, seeking out a place to sit. They found a small open table near the railing and sat down across from each other.

"Sam and Aaron will end up here," Cindy said. "We'll run into them."

June slumped in her chair and eyed her drink. Cindy started sucking hers up through her straw.

"I feel so awkward," June confessed. "With all these people. I've never been around so many paranormal people before."

Cindy paused sucking. "A lot of them I don't recognize. I bet they're with Aaron's group. At least everyone's being friendly."

"Well, isn't this whole thing about Kumbaya and brotherhood and whatnot?"

Cindy snorted.

"This is not a world I ever pictured myself in." June stirred her straw around in her drink. "Everything I knew about Sam until now was just a concept. This has been a little hard to swallow."

Cindy eyed her over her glasses, sucking on her straw.

June took a sip and winced. The drink was much stronger than she expected. "I guess what I'm saying is, I'm seeing who he really is now."

"You don't like it?"

"It's different from my life, that's all. Look at me. I don't fit in here."

Cindy folded her arms on the table. "Are you still worrying about this? Sam is a dynamo and a politician, yes, but he's not conventional. He never has been. I think that's what makes him so charismatic. He goes against the grain. That makes him attractive to a lot of people."

"Yeah, but I can't see him getting covered in tattoos and shooting whiskey in a dive bar. Or wearing leather and riding a motorcycle."

"Sam would totally ride a motorcycle."

June plucked the pink umbrella out of her drink. "We're two very different people. I'm wondering how it's supposed to work outside the context of everything we've been through. What about when life goes back to normal?"

"What if it never does?"

June twirled the umbrella between her fingers. "I don't know what he sees in me. He's shockingly the nicest, most attentive guy I've ever been with. I didn't expect that coming from him."

"Why not?"

She shrugged. "He just doesn't seem the most affectionate person. On the surface, anyway."

"Let me tell you something." Cindy tapped the table. "It doesn't surprise me at all. Sam has always had women chasing him. He's passionate. He cares about things. I can see that translating into a relationship, and the bedroom." She smirked. "He's good at what he does. And I've been with a lot of guys, so believe me, I can compare."

June started to take a sip of her drink and paused. "Wait, what? How do you know that?"

"Know how he is in bed?"

"Yes."

"Well, there was this one time...."

June stared at her.

"It wasn't like that." Cindy held up her hands. "He was just helping me."

"What?"

"My power, you know. Sometimes it can overwhelm me. Especially when I suppress it the way I do. It can cause damage. He saved my life, literally."

"You possessed his cock?" She didn't mean to speak so loudly.

"No! I didn't put any sort of spell on him. But when that power gets turned inward, it can rip you apart. He kept me from suffering, from dying maybe. Remember on the patio of Kevin's bar, I told you Sam is like my best friend, that he saved my life? That's what happened. It was a crazy situation, but I was suffering when I came to him, really suffering. I didn't know where else to turn. Everyone else would have made me feel bad about it or been scared of me."

June continued staring at her. "He had sex with you to save your life."

"Yes, but it wasn't that crude. He was caring and kind, and he made sure I didn't hate myself after. He loves his people; he really does. I honestly think I would have either gone crazy that night or killed myself. He was there for me. He was accommodating."

Now June's stomach started to turn, her mouth watering. She wasn't sure if it was the drink or the conversation.

"Why do you think it was appropriate to tell me this?" June asked. "That you had sex with my boyfriend?"

Cindy reared back. "We weren't in love. We weren't together. It only happened once."

June tried not to picture Cindy and Sam having sex—Cindy with all her boobs and butt, looking a thousand times more appealing than June's stick figure.

"You said you couldn't understand him being this good to you," Cindy said. "I was trying to explain he's a very good man to be in a relationship with. I think he'll surprise you in a lot of ways."

"Oh, I'm surprised all right." She grabbed up her drink.

Cindy slumped. "Don't be mad. For goodness' sake, did you think Sam was a blushing virgin? And besides, you've been with Micha the past few months. How do you think he feels about that?"

June sipped her drink, her outrage retreating slightly. Cindy had a point.

"Give yourself some credit," Cindy said. "You think Sam is smart and wonderful and attentive. So if he picked you, you must be a catch. You think a guy like him would pick a loser?"

June was silent.

"Take that hat off and let people see you're Sam Haain's girlfriend." Cindy reached over and whipped June's hat off.

"Hey!" June grabbed at it. "I turn to ashes in the sun!"

Cindy held it out of her reach. "You're covered head-to-toe in lotion. Quit being a crybaby. Take that wrap off, too, and show off your tattoos."

"Listen, bitch." June stood, trying to grab her hat again. "Not all of us have huge titties to flash around like some kind of—"

A commotion rose behind them. June looked over her shoulder. Surely, people weren't fighting already; the party hadn't even officially started.

But it wasn't a fight. Sam had arrived, Aaron at his side. Natalie bustled along behind them.

"Oh, good," Cindy said. "Now we can get our cabana."

"What?" June snatched at her hat again.

Cindy jerked it out of her reach. "Sam is renting one of the private cabanas up here. Much easier for him to hold court in."

Sam and Aaron made their way through the crowd. Aaron wore khaki shorts and a pink-and-blue Hawaiian print shirt, sunglasses, and leather sandals. He was suave and stylish, gold watch glinting in the sun. He actually made Sam look kind of frumpy.

Cindy waved to them. Sam brightened and walked over, people trailing behind him.

"There you are," he said. "Let me just talk to a few people, and we'll go to the cabana."

Cindy saluted him. June angrily sipped her drink.

Sam eyed the glass. "That looks refreshing."

"It's fucking terrible."

After he left, June set her drink down. "I'm gonna go find the restroom. I'll be right back." She didn't have to go, but she wanted to get away from all these people for a few minutes.

She started across the patio, weaving through the crowd. Midway, someone hooked an arm around her waist and stopped her.

"Come say hello to everyone." Sam tugged at her.

She cringed. "I don't think it's me they care about...."

"I don't think they realize who you are."

Despite her reluctance, she let him pull her across the patio and into the thick of the crowd. All eyes were instantly on her, like a specimen in a Petri dish.

"I know there's been a lot of speculation," Sam said over the chatter, which immediately ceased. "So I'm going to put the rumors to rest right now. June Coffin is my girlfriend."

June froze, holding her breath.

Sam smiled down at her. "We've been through a lot together. I don't know what I would have done without her. I'm glad she decided to stick around now that it's over."

She smiled faintly.

"I'm hoping if I become your new mayor she'll continue to stick around. God knows this city could use something a little less bland to look at."

Laughter erupted.

She became the center of polite attention. People complimented her tattoos, and before she knew it, she was pulling her cover-up off. They asked her questions about them, and her pride swelled as she explained she'd done many of them herself. She even momentarily forgot her ribs were visible, or that she had a scar on her right side.

"So when are you opening a shop here?" a guy asked. He showed her his heavily tattooed arm. "'Cause I'll be your first customer."

Other people clamored, saying they'd come to her shop too.

Her shop. In Chicago?

She got a few questions about her power, and if she was now part of the Paranormal Alliance, but most of the questions centered on her personally: her choice of tattoos, what they meant, where she was from, what it was like there, if her tongue ring hurt to have put in. No one asked her about the past six months or the Institute.

Sam eventually backed the crowd off and pulled her away. "Let's get out of the sun. We have a cabana. You can get a drink that's not pink."

"At least when I throw up later, it'll be festive." She looked over her shoulder as they walked away. People waved.

She waved back.

Chapter 16

The cabanas were little more than tent pagodas filled with colorful couches and stools, but June was grateful to get some separation from the masses. Sam ordered bottles of liquor, beer, and food. His officers would be joining them later, as well as some of Aaron's governing board.

"See, I told you," Sam said to Aaron. "A gathering to promote solidarity was a good idea." He sat next to June on a couch, his arm around her.

"The day is only beginning." Aaron sat in a chair across from them. "We'll call it a success when everything goes off without a hitch."

"As long as no one gets drunk and starts fighting," Cindy said. She sipped on a fresh drink. She was wearing June's hat beneath her own hat, like some crazy hobo lady.

"Everyone will get along," Sam said. "It's a hallmark day for paranormal people."

"Unless you're a vampire." Aaron looked out over the water. "Five hundred. That has to be nearly all the vampires in Chicago."

Sam played with June's bikini top strap over her shoulder. "I don't want to talk about it today."

"There's going to come a time when we need to talk about it. I know you don't keep company with vampires, and they aren't in your group, but they are paranormal, and this is a big issue."

"The vampires are going to do as they will." Sam waved his other hand. "No laws of ours are going to stop them. Nothing we talk about is going to keep them from whatever they want to do; it never has."

"No, and that's the problem. They didn't destroy nearly their entire population for no reason. This is the beginning of something."

June spoke up. "They wanted to cleanse their ranks. That's what Occam said. They only want old, powerful vampires left in the city."

"Yes." Aaron looked at her. "And what, I wonder, are those old, powerful vampires going to do now?"

June didn't want to contemplate it. She wanted Jason and Diego back safe before anything else happened.

"How many can there be?" Sam said. "It sounds like a very elite club."

"Enough to kill five hundred young ones." Aaron adjusted his sunglasses. "I would not at all underestimate them. They've just proven how many people they can kill in two short days. Pray they don't move on to other paranormal beings. Or normal ones."

Silence fell, the sounds of the party around them continuing, adding a surreal weight to Aaron's words.

A man stepped into the cabana then—a paunchy, spindly-legged older man, in khaki shorts and a T-shirt. He wore a floppy straw hat and dark sunglasses. He was holding one of the big pink drinks.

"I wanted to come say hello, Sam," the man said. "It's a pleasure to finally meet you."

Sam slid his sunglasses off and squinted. Aaron looked up at the man, pulled his phone out of his pocket, and started playing with it.

"Who are you?" Sam asked.

"A friend."

"A friend indeed," Aaron said.

The man smiled. "An admirer. I wanted to say how glad I am the Institute is finally getting what they deserve and that your innocence has been proven. I'm glad I could help in all aspects of that. I only hope everyone who deserves punishment has it coming to them."

Sam slid his arm from around her shoulders and sat forward.

"I also wanted to assure you," the man said, "that Eric Greerson is very much dead."

Sam stared at him. "How…are you so sure of that?"

The man took a sip of his drink. "Because, before his funeral, my friends and I paid him a visit. We opened his casket and cut off his head."

June blinked.

"A bit dramatic, yes. But I don't know any vampires who can survive with their head removed."

Sam sank back against the couch. June looked around at everyone in the cabana. Their reactions ranged from mildly surprised to bored, as if they heard this kind of shit all the time.

"Good luck with Robbie Beecher." The man tipped the brim of his hat. "I will do what I can, but I don't have any leverage against him. And you're welcome. I'm glad leaking the footage to the Internet was far more advantageous than anything else we've done."

He shuffled off and disappeared into the crowd.

Sam stared at Aaron. "That…that was…"

Aaron held up a finger. "No, that man is dead."

June kept her mouth shut. She'd just met the first head of the Institute, she was sure, the man who fished out evidence to clear their names. The man who took no chances with vampires. Michael Paulson.

"I should have thanked him," Sam said.

"He knows you're thankful." Aaron looked up from his phone. "Go on. Have a good time now, knowing your back is watched. Eat, drink, and be merry."

June muttered, "For tomorrow we may die."

June tried to have a good time. She ate a little, drank a little more, but then her stomach started acting up so she switched to water.

People drifted in and out of the cabana, visiting with Sam and Aaron. She got some attention as well, since the news had spread she was Sam Haain's girlfriend.

Cindy grew tipsier as the day dragged on, which meant she became even louder and more annoying. She insisted on taking selfies with June, and with anyone who would stand still. June avoided getting into conversations with her lest she drunkenly confess more things June didn't want to know.

News crews were all over the parking lot, but they weren't allowed on the beach. Sam mused he might go out and say hello, but he didn't seem in any hurry to do so.

"What, you don't want to address the voters?" Aaron asked him. "I would have thought you came prepared with a speech."

"Today is about having fun," Sam said. "I can campaign tomorrow."

Somehow, Sam dragged her out of the beach house and down to the water in late afternoon as the sun sank into the horizon. Plenty of people were already in the water.

"Come on." Sam tugged her hand. "You can't come to the beach and not go in the water."

"All right, but no farther than my knees. Who knows what's floating around in this lake? Didn't your river used to be filled with shit, and it emptied out here?"

Sam was already in to his ankles. "That was a thousand years ago."

"Oh, wow, I didn't realize Chicago was a millennium old."

Sam yanked and pulled her in. She hissed as she stumbled into the ice-cold water.

"Feels good, doesn't it?"

"Ew, it's all gritty." She wiggled her toes in the lake bed. "How do I know Jimmy Hoffa isn't floating around in here?"

"He is. When he comes by, wave."

She waded out to her knees but didn't budge an inch more, not able to see the bottom through the murky water at that point. She waded around while Sam talked to people.

Then Sam took off his shirt.

He sloshed toward her, muscles rippling in the low golden sun, like some kind of aquatic sex god. He slung his shirt over his shoulder, gripped the front of her cover-up, and yanked it open. She yelped.

"Come on. Get naked. Everyone's already seen your tattoos; it's no big deal."

She swatted at his hands. "I have this scar. What if someone asks me about it? The FBI says we can't talk about it."

"Tell them you got it in battle."

Sam worked her wrap off. The air gusted delightfully across her over-warm skin. She was still horribly self-conscious.

"You look awesome in that bikini." He draped the wrap around his neck.

She struggled to bolster some confidence. "I don't look nearly as good as Cindy in her suit."

"I don't look nearly as good as Pierce Brosnan in his."

"Young Pierce Brosnan or Pierce Brosnan now?"

Sam trudged toward the shore, working his hair tie out. He dropped his shirt and her wrap on the towels he'd brought and rejoined her in the water. He grabbed her hand and pulled her out farther.

"Hey, I'm not swimming!" She was quickly in up to her waist. Being short sucked.

"I'll swim. You hang on." He turned around and picked her up.

"Sam!"

After some kicking and screaming and sputtering at the cold water, she calmed down and attempted to enjoy it. Sam swam around, pulling her with him. She eventually clung to his back and rode him around like a dolphin. She even let her hair get wet.

"I can swim, you know," she said in his ear as he cut through the water.

"Yeah, but I like this better." His hair streamed heavy and wet down his back, and she stroked her fingers through it. "Man, I have to get back in shape. This is harder than it used to be."

"I like the shape you're in." She snaked a hand underneath him and pinched his nipple.

People watched them, saying hello as they passed. Thankfully, Sam didn't stop to chat. They passed Cindy who was whooping it up, having a splash fight with several guys.

"Hi guys!" She waved enthusiastically. "Can I hitch a ride?"

"No." June clung tighter to Sam's shoulders. "Faster, noble steed. Run from the dragon."

Sam took her out deep, almost to the buoys marking off the swimming area. She tried not to think about how far the lake bed was beneath them, or what might be down there. At least out there they were alone, and it was relatively quiet.

Sam stopped and they floated facing each other, June's arms draped over his shoulders, kicking her legs.

"I know this isn't your idea of a good time," he said. The features of his face were sharp and exquisite with his wet hair slicked back. His eyes were deep and dark as the water around them. "I needed this, though. Not just for my people, but for me."

"I know." She drifted against him, their skin brushing silkily together beneath the surface. "I needed it too. We needed something that wasn't suffering and worrying."

"I'm sure we'll have plenty more of that soon."

She wrapped her legs around his waist. "I keep trying not to think about where Jason and Diego are, how unfair it is that I'm enjoying the sand and sun and they're prisoners. And Micha, tucked away in that hospital."

"We'll get them all out soon. Even Micha." He slithered his arms around her. "I know it's hard to not feel guilty, but you deserve some peace of mind too. You deserve to have one day without suffering."

"Do I?"

He stroked his fingers up her back and plucked at the tie on her top. "Yes. You've committed no sin you should be punished for."

She brought her face close to his, her head slightly above him. She wasn't used to being the tall one. "We're all innocent, or as innocent as we can be, I suppose."

"It's not easy for me, either, you know. Robbie is always on my mind. That desperation to find him before he does something else, before he hurts any more people. And Muse…" He paused. "I miss her every minute of every day. She'd think this was the silliest damn thing I've ever put on. She'd be stunned her father and I would even collaborate like this."

June stroked his forehead, wiping away water droplets. "I could imagine her huddled under an umbrella with me, trying not to bake to a crisp."

He chuckled, but his eyes were sad. "I like to think she's here today, in spirit. This is also a celebration of her life, of the things she helped me accomplish. I wouldn't be here if she hadn't had my back all those years. I think celebrating with her father is fitting."

June kissed him and then pressed her forehead to his. They drifted silently in the water, bobbing together.

"No more good people will die," Sam whispered. "Not if I can stop it. And I will. With my last breath, if need be. Not my people. Not your brother. Not Micha."

She tightened her arms and legs around him. She wished, more than anything, that was a promise he was actually capable of keeping.

He continued playing with the tie on her top, and then moved his arm around to slip a hand up under one of the cups. Things were stirring below the water, as well.

She glanced toward the beach. They were still alone, but people were slowly encroaching. Sam was a magnet.

"We'd better behave." She gasped softly as he plucked her nipple. "We can get freaky in the tent later. Hopefully, none of your groupies will be lingering around then."

"That's what you think. Our sex video will probably be on the Internet by tomorrow morning."

"Good thing I got waxed, then."

"Yeah, I noticed." He reached lower and smoothed his fingers over the crotch of her swimsuit.

She convinced him not to fuck her in the water—not only because they had onlookers, but because water was a terrible lubricant. They swam around a bit more, letting Sam "relax" before they got out.

When evening fell, people lit lanterns, since they weren't allowed fires. Music was played and people danced on the sand. Quite a few were clearly drunk, even though the police were still patrolling and inspecting coolers to make sure no one had booze—like sneaking liquor onto a beach wasn't a time-old tradition.

She and Sam strolled around, hand-in-hand. Sam had his T-shirt back on. He'd left his hair loose, flowing in the wind.

"So," Sam said. "Anthony has spent all day at home, what a surprise."

She looked up at him.

"I started the program this morning. I've got it sending updates to my phone."

She breathed a sigh of relief. "I was worried I didn't get it on him right, that it might fall off."

"Unless it fell off at his house, no. If he hadn't said he was such a homebody, I might be worried. But it seems to be transmitting accurately."

"He's probably blogging."

Sam squinted toward the parking lot, where news vans were still clustered. "Maybe he wishes he were here with us."

"I somehow doubt that."

June slipped her arm through Sam's and stayed by his side, trying to get used to playing First Lady. Two young girls, pretty and pert and blond, ran over to talk to Sam. They seemed fascinated by her as well.

"The tattooed lady," one said. "You totally fit in with us."

Sam grinned slyly at June. "Welcome to the freak show."

June nudged him in the side. "Don't call us freaks. We're normally-challenged eccentric individuals."

The girls laughed as they walked on. "Sam Haain for president!" one called.

June rolled her eyes. "Oh my God, like, can I design your bumper stickers for the campaign?"

"You should get my name tattooed on your ass. That would be even better. Or a tramp stamp." He smoothed a hand over her lower back.

"If you don't be careful, I'm going to tattoo dicks on your face while you sleep."

* * * *

Eventually June was partied out and wanted to go to the tent. Sam joined her. She tried to brush as much sand off her body as she could before she crawled in. All their things were there. They rolled out their sleeping bags and made a cozy nest with the additional pillows and blankets they'd brought.

Sam left a lantern burning outside the tent and zipped the flap shut. June peeled off her bikini top, having brought a T-shirt and shorts to sleep in.

"Just in case." Sam indicated the light. "If anyone has to come fetch me, including the police. I have my fingers crossed no one gets us kicked off the beach before morning."

"You're quite the optimist." June unfurled her T-shirt.

"What are you doing with that?" He grabbed the shirt and tossed it into the corner of the tent.

She was naked from the waist up. The lantern provided a muted glow through the rippling canvas.

"I can't sleep in my suit," she said. "It's all gross and briny."

He cupped one of her breasts. "I agree, but you can't sleep in any clothes. It's the law of the beach."

"Is it?" She tugged his shirt up as well. "Then you'd better stop breaking the law, mister."

They both got naked. The air inside the tent was warm but not uncomfortable. She wrapped herself around him as they kissed, and it was oddly naughty being naked and frisky out there, even though they technically had privacy.

"You're so smooth," he murmured. "Everywhere."

"I almost forgot what it was like to be groomed. Or how much fun it was getting all my body hair ripped out."

He nuzzled her jaw. "I liked you even when I had to beat my way through the forest."

She pinched his ass. "Jerk."

They rolled around, kissing, caressing, teasing. Eventually, she ended up on top of him.

"Can I ask you something?" She gazed down at him, her hands on his chest. "Something personal?"

He sprawled beneath her, hair spread out on the sleeping bag. He dragged his hands up and down her body, over her breasts, along her sides.

"Sure."

She took a deep breath. "Did you sleep with Cindy?"

He fell still, his hands on her hips.

"What?"

"I don't mean, like, recently." She didn't want to kill the mood, but she had to get this off her chest. "I mean, in the past. Did you have sex with her?"

He dropped his hands. "Why are you asking?"

"Is that a yes?"

"Did she tell you that?"

"Yes. Earlier today. I thought it was really inappropriate, but you know Cindy."

He rubbed his face. "Why the fuck did she bring that up? To you, of all people?"

"I don't think she has a filter between her brain and mouth. She said you did it to help her. That she was suffering because of her power and you slept with her. I think she thought telling me was like a way of talking you up or something."

He took his hands off his face. "There are ways to diffuse the power without hurting anyone, but it's hard. Cindy turns her power inward, and that can harm her, badly. She came to me seeking help, and she was in a lot of pain, both physically and mentally. I offered myself in sacrifice, I guess you could say."

June pinched the bridge of her nose. "Seriously? So you let her possess your cock?"

"In a manner of speaking, yes. It was that or hospitalize her at the Institute."

June lowered her hand. "So she like...did to you what Zack tried to do to me?"

"Except I was well-aware of what she was doing, I consented to it, and I trusted that she would stop before she harmed me. I put my life in her hands, essentially."

"Why did you trust her that much?"

"She was always a good woman—loyal, strong, fiercely dedicated to our cause. Maybe part of it was also my martyr complex. I wanted to save her."

This sounded way too much like a porno fantasy, forced to save the girl with his dick.

"So what happened?" She tried not to sound petulant. "I don't mean what did you do in bed. What happened to you after?"

"I was down for a few days. But she was healthier, and she worked much harder after that to make sure she didn't get to the point where it nearly killed her again. She learned a lesson. She was ashamed of what had happened, but I told her not to be. I told her that we all have to grow through struggles."

June looked around for a blanket to pull around her, to hide in.

"She shouldn't have told you." He placed a hand on her stomach. "And I'm only telling you because I don't want you to think I'm keeping it a secret. It was a difficult thing to navigate. I have some regrets about it. I don't have any sort of feelings for her."

"I must be kind of a letdown, after being with a woman who has tits and ass like that." The words slipped out before she could stop them.

He gripped her hips. "Listen to me." His voice softened. "I've been with my share of women. Overflowing tits, tiny tits, ass, legs for days, short, tall, everything in between. I like the female form in all its shapes and sizes." He slid a hand onto one of her breasts. "I've never been with a woman covered in tattoos or with piercings everywhere." He moved his hand back down, between her legs. "But I'm damn well enjoying it. And you know what the best kind of woman is?"

"What kind?" she asked softly.

"The kind of woman I care about. Caring about her gives her a whole bunch of dimensions I can't get from a fling or trying to keep a sex witch from self-destructing."

June closed her eyes. "I don't fit your political lifestyle. I don't fit into the world you come from."

"I dated another politician once. It was awful. Imagine our egos clashing endlessly."

She opened her eyes.

"You're perfect," he said. "You're everything I could imagine wanting. You're my polar opposite. You keep the world spinning."

She leaned over, her hair sweeping around their faces. He sank his fingers into her, and she gasped.

"That's the absolute corniest line I've ever heard in my life," she murmured.

"Thank you." He gripped her around the waist and rolled her over onto her back.

For the first time—ever, perhaps—she let her guard down and let emotions flood in. They were raw and ungainly and scraped at her insides, but she needed to feel them. She needed to know there was part of her that was human, that was able to feel something decent and good after all the hell she'd been through.

She kissed him with the kind of passion she saw in movies—the overblown, dramatic kind she didn't believe existed—putting all of herself into it, letting him see what lay behind her walls. She prayed it wasn't a mistake. She prayed he wouldn't someday use it as a weapon against her.

He traced her body with his hands, touching everywhere, every curve, every indentation, each of her ribs. He even skimmed his fingertips across the rough skin of her scar.

"I don't want to lose you," he whispered. "I'll do everything in my power to keep you. We'll figure this thing out. We'll make you well."

She swallowed thickly. "I don't want to lose you, either. I don't want to lose this life. I think I finally like it."

Tears slipped down her temples, and she discreetly wiped them away. This was like the night Muse died, in Aaron's penthouse. His vulnerability and openness, the pain arcing between them.

He moved down and settled between her thighs. She closed her eyes and stroked his hair while he gently used his tongue on her, pushing his fingers into her as well. Not the frantic, hard finger fucking he'd given her at the storehouse, something more passionate, deeper, filling her with pleasure, making it build slow and hot.

She opened her eyes and stared at the canvas ceiling. She could almost see the stars through it. The wind rippled the fabric, like clouds passing across a summer sky.

He finally moved back up her body. His lips were hot and wet on her skin as he dragged his mouth up her stomach and chest. He paused at her nipples, to kiss and suck each of them, and she smiled.

"I should have always known," she said, "that you were an amazing lover. Someone as passionate as you."

He met her lips with his own. "I knew you'd be wild, hard to tame. I like a challenge."

"You want to tame me?" She gripped his cock. Firm. Ready. "You want to lock me up and keep me?"

"If I tried, I think you'd break the lock. And then probably strangle me with your bare hands. But that's kind of appealing too."

She stroked him, slow and smooth.

"What do you want?" she asked softly. "With me? With us?"

"I want…" His breath hitched, his hips twitching. "I want to at least hold you now and then. I don't want you tame. I just want you to be calm, with me, every once in a while."

"You belong here. This is your home. What if I can't stay?"

"We'll cross that bridge when we get to it." He grunted, pushing into her fist. "I don't want to think about it right now."

She squeezed him. "Let's just live in the moment."

"At this moment, I want to fuck you senseless."

"I want that too."

Sam had the foresight to bring condoms. He retrieved one from his bag, and she assisted him in working it on. Soon, she'd go to the doctor, and they could do it without this.

She gripped his shoulder blades and tried to keep her groan quiet as he pushed into her. Though the sounds of the party were far away, that didn't mean they were alone out there.

"God." He dropped his forehead against hers and pulled her knee up against his side. "I love how you feel."

"Yeah?" she breathed out. "I love the way you feel too." She caressed his back. "Give it to me."

He did, a solid deep fucking, not too hard or fast, just perfect. So good it made her head spin, made little pinpricks of light dance in her vision.

After a few minutes, he stopped, pulled out of her, and rolled onto his back, dragging her with him.

"I want to look at you." He cupped her breasts. "Ride me."

She sank down on him, a louder groan escaping her as he filled her again.

She braced her hands on his chest and bounced, driving him up into her over and over. Her eyes had adjusted to the dim light, and she could take him in, all his dusky skin, his hair spread around his head, his bottomless eyes, and that expression of helpless desperate pleasure on his face.

Screw Cindy and her boobs and ass. Her boobs bounced too as she rode him, tiny though they were.

He rubbed her, playing with the ring as she worked her hips against him. His heart pounded under her hands, which were still braced on his sweaty chest.

"Goddamn," he gasped. "You're so fucking hot."

She rode him harder, bouncing faster, whimpers escaping her throat. Her inner muscles clenched around his thick length. She tried to draw it out, loving the buildup to the explosion.

She couldn't fight it long, not with him rubbing her like that, not with the way he filled her. He pushed his hips up, meeting her, signaling he was getting close as well.

"I want to feel you come." His voice was low and thick in the hot close darkness of the tent.

Her thighs trembled. She gripped his shoulders, everything inside her tightening.

She had to bite down hard on her lip as the orgasm rippled through her, and even then she whined and moaned as she came around his cock. She shuddered helplessly on top of him, digging her fingernails into his flesh.

"Oh, yeah." He worked his hips still, fucking her through it. "There we go. Goddamn, June…"

She closed her eyes, continuing to quake. He worked his thumb on her ring, dragging it out, until it was too much and she had to push his hand away.

"Oh, fuck." He gripped her hips and started pistoning into her. She sat on him weak and limp, letting him use her body.

"Yes," she encouraged him. "Come on. Come for me, Sam. Come in me." The notion flashed through her mind that she could make him come with her voice if she wanted to. It was both tantalizing and horrifying.

She didn't need to, though. With a groan, he slammed up high and hard into her, and his cock throbbed. He clutched her hips, head thrown back, his body shuddering beneath her.

She caressed his slick chest. "That's nice."

He sagged against the floor. The wind flapped the tent. It was disgustingly humid now inside the small enclosed space.

She carefully slid off him, so as not to dislodge the condom, and collapsed in her own sweaty heap at his side. He rolled over and flopped an arm across her.

"I gotta confess," he panted. "I haven't had this much sex in a long time. It's pretty nice."

"Yeah, me neither. I've never been with anyone long enough to have this much sex with him."

June was parched and sweating, but being close to him was too nice for her to pull away.

"I'm sorry"—Sam stroked her face—"that Cindy told you about what happened between us. She had no business doing that. I'm going to give her hell for it."

"Did you fuck her the way you fuck me?"

"God, no." He cupped her cheek. "Not even close."

"Then it's okay." She kissed him. "She's just got a big mouth. I forgive her."

"It's never been with anyone like it is with you. I mean that."

"Me neither," she whispered.

They finally sat up, pulled T-shirts and shorts on, and Sam unzipped the tent to let some air in. June grabbed a couple bottles of water from the cooler.

"We should leave this open tonight." Sam batted at the flap. "No one is going to bother us, unless they're really drunk. Then I'll just have to kick somebody's ass."

She took a drink from her bottle. "Yeah, let the night in."

They stretched out on the sleeping bags, the cool air blowing across them and clearing out the overpowering reek of sex—a shame. That was her favorite scent.

"You gonna go back to the party?" she asked.

He shook his head. "I'm in for the night. I'm a social butterfly, but right now I need to be back in my cocoon."

"Butterflies don't go back in cocoons." She smiled. "Does that make me a caterpillar? I still like the cocoon and I haven't blossomed yet."

"You stay in there and let me back in every once in a while, deal?"

"You don't know anything about nature." She rolled toward him and kissed him.

Lying in the quiet, the tent flapping, the distant sounds of music and voices, the slosh of water, was more peaceful than anything she'd experienced in a long time.

Sam rolled his head toward her, bringing their faces close together. He threaded his fingers through hers between them.

"Can I tell you something?" he whispered. "Promise you won't freak out?"

"I can't promise," she murmured. "But go ahead."

He was silent a moment, and then he whispered, "I love you."

She stared at his face, her breath held. Then she found herself whispering in return, "I love you too."

God. That was certainly a development, wasn't it?

They didn't say anything else, didn't discuss it, didn't try to qualify it.

June clung to his hand, watching the night outside the fluttering tent flap. The world seemed peaceful for once, and so did the usual raging storm inside her head and chest.

Chapter 17

June awoke in the middle of the night with the distinct feeling she was being watched. At first she was disoriented, and then her surroundings rushed back to her and she remembered where she was.

Sam lay next to her, facing her, breathing slowly. He still held her hand but his fingers were limp and his eyes closed. Her palm was sweaty.

No voices or music in the distance, which meant the party had died down considerably or stopped altogether.

She lifted her head and looked toward the open tent flap. The lantern still burned outside, light shining through the canvas.

And someone was standing outside the tent.

She jerked upright, untangling her fingers from Sam's grip. She tilted her head, trying to look out the flap.

She couldn't see from her angle, though. The person stood off to the side of the tent, but close enough to the lantern that he was casting a shadow. Who the hell would be standing outside their tent in the middle of the night?

Her mind raced to Robbie, and then Occam. The police were keeping unauthorized people off the beach, but Occam was extremely good at sneaking into places he wasn't supposed to be.

She pushed the sleeping bag away and crawled cautiously toward the flap. Maybe it was just some drunken partier who couldn't find his tent.

Breath held, she pushed the flap aside and poked her head out.

No one was there.

She stared at the empty spot where the person had been standing, her brain momentarily unable to process the lack of information. She drew back in and looked at the spot on the canvas where she'd seen the shadow. An optical illusion?

The shadow was gone too.

Had someone been standing out there, heard her move, and ran off? Why didn't she see him run away?

She was wide awake now, debating what to do next. She could lie back down and be paranoid the rest of the night, or go investigate. Maybe the answer was simple and non-threatening: a drunken partygoer, one of Sam's groupies, a lost person trying to remember where their tent was.

Or maybe it was Occam.

She crawled out of the tent and got to her feet. She turned in a circle.

The sea of tents around them was quiet, most of them dark, shuddering in the wind. She didn't see or hear anyone. In the distance, a group of people was still sitting on the sand near the water, with lanterns around them. Their voices carried faintly on the wind.

A soft giggle erupted behind her, and she whirled around, eyes wide.

The giggle came from the direction of Cindy's darkened tent. The giggle sounded again, accompanied by rustling, and June scowled. Cindy had a visitor.

Could her gentleman caller be the person June had seen? Unlikely, given that Cindy's tent was zipped. The person would have had to walk past their tent—right in front of it, in fact—get in Cindy's tent, and zip it back up, all in those few seconds before June crawled out.

She looked around again. Had she been dreaming? Seeing things?

Or were vampires on the beach?

She crawled back in the tent and zipped the flap. After grabbing her bottle of water and drinking some, she lay down on the sleeping bag next to Sam again.

Sam stirred and draped an arm over her, mumbling in his sleep. She scooted closer to him.

She studied the spot on the canvas where she'd seen the shadow. Nothing appeared. Nothing stirred outside in the darkness.

So much for getting a good night's sleep.

* * * *

June opened her eyes to morning light and muffled voices. At some point, she had slipped back to sleep—not long ago, as she was groggy and didn't want to move.

She was hungry, also vaguely sick. Drinking yesterday hadn't been a good idea.

Sam was still asleep beside her, his arm across her chest. The canvas ceiling was bright now.

She grabbed her phone to check the time. A little after six AM. She had a text from her mother saying good night, and her chest tightened with guilt.

Megan Morgan

After a few minutes, she sat up and grabbed her water bottle. She would seek out the bathroom and get her morning barf over with if need be. Feeling like she would puke was worse than puking. At least once she puked she felt better.

What exactly had she seen last night? Occam was probably lurking around, watching her. She should have called out to him, tried to confront him. This seemed like a great idea in the light of day, not so much in the spooky night.

She grabbed her sandals and a hairbrush from her bag—pausing to stroke her fingertips over the picture of Jason and Diego—and unzipped the flap. Her queasiness wasn't horrible yet, but she didn't want to risk making a mess in the tent.

She climbed out into the cool morning air, shoes in one hand, hairbrush in the other.

And promptly dropped both.

Someone sat at the water's edge twenty or so yards away, back to her, shoulders hunched; however, even from a distance with the person's back turned, she was recognizable.

June stared, heart pounding, breath held. The ache in her stomach intensified, making her salivate.

It couldn't be. This couldn't be happening. Not another one.

June stood frozen, her mind racing. Maybe she was mistaken. Maybe it was someone else and she was losing her mind. She had to know, for her own sanity.

She walked slowly across the sand, toward the small white figure.

"Muse?" Her voice cracked.

The figure didn't move. Drawing closer, June could see the woman's white hair and tunic weren't being stirred by the wind. The same white tunic Muse had been wearing the night she died.

June could barely make herself take another step toward her, but she had to see her face, had to know for sure.

She forced herself to walk up to the water's edge, but stayed a few feet to the side. Muse stared out at the water, arms wrapped around her legs. She was pale and blank, unnervingly unnatural in her surroundings.

"What are you doing here?" June choked out. "You can't haunt me too, Jesus Christ."

Muse didn't respond or look at her. She had many of the same traits as Rose—unresponsive, elusive, still. Aggravating.

"Was that you outside the tent last night?" Something occurred to June then, like a punch to her queasy gut. "How long have you been trying to manifest?"

The shuffling at Sam's house, outside his bedroom and in the bathroom. What if Muse had been trying to appear and only had the energy to do so now? June had experienced other weird incidents at the hotel too—strange sounds and movements out of the corner of her eye. She passed them off as stress and imagination.

"Muse," June said louder. Could she use her voice on ghosts? "Look at me. Answer me."

Muse turned her head toward her, surprisingly and horrifyingly. Her eyes were blank and dead like Rose's, her face motionless. No lights on in the house.

June stared at her. "What the hell are you doing here? Why are you following me?"

They'd talked about the afterlife once. Muse wondered what it might be like. Tears stung June's eyes. This shouldn't have happened to her.

Muse spoke then. "He's in the home of our enemy." Her voice was listless and emotionless, like Rose's voice. "He's in the fortress."

"Who?" June clenched her fists at her sides. "Who are you talking about? Robbie? Occam?"

Muse didn't respond, staring placidly at June with her dead eyes. Maybe she was outside the tent all night. Maybe she was in Sam's house all the time. Watching them. Watching them with each other.

"Muse, I need you to be clearer with me."

Micha's ring made Rose more focused and responsive. Did Sam have anything that might help her with Muse?

"Find him where our enemy once was." Muse looked back out over the water and fell silent.

June wanted to throw herself on the sand and scream.

"I'm sorry, Muse." June trembled. "I'm so sorry this happened to you. I'm sorry you're caught and can't move on. It shouldn't be like this." She covered her face as the tears broke and spilled out. "I'm so sorry…."

When she lowered her hands, Muse was gone. She left no imprint on the sand.

June's stomach lurched. She stumbled to the lake and threw up, mostly water, and not much, but still miserable and painful as always. When she stopped heaving, she plunked down on the sand, head in her hands, and cried some more.

"June?" Sam's voice.

She lifted her head and wiped her cheeks. Sam appeared at her side and knelt, resting a hand between her shoulders.

"Sorry." She sniffed. "I was sick."

"It's okay." He rubbed her back. "You want me to grab you some water?"

She nodded.

He walked back to the tent. She raked her fingers through her hair. Should she tell him? How would he handle it?

He returned with a bottle of water. She took a few sips, soothing her burning throat. The experience was more awful when she didn't have much to bring up and it was mostly stomach acid. She fought the urge to curl up in a ball and cry over everything. Cry at the injustice of it all, the pain.

Sam sat down beside her. "At least the beach doesn't look too beat up. Cleanup won't take that long."

She capped the bottle, hands shaking. "I guess it was a success, huh?"

"Yeah." He rubbed her shoulder. "It was a big success."

She couldn't bring herself to tell him, at least not right there.

They had to be off the beach by eight AM, so Sam made rounds waking people up and getting his crew together. People exited their tents and started packing up. Judging by the reduced number of tents some had already left during the night. June crawled into theirs and packed while Sam took care of business.

Cindy poked her head in as June was rolling up her sleeping bag.

"Good morning," Cindy said. She had sunglasses on, her hair wild. "Sam has to stay here and oversee the cleanup, so I'm gonna drive you and the stuff back to his place."

"Okay."

"Did you have fun yesterday?"

"It was more fun than I thought it would be, yeah."

"Did you have fun last night?" She smiled.

"About as much fun as you did." June eyed her. "I heard the giggling over there."

Cindy smiled wider. "Yeah, it was a lot of fun."

June moved through the morning in a trance, her mind still caught on the image of Muse sitting at the water's edge. She would have to tell Sam, if for no other reason than to pass on Muse's message. Maybe he could make more sense of it than she could.

Before they left she found Sam, and he paused talking to a group of people to kiss her good-bye. Hoots and catcalls went up.

"I'll be along soon," he murmured. "Don't worry about unpacking. I'll do it when I get home. You just relax." He patted her ass. More hooting.

"It was nice to meet you, tattooed lady!" a girl called out.

"Is that my new nickname?" June smiled. "Am I finally part of the circus?"

"You know me; I'm the ring leader."

Cindy drove them back to Sam's place. They were silent as they sped down the freeway, the beach shrinking away in June's side mirror. She watched it until it disappeared.

"Hey, listen," Cindy said. "I'm sorry about yesterday, about what I told you. I've got a huge mouth."

"It's all right." It actually was. "I know he was just trying to help you. It didn't mean anything."

"Sam's a good guy."

"He must be, to offer his dick in sacrifice." June shook her head. "So noble of him."

"I was literally gonna die. It was really unpleasant."

"Yes, his dick is nearly unbearable. I don't know how I take it as often as I do."

Cindy huffed. "I meant for me, the way my power was eating at me. I had nowhere else to turn. I was scared I'd hurt or kill someone."

"I know. I forgive you. Just…no more TMI, all right?"

"Promise."

Back at Sam's place, June collapsed on the couch, still sluggish, slightly sun burned, and gritty everywhere. Dipity walked on her, purring and sniffing.

"Do I feel like a litter box?" June asked. "Please don't poop on me."

Cindy stuck around, and June took a long hot shower in the downstairs bathroom. She kept peeking around the curtain and listening. Hopefully, Muse would have the decency not to show up while she was in the shower. As the hot water poured over her, she struggled with what to do, how to tell Sam.

Sam came home a couple hours later. June sat slumped on the couch, watching the news. They were still talking about the vampires.

"Hey," June said listlessly. "Beach all cleaned up? No fines?"

He held his phone, peering at it, frowning.

"All is well. Everyone behaved themselves." He leaned over and kissed the top of her head. "You smell clean. I can't wait to shower." He strode out of the room.

He returned a few minutes later with his laptop, still frowning.

"What's up?" June asked as he plunked down on the couch beside her.

"Anthony. He's not at home anymore."

She leaned over so she could see the screen. He had a map up, a red dot in the middle of it.

"When did he leave?" she asked.

"Early this morning." Sam zoomed in on the map. "He was downtown earlier, according to the app on my phone. Now"—he stopped zooming and tapped the screen—"he's here."

"Where's here?"

Sam looked at her. "The Medical District."

"Maybe he had a doctor's appointment or something?"

"You know what's in the Medical District, right?"

She sat up, a light bulb popping on in her head. "The Institute?"

"Yes, he's close to it. I don't know how accurate this thing is, but it says he's within a block of it. He's been there for over an hour."

"Maybe he went to see the protests. There's always people outside, from what they show on TV."

"Does he seem like the type of guy that would go to a protest?"

"What the hell would he be doing there, then?"

"That's the question." Sam remained focused on the screen. "It's not like I can ask him without blowing our plan."

"Maybe he followed one of Robbie's spies there."

"What would Robbie's spies be doing at the Institute?"

June shrugged. "Keeping an eye on things?"

Sam stood up, taking the laptop with him. He stood in front of the TV, staring across the room, and then he turned to her.

"We should find out what he's doing," he said. "Go spy on him."

"Isn't that what we're doing? You want to go to the Institute and see what's going on there? You realize if anyone sees you, they're going to eat you alive. Not to mention the FBI will be just a tad bit anxious, don't you think?"

"I'll use my power. No one will even know we're there."

"We," she said dryly.

"You don't have to come with me if you don't want to, but I've learned better than to tell you to stay put."

She sighed. "Are we taking one of your cars?"

"I'll ask Cindy if we can borrow hers. Mine might be recognizable. We won't tell her what's up. I don't want anyone else in on what we're doing, just in case Anthony talks to them."

June sighed again. "All right. I suppose it's a good idea to find out what he's up to, especially since he's not one to leave the house. Maybe he does have a doctor's appointment or something."

"I hope it's as benign as that."

Chapter 18

As much as June wanted to spend the day in a vegetative state, she couldn't let Sam go by himself. He took a quick shower, and she monitored the app on his phone while he cleaned up and dressed. Anthony didn't move.

Cindy gave up her car without questioning. As they left, Cindy waved good-bye from the porch, holding Dipity, whom she also made wave with her paw. June waved back.

"Are you waving at the cat?" Sam asked.

"You're a hater, Sam. Just a hater."

The guards were still at the gate, but no reporters or gawkers.

"Vampires," Sam griped. "Stealing the spotlight. Am I the only one left in this city not willing to slaughter people for attention?"

"Your cameras are probably still at the beach. I can't believe you didn't go talk to a single reporter yesterday."

"Yesterday was about having fun." He softened his voice. "I meant what I said last night. What I told you. It wasn't just the heat of the moment."

"I know. I meant it too."

She did.

On the way, she struggled with whether or not to tell him about Muse. Maybe she'd wait until they found out what Anthony was up to. Muse's words were certainly important, but maybe they wouldn't be vital until they had context. Maybe she'd been talking about Anthony.

In the Medical District, they parked a few streets away from the Institute. June had been keeping an eye on the phone while Sam drove, and she handed it to him.

"Nothing yet," she said. "He's just sitting."

Sam peered at the phone. "I wonder if he somehow discovered the chip and dropped it somewhere to confuse us."

"Why would he drop it here? If I was gonna mess with somebody, I'd stick it to a dog or something. Why is Anthony digging through garbage cans and running through the park? Why does he stop at every fire hydrant?"

Sam opened his door. "Let's go find out what he's up to, then."

They got out. June slipped her sunglasses on, as the day was bright and hot, like yesterday. At least she wasn't at the beach.

Sam walked around the car and took her hand. Tingles rushed over her skin.

For once, Sam actually made himself look like a man. A blond man with a deep tan. She was a blond woman in a pink dress.

"Are we...Barbie and Ken?" She plucked at the skirt.

"We're the exact opposite of ourselves. No one is going to recognize us."

"You sure you don't wanna be Barbie?"

"I'm trying out your boring being a man thing, all right?"

They walked about a block until the Institute loomed into view. Being in that area, seeing it up close again, she developed a serious case of the heebie-jeebies. She looked up at the building as they approached, her mouth dry and throat tight.

"He's somewhere close." Sam stared down at his phone. "What in the hell could he possibly be doing?"

As seen on TV, the area in front of the Institute—the sidewalk, the courtyard, even a parking lot off to the side—teemed with protestors. People were holding up signs. Camera crews were everywhere. Tents had been erected in the parking lot. Apparently, this was Occupy The Institute.

"This is heartening to see," Sam said as they crossed the street toward the crowd. "This is all because of us."

She tightened her grip on his hand, getting flashes of what happened the last time they joined a protest. "We shouldn't get too close. We didn't come here to gloat."

They stopped on the sidewalk behind the crowd. June stretched up to see. A thick line of police officers in riot gear prevented the crowd from encroaching fully on the darkened front doors. Someone was speaking through a bullhorn nearby, raging about the Institute being "built on a mountain of lies." Someone held up a sign that said "Paranormal Oppression = Hitler's Wet Dream."

"I see they brought out the classics," June murmured. "Is Anthony here?"

Sam squinted at his phone. He looked up and around at the parking garages lining the street. "No, I don't think so."

No cars around, as the street was blocked on both ends by police barricades. The garages were empty.

Sam tugged her hand. "Come on."

They walked back across the street, past lines of police tape and watchful cops. They started down the street, back the way they'd come.

"Where are we going?" June asked.

"We can't get to where we need to from there. We need to sneak in. Too many cops around."

"What are we sneaking into?"

He didn't answer. They walked to the next street over. Sam stopped in front of a towering parking garage and looked up. The place was empty, the gate to enter it blocked by a big metal barricade.

"This is one of the garages for the Institute," he said. "If I'm not mistaken, it's the one that has the walkway that goes over to the Institute itself."

"He's…here?"

He showed her the phone screen. They were right on top of the red dot. "He's either in there or we're standing next to him and he's invisible."

"Is invisibility a possibility? I mean like…for anyone?"

"For Occam it clearly is." He jammed the phone into his pocket. "Come on."

"How are we going to get in?" She let him drag her toward the gate. "It's locked up."

"It's locked up to cars."

Indeed, they found a door with the words "after hours entrance" on it, and it was unlocked. As they entered the shadowy cement cavern of the garage, June grew paranoid. Parking garages creeped her out. She'd seen Rose meet her end in one and almost met her own end in the same one.

She looked up the sloping floor they stood on. "Where do we go?" She kept her voice down. "How do we find him in here? What's he even doing in here?"

Sam walked over to a guide on the wall, which detailed the floors. "Level six," he said. "That's where the walkway is. We'll check there first. You up for some exercise? We can't take the elevators; they're probably not even operating."

"Sure. I'm the picture of health, after all."

They walked through the empty garage, climbing each floor up to the next. June kept looking around, filled with paranoia, jumping at every sound from the streets below. They had to keep stopping so she could catch her breath.

"Want me to carry you?" Sam rubbed her back as she slumped against a railing. One more level.

"Not that your arms aren't big and strong, but I'll crawl before I'm carried." She pulled in a deep breath. "It's just the malnutrition and bullet in my lung getting to me, you know?"

"I feel your pain. I stubbed my toe the other day. It hurt like a bitch."

She straightened up. She pulled in another breath, this time to brace herself. "Listen, Sam. There's something I need to—"

Sam held up a hand, stopping her words. He stared up the ramp to the next level. "Did you hear that?" he whispered.

She held her breath and listened. Voices, muffled and indistinct.

"Someone's up there," Sam said.

"You think it's Anthony?"

"If it is, he's not alone. Unless he's talking to himself."

"Could be police or security guards. I don't know how fast I can run right now."

"That's the floor where the walkway is." He tugged her arm. "Come on."

They crept up the ramp to the next level. June's heart hammered in her ears from exertion and trepidation. They didn't go all the way up the ramp, just far enough they could peek over the wall to the next floor.

The level was empty like the others. This one had a big arch in the middle that opened onto a walkway stretching across the street.

A group of people was standing in front of it.

She and Sam quickly ducked down behind the wall and looked wide-eyed at each other.

"Maybe it's guards," June whispered. "Making sure people don't go across."

They inched back up. June stood slightly farther up the ramp, so she and Sam were the same height.

If these were guards, they weren't in uniform. Four men.

One was Anthony.

She and Sam looked at each other again.

"We have to make sure we don't interact with them," Sam murmured. "Or he'll see it."

Across the distance, their conversation was impossible to make out. Anthony seemed nervous, rubbing his hands together, shifting from foot to foot. The other three men surrounded him. One was talking to him, gesturing in his face practically.

Sam eased down behind the wall. He frowned, brow furrowed.

June eased down too. "What?"

"I recognize one of those guys. The other two seem vaguely familiar as well. Members of the Paranormal Alliance. Past tense, I'm assuming."

"That means…"

"Robbie's people. What are they doing here? What's Anthony doing here?"

The answer could only be found in the men themselves, so they peeked back up over the wall.

The conversation seemed to grow heated. The man talking raised his voice, and June caught a few words: "prove it," and "orders." Anthony backed off, hands lifted, shaking his head. One of the other men grabbed his arm.

Anthony struggled. He shouted, "Okay! All right!"

The men filed into the walkway. As they did, all three hunched down, ducking below the windows. Anthony walked in last.

"What's going on?" June whispered.

The men disappeared down the walkway. June and Sam sank behind the wall.

"Why are they going into the Institute?" Sam spoke to the air. "And if it's so easy to get in that way, why isn't it being guarded?"

June had no answers. She couldn't imagine why anyone would want to creep into the Institute, let alone Robbie's minions. Maybe they were stealing things? Maybe paranormal people were still inside and they were liberating them?

"We better get out of here," Sam said. "If Robbie's people are around, I'm more concerned about running into them than the police."

* * * *

"What would Robbie's people be doing inside the Institute?" Cindy paced the kitchen floor, swishing back and forth like an agitated cat. "How the hell would they even get in there?"

"I don't know." Sam stood at the counter. "Robbie's machinations are beyond me." He picked up his phone. "I haven't heard back from Anthony yet. I texted him and asked him to stop by tonight."

The tracking device showed Anthony had left the Institute an hour after he entered it and returned to his house.

"We have to be careful," June said. "You can't say too much when you interrogate him. See if he gives up the information himself. If he does, then we know we can trust him."

"And if he is trying to betray us to Robbie," Sam said, "I'm going to string him up with his brother. In fact, I'll string him up to lure his brother out."

Cindy stopped pacing. "None of this makes sense. When the hell is all this convoluted bullshit going to end?"

June glanced at Sam. "Can I talk to you out on the patio?"

Sam put his phone down and looked at Cindy. "I want a list of all the Paranormal Alliance members who jumped ship to Robbie."

Cindy frowned. "That might be hard. Some we know for sure; some we're not quite clear on. Some just fled Chicago, trying to get away from this mess. They haven't jumped to Robbie, but they're unaccounted for too."

"Then get a list of everyone unaccounted for. Confirm things. I want a clear picture. Get the others off my campaign and on it too."

Cindy nodded and left the room.

"Come on." June motioned Sam toward the patio.

Sitting in the slanting afternoon sun, June gazed into the overgrown foliage around the patio, collecting her thoughts. Sam sat beside her.

"I have to tell you something." She clenched her hands on her knees. "It might be difficult to hear, but it might give us some kind of clue."

"Okay." Sam arched an eyebrow.

She spat out before she lost her nerve, "I saw Muse."

He blinked slowly.

"This morning, at the beach. I woke up in the middle of the night and thought someone was outside the tent, but… I guess it could have been a dream." She tightened her fists, her newly manicured nails digging into her palms. "I came out of the tent this morning and… She was there. Sitting by the water."

"Her ghost?" Sam whispered.

She nodded. "I wish it hadn't happened. I mean, surely it means she's not at peace, the way Rose isn't. I haven't seen Rose in a while, though. I suppose Micha is her concern and… Well, we know how that sits."

Sam looked at the floor, then back up at her. "She spoke to you?"

"Yes. It was a lot of ghostly nonsense, the way Rose talks to me, but maybe it's about this. It didn't make sense at the time, but now that we know Robbie's people are sneaking into the Institute…."

"What did she say?"

June tried to recall the exact words. "She said 'he's in the home of the enemy. He's in their fortress.'"

Sam stared at her.

She let out a breath. "It must mean the Institute," she said. "She was trying to tell me that someone—Robbie, Anthony—is inside the Institute. I'm sure of it now."

Sam looked down again. "Why—and how—would they be inside the Institute?"

"I know." June glanced around. "I figure this means I'll be getting another visit from her." She decided not to mention Muse had possibly been trying to manifest inside the house.

Sam was silent, staring at the floor. June didn't move or speak.

Finally, he lifted his chin. "You can control Rose with Micha's wedding ring, right? You can make her appear?"

June held up a hand. "I'm not making Muse appear. Ghosts are not that helpful, trust me. Even with the ring, Rose speaks in riddles. I'd rather get the answers on our own."

"Maybe we can't find the answers on our own."

"I'm not making her appear, even if you can give me something that works. Let her rest, if she can."

He rubbed his hands together. "How did she look?"

"Dead. Because she's dead, Sam. Her ghost isn't her. Even if I summon her, you won't be able to see her." She paused. "I'm sorry she's still restless. It's not fair, after everything she went through."

Sam stared across the patio. "It's unfair you have to deal with ghosts, too, after everything you've been through."

"Occam believes it's because of my power. He says I'm a necromancer now. I can talk to the dead. One of the perks of having a terminal case of superpowers."

"Muse would sometimes have bursts of telekinesis. Nothing she could control, much like you seeing ghosts."

"Makes me worry what other powers Robbie is developing." The thought chilled her to the bone.

"Maybe if you summon her just once, you could ask—"

"No." June got to her feet.

"You can't deny Rose has given you guidance in the past."

"I'm not doing it, Sam." She opened her arms. "She doesn't deserve that. This is our shit now, and we have to deal with it. She doesn't have to anymore."

Strain showed in his features, a deep pain in his eyes. "This isn't about me seeing her. It's not like that."

"And this is not about me being jealous. This is about having some respect for the dead." She turned toward the house. "No, Sam. Just no." She went inside.

Cindy and the rest of Sam's crew worked in the dining room, put to their new task. Anthony finally texted Sam, saying he would stop by at seven.

"Keep your cool," June warned as Sam paced in the living room. "Let him tell you. If he doesn't, we know we can't trust him, and we'll figure out what to do."

"If he lies to me, I can't allow him to leave here. It means he's playing us into Robbie's hands."

"It's not like Robbie doesn't know exactly where we are. Anthony doesn't know anything that Robbie wouldn't already know."

He stopped pacing, his eyes stormy. "I'm tired of being played for a fool. This ends here."

She sighed. "Then let me be there when he comes over. If he does something shady I can—I'll use my voice on him or something. He can see it coming, but it's not like he can stop me, right?"

"I don't know how much he'll want to talk with you there. He's afraid of you, remember?"

"If he legit wants to help us, he's got nothing to be afraid of."

He raked his fingers through his hair. "Fine. But don't spook him. Let me take the lead. This could get ugly."

"I have a feeling it's going to get ugly no matter who takes the lead."

They waited in Sam's office for Anthony to arrive. June checked out the encyclopedia-thick books in Sam's bookcases: books on politics and government, books about law and democracy, books about supernatural sciences.

"You don't like the Institute." She studied the spine of one titled *Paranormal Biology and Physiology*. "But you still respect the science?"

Sam sat at his desk. "Of course I do. If people like Trina were the only ones studying it, I wouldn't mind."

"How do you manage to hide that you're a shapeshifter? I realize it's to your advantage, but how on earth do you do it?"

"There's no law saying I have to disclose what I am. Certain people in the Paranormal Alliance always knew and vouched for my validity. Our mission and intent has nothing to do with what I am. It's my work people admire and follow. My work has nothing to do with me being a shapeshifter."

"What about the normals? If you won't tell anyone what you are, how do they know you really are anything?"

"They don't. And that's to my advantage too. You can't persecute me for being paranormal if you don't even believe that I am."

She turned from the bookcase. "Now do you understand why I denied what I am for so many years? Why I hid it?"

He stared at his computer screen. "We all get outed, sooner or later. I've just managed to hold on this long."

Anthony announced his arrival via text. Sam went to let him in through a side door, far away from the rest of his guests. She remained in the office. She had sneaked into boy's houses when she was a teenager with far less drama.

When Anthony entered the office, he was visibly tense: jaw tight, eyes wide, shoulders hunched. He eyed June, though surely he must have seen she was there.

"Hi, Anthony." June kept her voice polite and even. "I thought we should try to be friends. We've had a lot of misunderstandings."

Anthony didn't speak, wrapping his arms around himself and glancing around the room. His eyes flashed.

No matter how it went, no good could come from this conversation.

Chapter 19

Sam leaned against the desk. "I was wondering if you had any updates on Robbie."

Anthony swallowed, his Adam's apple bobbing. "Yeah. I got an update for you all right."

June held her breath.

"Robbie is planning something big." Anthony shifted from foot to foot. "I talked to him. Directly. I met with him today."

Sam stepped away from the desk. "You saw him?"

Anthony nodded. "I…yes. I convinced some of his guys to take me to him. I pretended I'm thinking about joining him."

The air crackled with tension. Suddenly, Anthony lurched back, jerking his shoulders up around his ears. This was a precursor to Sam rushing forward and grabbing him by the arms. June gritted her teeth. So much for playing it cool.

"Where did you meet him?" Sam demanded. "Where is he?"

"Sam," June warned.

"Tell me where he is." Sam spoke in his face.

"He's inside the Institute!" Anthony yelped.

Sam released him. June stared at Anthony, relieved but chagrined. She had some apologizing to do. She also had a hell of a lot of questions.

"What do you mean he's inside the Institute?" Sam asked.

Anthony huddled in on himself. "He's hiding inside the Institute. His guys took me in to see him."

"How the hell is he inside the Institute?" Sam took a step back. "That place is locked up. There's cops everywhere. No one can get in."

"You underestimate my brother." Anthony shuddered. "I mean, not that you're not smart—"

"He did underestimate your brother," June said. "I think everyone did. Are you going to tell us how the hell you got inside to see him?"

This was a back-up test, another layer of reassurance. If he told the truth, he was good.

"There's this walkway." Anthony looked warily at her. "They took me through it from inside a parking garage, after they made me wait forever while Robbie was busy. He had to make sure I was reminded we always do things on his time." He grimaced. "Remember I heard him say something about hacking into a security system? Him and his people have taken over the security system inside the Institute. No one knows they're there. They can get in and out, and they can move around unmonitored."

Anthony's eyes flashed. He scrunched up his face and touched the back of his arm. June walked over to him.

"We put a chip on you." She gripped his shoulders and turned him around. "We've been tracking you."

She brushed her fingertips down the back of his arm. He cringed but didn't pull away. She found the edge of the chip and carefully peeled it off. He turned back around.

"Remember when I grabbed your arm?" She lifted the thin piece of plastic in front of his face. "We had to make sure you weren't playing us, that you weren't working for Robbie."

Anthony gaped at the chip.

"I'm sorry." June handed the chip off to Sam. "I'm also sorry that I've doubted you and treated you badly. You can understand why I had misgivings."

"I guess." Anthony spoke tightly. "You had to be pretty clever to get that on me without me seeing it."

"Yeah. We've learned to be clever. Survival."

"How did your brother get inside the Institute?" Sam asked. "Did he tell you?"

Anthony nodded. "Robbie has always had people inside the Institute feeding him information, helping him. Some were in the Paranormal Alliance."

Sam clenched his jaw. "So Robbie used his inside men to get in?"

Anthony nodded again. "He said this has been in the works for years. He said he let you do all the grunt work. His plan was to get the Institute shut down—which you did for him—and then get inside. They've locked the place up, but his ways in were left open. His people made sure."

"That's insane." June marveled at the information. "That's a hell of a lot of moving parts. Risky too."

"He's smart, and bold." Anthony looked down. "The people guarding the Institute right now are his people. No one is going to get inside without him knowing about it. Not cops, not FBI, not anyone."

Sam turned in a slow circle. "All right… So he's inside. I unwittingly helped him get in there. I'll accept that. But." He turned back to Anthony. "Why? Why is he inside the Institute?"

Anthony looked up. His eyes flashed.

"Because he's going to blow the place up."

June stared at him. Sam stared at him. For a moment, June was sure she'd stepped into some cheesy action movie. Blow up a building?

"What?" Sam said. "Blow it up?"

"He bragged about it the entire time I was there. He hasn't changed a bit, except he's a lot more powerful than I remember. I can feel it rolling off him, see it under his skin. It's terrifying."

"He's going to blow the building up?" June tried to wrap her mind around it. "How is he going to manage that?"

"They've got the place wired. He said it's not ready yet, but it will be soon."

"While I support the idea of that place falling into ruins," Sam said, "isn't that a bit grandiose, even for him?"

"He says it's all part of the plan to ensure his place among his followers." Anthony chewed his lower lip. "He's giving them a gift. He's putting a real end to the Institute. He says they'll follow him to Hell and back when he's done. Or to war."

Sam walked over to the windows. "This is absolutely insane…."

"I wouldn't believe it if I hadn't seen it."

"I believe it," June said. "This sounds exactly like his brand of megalomania."

Sam turned from the windows. "Did he give you any idea when this Bond villain scheme of his is going to take place?"

"Soon." Anthony's voice fell. "I have two days."

June frowned. "Two days?"

"To make my decision."

"What decision?" Sam asked.

"To join him or not." He rubbed the back of his arm where the chip had been. "He wants me by his side. He says we'll be unstoppable together. If my answer is yes, I'm supposed to go back to the Institute and join him."

June gazed at him. "And if your answer is no?"

Anthony gazed back at her, silent.

"We'll figure something out," Sam said. "We'll get you the hell out of town."

Anthony laughed bitterly. "There's nowhere to hide from him. Not for me. I could go to Antarctica and he'd find me. And knowing what he's up to?" He shook his head. "He wouldn't let me get away. I'm trapped. That's the way he wants it. He gets his little brother back, one way or another."

All three of them had brother issues, in vastly different ways.

"I can't let Robbie do this," Sam said. "I can't let him get away with it."

June drew a deep breath. Her side ached. "A lot of people could get hurt if he brings that building down. There's always people out front."

"It's not just the people." Sam's voice was grim. "Or even the building. I don't care about the building. Let it crumble. But Robbie is right. If he does this, his followers will rally behind him with monstrous ferocity. The fence sitters will fall off onto his side. His army will wash this city in blood and kill every person who doesn't agree with them, paranormal and normal alike. The Institute won't be the only thing in ashes."

A chill raced down June's spine.

"You're right," Anthony said, soft and distant. "This is his way of kick starting the apocalypse."

However, no man was an island, and neither was Chicago.

"He can try to take over," June said, "but he can't take over the world. This is just one city."

Sam's eyes were ablaze. "Yes, but it's my goddamn city."

* * * *

Mr. Capelli had silver hair and blue eyes. He had a warm smile, wide and white. The soft sagging lines on his face reminded June of her mother's favorite white leather armchair, all squishy and fold-y.

June and Jason were ten. They'd been living in California for a year, and it was completely different from Rhode Island. Always sunny and hot, no seasons. No leaves turning colors, no snow on the ground. Sometimes in winter, it got chilly and gray, but that was it. June still hadn't adjusted, but then, she hadn't adjusted to a lot of things: the absence of her father, the constant tension in her mother's voice, the way she felt like an even bigger weirdo at school than she ever had in Rhode Island. Everyone seemed richer and smarter and more popular than she was. She got made fun of for being short, for being skinny, for not eating most of her lunch because it made her sick.

Mr. Capelli's visits were the one part of her new life she liked. He came over every other weekend and stayed for a few hours, talking to her and Jason about their voices. June's voice was another source of weirdness for her. The anxiety-inducing levels of attention she put into not saying the wrong thing or hurting anybody, or not ruining anyone else's family, made her miserable. Jason never used his voice. He hadn't for a long time, since Katie died. She envied him, how it seemed so easy for him.

Mr. Capelli showed them books about people with supernatural powers. He talked about all the different powers people had and how they struggled with them. He taught them techniques for using their voices safely, how open-ended commands caused the most harm, how they had to make sure the tasks could be completed so the spell would break. June practiced with him, but Jason never did. Their voices didn't affect Mr. Capelli, but he didn't explain why.

Sometimes after a lesson, he would take them for ice cream or to the park. His voice was soothing, and she liked to listen to him talk.

"I know you feel like the strangest person in the world," he said to her, one bright Saturday afternoon. They sat on a bench in the park near her apartment. Jason climbed on a nearby jungle gym.

"There's lots of strange people, aren't there?" June asked.

"Yes. And people without powers will try to make you feel bad about it. They'll try to make you feel like a freak. But remember, you're important and useful. You're special, and you'll do special things in your life."

"What will I do that's special?"

He looked down at her. "You'll do greater things than you could ever imagine. Even if you're scared, even if you don't know what to do next, you'll find the specialness inside you and do what has to be done. You'll save people."

Jason sat on the jungle gym, way at the top, legs dangling through the bars.

"Like a superhero?" June asked.

He chuckled. "Yes, like a superhero."

"How do you know I'll do those things?"

"Because I see it inside you." He leaned closer, lowering his voice. "Being a hero means doing the right thing, doing the hard thing, even when it doesn't benefit you. Being a hero is about sacrifice, and it takes a strong person to sacrifice. The strongest kind of people. I see that strong person inside you."

"What is sacrificing?"

"It means giving up a part of yourself to make someone else happy, or to save them. It means your love for someone or something else is stronger than your love for yourself. Like your mother. She's given up many things for your happiness, because she loves you."

That didn't sound so great. In fact, it sounded scary. But she loved her mother, and she wanted to be just like her.

"I want to be special." She nodded. "I want to be a hero."

"You will be. But you must give it time. The day will come. I see many things."

"What kind of things do you see?"

He smiled. "All things."

"How do you see everything?"

"I'm special too. We're all special in our own ways."

"It must be hard to see everything. Isn't that a lot to see?"

He squinted over at Jason. "Oh, yes. But sometimes I get to just sit on a bench and talk about it, and those are the nice times. Especially when someone is listening."

She swung her legs, sneakers scuffing the ground. Jason swung down off one of the bars in the middle of the jungle gym and dangled in mid-air. She thought about love and about being special. She thought about being a hero.

Sacrifice.

Chapter 20

Sitting on the couch in the silence, the night thick outside the windows, June stared down at her phone. Her mother's voice still rang in her ears. The constant litany of "I miss you, I miss you, I miss you," as June continued pretending everything was all right, that they were coming home soon, that Jason was fine.

The sound of her mother singing her opera rang in June's ears, too, down through the years. The scales and harmonies, the way she'd sing in the kitchen in the morning, the pieces she'd practice for auditions. But the auditions became fewer and fewer as the need to work and provide swelled over her dreams. The sacrifices she made for her children slowly took her voice away.

June looked at the front door, everything inside her as still as the house.

Mr. Capelli never explained how much being a hero sucked, how nobility was far less pleasant than self-interest.

She stood. The door was open to the night. She walked toward it.

Outside on the porch, Sam sat in a chair. He looked like he had the night Muse died, lost and vacant.

June walked over and sat down in the chair adjacent to him. She looked toward the spot where Occam had dumped the body.

"I don't know what to do," Sam said. "I can't pull one idea out of my head."

June didn't speak.

"I have to stop him. If I don't stop him, this will be catastrophic. What it will bring down on this city will be terrible and irreversible."

"I know," she whispered.

"How can I possibly get in there? Even if I change my appearance, getting past Robbie's watchful eye will be nearly impossible."

June looked down at her hands, folded between her knees.

"And even if I do get in there." He shook his head. "What do I do? How do I stop him? I can't fight that man. I can't do anything to him. He can end me with a thought."

June clicked her nails together.

"Maybe we should tell someone." Sam sat forward. "Leak the information, let someone go in there and find out." He paused. "But I don't know if that's a good idea. That's just throwing victims in Robbie's pit."

June spoke softly. "No authority is going to bring him down. He's already proven that."

"So it has to be me." He pushed his hands through his hair. "I have to get in there—somehow—and stop him, some way. Even if I tell Anthony to go in there and pretend he's with Robbie, what good will it do? Unless Anthony can stop him, assassinate him maybe. But Robbie's not alone."

"No, he's not." She looked up. "And if Anthony kills Robbie, Robbie's goons will kill Anthony."

"I won't throw him to the wolves like that. I can't ask that of him."

"He wants to end his brother too. But Robbie is much more likely to end him. Much more likely to end all of us."

Sam growled. "He can't win like this! We can't let this happen, not after everything we've gone through, everything we accomplished. He has to be stopped."

June nodded.

"Even if I have to give my own life," Sam said, "I will stop him. I won't let him have this city."

Sacrifice. Loving something more than you love yourself.

"I never had dreams of martyr-hood." Sam's voice fell. "Despite what everyone believes. I think heroes are much more effective alive."

June got up. The night seemed to watch her every move, tracking her, waiting with breath held in the balmy silence.

Sam's face was obscured in shadow, but his eyes gleamed. "I have to make some phone calls," he said. "We'll try to keep this to ourselves as much as possible, but I need help."

His friends had left earlier. Sam hadn't said anything to them, not even Cindy. Anthony left, too, even more distraught than Sam.

Wordlessly, she walked into the house, the eyes of the night still on her back.

The house was deathly quiet. She stood at the bottom of the staircase. Her thoughts ran to a million things, a million ideas, outcomes, worries. A million emotions.

Dipity sat on the first landing, gazing down at her.

June climbed the stairs. Dipity streaked past her into the darkened hallway above.

June didn't turn on the lights. She stopped outside Sam's bedroom door. She considered the door across from it, though. Dipity wound around her ankles.

She reached out and opened the door—the door to the giant master bedroom with the French doors and balcony.

Light filtered in from the security lights outside. June felt around for a switch, found one, and flipped it. The lamps around the bed and a chandelier in the center of the ceiling switched on. The darkness vanished, making her wince.

Dipity sat in the middle of the hallway, staring at her. She didn't move to follow June in.

"Wise choice," June said. "You don't want to watch this."

She stepped in the room and pushed the door shut behind her.

A vanity sat opposite the balcony doors, a massive mirror hanging above it. Toiletries sat on top the vanity. The room was nicer than some of the hotels she'd been camped out in recently.

She walked across the room to the French doors. Sheer white curtains hung over them. She pushed the curtains back and lifted the latch, and pushed the doors outward.

The balcony had stone railings. Flowerboxes sat on them, badly in need of tending.

The grounds spread below her, cloaked mostly in darkness, except where the security lights shone. She stood at the railing. The sky was clear and splashed with stars. The orange glow of the city burned in the distance.

"Come on then," she said to the night. "Let's do this."

She turned and walked back through the doors, leaving them open.

The mirror over the vanity caught her reflection, her form skeletal and pale. She walked over and pulled out the stool beneath it, and sat down.

The mirror was covered with dust. She wiped it away with her hand, clearing a space big enough to see herself and the room behind her clearly, to see the balcony doors.

The things on the vanity were meant for guests: lotion, shampoo, soap, cologne. A hairbrush, wrapped in plastic. She picked it up and peeled the plastic off.

Her face was so gaunt, her lips dark, her eyes burning green as always, though oddly, once again, not with as much intensity as before.

She started idly brushing her hair. The brush was a good salon-quality one; it deserved some use. Sam was unlikely to have guests again anytime soon.

Except for one guest, and he arrived shortly.

A shadow moved outside the doors. Momentarily, the shadow materialized into something more solid, stepping into the light.

Occam was no vision of the classic romantic vampire. He wore jeans, battered sneakers, and a ratty stained T-shirt. He leaned casually against one of the doors, hip jutted out.

She paused brushing, and then resumed.

He gazed at her, silent; finally, he stepped away from the doors and walked across the room toward her.

She placed the brush on the vanity and watched him in the mirror.

He stopped behind her and bent down so his face was next to hers. His gray, pale eyes reminded her of Robbie's, though somehow more sinister. He gently smoothed her hair over her opposite shoulder, baring her neck. He didn't smell as repulsive as he usually did. Maybe he'd taken a shower for the occasion.

"You don't have to invite me in," he said. "That's just a fairy tale."

"Yet you waited."

He continued stroking her hair. His touch made the back of her neck prickle.

"You've been a busy man lately," she said. "I'm surprised you have the time to watch me."

"I didn't kill them all. I am but one drone in the hive."

"You were the one burning out their eyes. You still have the light."

He chuckled softly, a flash of fangs peeking out between his cracked lips. "At least Sam knows it's being put to good use."

She tilted her head as his fingers dragged through her hair, pulling it.

"I want to ask you something," she said.

He made a soft sound of assent. His closeness was terrifyingly intimate.

"Can you get me and Sam inside the Institute?"

"Where Robbie is."

"Yes." She blinked at their reflection. "Can you get us in there? Get us to him?"

"He'll kill Sam."

"Maybe. But can you at least get us in there?"

His eyes glittered. "I can." He ceased stroking her hair and rested his hand on her shoulder. "We've been monitoring his ridiculous antics. He thinks he's so clever."

"If he goes through with what he's planning, his followers will destroy this city."

"What a pity." Occam stroked his fingertip up the side of her neck along her jugular.

She pulled away and turned on the stool. "I need to ask two things of you."

He stood upright and stepped back. He opened his hands. "Ask."

"I want you to get us inside the Institute."

He gripped her chin, tilting her face up. "And the other?"

"I want Jason and Diego returned to me. Safely." She stared up at him.

He rubbed her chin with his thumb. "And what do I get in return?"

She gripped his wrist. He stilled his rubbing. She took his hand, opened his fingers, and pressed her lips to his palm. His skin was rough, and he smelled like something raw and visceral, like—blood?

"Everything you want," she whispered.

He cupped her jaw. She held his arm tight, above his wrist. He was solid, warm, not undead.

"But not," she spoke tightly, "until you fulfill both parts of the bargain."

His eyes blazed, his gaze cutting through her. She felt fragile under his touch, like he could twist her head off any moment. He could too.

"How do I know you won't run away?" he asked. "How am I supposed to trust you?"

"Where am I going to run from you inside the Institute? Who's going to protect me? Do you think I'll run to Robbie?"

"Your beloved Sam will die at Robbie's hands. If I take you inside, Robbie will kill him." He bent down. "I won't let him kill you, though."

She swallowed, staring into his eyes. "We'll think of something."

"No, you won't, Little Red." He moved his thumb to her lips and dragged it across them. "But I will do what you ask, both parts, if you promise not to run away from me when the time comes."

"I promise," she whispered.

"If you do deny me, I'll rip out Sam's throat. Do you believe me?"

She nodded.

"Then it's a deal."

She drew a deep breath. "This has to happen in the next two days. Robbie is going to kill his brother if he doesn't join him."

"Ah, the seer. Sniveling little thing that he is." He removed his hand from her face. "Very well. Two days. You must be ready when I come for you. No hesitation. When I say we go, we go."

She nodded.

"I take it you haven't discussed this with Sam? I can't imagine he would be happy."

"I'm my own woman. I make my own decisions."

"Yes, you are. Your strength is what I admire most about you. You'll make a fine addition."

She shuddered. "But I won't allow you to put your teeth in me until you do what I ask, all of it."

Occam brought his lips close to her ear. She closed her eyes tight, turning her head.

"Darling," he whispered. "I could have put my teeth in you so many times already. It's just that I'm much more aroused by the idea of you giving it willingly."

She kept her eyes closed, trembling, though she wasn't sure if it was anger, fear, revulsion, or all three.

He drew back slightly. She opened her eyes, but then closed them again as he pressed his lips to hers.

Surprisingly, his mouth didn't taste terrible. In fact, it didn't taste like anything at all. His lips were dry but plump and firm. She almost responded to the kiss when he pulled away and stepped back.

"Two days," he said. "We'll make each other's dreams come true."

With that, he vanished. Into thin air—one moment he was there, the next he was gone. She looked toward the open doors. Nothing moved on the balcony.

She touched her lips where the pressure of Occam's stolen kiss remained.

She rose and left the room. Dipity was no longer in the hallway. June walked downstairs.

Sam sat at the counter in the kitchen, laptop open in front of him and phone in hand. He looked up.

"You all right?" he asked. "I thought you went to bed."

She wrapped her arms around him and rested her head on his shoulder, looking at his laptop screen. He was on Anthony's blog.

He kissed her hair. "I'll figure something out. I'm still the smartest man in this city. Don't worry."

She lifted her head and looked into his eyes. So unlike Occam's or Robbie's or hers. She gripped his jaw and kissed him.

He wrapped an arm around her waist and pulled her close. His grip was reassuring, comforting, strong. She hoped she would feel it again, someday, somehow.

She broke the kiss and pressed her forehead to his. She dragged her tongue across her lower lip, tasting only him, feeling only the pressure of his kiss now.

"It's going to be all right," she said softly. "Everything is going to be all right. I promise."

Chapter 21

Dull morning light streaked the bedroom ceiling. Sam's arm lay across June's stomach, heavy and protective, his breathing slow against her shoulder.

She'd slept fitfully, jerking awake at every sound. Dipity was curled against her side. She envied her cat and boyfriend that they could rest, though she suspected Sam's sleep was just as sketchy as her own.

The only sound now was the first chirpings of birds outside. Nothing stirred in the house, living or dead. She glanced toward the bedroom doorway, for once hoping a ghost would show up with some advice, however vague and incomprehensible.

But there was no advice now. She'd made her choice—the only choice she could make, the only one that would help them.

She closed her eyes.

A few minutes later she snapped them open, tensing, as the intercom on the wall beeped. The system was connected to the front gate.

Sam lifted his head. He looked around blearily. He rolled over, glanced at the clock, and sat up.

"It's barely six AM." He got out of bed and stumbled over to the panel. "What the hell?"

June sat up, her heart in her throat.

Sam punched a button on the panel. "What?"

"Mr. Haain." One of the guards. "There's someone at the gate."

June threw the blankets off. Dipity leaped up and jumped off the bed.

"Right now?" Sam said. "Who's here at this hour of the morning?"

The man's voice came back. "They say they're here to see June. Two men."

June scrambled off the bed.

"Tell them to open the gate!" She looked around for her pants, but she was too discombobulated to function. She wore one of Sam's T-shirts, way too big on her, hanging past her panties.

"What's going on?" Sam asked her. "You're expecting someone?"

"Tell them to open the gate." She ran out of the room.

"June!"

She raced downstairs and to the front door, and flung it open. The morning was cool, the lawn still steeped in shadow. Sam caught up to her on the porch and gripped her arm.

"Who's out there?" he demanded.

She didn't answer. She pulled out of his grip and hurried down the porch stairs, her bare feet slapping on the wood. She felt like she was moving underwater, unable to push forward fast enough, like being trapped in a nightmare.

The nightmare was about to end, though, at least part of it.

When she reached the driveway, she stopped. She stared down it, breath held.

"June." Sam followed her. "Tell me what the hell is going on!"

She pulled in deep breaths. Her hands were clenched in shaking fists at her sides as she waited, for what seemed like an eternity.

Then, two figures appeared, materializing out of the thick shadows around the bend in the driveway.

With a strangled shout, she ran toward them.

Her feet stung as they pounded on the pavement, but she didn't slow down. She bolted toward the two figures until their faces became clear and then blurred as tears spilled from her eyes.

She flung herself against her brother's taller, bulkier frame. He wrapped his arms around her, as did someone else, from the side. She reached out and snaked an arm around Diego's slender waist.

They both stunk horribly—sweat and body odor, and that awful rotten musty smell of Occam's vampire shambles—but she had never been happier to have her nose offended. She cried, pressing her face to Jason's dirty T-shirt.

"You're alive," she choked out. "You're really here."

She was hugged and kissed and clutched, with no clear idea who was who, but it didn't matter. She tangled herself with both of them, her heart slamming against her ribs. Her side ached fiercely, but she closed out the pain, melting into their embrace.

She finally managed to draw back, taking them in through tear-filled eyes, a heavenly vision. She gripped Jason's face.

"Are you all right? Are you both all right?"

"We're fine." Jason's voice was strained. "I'd kill for a sandwich and a shower, but they didn't hurt us."

"I hate vampires." Diego seethed. "Fucking monsters. They kept us like animals, but Jason's right. We're okay. They never harmed us."

June couldn't stop crying. She looked them both over for reassurance. They were dirty, their appearance as awful as their stench, but no cuts, no bruises. Only the old pink scar on Jason's wrist. She had to give him back his watch.

"Oh, God." She wept anew, clinging to both of them. "Thank God. Thank God you're all right."

Jason wrapped his arms around her again and lifted her off her feet. She clung to him, dangling. He placed her back on the ground and nodded to someone behind her.

"Sam," he said. "God, it's good to see you again too."

June turned, sniffing.

Sam stood in the middle of the driveway, brow furrowed, mouth open. He stared at June.

"Occam let us watch you guys on TV," Jason said. "The press conference. He thought it was funny."

"I didn't tell the FBI where you were." June gripped her brother's arm. "I was too afraid of what Occam would do."

Diego squeezed her hand. "Yeah. He kept saying you wouldn't be dumb enough to send anyone after him. He said if you did, something bad would happen to us."

Jason looked around. "This is your place, Sam? Damn. Right now I'd settle for a hovel if it didn't belong to a vampire, but this is pretty impressive."

Sam walked slowly toward them, still staring at June.

"Sam," she said softly. She trembled all over, from joy, from terror of what lay ahead.

Sam stopped. He shook his head. "June," he whispered. "What the hell have you done?"

* * * *

"We can't get inside the Institute on our own." June stood in the middle of the living room, arms folded, chin up, trying to appear much more confident than she felt. "There's no way we can get past Robbie's surveillance."

Sam sat on the couch in front of her, his head in his hands. Jason and Diego stood behind her.

"We need Occam's help," she said. "He can do it, or he can at least help us do it. Isn't that why you involved the vampires in the first place, because they can do all kinds of things we can't?"

Sam lifted his head and pressed a hand over his mouth. He stared at the floor.

"There has to be some other way." His voice was hushed. "There has to be—"

"There isn't," she said. "Sam, we're fucked. We're fucked really, really hard. The only way we can hope to stop him is by using extreme measures. Even if we could somehow get inside undetected, how are we going to stop Robbie? Tell me that. How are you going to bring him down? He can kill both of us without lifting a finger. And he will. He won't play around this time, mark my words."

Sam lifted his gaze to her.

"But he can't hurt vampires," she said. "It's a vampire who has to take him out. It's the only way."

Sam lowered his hand. "Why would you make this deal with the devil behind my back? Why didn't you tell me?"

"Because you wouldn't have let me do it."

He slapped his hands on his knees. "No, I wouldn't have let you."

"There's no other way, Sam."

Jason cleared his throat. He stepped up beside June. "She's right, Sam. If this is something you guys have to do, you can't get rid of Robbie on your own. Even with Muse around, she can't read his thoughts, right? He's blank to her?"

June cringed. She turned to him, biting her lip.

"Muse is dead," she said softly. "Robbie killed her."

Jason's face sagged.

Sam got up. He walked over to June, glowering.

"Jason," Sam said, "do you understand what your sister is saying?"

She glowered at Sam in return.

Sam gestured at Jason. "Do you think Occam let you go out of the kindness of his gentle vampire heart? Do you think he's going to help us just because it'll make him feel good? Your sister has struck a bargain with him. That's why he's willing to help us. That's why he let you go."

June squared her shoulders. "Jason"—she turned to him—"a lot has happened since Occam took you prisoner. There's things you don't know, things about me. Things I didn't even know until a month ago."

"I'm not letting him take you," Sam said lowly.

"Shut up," June told him.

Diego looked between her and Sam, eyes narrowed. "Are you... Are you saying you're going to become a vampire, June?"

"What?" Jason said sharply.

She held up a hand. "I have to explain some things. And you have to listen."

Jason shook his head. "Why would you even consider—"

She pressed a hand to his chest. "I'm dying."

He blanched, his eyes going wide. "What are you talking about?" He stared at her.

"My food allergies, they're not allergies. It turns out it's my power killing me. Eating me from the inside out. The way Muse's power was destroying her. The way Robbie's power is destroying him. That's what's happening to me."

"June." Diego stepped toward her. "Oh my God..."

"How do you know that?" Jason gripped her hand on his chest.

"Occam told me. It's what happened to him, before he was turned. It'll eventually kill me—either starvation or my guts will dissolve or something equally horrible. That's my fate."

"You believe him?" Jason asked.

"Yes," she said softly. "We've been trying to find some medical way to combat it, but... They haven't been able to save any of us yet, have they Sam?"

"There's a first time for everything," he said grimly behind her.

"So you're going to become a vampire?" Diego asked.

"If I become a vampire, I'll survive. It'll even fix some of the damage. Robbie has been trying to convince a vampire to change him, to fix his issues, too, so he can live and continue destroying the city."

Jason gaped. "That...would make a monster."

She nodded. "I don't know if Occam told you, but recently they cleansed their society. They killed most of the vampires in the city. Supposedly, because they only want strong vampires around, but they also don't want anyone turning Robbie, and the old vampires—the ones who can really help him—would never do that."

Jason and Diego stood silent, their horror seeming to radiate on the air.

"I made a deal," June said. "I'll become a vampire, if Occam helps us stop Robbie—and gave you and Diego back to me, unharmed."

"We can find another way," Sam said. "We'll figure it out."

She pulled her hand away from Jason and turned to Sam. "If I become a vampire, what do you think is going to happen? I'll still be me. Do you think I'll turn into Occam? I'm less inclined to believe Occam's personality is a result of his vampirism and more just him naturally being an asshole."

Jason gripped her shoulder. "June, you really believe this? You really think you're dying?"

She looked back at him and pressed a hand to her stomach. "Yes. In my gut, trust me. And it's getting worse every day. I don't want to die. I don't want to face what I can feel in my body is happening."

Sam drew a sharp breath. "I can't lose you to the vampires. Not after everything. If I lose you…"

June looked back around at him. "If I don't become a vampire, you're going to lose me completely, forever."

"What the hell else has happened?" Jason asked. "All this stuff, just since we've been kidnapped? Where's Micha?"

June rubbed her forehead. "You guys need a shower and a decent meal, and then I'll tell you everything."

Sam's face was stony, but his eyes were full of fear, of anguish. She wished she could kiss away his anxiety. She wished she could expel her own.

"Occam will be in touch soon," she said. "He promised we would act before Robbie kills Anthony."

Sam stepped up to her. "I'm not waiting on a vampire. And I'm not letting him turn you. We will figure this out." He turned and stormed off toward the kitchen.

June wrapped her arms around her aching, empty stomach. "There is no other way," she whispered.

While Jason and Diego showered, and with Sam brooding in the kitchen, June sneaked a phone call out on the porch.

"Do you think you can slip your cell phone to Micha?" she asked Trina, keeping her voice down. "I need to have a conversation with him. It's very important."

"I don't know. Possibly. But I don't know how he could talk to you without them listening in." She paused. "What's going on? You sound odd."

"I just need to talk to him. Can you try?"

"I'll see what I can do. If he can get in touch with you, I'll have him text you right before he calls. Keep your phone on you."

"I will. Thanks a lot, Trina."

"Are you sure you're all right? Make sure you don't miss your appointment on Monday. I've got a new regimen of vitamins I want to try out."

June swallowed. "Sure. I won't miss it."

Jason and Diego looked much better showered and in fresh clothes—some of Sam's—and they looked much happier with real food in front of them. June didn't want to spoil their appetites, so she didn't start talking until they were mostly done eating. She filled them in on all the sordid details from the past month.

"So you're with Sam now?" Jason jerked the water bottle he was holding toward the dining room, where Sam had relocated and sequestered himself. "Gotta say, I'm not surprised."

June sat across from them, too much a bundle of nerves to eat. "I'll always care about Micha. Trina is going to find a way to save him. It's not fair he should die after all he's been through."

Diego lowered his fork. "Maybe he can become a vampire too."

June sighed. "Everything is really complicated right now. Who knew being out of hiding was worse than being in it?"

They were all silent. Seeing them in front of her was the first awesome thing that had happened in a while. So much better than a picture.

"What went on with Occam?" she asked. "What did he do to you guys?"

Jason shrugged. "Nothing. It was boring as hell. He locked us in a room. Sometimes we didn't see him for days. No vampires ever touched us, but I think they were trying to break us with sheer mind-numbing boredom."

"When he did come by," Diego said, "it was just to mess with us and drop off food and water. Vampires think humans can live on Cheetos and Pepsi."

"He did let us watch the press conference," Jason said. "That was a fun outing."

"I was worried you'd resist him and he'd do something to you." She looked at Diego. "Especially you. There was—right after he kidnapped you, I didn't know it yet, but he came to talk to me, and he smelled like your cologne. I was worried you'd fought him."

Diego rolled his eyes. "No. We were getting ready to leave Chicago and we were at the hotel where I'd been staying, picking up my things."

"And I wasn't very happy with you," Jason cut in, eyeing her. "I wanted to find you and put my hands around your throat, to be honest."

"I figured." She still felt guilty about it, especially given the outcome.

"Occam showed up," Diego said. "Like some friggin' ghost, he just appeared. He was being an asshole. He went through my suitcase, took a bunch of my stuff. He sprayed my cologne on him, said it would make you like him more."

"Occam is always an asshole," she said. "I'm glad you didn't try to fight him."

"I wanted to." Diego grew snippy. "His goons swarmed in and took us out of there. I still have no idea what happened to my stuff, or even my car."

Jason continued eyeing June. "And now we're all safe, and you want to put yourself in danger again. Going into the Institute is a really dumb idea."

"Not going in there is an even dumber idea. If Robbie blows that place up, his followers will devour the city."

Diego muttered, "I'm inclined to let them have it."

"I used to feel that way too," June said. "Now—I don't think it's right. It'll set the paranormal community back decades. Normals will fear us again."

Jason smirked. "I can for sure tell you're dating Sam now."

She glared at him. "Do you really think what Robbie wants to do is right?"

He was silent a moment. "No, I don't. But I wish it wasn't you that had to take care of it, and I sure as hell wish you didn't need Occam. What if you die in there?"

"I'm going to die if I don't go in there." She sat back. "If you want me around, this is how it has to be."

A commotion rose in the living room. A moment later, Cindy appeared in the doorway, blustery and wide-eyed.

"You're really here!" She rushed in.

Jason stood. She was as tall as him in her heels. They embraced, Cindy clinging to him, her face pressed against his shoulder.

June side-eyed Diego. "I guess that answers my question," she murmured. "About if you and Jason got up to anything to pass the time."

Diego tilted his head, giving her his patented death stare. "It wasn't exactly a porno fantasy."

"You must be slipping."

"Just because you can get laid in a crisis, June."

Cindy drew back, still clutching Jason. "Occam let you go?" She looked at June. "What the hell is going on? Sam is fit to be tied, and he's not answering any of my questions. Why is he all wound up?"

"You'll find out soon enough." June got up and walked over to them. She squeezed Jason's shoulder and pulled her phone out of her pocket. "There's someone I want you to say hi to."

She tapped the screen to get to her contacts.

"You were held for questioning by the FBI," June instructed him. "You weren't allowed to talk to anyone." She pressed the call button and held the phone out to him. "Dodge as many questions as you can. Say the FBI has a gag order on you."

Jason took the phone from her and hesitantly placed it to his ear.

June wandered out of the room. She smiled when Jason's happy, surprised gasp followed her.

"Mom!"

Chapter 22

The hot, humid day gave way to a warm, sticky night. If June ever got back to Sacramento, one thing she wouldn't miss—among plenty of other things—was the lake-fueled humidity.

She sat on the edge of the porch, dangling her legs over the side. The ground was a good ten-foot drop below.

She was waiting.

She tilted her head back and took in the sky. As a child, she'd wished on the first star that appeared every night, something her mother had taught her. She couldn't remember any of those wishes. She couldn't remember if any of them came true.

Her phone rang in her hand. She'd gotten a text a few minutes ago.

Her mouth was dry as she answered. "Micha."

"I don't have much time," he whispered. "Luckily they don't have cameras on me in the can. What's up?"

She smiled. "It's good to hear your voice. I don't know why we didn't think of this before."

"It's risky. If they catch me talking to you, we'll both be in trouble."

She took a deep breath. "Something is going on. I wanted you to know about it, just in case something happens. We're going into the Institute. I'm not sure when, maybe tonight, maybe tomorrow."

Silence on the other end, and then he spoke, sounding bewildered. "What? Why are you going in there?"

"Robbie's in there."

"Robbie's inside the Institute?" Micha's voice got louder.

"Yes, and we have to go in after him. He's going to blow the place up. We found out from his brother."

More silence.

"I…have a lot of questions," he said, "but my main one is why would you stop him from blowing that place up?"

"If he blows it up, his followers will rise up and destroy the city. I'm not too fond of the place, either, but I can't let that happen. We can't."

"You guys could get killed."

She wished she could tell him one good thing. "Occam is going to get us inside and help us get to Robbie. Robbie can't affect vampires."

"Occam?" He dropped his voice back to a whisper. "You're working with the vampires?"

"It's the only chance we have. There's something I need to tell you, about me."

A faint knock sounded in the background. Micha called out, "I'm almost done!" He spoke into the phone. "I can't stay on much longer. Why the hell would you work with Occam? You said he kidnapped Jason and Diego."

"He brought them back." Her heart pounded. "It's a lot to explain, obviously I can't do it right now. Listen… You're not the only one suffering from an illness brought on by supernatural powers. We're in the same boat."

"What?"

"You know how Muse's powers were killing her? Well, mine are killing me too. I don't know how much time I have left."

"Jesus Christ."

"But there's a way to save me. I made a deal with Occam. That's how we do this. That's how we get out alive."

Silence for a moment. "Are you…saying you're going to become a vampire?"

"I have to."

Another knock.

"Be right out!" Micha yelled. Water came on. "June, you can't do that."

"You want me to die?'

"No. But there has to be another way."

"If there was one, I'd be trying it already. Listen, I know you have to go. I just wanted… I wanted to let you know what's going on, and I wanted to tell you if anything happens, I really enjoyed the time I spent with you, and I'm sorry for what they did to you." She blinked a few times. "Who knows, maybe vampirism is the answer for you too. Maybe it's not so bad."

"Maybe it's not, but their society sure as hell is. June, don't say good-bye this way."

"I have to. Hang up so you don't get in trouble. I'll text Trina when everything is about to go down so you know. You should probably keep an eye on the news too."

"June."

"I'm sorry, Micha. Good-bye. Good luck."

She hung up. She closed her eyes, pulling in a shaky breath, and clutched the phone against her chest. She fought back tears.

She had a wish now. To move forward. To get this show on the road.

Miraculously, instantaneously, her wish came true.

She opened her eyes at the soft whisper of footsteps on the grass below. Occam crossed the lawn toward her.

Her stomach crawled into her throat. She dropped the phone on the porch floor.

He held up a hand. "It's not time yet, don't get excited."

She suspected she only heard him coming because he wanted her to.

"We need to make some arrangements." He stopped below her. "This isn't going to be easy, even for me."

She gripped the edge of the porch, staring down at him.

"I need you and Sam to do some things," he said. "Is he around?"

"He's not very happy with me right now."

Occam chuckled. "I don't guess he is."

She looked across the yard. "How do you get in here? There are guards at the gate. Sam's got the security cameras on now. How do you keep getting onto the property?"

"I'm a shapeshifter, darling."

"You're good enough you can glamour objects, okay. Does that mean you can make yourself look like a tree or something?" She pictured a tree scuttling across the grass.

"No. I can make myself invisible."

She raised her eyebrows.

"So to speak. I can take on the patterns of things around me. It's more like camouflage than shapeshifting. It comes in handy."

This actually sounded fascinating.

"That explains a lot," she said. "Like all the times you just seemed to disappear." She cringed. "You weren't really gone, you just…blended in."

"Yes. And then I slipped away."

"How long have you been creeping around here, blending in and watching me?"

"As long as I needed to."

"Have you been inside the house?"

"Only when you asked me in."

The sounds she'd been hearing were caused by Muse trying to materialize, then. But why? June had seen Rose readily. Why did Muse have a hard time?

"There are a lot of things I need to know," she said. "Before I come over to the dark side. I'm curious what I'll be able to do."

"Well, you won't be able to do the things I do." He strolled over to the porch stairs. "I can do those things because I'm a shapeshifter. You bring your own unique talent to the table. In time, who knows what you'll be able to do with it."

"But I won't age, right? And I won't die from any disease. The only way to kill a vampire is to destroy a vital organ."

"Yes." He stood at the bottom of the stairs.

"What about being maimed? Can you be scarred or lose body parts?"

"You can't be scarred. The damage will heal itself. Mortal wounds quickly seal up enough to sustain life and then gradually heal completely. As for losing body parts—unfortunately, it can happen, and has. Healing and regeneration can only go so far. Human DNA is not coded to re-grow lost parts."

"Do you get more strength? Sam said you once decapitated someone with your bare hands. Internally, anyway."

Occam waved a hand. "It was during a fight with another vampire. I was hopped up on heroin and it was a lucky break, pun intended. But I do enjoy using the legend to scare people."

She cringed. "So you...pulled his head off, and... Did he heal? Did it reattach?"

"It did heal. He was never quite the same. We purged him recently. He was a weakling and a hot head. We don't have room for that."

But they obviously had room for violent heroin junkies.

She swallowed. "I'll have to be part of your society, at least a little bit. I don't guess I can just go on living my life normally."

"You won't want to."

"I want to stay with Sam. I want to be able to see my family. I want to go home to California for a while and see my mother. I know I'll have issues. I'll need blood. I'll have to travel at night. I'll join your vampire crusade, but I have to have my life as well."

"You'll be different, not just physically. Your desires will change."

"I think that's bullshit. You just killed a whole bunch of vampires who were living normal lives. So it's possible."

His eyes gleamed in the twilight. "Yes. We just killed them."

Footsteps sounded inside the house. The front door opened. Sam stepped out.

"I thought I heard—" He froze at the sight of Occam. "You."

June quickly got to her feet. "Sam."

"It's not time," Occam said. "I came to make arrangements. We have to work out a few things before we go in there."

"I'm not going anywhere with you." Sam gripped June's waist. "And neither is she."

"Sam"—June placed a hand over his on her hip—"just hear him out."

Occam started up the stairs. "I went to the Institute today, had a walk around inside, got the lay of the land. There's a bit of good news." Sam moved her back as Occam reached the top of the stairs. "Robbie has taken over the security system, but he's only running the cameras at the entrances to the building. He doesn't want anyone picking up a feed from inside, so those are all offline."

"You walked around the Institute?" Sam asked. "How? No one saw you?"

Occam looked at June. "You want to explain what I just told you about me? I don't feel like repeating myself."

"It doesn't matter right now." She pulled out of Sam's grip. "So there's no surveillance inside, just at the entry points."

"Yes," Occam said. "Robbie has a team in there—not too many, maybe twenty people. Enough to help him out, but not so many they can't be stealthy. They're rigging the structure with explosives. I do hope they're actual engineers or explosive technicians and not just looking things up on the Internet; otherwise, it might go boom ahead of schedule."

"Then it's easy for us to creep around too," June said.

"The FBI hasn't begun their physical investigation yet," Occam went on. "But they will soon, so he has to do the deed in the next few days. He's played a long game, ever so patient, making sure everything was in place before he took action." He focused on Sam. "Smart man. Too bad you're not as nefarious as he is."

Sam glared at him.

"Robbie is camped out in the executives' quarters on the top floors. Where all the big wigs work—or used to. Unemployment lines are awful long these days."

"So we just have to get up there, undetected, and take him out," June said. "But first, take his twenty or so people out."

"His twenty or so people will be whittled down to just a few by the time we walk in. My vampire friends are very good at clearing spaces. I don't like a bunch of icky obstacles."

Megan Morgan

"Robbie is a telepath," Sam said. "How the hell would we sneak up on him? You can, but we certainly can't."

"Robbie is powerful." Occam nodded. "But he can't hear the entire building. Maybe most of the floor he's on, but nothing beyond that. He can feel something coming, but only when it gets in his vicinity."

"Which means you have to sneak up on him," June said. "If you're willing to do that."

Occam gazed at her. "It depends. Are you willing to change your lifestyle?"

She tensed. "That's not fair."

Occam shrugged. "You're asking a lot of me. If you think I'm completely immune to Robbie, you're mistaken. He can very much drive something through my chest if he gets the urge."

"But he needs you." She stepped closer to him. "He wants what you have, so he's going to be nice to you."

Occam tilted back. "This has gone from 'get me inside' to 'kill Robbie for me, big bad vampire.'"

Sam walked over to them. "We don't need you. We'll figure something out. If Robbie's going to die, it's going to be by my hand."

Occam laughed. "Okay."

"We just need to stop him from blowing up the Institute," Sam said. "We need to undo those charges."

Occam scoffed. "So you're an explosives expert? Or will you be learning how to defuse bombs in two days?"

"All right." June's voice caught. "Maybe… You should make me a vampire before we confront him. Then I can kill him myself."

"June." Sam spoke sharply.

"You can't just walk up and pop him." She looked at Sam. "I know you want to do this some other way, but we can't. You will die trying. This way, we have a chance. We live." She lowered her voice. "I live. If I don't do this, if I don't let Occam do this to me…"

Sam held her gaze, his eyes shining.

"Okay." Occam tapped his foot. "That's settled. Now, I need you to do something for me. You need to bring Anthony along when we go inside."

"Why?" June asked.

"It'll be easier that way. Anthony needs to act like he's joining his brother. Nepotism is so ugly, I tell you."

"Anthony may not want to go with us," Sam said.

"Does he want to die?" Occam opened his arms. "Because Robbie has no qualms about making good on his promises, trust me. And if he doesn't come, we can't do this."

"We'll get him to come," June said. "Just tell us when you intend to do it."

"June," Sam said. "We need to discuss—"

She held up a hand. "When, Occam?"

"Tomorrow evening," he said. "At nightfall. I'll come for you. Be ready. Bring whatever you like, whatever you think will help. And make sure you bring Anthony, even if you have to force him with that sweet voice of yours."

"He wants to see his brother dead too." June paused. "And—how will we do this? Are you going to turn me?"

"We shall have to see how things play out, won't we?"

She pulled in a deep breath and nodded.

Sam stalked back in the house. June watched him a moment and then looked back at Occam.

He wasn't there.

She scanned the darkened yard. No movement, no sound. A shudder raced down her spine, and she followed Sam inside.

She found him in the dining room, slamming things around.

"Sam." She stood in the doorway.

"I don't want to hear anything you have to say right now." He didn't look at her. "You've made your choice."

"So have you. You've made the choice to save this city from Robbie." She walked into the room. "You could let him do what he wants, and none of this has to happen with Occam."

"I can't let him do what he wants." He leaned over with both hands on the table.

"Then we can't do this without Occam. Surely, you can comprehend that us going in there alone is a death sentence."

Sam said nothing.

"With Occam's help, we have a chance. And what's the price for his help? That I get to live?"

He looked up. "I'm going to lose you."

"You're going to lose me if I don't let Occam do this, much more horribly."

"Trina is looking for a cure."

"Her vitamins?" June tilted her head. "Sam, do you think she can fix what no one could fix for Muse? It might work for a while, but it won't work forever. I don't want to die."

He pushed away from the table and walked over to the windows.

"Get in touch with Anthony," she said. "Right now."

She walked upstairs, numb and in a daze. She was beyond fear, beyond anguish, even beyond hope. She simply focused straight ahead on what needed to be done.

In the hallway, she paused outside one of the guest room doors. Jason was sleeping inside. Diego was in another. The urge to check on them, to make sure they were still there, overwhelmed her. Quietly, she turned the doorknob to Jason's room and eased the door open.

The room was dark. Jason was asleep on the bed.

He wasn't alone.

Cindy lay next to him. They were facing each other, Cindy's arm draped over Jason's side. Both were fully clothed. The sight made June's heart ache.

She closed the door and bowed her head, considering the future, considering Jason's future, her mother's future. Maybe they would be better off if they didn't see her again after she became a vampire.

She turned, intending to check on Diego next, and nearly yelped.

A short distance down the hallway, a small white figure stood. Still as the grave, staring blankly.

Muse gleamed in the darkness. Like Rose, she appeared solid but dead, like someone had propped her corpse up.

June glanced back, toward the stairs. If Sam came up he wouldn't see her, but June would have a hard time acting like she wasn't there.

"The answer is inside you," Muse whispered. "It will change you."

June stared at her. Those words made no sense, not like she expected them to, but they did seem ominous.

"Are you talking about Occam?" June asked. "About him making me a vampire?"

Muse didn't reply. How much of a human's personality remained in a ghost? Were they just an empty shell, an afterimage?

June inched toward her. "We have to do something dangerous tomorrow. If you can help us at all, offer any advice…"

Footsteps sounded on the stairs. June looked around, then back down the hallway. Muse had vanished. A chill lingered in the air.

"I guess not," June murmured.

Sam stepped into the hallway, holding his phone.

"Anthony will come," he said. "Happy now?"

She drew a slow, deep breath. "No. But I guess we just wait for our ride now."

Chapter 23

June descended the porch stairs at twilight, another twilight, twenty-four hours from the last. Things were in motion, barreling toward a brick wall or the open sky—the next few hours would tell.

Three figures stood in the driveway: Jason, his arm around Cindy's shoulders, Diego standing next to them.

A gun rested on June's hip. She hadn't gotten to practice for a while, but she wouldn't be shooting Robbie, anyway. Having it there just made her feel more secure. She could shoot other things, if need be.

"I guess this is where you wish me luck," she said as she approached the three. "Occam will be here soon."

Jason let go of Cindy, wrapped his arms around June, and squeezed. "You better return in one piece," he whispered. "We just got each other back."

She clung to him and closed her eyes. "Remember what we discussed. If I don't, you have to take care of Mom."

Jason squeezed her tighter, nearly cutting off her breath. "Don't make me have that conversation with her."

He drew back, still holding her, and looked into her eyes. He had their mother's eyes. Not like June's. They had never been that vivid.

Diego inched up beside them. She untangled herself from Jason.

"And you," she said. "You have to make sure the shop stays open. Keep the dream alive."

Diego threw his arms around her.

"You'll be back in the shop soon." His voice trembled. "Tattooing some surly drunk biker. You'll be giving all of us hell for slipping freebies to our friends."

She blinked tears from her eyes. That seemed like another lifetime. How the hell had she ended up here?

Diego pulled back and wiped his eyes. "I don't know if I can deal with you as a vampire, but if it means not losing you, I'll take it."

Jason squeezed her shoulder. "Me too."

Cindy stepped up to her, eyes shining. "You're my best friend, June." She clutched June's hands. "Fighting by your side has been an honor."

June hugged her before she said anything else dramatic and stupid. She was smothered in boobs.

The door to the house opened. June let go of Cindy and turned.

Sam and Anthony stepped out on the porch. Everyone in the driveway stood silent as the two descended the stairs.

"There's a car at the gate," Sam said. "I'm assuming it's our ride."

June braced herself. She took in Anthony as he walked over to them. "Can you see how this will go?"

Anthony's eyes flashed. He shook his head. "Too many winding paths. I can't even see my own fate."

"I guess that's a good thing," June said. "The future is wide open."

Cindy rushed over and hugged Sam. He wrapped his arms around her, gazing at June over her shoulder.

"Please come back to us," Cindy begged. "We need you now more than ever."

Sam drew back and gripped her arms. "If I don't, I've left instructions on what I want for the Paranormal Alliance. Promise me you'll honor my wishes."

Cindy sniffed and nodded. "We'll carry on, Sam. I promise."

June pulled her phone from her pocket and texted Trina: *Tell Micha it's happening.*

Jason hugged her one more time. "I love you," he whispered. "You gotta come back, even if you have fangs."

She clutched him tight. "I have to get those put in."

If she didn't turn away from all the sad faces and go, she would lose her courage.

June, Sam, and Anthony strode down the driveway toward the gate. She glanced at Sam.

"We're going to stop him," she said. "We'll come back from this."

He stared straight ahead. "We won't come back the same."

A black car sat beyond the gate.

"No," she said. "We won't."

Occam sat in the front passenger seat, Zack driving. They both turned and watched the three of them as they piled into the backseat, June in the middle.

"My favorite vampires," June said. "I see you survived the cleansing, Zack. I'm relieved."

Zack chuckled darkly.

"Soon, he'll be your brother." Occam swiveled farther to look at Anthony behind him. "You're the seer."

Anthony stared at him. His eyes stayed dark.

"You look like your brother," Occam said. "You must be so proud."

Anthony stiffened. "I'll be prouder when he's dead. I don't consider him my brother."

"Let's just go," June said. "We can't waste time."

"Indeed, we can't." Occam turned back around. "Robbie has his finger on the trigger."

They drove away from the house. June didn't look back.

They seemed to be hurtling forward at the speed of light, yet the neighborhoods slid by painfully slow. An agonizing long time passed before the buildings of downtown loomed on the dark horizon, their lights gleaming against the night.

"Would you like to hear the plan?" Occam finally broke the silence. "Or are you just going to stumble after me like good little sheep?"

"I figure we're at your mercy," June said. "But what do you have in mind?"

"I'm glad you asked. We'll use Anthony to get inside. Sam and I will use our powers. Do you think you can stop pouting long enough to help, Sam?"

Sam said nothing, staring out his window.

"My helpers are inside," Occam said. "Most of Robbie's minions will already be bloodless by the time we show up. Any strays, they'll let me know about, as well as Robbie's whereabouts. Hopefully, he's still on one of the upper floors. We'll send Anthony up to say hello and keep him distracted. Then we'll move in as close as we dare."

"And then what?" June asked.

Occam turned around. "It depends. I can go up and pretend I'm there to give him what he wants from me. Or I can turn you, and you can greet him."

June swallowed.

"However." Occam eyed her. "Robbie will be happy to see me—you, not so much. And you'll still be no match for him. That gun on your hip won't help. He may not be able to throw you around when you're a vampire, but he can throw everything around you."

"Then it has to be you," June said. "You have to kill him. And then we have to find all the charges and defuse them."

"'We'll watch you do all the work for us,' is that what you're saying? You don't have a plan of your own?"

"We do," Sam spoke up. "You don't need to do our dirty work. You only need to get us inside and tell us where Robbie is."

June glared at Sam. "Nice of you to share this plan with me."

Sam looked back out the window. "If you can throw yourself on the blade, so can I."

"My only interest is June." Occam shrugged. "She made a promise."

"I'll keep it," she spoke tightly. "If you keep yours."

"I will. My concern is that he doesn't kill you. I won't allow that to happen."

Was she supposed to be relieved?

"Fine, then." She looked at Sam. "Since we have a plan."

They fell back into silence, the car rushing along the lake shore, the pathway to their doom as it was back in January.

The drive to the Medical District was agonizing, crawling through traffic, passing through the normal world where people were going obliviously about their lives: walking and talking and laughing, going into bars, getting on buses, hugging, holding hands. Would she ever get back to that world?

When they arrived, Zack drove them to the parking garage she and Sam had snuck into. He stopped the car at the curb in front of it.

"Park nearby," Occam told Zack. He said to the others, "This is our only getaway car so you have to follow me back to it." He turned and focused on June. "Don't be afraid, Little Red. Just hold my hand."

As they were climbing out, June's phone buzzed in her pocket. She pulled it out. A call from Trina. She let it go to voicemail.

She had two texts from her, as well. The first one asked, *What the hell is going on?* The second said, *June, call me! Please!*

June pushed the phone back into her pocket. Zack pulled away from the curb. They hurried into the parking garage.

As they marched up the sloping floors, Occam filled them in further.

"Robbie's goons will be at the entrance to the walkway. Anthony, I need you to lure them away, out of sight of the cameras." He smirked at Sam. "We're going to commit some bodysnatching."

Sam strode along, staring straight ahead.

June walked behind them. "Why don't we just sneak in the way your vampires sneaked in? Why go knocking on the front door?"

"Do you think that's a good strategy?" Occam asked over his shoulder. "How many telepaths do you think Robbie has in the house? Vampires can't be read. Could you block your mind while you're breaking in, unsure where the listeners are?"

He was a bastard, but he was a clever bastard.

Floor after floor, they made their way up, until they reached the ramp leading up to the floor with the walkway. As before, they stayed behind the wall, peeking over.

Three men stood at the entrance to the walkway—the tube was lit up, stretching across the darkness to the equally darkened building.

"Fortunately," Occam murmured, "these are not telepaths. That's why they're out here." He turned to Anthony. "Tell me where the edge of the camera's sight is."

Anthony peered over the wall, his eyes flickering.

"The camera only sees the entrance to the walkway," Anthony said. "A few feet out from it."

"How do you know that?" June was boggled.

Anthony looked at her. "I see them walk out of the camera's sight in a minute."

"You can see stuff like that?" She gaped, momentarily forgetting their dire situation in her wonder.

"I see everything." His eyes flickered again. "I can tell you their blood pressure and heart rate for the next few minutes. I can tell you what radio signals and light particles they pass through."

"Wow," she murmured.

Occam crouched behind the wall. "Go. Tell them you want to speak to Robbie, that you've come to join him."

Anthony took a deep breath and walked up the ramp. They peeked over again. June clung to the top of the wall, her heart hammering against the concrete.

Anthony walked across the floor toward the walkway. When the three men noticed him, they all drew guns. Anthony held his hands up and stopped.

"It's me!" His voice went high. "Anthony, Robbie's brother. I've come to talk to him."

The men lowered their guns but didn't holster them. They walked over to Anthony, a man with blond hair at the front.

"He told me to come back when I'd made a decision." Anthony backed away. "I've made one."

The blond man grabbed him and started frisking him. The other two watched.

Occam ducked down and looked at June, his eyes gleaming. "I hope you're ready for some blood."

June tensed.

He vanished.

Sam started. "Where the hell did he go?" he whispered.

She clutched the top of the wall and looked over.

The blond man was still frisking Anthony, his back to the other two.

Suddenly, Occam appeared in front of the two men. Before they could so much as gasp, Occam whipped his arms out in opposite directions. Something metallic glinted in both hands. The men reeled back, clutching their throats. Blood sprayed the concrete.

Occam wheeled around as the blond man turned from Anthony. The man only shouted, "Hey!" before Occam flung whatever was in his hand at him. The object embedded in the hollow of the man's throat and he stumbled back. Anthony scurried away.

June fought the urge to scrunch down and cover her eyes. She had seen worse than this.

The two men with their throats slashed tried to stumble toward the walkway, but Occam tripped them and they collapsed. One writhed and scrabbled at his throat, making wet choking sounds. The other lay shuddering and twitching, a pool of blood expanding around his head.

Occam turned and marched toward the blond man, who was reeling and clutching at the object buried in his throat.

Occam yanked it out and slashed his throat with one stroke. He crumpled.

Sam ducked down, breathing hard. "Jesus Christ."

June was frozen, clinging to the wall and staring.

Occam turned toward them. June could make out the blades now—a pair of straight razors. Anthony stood away from Occam, his hands fisted in his hair, shoulders up around his ears.

"When you've been alive as long as I have," Occam said casually, "you learn a few tricks. Come on." He swung one of the blades and blood flew from it.

Numb, June walked up the ramp. Sam followed her.

She tried to stay as far as possible from the bodies. The blond man was still twitching. The scent of blood hung on the humid air.

Occam pushed the blades into the front pockets of his jeans. "Pick one, Sam. In fact, pick two. One for you and one for June. I'll be the other guy." He looked at Anthony. "You just be yourself, young man."

Anthony lowered his hands, shoulders still hunched. His eyes flashed erratically.

Sam walked over to the two men. He bent hesitantly, peering at their faces.

"It doesn't have to be exact," Occam said. "I doubt anyone is left watching the cameras. But just in case. We'll move quick."

"I don't want to learn how to do this," June said. "I'll never be this vicious."

"Of course you feel that way right now, Little Red." He cupped her cheek. His hand was warm and sweaty. "But once the world doesn't have its foot on your neck, you may be surprised how much you like to strike back."

"Occam," Sam said. "We need to do this. Let's go."

Occam dropped his hand from her face. Sam was now one of the dead men. He held a hand out to her.

Occam turned into the blond man. "Yes, let's get this party started. I'm sure Robbie can't wait to cut the cake."

June walked over to Sam. She gripped his hand and tingles washed over her skin. She changed into the remaining man.

"Come," Occam said to Anthony. "Let's have a play date with your brother."

Chapter 24

They moved quickly into the walkway. Occam went in front, Anthony behind him, June and Sam following.

An arched glass roof looked out on the Institute and the street below. People still crowded the area in front of the building. Occam ducked down, and they followed suit, crouching below the waist-high wall beneath the windows.

"Is there a camera at the other end?" June whispered.

"I don't see us walking through one," Anthony murmured. "Maybe they disabled it."

The walkway was about fifty yards long, and being crouched down wasn't easy on the back, even for someone as short as she. When they reached the other end and stood upright, June drew a sigh of relief.

The walkway opened on a small foyer and a set of glass doors. Occam pulled one open. He gestured inside.

"Step into the funhouse."

June reluctantly passed through the door, into a darkened hallway. A security light shone at one end. Her skin crawled being back in the place, though she had never seen this part of it.

Sam let go of her hand.

"This way." Occam jerked his head toward the light. "Be on your guard until I know what's up."

They started down the hallway. June placed her hand on her hip, over the gun.

The place was eerily quiet. They walked through a series of hallways, past windows looking down on the courtyard. Eventually, they came out into a wide-open space with a huge bank of windows reaching up to a high ceiling. As they crossed the area, June started in recognition.

This was the atrium she had stood in and watched Micha talking to his supporters, after their first meeting; however, she'd been on the other side, which wasn't enclosed and where people congregated to smoke. She looked down into the atrium, the space dark and silent. In her mind she envisioned Micha walking across, a line of young people following him.

They entered a doorway on the other side. After a short distance, June slowed, her heart crawling into her throat. Footsteps, not their own. A figure appeared at the other end of the hallway and June froze, her hand on her gun.

Occam looked over his shoulder. "Steady. Don't shoot your sister, now."

Belle stood in the glow of a security light. June didn't relax much. They walked toward her.

"What's the situation?" Occam asked.

She handed him something: a walkie-talkie.

"Robbie is upstairs." Belle's voice was light and soft. June had never heard her speak before. "In the executive offices. We've taken all but two of his men; they're on the floor with him. Too close."

"Excellent." Occam played with the radio. "We should move before the two left start trying to communicate with their fallen comrades."

"Why didn't you just take them all out?" June asked. "It's not like Robbie can hear you coming."

Occam jammed the radio into his back pocket. He leaned toward her and whispered, "Do you know what sort of thoughts go through a man's mind as he's dying? Robbie would hear that."

June shuddered.

Occam leaned back. "Is everyone on the vampire floor?" he asked Belle. She nodded. "They're having fun."

Occam turned to June. "I'm going to stash you and Sam there for the time being, so you have someone to watch over you." He pointed at Anthony. "You and I are going up to pay big brother a visit."

June frowned. "Why are you going up with him?"

Occam sighed. "It's a good thing I'm here to think one step ahead, isn't it? Of course Anthony could go up and see his brother alone, but isn't that going to seem a bit odd?" In a blink, he turned back into the blond man he'd murdered.

"And Robbie won't realize it's you?" June asked.

"He didn't realize it was me the last time I saved your ass, did he?"

She flashed back to the night Muse died, when Occam disguised himself as a henchman.

Occam tapped the side of his head. "Shapeshifting isn't just physical, if you're good enough." He winked at Sam. "But you won't live long enough to perfect it."

Sam glared at him. "Find out exactly where Robbie is, and then come back for us. He's going to pay, and he's going to pay at my hands."

Occam shrugged. "Whatever you like. I'm just doing what I was bribed to do." He nodded at Belle. "Take them to the vampire floor. I'll contact you when I'm coming back down."

He motioned to Anthony and started down the hallway. Anthony—his face blanched even in the dim light—quickly followed. June prayed that somewhere, deep inside, Robbie actually felt some brotherly love.

Did Robbie feel anything besides spite and malice?

Belle led June and Sam to an elevator. The lights were off, but the electricity was still on. As they climbed, June stood tense, hands clenched at her sides. She had no good memories of elevators inside the Institute.

When they stepped out on the vampire floor, they were greeted by the sound of breaking glass and laughter.

June stopped short. "What the hell is going on?"

"We're having a party," Belle said. "Come on."

Reluctantly, June followed her. The vampire research floor was alive with—vampires. Vampires who were gleefully trashing everything. They were tearing things out of filing cabinets and desks. Furniture was toppled over, pictures ripped down, anything that was breakable broken. A woman was spray-painting one of the hallway walls. She had oh-so-creatively written "Death to Normals." Slightly more foul, one man was taking a piss on a pile of papers. He sneered at Sam and June as they passed.

"Guess they don't like science," June said.

They stopped outside what appeared to be a lab. The lights were on in the room, the place in massive disarray. Carts and shelves were toppled over, broken glass everywhere. Two vampires were busy smashing samples on the white tile floor, turning it red.

A third tall, wiry man with short brown hair and a long goatee strolled over to them. He held a tube full of blood. He popped the stopper and sucked it down like a shot, focused on June.

"Is this her?" He tossed the tube over his shoulder, and it smashed on the floor. "Our new sister?" He moved closer to her.

June cringed, but held his appraising, curious gaze.

"Yes," Belle said. "No touching, Logan. Occam wants to do the honors himself."

Logan looked her over. He was even creepier than Occam, gangly and hunched, and he had a weird fluid way of moving as he eased toward her. She tilted her chin up, refusing to be intimidated.

"Not bad," he murmured. He narrowed his eyes at Sam. He smiled a broad, not entirely charmless smile. "Sam Haain. It's an honor to meet you."

"Is it?" Sam said coldly.

"Why, of course. After all, I was one of the vampires who bled your brother's killers dry. That was so much fun."

Sam stared at Logan.

Logan waved a hand. "Apart from Ethan Roberts, of course. He escaped. That's the problem with those pyros. They're so good at creating a smokescreen."

Sam gasped. He took a step back.

Logan lifted his eyebrows. "You didn't know Ethan Roberts was the fourth man?"

June gripped Sam's arm. This wasn't the place for emotional revelations. They needed to concentrate on the imminent danger ahead of them.

Logan chuckled. "I don't know how the knowledge escaped you. Your brother was badly burned. You knew it was a pyro that killed him. How did you not suspect Ethan?"

"He's not the only pyro in the city." Sam spoke tersely. "And he'd been a friend of the Paranormal Alliance for a long time."

"He was a friend of Robbie's, always." Logan pointed upward. "Don't worry. If you live through Robbie, you can make Ethan pay too. He's not here, which means he's out there, somewhere. The hunt is still on."

Sam clenched his jaw. His eyes glittered. His muscles were tense under June's fingers.

"Why don't you two sit tight?" Belle said. "Occam will call soon."

Logan smiled widely. "Yes, enjoy our hospitality." He motioned around the room. "If you want to help us get rid of the trash, you can."

They declined and instead sat in chairs in the hallway, two that were still upright. Sam sat across from her, staring at the wall above her head. June flinched every time something broke, her nerves at their snapping point.

"You didn't ask Muse?" she said. "When I gave you the Oracle?"

"I couldn't bring myself to do it. She didn't deserve her peace disturbed like that."

"We have bigger things to worry about right now. Try to put it out of your head." She couldn't coddle him at the moment.

"After I found out Ethan betrayed me, I should have realized it."

"You can find him and make him pay after you take out his boss." She could barely catch her breath, her chest tight with fear and tension. "I'm sorry. I'm sorry he did this to you, to your brother, but he's not our concern right now."

"You're right. I have to take Robbie out first. His sins are even greater."

She slid to the edge of her seat. "You can't face him, Sam. He'll kill you. What are you planning?"

"Why should I tell you? You didn't tell me your plans."

She bristled. "You cannot walk up to Robbie and take him out."

"Probably not." He sat forward too. "But there's no other way. I have to stop him."

"Don't be an idiot!" She slammed her hands on the arms of her chair. "We came here to stop him from blowing the place up. That's what we have to do."

"Do you think if we stop him from blowing this place up, he's just going to fade into the woodwork?" Sam got to his feet. "He has to die tonight. He can't be allowed to plan anything else. And I'm going to end him. Me." He pointed forcefully at his chest. "It's me he's ripped the most from, and I'm going to shred him to pieces."

He walked away. Her heart was in her throat. This was a nightmare she couldn't wake up from. She couldn't talk him out of it. She couldn't stop his impending doom. But she also couldn't end the night looking at his corpse. She had to find a way, or save him.

Would Occam be willing to make him a vampire? Would Sam allow it? Maybe if she convinced him, they could remain together....

She looked around, trying to breathe. Then, she stopped breathing entirely.

Someone stood down the hallway, motionless and staring into one of the rooms. Not a vampire.

Rose.

June got to her feet. Curiosity overrode fear. A ghost sure as hell wasn't as scary as the living right now.

June walked toward her. A few feet from the ghost's stone-still figure, she stopped. Rose stared through the open door of a darkened office. Her gaze was blank, but something seemed different about her expression. It was forlorn, despairing.

June edged past her and into the room. The vampires had already trashed it, papers everywhere, furniture overturned.

"Was this your office?" June asked.

Rose didn't respond. The nameplate on the door didn't bear Rose's name, but then, Rose had been dead since January.

"I was a means to their end," Rose whispered.

June flipped on the light.

The windows were covered with the same light-blocking blinds as the rest of the floor. No one would see them up here, no matter how long the vampires partied.

June picked her way across the room. Rose remained outside the doorway. The ghost wasn't merely staring into the room, but at something.

The desk.

June approached it, stepping over the toppled desk chair. Everything on top had been pushed to the floor, including the computer, the monitor lying broken against the wall.

"Underneath," Rose whispered.

June's skin prickled. She bent over.

"Where?" June peered beneath the desk. "I don't see anything...."

June dutifully searched under the desk, running her fingers across the carpet. She tugged at it, testing to see if a piece was loose and could be pulled back, but it stayed in place.

"You have to tell me where," June said.

Rose remained silent.

June attempted to push the desk across the floor in hopes of revealing something. She pushed it a few feet but found nothing. She got down on her knees and felt around on the carpet again.

"Underneath," Rose whispered again.

June's heart thudded in her ears, her breath quick from the exertion of pushing the desk.

She pulled out one of the side drawers. Papers fell out. She flipped the drawer over. Nothing.

She did the same with the one below it and pulled out the middle drawer beneath the desk. Pens and paperclips scattered on the carpet. Laughter erupted from the doorway.

June jerked her head up. The vampire who had been graffiti-ing the wall. She breezed past Rose.

"That's the spirit!" the vampire called. "Destroy the lies!" She moved on down the hallway.

June looked down at the broad, flat drawer in her hands.

Something was taped to the bottom of it—a large manila envelope.

June stood and plunked the drawer on the desk.

"You put this here?" She scrabbled at the edge of the tape and started peeling it back. "You wanted me to find this?"

Rose continued staring, that same forlorn expression on her face.

June removed the envelope. The flap was tucked but not sealed. She opened it.

Inside was a half-size spiral notebook and a USB stick. June held them up. Rose was no longer staring at the desk but at the objects in June's hands.

"This is yours?" June asked.

For the first time, Rose eased out of her corpse-like posture. She sagged, including her face, as though melting in relief.

"Micha," Rose whispered, her voice filled with anguish. Her eyelids drooped.

Then, she faded—she didn't vanish all at once, but lifted onto the air like a puff of smoke and was gone.

June stared at the blank spot where she'd stood, quietly amazed.

"You're welcome."

Chapter 25

"Bit of an odd time for reading, isn't it?" Occam said from the doorway.

June looked up. She sat Indian-style in the middle of the trashed office, the notebook open in her lap. Her eyes burned with unshed tears.

Occam leaned in the doorway, arms folded. Belle and Sam stood behind him. The commotion from the rest of the floor had dwindled. Maybe they were running out of things to destroy.

"She was set up." June's voice was thick. "The Institute, they tricked Rose."

"Imagine that," Occam said.

"She didn't feed Micha to them. She was trying to do the right thing, but they had her cornered." She wiped her eyes with the back of her hand.

"What is that?" Sam asked.

June touched the notebook. "She was keeping a record. She wanted to find someone to expose the Institute. She knew about the serum. They came to her and wanted her to work on the project, but she refused. So they threatened her."

Sam moved into the room. He stepped over the mess, and she held the notebook out to him. He took it.

"They told her if she didn't cooperate, they would give Micha the vampire vi—" She stopped short of saying "virus." Occam was staring at her. "They would make Micha a vampire. After what happened to her sister, it must have terrified her."

Sam flipped through the pages.

"One of the higher-ups came to her," June said. "Her name was Lena Burke. She told Rose she wasn't willing to work on the serum, either, and she would help expose them. She gave Rose the powder with the receptors in it. She told her it was a secret project they were working on that would block vampirism, and she should give it to Micha to protect him."

Occam barked out a laugh. "There's no such thing."

"We know that." June climbed to her feet. "Rose didn't know that. She was frightened and desperate. She started giving it to him, but then she got suspicious." She held up the USB stick. "She began testing the powder."

Sam eyed the stick. "I take it those are the results of her tests? It could tell us a lot about that serum. The FBI would take a keen interest in it."

"They knew she was a liability." June squeezed the stick in her palm. "They knew she could expose them. That's why they killed her. That night in the parking garage, they weren't trying to kill me or Jason. When they saw she was helping us, they probably ordered the security guards to take her out. It solved their problem."

Sam closed the notebook and held it out to her. "This clears her name, then."

June took the notebook. "She doesn't care if anyone in authority knows the truth." She clutched the notebook to her chest. "Micha has to see this. He has to know his wife wasn't using him as a guinea pig. She was trying to protect him."

"This is all very touching," Occam said. "However, there's a man upstairs who's very happy to see his brother and very distracted as a result. What would you like to do with him?"

June jammed the notebook into the back pocket of her jeans. She pushed the stick into a front pocket. No time for being emotional, like she'd told Sam. Focus on the enormous obstacle in front of them.

"He has a blueprint of the explosives," Occam said. "I peeked. They're on the desk in the office where he's camped out. Sorry I couldn't snatch them. That would have looked a bit funny."

Sam turned to Occam. "Take me up to him."

June stepped forward. "No, Sam."

"I have to. I'll go up and take my best shot. Maybe it'll work."

"We're here to stop him from setting off those charges." June gripped his arm. "We can't kill him."

"We have to kill him." He looked into her eyes. "We can't stop this place from blowing up without killing him. It's not going to happen."

"Then let Occam turn me now. As a vampire, I can take him on. Maybe."

"No." Sam pushed her hand off his arm. "I want you to get the hell out of here. You've done your part."

"Are you out of your fucking mind? Do you think I'm going to walk out of here and let him kill you? We have to stop the bombs!"

"I can't defuse a goddamn bomb." He gripped her shoulders. "Certainly not as many as he's probably got set up. The only way to stop this is to stop him, and then we can get people in here who know what they're doing. I promise you, though, if he takes me out, he's coming with me."

"No." She shook her head wildly. "No, Sam! That's not how this works."

"I have to stop him." His voice cracked. "I let him kill my brother. I let him kill Muse. I let him kill my followers. I didn't see what he was doing, for years. I was blind while he worked against me. I have to stop this, here and now." The unshed tears in his eyes spilled over, slipping down his cheeks. "I can't let him destroy anything else I care about."

Tears fell from her eyes as well. "Then I'm coming with you. We do this together."

Occam flung his head back, as though exasperated, and looked at Belle.

"We do this together," she repeated, trembling. "Like we've done everything. If you go down, so do I."

Sam pulled her against him. She wrapped her arms around him. His heart pounded against her chest, matching the rhythm of her own.

"Maybe one of us can survive him," she said, muffled against his shoulder. "But if not, he won't survive both of us."

Occam sighed and stepped away from the door. He wouldn't let June die, but maybe he wouldn't let Sam die, either, if she begged him.

Sam drew back. He wiped his eyes and looked at Occam. "Take us to Robbie."

Occam gestured dramatically into the hallway. "Right this way, fearless heroes."

June felt like anything but.

Occam led them through the vampire floor, Belle at his side. June clung to Sam's hand. She had faced certain death before and come out on top. She could do it again.

The vampires watched them pass. Logan smirked at them, standing in the doorway of the lab.

Occam led them to the elevator they'd come up in. They filed inside the car and the doors slid shut.

"Here we are again," June said softly. "Part of me wishes we could let this place crumble."

Occam stared at the numbers above the door. "Robbie will know you're approaching as soon as we step out. I would strongly suggest you not go running at him with guns blazing. He's certainly going to know your intentions."

Sam wrapped an arm around June's shoulders. "I don't suppose we can disguise our thoughts from him? He's too powerful for that."

"You're not powerful enough for that." Occam huffed. "Let me do the talking, all right? It'll at least keep him from immediately crushing you like a bug."

June stared at the doors. A creeping sensation washed over her, like she could feel Robbie's mind reaching out and gripping her.

The doors opened to a darkened hallway. Occam stepped out.

"His office is here." He looked back at them. "Come on, you're so eager to die."

They followed him out of the elevator. June's vision and hearing sharpened with the adrenaline pumping through her veins. Despite Occam's suggestion, she drew her gun. Even if she was being bludgeoned to death by a telekinetically levitating chair, she would do her damndest to crack off a few shots at him.

They strode down the hallway, she and Sam holding hands again. Occam and Belle walked in front of them.

Someone stepped out of a doorway and June jumped. Not Robbie, a man she didn't recognize. He fumbled for a gun on his hip.

"What are you doing in here?" the man demanded. One of Robbie's two remaining lackeys.

Before he could pull his gun, Occam whipped one of the blades from his pocket and flung it at him. Like in the parking garage, it embedded in the man's throat. He scrabbled at it, choking and stumbling backward.

June made a mental note: if she survived this, she was going to learn how to use a blade.

Occam walked up to the man and yanked the razor out of his throat. The man crumpled to the floor. Occam turned to Belle, giving the blade a quick swipe with his tongue.

"Go find the other one," he told her. "Make him regret his life choices."

Belle rushed down the hallway.

Occam motioned with the blade. "Come on. We're expected."

They continued down the hallway, stepping around the gurgling, shuddering man on the floor.

Occam led them to a set of wooden double doors and stopped. "Ready to make an entrance?"

Sam let go of June's hand and gripped her arm. He pulled her toward him and kissed her, hard. She clutched his hair and kissed him with equal intensity, squeezing her eyes shut. Heroes had to sacrifice.

Occam made a disgusted sound. "Maybe you can just repulse him to death."

They broke the kiss and June stepped back, taking Sam's hand again. "I doubt Robbie is repulsed by much. That's the advantage of being the most repulsive thing in the city. Let's make sure he doesn't offend anyone else."

Sam smiled. "You did it."

"Did what?"

"You said you always wanted to say something cool and inspiring. There you go."

She grinned.

Occam pushed the doors open.

The room beyond looked like the office of some high-ranking official in some fancy government mansion. An enormous room, with bookshelves lining the walls and swanky furniture. Windows looked out on the nighttime city. Gigantic paintings hung around the room—one depicted Eric Greerson, another the man they'd met at the beach, Michael Paulson.

Robbie was certainly expecting them.

He stood in the middle of the room, facing the doors. His presence filled the air like pulsing radiation.

He was dressed startlingly normal: a pair of black pants and a white dress shirt. This made June's brain short out. She expected something more—armor, spikes, a dragon's spines, something. Not business casual.

The dark, ragged scar traversed his pale face. His eyes were as white as his shirt.

Anthony sat on a couch behind him, clutching the cushions. His eyes flickered like a strobe light.

"What are you doing here?" Robbie demanded as Occam strolled toward him. "How the hell are you here?"

Occam spread his arms. "Vampires, Robbie."

Robbie jerked his head toward a huge desk sitting across from the couch. Papers were scattered across it. A phone sat there.

"No use calling your lackeys," Occam said. "We already made snacks out of them."

Robbie jerked his head back around to face Occam and gritted his teeth. He then stepped sharply to the side, looking at the two of them.

"You." His voice was venomous.

Sam let go of her hand. "Me, Robbie."

Chapter 26

The doors slammed shut behind them, and June jumped. She fought the urge to lift her gun, because if she did, Robbie might rip it away. Not that he couldn't take it from her side, but it was less a focus down there.

"What is this?" Robbie demanded of Occam. "Haven't you tormented me enough? I don't want anything to do with your precious siren."

"She wants to do with you, though. I brought you your brother." Occam gestured to Anthony. "Aren't you grateful? It's a family reunion."

Robbie whipped his head around to look at Anthony, like a snake sensing prey. Anthony scooted across the couch.

"Did you know about this?" Robbie asked him.

Anthony shook his head, but then suddenly, began to choke. He gripped his throat, his eyes popping wide.

"Robbie," Occam said. "Come now, let's not be hasty. I'm not here to mess with you. I have a proposal. Hear me out before you strangle anyone."

Robbie turned back to Occam. Anthony sagged against the couch, drawing heaving breaths.

"I completely understand." Occam held up his hands. "You could kill all the humans in this room with a thought. You could tear their skulls from their faces. You could throw them out the window. I get it. Hell, I even appreciate it. Now me, you'd have to wrestle with a bit." He smiled knowingly. "You couldn't take me out so easily. Maybe not at all."

"You're arrogant," Robbie said. "Getting in my way once again, for no reason."

"Yes, Robbie, I'm the arrogant one. I'm not the one who commandeered an entire building and plan on blowing it up."

"What do you want?" Robbie strode over to him. "Why did you bring them?" He pointed at Sam and June.

"To sweeten the pot. To make you consider my proposal more seriously."

June narrowed her eyes.

"What proposal?" Robbie sneered. "There's only one thing I want from you, Occam. And you and your kind certainly went out of your way recently to make sure I didn't get it."

"Yes, you want to be king of the world. I can make you king of the world, forever. And I will, for half."

June stared at the back of Occam's head, her breath stilling.

Robbie reared back, crinkling his brow. His white eyes shone. "Half?"

"Half of this city. I want to be king too."

June's bewilderment turned to horror.

Occam thumbed over his shoulder. "I know you don't like to share your toys, that's why I tricked them into coming here. I figured if I handed them over, you'd be more inclined to say yes."

Robbie focused on them.

"You son of a bitch!" Sam lurched forward.

"Occam," June said. "How could you do this? You don't care about this fight! You don't want power."

He looked at her, affecting a pout. "I lied I'm afraid. It's something I do."

June tensed, clutching the gun tighter. She backed up to the door, but there was nowhere to go.

"I would like to rule this city," Occam said. "Think about it, the vampires in charge? No more lies, no more science done on our behalf. No more Rose Bellevues. That would please me greatly." He stepped up to Robbie and clamped a hand on his shoulder. "And you'd be one of us."

Robbie's sightless eyes were still focused on Sam and June.

"I'll turn you." Occam spoke close to Robbie's ear. "I'll heal you. And then we can have some fun with these two. I know I'd certainly like to have some fun with her." He looked June up and down.

June backed up farther against the door.

"And I'd love to have some fun with him." Robbie focused on Sam.

"So what do you say?" Occam asked. "You, me, forever?"

Robbie pulled away from Occam and glided toward them. Sam backed up too. June considered putting the gun to her head.

"It's true I don't like to share," Robbie said. "But I think this city is big enough for both of us."

Robbie herded them away from the door and into the room, between the desk and couch. June's gun flew from her hand and bounced across the carpet.

Occam stood back, watching with a smug smile. She should have run from him long ago. She never should have listened to anything he said, much less solicited his help.

She sought an escape. Another door across the room, between two bookcases. Getting there would take a few seconds—if it was even unlocked—but Robbie would need only a few seconds.

"Robbie"—Sam stepped in front of June—"This is between us. Let her go, and you and I can do this one-on-one. You already said you don't care about her."

"I care about her," Occam said.

June moved from behind Sam. "Sam, no…"

"One-on-one?" Robbie tittered. "How long do you think you could last?"

Sam winced, gripping his side. He doubled over.

"Stop!" June pleaded.

Robbie stared him down. "All I need to do is apply pressure in the right place, and our one-on-one will end. Do you still want to fight me, Sam?"

Occam chuckled. "Robbie. You should leave the torture for after I turn you. I guarantee it will be much more fun."

Sam sagged and then stood upright, breathing hard. June clutched his arm.

"You're right," Robbie said. "I'm tired of his over-confidence. Every time he thinks he has some sort of upper hand, I show him otherwise. I don't know why he's still flinging himself at me."

"Because you can't do this." Sam was still wheezing. "I can't let you do this. Even if I die trying, I have to stop you."

"Do you love the Institute so much?" Robbie opened his arms. "This place that would have destroyed all of us, given enough time? That would have taken our powers from us and given them to others who don't deserve them? What attachment do you have to this place that makes you want to stop me from putting an end to it once and for all?"

Sam took his hand off his side, standing up straighter. "I have no attachment. I would love to watch it burn. But I know what that burning means. What it means to your followers. If I allow you to go through with this, they will be unstoppable."

"That's what you fear? That we'll burn down the city? That all your followers will do the right thing and finally turn to me? Maybe you should have thought of that long ago, Sam. Maybe if you were stronger and smarter, you'd be in my place right now."

"What do you think is going to happen?" Sam gestured toward the windows. "If you take this city, there's still a whole world out there. Your crazy ideology isn't going to reach beyond the city limits. They'll take you and all your followers down with you."

"You think so? A bit hard if I'm invincible."

"You won't be invincible. You will still have weaknesses. They'll drop a fucking bomb on your head if they have to."

Robbie laughed, high and tittering.

"You're a monster," June snarled. "Nothing but a soulless, heartless monster! You're not representative of our people. The only thing you're going to do is set our kind back centuries."

Robbie strolled toward her. She stood her ground. He started circling her. An electric tingle danced across her skin, his power palpable.

"What makes you think"—he passed by her shoulder—"our kind were ever meant to mingle with the normals? That we're supposed to put on some sort of good face so they accept us?"

She clenched her jaw, staring at Occam.

"They only want to kill us."

Her hair shifted and she flinched. He hadn't physically touched her.

"They want to steal from us, hurt us, terrorize us. Why shouldn't we do the same to them?"

"Because we all have to live on this planet," she said. "And we can't make any progress if we spend all our time terrorizing each other."

He stopped in front of her. Up close, through the milky white of his eyes, she could barely make out his irises.

"Do you know how I've spent my life?" he said. "Mistreated, feared, tortured, taunted. Always someone pushing me around for being different—for being paranormal, for being deaf, for being too weird, for being too bookish, too smart, too anything. I didn't fit their mold, so they wanted to beat me down and get rid of me. Do you understand why that creates a 'monster?'"

"Yes." Tears slipped from her eyes. "I know what it's like." She held out her arms. "Do you think I look like this because I want to fit in, or because I finally gave up trying to be one of them?"

He gazed at her, silent.

"I know what it's like." She lowered her arms. "I never fit in anywhere. I watched people I cared about suffer because of me. *I* suffered because of me. I was always the weirdo. I will always be the weirdo. I just embraced it, finally. If I was going to be strange, I was going to be as strange as I could possibly be. But I sure as shit didn't go on a killing spree."

He still gazed at her. He was like an alien being, studying her, trying to figure her out.

"I know what it's like to be dying from it too." She pressed on. "I know how it makes you afraid and desperate. I know how it feels to know this thing that sets you apart is also going to eat you alive. It's not fair,

Megan Morgan

and it hurts, and it feels like if there is a God, He hates you and wants you to suffer."

The room was intensely silent. She couldn't even hear her own breath or feel her heartbeat. She was caught in the white of Robbie's eyes, in the strange, intense otherness of his face. Yet he wasn't so strange at all. Behind that grotesque mask was something frail and vulnerable and human.

Maybe she could reach that human.

Robbie shifted closer to her. He spoke lowly. "I see much of myself in you. I know you understand me."

More tears fell from her eyes.

"But unlike you, I have the will to fight the thing inside me that's trying to destroy me. I have the will to fight the ones outside who destroy me. I'm not hampered by a conscience that would only stay my hand when it needs to move."

She closed her eyes. If a human being was in there, he was buried much too deep.

"What about your brother?" She opened her eyes. "I can't imagine hurting my own brother."

Robbie sneered. "We may come from the same mother, but our similarities end there. He's always been far too complacent. Never trying to use that amazing, rare power he has. And I was always willing to tutor him." He turned and walked over to him.

Anthony cowered.

"Look at him. Look at what he is. This is not my brother." Robbie spat on him.

Anthony yelped.

Sam looked down at the desk. He glanced at June.

Robbie turned. "Yes, Sam. Those are the locations of the explosives. Even if you could get to each of them, do you think you could disarm them? My men have been in here for years, putting down the foundations for this. It's extremely complex, and several of my men are—were—" He glared at Occam. "Very intelligent engineers and explosives experts. Tell me, Sam, do you think you know more than them?"

Sam didn't reply.

"I've spent years putting the right people in the right places. Gleaning information, deploying spies, worming through their infrastructure. This has been in motion for longer than you can imagine. A few snips on your part are not going to put an end to all my careful construction and planning. If you want to try." He motioned to the doors. "Go right ahead.

We can pretend it's a game. See how many bombs you can defuse before Occam turns me and I come after you."

Sam looked across the room, toward the doors. He didn't move, though.

"Did you think teaming up with my brother would give you some advantage? Ah, but you have a soft spot for brothers, don't you? I thought when I had yours killed, it would stop you from making that treaty with Aaron. I have to give you credit, you were tougher than I thought."

Sam glowered at him. "You've taken enough from me, Robbie. You might take my life, too, but I'm going to make sure you suffer before I leave this world."

Robbie laughed. "Of course you are. I do admire you, Sam, your reckless tenacity. I would have found you a useful partner if you'd had any real sense and joined me. Even now, in your last minutes, you can't quit pontificating. I wouldn't expect any less. I'm sure Chicago would have found you a fine mayor."

"With my last breath"—Sam pointed at him—"I will fight you. I will leave scars on you. If I can't take you with me, I'll make you wish you were dead."

Occam spoke up. "How long are we going to posture? While this is all spectacularly emotional and gripping, I'm a busy vampire. I'm eager to get on with ruling the world."

"You're an asshole." June seethed at him. "You lied to me. I was actually starting to trust you. Hell, I was even willing to become a vampire!"

Occam tilted his head. "You're a naïve little girl. How was anything I ever said believable? That I didn't want power? That I didn't want to own this city?"

"You said you wanted to own it on your own terms." She clenched her fists. "You said vampires would own this city one day, but you'd do it your way."

He opened his hands. "This is my way."

"You protected me!" Her rage spilled out. "You were so focused on having me. That was all a lie? Why did you interfere with Robbie's plans once already, if you wanted to rule this city with him? Why didn't you let him kill us last time?"

Occam was suddenly in front of her. He grabbed the back of her neck, bruisingly tight. "You talk too much, siren. You should swallow that voice for once."

"Let her go," Sam growled.

Occam instead turned her to face Sam, his hand still on her neck. His fingers bit into her flesh. He rested his chin on her shoulder.

"I'm going to make him watch," he murmured next to her ear. "What I do to you."

Sam stared at Occam, his eyes blazing. "You'll never get the chance, Occam. If I can't take Robbie with me, I will certainly take you."

"So impotent in his rage." Occam let go of her and stroked his fingers across her jaw.

She was shaking.

"Is he always so limp and ineffectual?"

June waited for those fingers to grip her throat, or worse. Instead, Occam stepped away. She stumbled toward Sam. He wrapped a protective arm around her.

"Come on, Occam," Robbie said. "Let's do this. I was planning on setting off the charges tomorrow night, but since they're not all wired yet and you killed my men..." He ground his teeth. "After we dispose of them, I'll have to finish the job myself and get rid of the rest of the trash." He gestured disdainfully around the room and waved at Anthony. "Including that."

Could Anthony see his own death coming?

Occam focused intently on June, the corner of his mouth pulled up in a smirk. He winked and turned to Robbie. "A fine plan."

June blinked.

Robbie tilted his chin up. "I've read about vampires, about the process and the changes, the healing that takes place. I'm ready for it. I'm looking forward to seeing how it enhances my power as well."

"Trust me when I say there's much you can't learn in books." Occam stood in front of him, only a few inches taller, yet seeming to loom over Robbie's frail frame. "Science will never be our friend."

"Science has never been my friend."

June gripped Sam's hand on her shoulder. Sam looked down at the desk again.

Robbie turned away from Occam. "Perhaps first, we should discuss our arrangement after the change. After all, I've done all the work here, and you've—" He stopped short.

Robbie stared toward the double doors. June widened her eyes.

Muse stood there.

Occam's words flashed into June's head. With increasing powers, other powers could be activated. Robbie was a necromancer as well.

"You," Robbie snarled. "You think you're going to come from beyond death to stop me again? Where's your blade now, lap dog?"

Muse remained, her dead gaze fixed on Robbie's face.

"Robbie," Occam said, his voice tinged with bemusement. "Leave the ghost alone. She can't do anything."

"I'm not going to let her stand here and mock me during this. She's already plagued me enough. I thought when I killed her that would be the end of it."

June glanced at the desk as well, at the bomb blueprint, and then at her gun on the floor a few feet away. Robbie was distracted.

Muse suddenly spoke, still looking at Robbie. "It's a precarious game he's playing." Her voice was emotionless and flat. "Run."

June stared at her. Robbie stared at her, his face screwed up in an angry grimace. "What are you talking about?" he demanded.

But Muse was speaking to her, because Muse was attached to her, not Robbie.

June sprang into action, jerking away from Sam and diving for her gun. She snatched it from the floor. Sam reacted as well. He grabbed the blueprint, and they both ran full tilt toward the door on the opposite side of the room.

Robbie's cruel laughter followed them. "Where do you think you can run?"

"I got them," Occam said.

As they reached the door, Sam turned the knob, and it blessedly opened. June spun around and lifted her gun. She fired.

Occam was coming at them, and the bullet hit him. He yelped, jerking back, a spray of blood erupting from his shoulder. For a moment he seemed stunned, and then rage filled his eyes.

She didn't have time to savor it. They rushed through the door and into another smaller office. They crossed it and burst through the door to the hallway.

They paused briefly, Sam staring at the paper. June sucked in breaths, limbs vibrating with energy and fear.

"This way!" Sam grabbed her hand.

They ran.

Chapter 27

June expected Robbie to rush down the hallway after them like a dragon breathing fire. He was probably occupied with being turned into a vampire, though. How long did it take? How far could they run before the inevitable?

They made it to the door of a stairwell. Sam pushed it open.

In the stairwell, to June's surprise, Sam dragged her up the stairs instead of down.

"Where are we going?" She clutched his hand as they pounded up the steps. "We should be going down to get out!"

"We're not getting out."

She struggled with the pain in her side and the burning in her malnourished limbs, but they couldn't stop. She'd rather die moving.

"They're going to come after us," she panted. "What about Anthony?"

"Anthony is screwed, just like we are."

They ran up four flights of stairs, June's body flagging further with each additional step. Sam finally flung open another door. They stumbled into a hallway. Sam looked at the number plate next to the door, then down at the blueprint.

"Forty-five," he said. "This is it. Come on." He hurried down the hallway.

"Where the hell are we going?" She loped after him, fighting to catch her breath. "We can't hide from Robbie."

They stopped outside a door with a plate on it that said "electrical room."

"I think this is it." Sam pushed the door open, and they stepped into a cavernous room.

A deep hum filled the air. Hulking banks of machines rose around them, creating a maze. The high ceiling was held up by thick columns.

Sam took her hand, and they rushed between the rows of machines.

"What are we doing in here?" she asked. "What's in here?"

"I'll tell you if we find it."

As they navigated around the machines, June noticed something odd: many of the support columns were wrapped in black foam. Wires stretched between them, like a techno spider web.

"What are those?" She stared up as they ran beneath a tangle of them. "Are those normal?"

"Those are explosives. It's normal if you're about to blow up a building, yes."

They turned a corner into an open area. The walls were lined with rows of meters. Several tables sat in the middle of the space, piled with tools and electronics.

"Yes!" Sam let go of her hand and hurried over to the tables. "This must be it."

She followed him. "What is it?"

Sam dropped the blueprint on a table. "This is just a rough layout of all the explosives." He pointed out the spots on the paper, his hand trembling. "It's not detailed."

Indeed, the blueprint showed only which floors the charges were on with rough sketches of how things were connected.

Sam pointed to a box in the corner of the sheet. "That's where we are right now."

Above the box were the words "Control Room—Floor Forty-Five." Inside the box were the words "electrical room."

Sam patted a huge sheet of paper laid out on the table beneath his blueprint. "This is the real deal. All the information." He lifted the smaller one off and tossed it away.

June peered at the big blueprint. The building was intricately detailed in this one, with notes added, the bombs and all their connections mapped.

"I read up on building detonations." Sam pointed to the lower floors. "The first blasts will happen at ground level, and they'll work their way up. It has to compromise the structural integrity starting at the bottom. The charges should be in the middle of the building, so it falls inward. Ideally, anyway, for safety—but I'm sure Robbie doesn't give a shit about keeping the buildings around us intact."

"You're going to stop the bombs?" June looked up at him. "There's a lot of them."

"No." Sam walked over to a pile of electronic parts on one of the tables. "I'm looking for something else. Robbie is right. I'm not a blast expert."

As June walked around the corner of the table, she tripped on something. Something large and resilient.

She shrieked, jerking her gun out in front of her, though obviously she didn't need to shoot the person. He was already dead.

The man lay face-up, a pool of blood around his head. His blank eyes stared at the ceiling. A ragged, bloody hole had been torn in the side of his throat. He was holding a long industrial screwdriver in one hand. If he'd been trying to use it as a weapon, it hadn't worked.

Sam rushed over. "Occam's vampires came up here and took out Robbie's goons. I bet if you look around, you'll find more." He hurried back to the electronics. "At least they did us that favor."

June got the hell away from the dead body, trying not to look at it. Sam pushed things around on the table, frantically rooting through the stuff.

"What are you trying to find?" She laid her gun down on the table. "Tell me and I'll help you."

"I'm trying to find the detonator."

She had no idea what that might look like. She pictured something like an old-timey push switch that villains in movies blew up train tracks with.

"None of this may be done right." Sam looked up at the wires strung between the columns. "He said it wasn't all hooked up yet. The explosives might not be in the right places. The detonation might only bring part of the building down. I don't know how precise he's managed to get it."

"I'm sure Robbie doesn't care how precise it is, as long as he causes some destruction."

Sam opened up a black case, and froze. He stepped back, hands open. "I think this is it."

She leaned over to see.

He took out what looked like a yellow walkie-talkie, with two big buttons on it—a black one with the word "arm" above it and a red one with the word "fire" above it.

"That sets off the blasts?" June asked.

He flipped a switch on the bottom and the buttons lit up.

"If the blast caps are connected, yes." He looked up at the wires again. "Like I said, the explosion would start on the bottom floors."

"Can it stop the explosions too?" She widened her eyes at the box. "Is that why you were looking for it?"

Sam gripped her shoulder. "We're not going to stop the explosions."

She stared at him.

He held up the detonator. "We're going to set them off."

She was struggling to catch her breath still, her wounded lung working hard. Her whole body was numb, her brain a flat line. "What?" It was the only word she could get out.

"We're dead." His voice was grim. "This is the only way we can take him with us."

She looked at the detonator, her vision narrowing like staring down a long tunnel.

"And that fucking traitor Occam," Sam said. "We can't let them win."

Despite the logic, despite the knowledge they had no other choice, everything inside her rebelled, the will to live too strong.

"Sam, there has to be another—"

"There isn't. We go, they go. End of the line, for all of us."

She'd never dreamed this would end in a literal blaze of glory.

She opened her mouth to speak, but a sound echoed through the room. A clang, the sound of the door being slammed open. Footsteps.

She snatched up her gun. Probably pointless, but she had to try.

"I need a minute to arm the blasts," Sam said. "Stop them if you can."

The footsteps approached fast. June lifted her gun in both hands, her arms turning to stone, unflinching.

Neither Occam nor Robbie appeared around the bank of machines. Instead, Belle popped out. She stopped. She had her radio in hand and lifted it to her mouth.

"Occam," she said. "They're in the electrical room."

June pulled the trigger. The blast echoed through the room. Belle yelped and collapsed to the floor, her radio flying out of her hand and skittering across the concrete.

June ran over to her, and to make sure, shot twice more directly into her head. Blood sprayed June's legs, along with chunky bits of skull. Belle was still.

She turned to Sam, breathing hard. "Hurry. They're coming."

Sam figured out the detonator—it was simple, really. He pushed the "arm" button first. Nothing noticeable happened, but a moment later a light above the "fire" button blinked on, glaring red.

"This is not how I imagined the end." June's voice shook. "This is not how I imagined our end."

"Me, neither."

She stood in front of him, gun dangling at her side. She pictured the glass at Navy Pier with the angel leading the man into death. "Do you think it will be like the glass? The way you imagined for your brother?" She gazed up at him, like the man in the glass gazing up at the angel.

He cupped her cheek, a sad smile breaking his lips. "I always hoped, but I'm not at all a believer in angels. It was just a nice fantasy. At least you're here with me. Neither of us is an angel, but it's better than dying alone."

She looked down at the gun, considering a quicker way. But it was only one gun. Could she watch him go first? Could he watch her?

"I don't believe in angels, either," she said. "But I've certainly come to believe in demons."

He pulled her close, sliding his hand around the back of her neck, and kissed her forehead reverently. She closed her eyes. She felt almost at peace. Giving up the fight was more of a relief than she ever could have imagined.

"I'm sorry this became your world," he said softly. "I'm sorry you were pulled into this. If I could go back and change it for you, I would. I'd make sure you never came to Chicago."

She eased forward, to rest her head on his shoulder. "Then I wouldn't have met you."

"All things considered, that would have been the best thing that could have happened to you."

She focused on the detonator. The glowing red light shone back at her.

"Maybe we can still get out," she said. "Maybe we'll be able to run when the explosions go off."

He drew back and looked up. "If these are armed, there's no way. It'll happen fast, at least. If they aren't hooked up, the building will still crumble from the bottom. We won't be able to get out. We'll never get down fast enough."

"What if the ones on the bottom aren't armed yet, either?"

He laughed ruefully. "Then our death will be much slower and much more painful. At least mine. Occam might still spare you."

"I can't imagine the kind of life he'd spare me for." She shook her head. "What about all the people outside, the protestors? Who knows how many people we'll take with us?"

"If we don't do this, Robbie will kill them instead."

This truth was the hardest to bear. They'd made mistakes, done bad things, tried to do good things, got caught up in a web they'd woven themselves. Maybe they kind of deserved this, but the innocent bystanders below didn't.

"All right," she said. "It's this or what's coming up behind us."

As if on cue, the door clanged open again. She stiffened. Sam lifted the detonator.

Occam's voice boomed across the machines. "Do not blow up the building, you godforsaken imbeciles!"

June clutched Sam, her gaze locked on the spot where Belle had popped around the corner. Footsteps approached.

"Don't do anything!" Occam called out. "Until you see what I have for you."

She looked up at Sam. He frowned.

"I promise"—Occam's voice drew closer—"if you don't like what you see, you can bring the place down."

June swallowed, her heart thudding in her ears. Doom closed in, the walls set to fall and crush them.

Then Occam stepped around the corner.

He was a shocking sight. Blood oozed over his lower lip and streaked down his chin. His shoulder was equally bloody where June had shot him. Most startling of all, though, was the load he carried.

He held Robbie bridal style, Robbie's head hanging, one arm dangling limply. Robbie's shirt sleeve was soaked with blood, and it dripped from his fingertips. The blood emanated from a gaping wound in the side of his neck.

June stared at them, confused, disbelieving. Occam looked down at Belle.

"For fuck's sake!" Bloody spittle flew from his lips. "Vampires are your friends, June Coffin. Stop fucking shooting them!"

June couldn't respond. She opened her mouth, but nothing came out.

Occam stepped over Belle, his load swaying. He carried Robbie across the room, toward the tables, a trail of blood following them.

As Occam approached the tables, the items on them moved, pushing back slowly like a magnet repelling another. Objects clattered to the floor. June took a step back. One of the meters on the wall popped, the glass cracking. She jumped.

"He's still alive," Occam said. "A fighter, isn't he?"

June and Sam slowly approached the tables from the other side. The overhead light shone on Occam, his skin flushed, the blood continuing to drip from his lower lip. Despite the obvious psychic hysteria on Robbie's part, he didn't stir in Occam's arms.

Occam tossed Robbie's limp body on the table in front of him. Blood splattered across the blueprints. June jerked back. Robbie's eyes were open a slit, his mouth slack.

Occam licked his bottom lip. "You're right. What would I want with this fucking city?"

Chapter 28

"What are you doing?" June finally managed to speak. "I thought you were going to turn him."

Occam slammed his hands on the table. His eyes were glazed, like he was drunk.

"I never betrayed you," he said to June. "But I sure as hell couldn't tell you my plan, now could I, seeing as this asshole here is a mind reader. It had to seem legit. You had to be scared. You had to think I was going to sell you out."

The numbness encasing her broke. "You...never meant to give us to him?" Tears of relief spilled from her eyes.

"Does it appear that way?" Occam looked at Sam. "Could you please put down the goddamn bomb?"

Sam placed the detonator carefully on the table.

"But why?" June choked on her words. "You actually care about stopping Robbie from destroying the city?"

Occam rolled his eyes. He wiped a hand across his chin, smearing blood. "No, I don't. I've told you that a million times. Destroy it. It'll be easier for us to pick through the wreckage and take what we want instead of trying to wrestle it from you nattering, incompetent shitheads."

"Then why?" Sam asked. "Why are you doing this?"

"Not that you're complaining, right?" Occam smacked his lips. "I don't care about Robbie. I only have one thing I care about. I told you this."

June could finally pull in a deep breath. "You wanted to keep me alive."

"Correct. The only thing I give a shit about is getting you out of here, in one piece, for me. And this moron"—he waved at Sam, flinging droplets of blood— "decides to run into the arms of certain death, and you follow him. So what do I gotta do?" He opened his arms, indicating Robbie. "This. And let me tell you, he tastes like shit." He spat a bloody wad of saliva on Robbie's chest. "His blood is diseased. Like you, Little Red. Oh, I remember the taste of your blood."

He'd tasted June's blood on the porch of his house and claimed he could tell she was dying.

Another meter broke, the glass shattering. June flinched.

"So this was a double cross," Sam said. "You convinced him to let you drain him."

Occam made a tah-dah gesture.

The relief shining in Sam's eyes matched her own, but something else shone in his eyes too—grief, bitterness. His nemesis was defeated, but not by him.

Occam watched a tool box scoot haltingly across the table. "He's still trying to lash out. But he won't live long. Even an ultra-telekinetic, mind-reading psycho can't live without his blood."

Robbie appeared so deceptively fragile lying there limp, pale, oozing away his life. June's gun was suddenly yanked out of her hand and skittered away under the table. She didn't need it now, anyway.

"So before that happens." Occam delved into his pants pocket. He pulled out one of the closed razors and held it out to Sam. "Do the honors. He's aware of what's going on. He'll feel it."

Sam stared at the razor.

Occam pointed at June. "And then she comes with me."

June looked between them.

Slowly, hesitantly, Sam reached out and took the razor.

June stepped back. Her side ached. Her vision swam.

The razor shook in Sam's hand. Not because his hand shook—because Robbie was trying to pull it away. If he just faded out, the worst monster she'd ever known, it would be an anticlimactic, fizzled end to a terrible life. He didn't deserve to get off so easy. He didn't deserve to die peacefully. If Sam didn't kill him, she would grab the razor and do it herself.

"Do it, Sam," she said. "Before he bleeds out."

Fear shone in Sam's eyes, and pain, the kind she'd seen the night Muse died.

"I've never harmed another paranormal person." His voice was strained. "This isn't who I am. This is the opposite of what I built the Paranormal Alliance on."

"This man killed your friends," June said. "He killed your brother. He deserves this. You're saving the people you want to protect."

"I helped," Occam muttered.

A few tools fell off the table, but fewer things were moving. Robbie's chest hitched with shallow breaths. His skin had gone gray. The blood pooling around him had reached the edge of the table and trickled over the side, next to Occam's feet.

"Do it," June said. "Do it now, while he still knows it's you who did it."

"Time's running out, chump." Occam drummed his fingers on the table. "He's about to draw his last breath. Are you telling me you don't have the balls to kill a man who's already dying? I knew you were weak, Sam, but this is a whole new low."

Sam's face hardened. June stayed at his side, silently encouraging him.

Sam was still for a moment, but then he reached out and grabbed the top of Robbie's hair.

June had already seen so much death she didn't flinch. Part of her, some part that had gotten severely twisted, surged with excitement.

Sam yanked Robbie's head off the table and brought his face close to his. Robbie's eyelids fluttered, a hint of white peeking out.

"Can you hear me?" Sam's voice had gone dark. "Do you know who has you right now, Robbie?" He flicked the blade open.

Robbie let out a gust of breath, his lips, mottled dark, opening slightly. His eyelashes fluttered harder. The blade vibrated.

"It's me, Robbie," Sam said. "The one you tried to destroy. I hope it was worth it. I hope you got everything you wanted, you fucking monster."

June clenched her fists.

Sam looked at the blade. "You're too weak to fight me now. Too weak to hurt those who aren't you. Is this how you wanted to go down? In the end, you were the shortsighted one. Never trust a vampire, Robbie."

Occam snorted.

Robbie let out a weak cough. The blade shook, but Sam kept a grip on it.

Sam jerked Robbie's head. "Tell my brother I said hello. And he's welcome."

Sam sank the blade into the side of Robbie's throat, into his jugular, and dragged it across his neck.

Robbie's head thumped back on the table as Sam let go of his hair. He made a wet strangled sound, the narrow bright red slit across his throat bubbling out blood. More spurted from the side of his throat, a meager pulse. He'd already lost so much.

Sam took a few steps back and dropped the blade on the floor. June gripped his arm.

Robbie's limbs twitched. The blood spurting from his jugular grew less and less, and he slowly stilled. A rattling breath wheezed from between his lips, and his chest didn't rise again. His eyes, half-lidded, stared blankly at the ceiling.

June pressed against Sam's side, gripping his shirt. A raw coppery scent hung on the air.

"It's over," she whispered. "It's over." She gripped Sam tighter and buried her face against his chest.

He wrapped his arms around her and drew a shaking breath. "It is."

Occam clapped. "Congratulations."

June lifted her head and looked fearfully at him. Occam extended an arm, holding a hand out to her.

"Come, darling."

Sam tightened his arms around her.

"You're mine now," Occam said. "That was the deal. You don't want to betray me, do you? I have a way of dealing with people."

She untangled herself from Sam. She was resigned to this. She was ready.

Sam clutched her shoulder. "June…"

"It's all right," she said. "This has to happen. It'll be all right."

She pulled away and walked slowly around the table toward Occam.

Robbie's blood dripped on the floor, the only sound in the room apart from the hum of the massive machines around them.

"What's going to happen?" June asked. "How does it work?"

"It's easy." Occam beckoned her closer. "I'm a bit full right now." He patted his stomach. "But it doesn't matter, you don't need to drain someone first; that's where Robbie was ignorant. I do like a bit of ceremony, though. I like at least a taste before I turn someone—especially you, Little Red. Something to remember through the many, many long years we're going to spend together."

June stopped in front of him.

"And then I'll give you a drink of my blood." He touched his chest. "That's all it takes. Within the hour you'll start to feel the change. It'll be a bit uncomfortable, but not painful. You'll see the world in a whole new way. I think you'll like it."

She swallowed. "And then what? What happens after I change? What will you do with me?"

"Whatever you like." He moved closer. "We'll take a little trip. Get away from all the stress." He looked over at Sam. "You won't need these people anymore. You won't even think about them in time. Your new life will be so enriching compared to this."

"I can't leave behind everyone I love. You have to let me see them."

His eyes darkened. "That wasn't the deal. I do this for you, and you come away with me, forever. You become mine."

"Occam," Sam said.

"And I let them live." Occam pointed at Sam, still looking at her. "I don't let any harm come to the people you love."

June blinked back tears and looked at Sam. "I'm sorry. I love you. Tell Jason and Diego I'm sorry and I love them too. And my mother. Tell Jason to take care of her."

"June." Sam gazed desperately at her.

She turned back to Occam, tears escaping down her cheeks. "You did what you promised. Even more. I won't fight it."

Occam gripped her arm. "I'll let you watch, Sam. It's not going to hurt her. Just you."

Sam started around the table. She held a hand out and he stopped. Occam would kill him if he interfered.

"Just let it happen," she said. "It's all right, Sam."

It wasn't all right, but it didn't matter. She'd made her sacrifice.

Occam slipped the other razor out of his pocket and flicked it open. She hissed as he slashed the blade across her forearm.

He'd made only a small slit—enough for blood to ooze out and streak down to her wrist.

"Don't worry, darling." Occam lifted her arm. "That's the last time I'll hurt you."

He locked his mouth over the wound. She closed her eyes and turned her head to the side. The sensation of his lips pressed to her skin, wet and warm and slimy, repulsed her. After a thankfully brief taste, he drew back.

She looked back at him, gritting her teeth.

He licked his lips, as though savoring her taste. Hopefully he was right and her mind changed once she transformed, because the idea of spending eternity with him right now was unbearable.

He furrowed his brow.

"What?" she asked.

He tightened his grip on her arm and she winced. He smacked his lips. "Your blood...tastes different."

He leaned forward and licked up her arm, lapping up the trail of blood. The hot caress of his tongue made her shudder.

His confusion appeared to deepen. He worked his tongue around in his mouth.

She didn't understand.

Then, his confusion turned to anger. "You're not dying."

She blinked. "What?"

"I could taste it before—the way it was eating you. The disease. Just like him." He jerked his head at Robbie. "It's gone."

He tightened his grip painfully and she yelped.

"How am I not dying?" She tried to pull away. "I've been sick. I've been throwing up every day!"

His crazy, furious gaze frightened her. He locked his mouth over the wound again.

She pushed at his shoulder with her other hand, but couldn't budge him. "Get off me!"

"Occam!" Sam barked.

Occam jerked up, blood smeared around his mouth. His face sagged. "Oh my God." He gritted his bloodstained teeth. "Are you fucking kidding me?"

She tried to yank her arm out of his grasp.

"Are you fucking kidding me?" He jerked her toward him. "Are you fucking kidding me!"

She struggled. Sam approached them, but stopped a few feet away. "Occam, let her go!"

Occam snarled. "Did you do it on purpose? Did you think it would save you from me?"

She squealed in pain. "I don't know what you're talking about!"

"Let her go." Sam had the other razor in his hand.

Occam yanked her against him. He stared into her eyes, his face a few inches away. "Did you do this to stop me? Did you think it would work?"

"I don't know what the hell you're talking about." June tried to pry his fingers off, on the verge of sobbing.

"Does he know?"

She stilled, staring into his eyes. Her arm throbbed in his grip.

Occam tilted his head. "Do you even know?"

She couldn't process what he was saying for a moment, and then the pieces horrifyingly clicked together. The nausea, mainly in the morning. Putting weight back on. The way her eyes were fading. Her period hadn't started yet. She flashed back to the news program, the day they'd kidnapped Trina. How the woman had a baby and her powers disappeared.

He let go of her arm, and she stumbled back, gaping, and placed a hand on her stomach.

Occam started laughing, loud and cruel. She gripped the cut on her arm and looked over at Sam, eyes wide. He gaped back at her, his expression mirroring her shock.

"Your powers are what make you beautiful." Occam continued chuckling, wiping at his eyes with his forearm, the blade still in his hand. "Do you think I like you for your personality?"

She clenched her arm across her stomach, backing toward the tables.

"And now they're fading!" Occam snarled. He stalked toward her, blade raised.

She screamed, stumbling back.

"Leave her alone!" Sam shouted.

Occam jerked the blade at him. "I will put you on that table with Robbie. I can do it faster than you can do anything to me, mark my words."

June hit the corner of the table, her ankle catching on the leg, and tumbled to the floor, next to the dead man.

Her gun lay under the table, too far away to reach. She scrabbled for the nearest thing—the screwdriver in the man's hand.

Occam swooped down on her. She screamed again, trying to scramble away. He landed on top of her and gripped her throat. His eyes blazed, blood running from his lips.

"I did all of this for you!" He tightened his fingers and she choked. "I risked myself and killed for you. I moved heaven and earth for you, gave you everything you wanted. And now you're useless to me. Useless! You're both going to pay for this betrayal." He swung the blade up in his other hand.

She reacted out of pure instinct, bringing her arm up, the handle of the screwdriver clutched tight. She slammed the length of it up into his chest.

The force was more than she imagined herself capable of, fueled by sheer terror and survival instinct. Something snapped in her wrist as she drove the screwdriver between his ribs. First she felt resistance, and then a sickening give as it skewered his heart.

He pitched forward with a heaving gasp. The razor fell out of his hand. Pain shot up June's arm, followed by swift numbness. She let go of the screwdriver and scrambled out from underneath him.

"June!" Sam was there, pulling her up.

They hurried away from him, Sam holding on to her.

Occam struggled to his feet, his hand around the handle of the screwdriver. The tool was embedded all the way to the hilt in his chest, a foot of cold, unforgiving metal.

She gripped her wrist. Sam drew her back farther as Occam lurched toward them.

Occam wheezed, his shoulders hunched, teeth gritted. He slammed his other hand on the table as he wobbled. He focused on her with burning eyes.

Sam gathered her back against him. She clamped her good hand over her mouth, staring at Occam. She didn't move. She didn't breathe.

Occam leaned heavily against the table, his knees buckling. He'd gone pale. Saliva and blood dripped from the corner of his mouth.

Then his pained, furious gaze softened. His face sagged. He smiled, slow and cruel.

"This is the end," he said.

He grabbed the detonator off the table and smashed the red button.

June took her hand off her mouth and screamed, lurching in Sam's arms.

In the distance, a deep rumbling started, like the thunder of an approaching storm. The floor vibrated. The lights flickered.

"Oh my God." June wheeled around, looking at the ceiling. Nothing happened, though. The charges above them weren't attached.

But some of them were.

Occam stumbled and collapsed, the detonator in one hand and the other still around the screwdriver.

Another rumble sounded from deep in the building and everything around them shook.

"What are we gonna do?" June asked.

Sam grabbed her arm. "We have to get out of here. Now."

Chapter 29

They dashed through the electrical room and into the hallway. They ran toward the stairwell they'd come up, moving on pure instinct. Where could they go in a collapsing building?

"We have to get Anthony on the way down." June was huffing for breath as they entered the stairwell. "If he's not dead."

"We can't waste time!"

"We can't just leave him here!" She gripped Sam's arms and gritted her teeth as her wrist throbbed. "We got him into this situation. We have to get him out of here if we can."

"Fine. Come on."

They rushed down the stairs. The stairwell creaked ominously. June functioned in a frantic bubble of terror, one that sharpened her senses and focused her mind. If they could get downstairs in an elevator before the electric failed, they might have a chance. Of course, that was if there was even a downstairs left to get to. The fact that the whole building hadn't gone down already told her not all the charges were armed—just enough to put it on the precarious brink of collapse, buckling under its own weight as the foundation crumbled.

They reached the floor with Robbie's office and ran toward it. The lights continued to flicker. Glass shattered somewhere.

They burst into Robbie's office. A puddle of blood lay in the middle of the floor, a trail leading from it to the doors. The spot where Occam had bled Robbie.

Anthony lay on the couch, curled up on his side, arms over his head. June ran to him and gripped his shoulder. He wasn't bleeding. He was shivering.

"Anthony." She rolled him onto his back. "Can you hear me?"

He shuddered, his eyes flashing rapidly. He drew heaving breaths.

"He's overloading." Sam nudged her out of the way and started gathering him up. "We can't drag him between us. It'll take too long."

June backed up to give him space. The walls vibrated. Plaster dusted down from the ceiling. She looked around wildly as Sam heaved Anthony up and across his shoulders in a fireman carry.

She froze. Muse stood in front of the double doors again. She stared blankly at June.

"Go up," Muse said.

June stared at her. The building creaked.

"Answer your phone," Muse said.

June snapped out of her stupor. She patted her pocket and fumbled her phone out. The screen was blank and she had no missed calls. She turned the ringer on and jammed it back into her pocket.

"Come on!" Sam hurried toward the doors. Muse vanished.

June rushed after him. As they entered the hallway, she grabbed his arm and pulled him toward the stairwell. "We have to go back up."

"What?"

"We have to go up. Muse says so."

"We can't go up. We have to get out of here! If this building comes down, we can't be on top of it."

"If it comes down, we can't be under it, either." She pushed into the stairwell and started up the stairs. "I've learned to listen to ghosts."

"June!" He followed her.

She dashed up each flight of stairs, adrenaline fueling her, though her body was exhausted. Eventually it would give up—puke, pass out, die, or all three. She didn't know how much fuel she had left. Her chest burned with each breath, her side locked in a tight cramp.

Two levels above the electrical room, a sharp trill made her jump. She stopped on a landing, panting, and pulled out her phone.

Trina was calling.

June answered. "Trina!"

"June, are you still inside the building?" A frantic voice, not Trina's. Micha.

"Yes." She looked up the next flight of stairs.

Sam slumped against the wall, a few steps below. His face glistened with sweat. Anthony dangled from his shoulders, twitching.

"Please tell me you're on one of the upper floors," Micha said.

"Yes." She gripped the railing as her head swam. The lights flickered. "We're going up."

"Get to the roof. Keep going."

"How do we get to the roof?" She looked back at Sam.

Micha spoke fast. "There's a service elevator on the fiftieth floor. Take it all the way to the top; there's a button that says HP. When the elevator opens, you'll be in a hallway. Go all the way to the end and open the door."

"What if the electric goes out, we'll be stuck in the elevator. It keeps flickering!"

"Even if it does, the elevators are on backup generators. Go! Go!"

She threw the phone down and dashed up the stairs, taking them two at a time. Sam quickly followed. At the next landing, the number forty-eight was painted on the exit door. Two more floors.

She dug deep for the last of her energy. They were almost there—though she had no idea where "there" was or what would be waiting. She tried to keep faith in Muse.

Sam lagged behind, and when she reached the door for the fiftieth floor, she had to wait for him. He caught up, panting and staggering. She opened the door and grabbed his arm, trying to support him.

They were in a hallway. Not far away was an elevator. She led him to it and hit the button to go up.

The building groaned and wheezed, as though it were alive and suffering. Dust fell from the ceiling. Crashing and clanking sounded all around them. The lights dimmed. All of it combined was terrifying.

Thankfully, the elevator opened quickly. They stumbled inside and June prayed it was the right one. The HP button shone like a beacon, and she pounded on it.

The doors slid shut. They ascended.

"Where are we going?" Sam panted.

"The roof." She stared at the numbers above the door. They had to go up five levels.

"What's on the roof?"

Every inch of her trembled. This was the last horrifying elevator ride she would ever take in this place, for better or worse. "I don't know."

The three of them would not die like this. Four. She pressed her good hand to her stomach.

The doors opened to a long windowless hallway, a door at the other end. She slipped out of the elevator and motioned to Sam. "Come on. This is how we get out on the roof, I think."

They hurried down the hallway, their footsteps clattering and echoing. The door loomed ahead—the door to freedom? To salvation? June dragged her hand over the smooth painted wall as they ran to keep herself steady. She was on the verge of collapse.

About a hundred feet from the door, everything went black.

The darkness was startling and made her vertigo worsen. She stumbled but didn't stop. The wall shook.

"Keep going!" she yelled.

She was running full tilt and slammed hard into the door, her breath knocked out of her with a painful whoomp. The door burst open and she stumbled out into the humid night air.

Her head spun and her vision blurred. She stayed on her feet, rubbing her eyes. She lowered her hands and blinked, trying to figure out where they were.

Ventilation shafts rose around them. The faint sound of screaming sirens came from below. The acrid scent of smoke filled the air. Clouds of it rose into the sky, drifting up the sides of the building.

Another sound came from above, a rhythmic chopping sound. June looked up.

A helicopter hovered over the building. A spotlight on the bottom of it raked across the roof.

June lifted her arms and waved frantically. If it was fire rescue and they were about to be saved, or the police and they were about to go to prison for a long time, she didn't care. They weren't going to die in an explosion, at least.

The light passed over them, and she winced at the blinding brightness. She dropped her head and kept waving. The light stayed on them.

Then it blinked off and the helicopter began to descend.

Across the roof was a helipad—that's what the HP stood for. Probably to bring in supplies, patients, dignitaries, and of course, unethical scientists.

"Come on!" June motioned to Sam. They hurried toward the pad.

As the helicopter lowered, the air kicked up around them, buffeting her and tossing her hair around her face. She squinted at the helicopter, pressing against the onslaught. When it lowered enough she could see the side door was open, her heart nearly stopped.

Two people leaned out, a man and a woman.

Trina and Micha.

June lifted her arms again, raising her hands to the sky, and wept.

As the helicopter settled on the pad, the wind and noise from the propellers were overwhelming, but they certainly weren't the worst thing they'd faced that night, and she joyfully walked forward. Micha leaned out, his arm extended to her.

Getting up into the helicopter was a task, especially for someone as short as she was. Micha grabbed her arms. She shrieked in agony as her wrist was pulled. He hauled her up and in. She collapsed against him.

Sam heaved Anthony in first. "If this building goes down," he yelled, "the shockwave is gonna suck this copter down too!"

"Then get in!" Trina reached for him.

He gripped her hands and boosted himself in. He collapsed next to June. Micha pulled June away from the door, and Trina closed it.

In the cockpit, June didn't recognize the pilot, but Aaron sat on the other side, looking back at them.

Sam lifted his head and blinked at him. "I didn't know you had a helicopter."

"It's a rental," Aaron snarled. "And you're fucking reimbursing me for it!"

As they rose away from the roof, June looked out the window in the door. Sam sat up. Arms wrapped around her, multiple people holding her protectively.

The scene below opened up in horrifying detail.

The lower portion of the building was on fire. Flames licked up the sides, emitting thick plumes of black smoke. Debris was scattered around the building and filled the courtyard. People were running down the streets around the Institute. Chaos.

Suddenly, a roar rose over the sound of the helicopter blades. Half the building crumbled, cascading down in a shower of debris and white smoke. The collapse happened surreally fast, expanding the rumble pile around the building. June gripped one of the arms across her chest, heedless of her wrist.

"Jesus Christ," Aaron said from the front.

The sight was boggling, so much fire, so much smoke, the standing half of the building jutting out of the flames like a broken ruin. The rest of the city spread out around it, calm and glittering.

Sam sat on her right, Micha on her left. Both of them held her. They looked at each other and then at her. She didn't know what she felt. Horror? Relief? Joy? Her emotions had shut down at the enormity of it all. She looked down. She had gripped Micha's arm. Every inch of her body ached and her muscles were useless, but strong arms held her up.

She looked back at the broken building dwindling in the distance, orange with fire, black with smoke.

"This is the end," she whispered.

Chapter 30

When they landed, June had no idea where they were—just an airfield, a small one, with a domed hangar near the runway. As they settled gently on the ground, she made out three figures standing next to the runway. She squinted, her mind barely functioning, let alone her senses. The three rushed toward the helicopter, and she caught a flash of brilliant red. Cindy, Jason, and Diego.

The motor wound down and the blades slowed. The quiet that poured in made it obvious her ears were ringing. Trina opened the door.

Cindy was sobbing. "Oh my God. Oh my God!" She opened her arms as Sam jumped out. He wobbled, even more so as she slammed into him and wrapped her arms around him.

Jason and Diego helped pull June down, Micha above her. They were crying, too, as they gathered her into their arms. They held her upright, because her legs were no longer working.

Micha sat in the helicopter, legs dangling over the side, hands on his knees and shoulders slumped. He looked exhausted and still sickly.

"Robbie is dead," Sam said.

Cindy clamped a hand over her mouth. Her eyes shone.

"So is Occam," June said weakly, clinging to Jason.

Jason clutched her tighter and kissed the top of her head.

"So is the Institute," Sam said. "It's gone."

Cindy took her hand from her mouth. "Like…*gone* gone?"

"Gone."

Trina climbed out of the helicopter. Aaron had gotten out too. He walked over to them, fists and jaw clenched.

"Now that you're all alive and well"—his voice was clipped—"how about I fucking kill you? What part of this did you think was a good idea, Sam?"

Sam waved a languid hand. "Please don't punch me right now. Let me get my breath first."

"Muse saved us," June said. "She told us to go up instead of down. We never would have made it to the helicopter without her."

Aaron frowned at her, furrowing his brow. She didn't know if that would be the last of Muse, if she was at peace now or still had work to do.

June looked into the helicopter and then stumbled over to Cindy. Jason followed, holding her up.

"Cindy." June reached for her.

Cindy let go of Sam and reached for June too.

"I need you to do something. Do you have your car?"

Cindy blinked, tears slipping down her cheeks. "Yes."

June pointed to the helicopter. "I need you to get Anthony. Put him in your car. Drive him out to the storehouse."

Cindy tilted her head.

June looked at Sam. "Beyond human energy. There's nothing to see out there. Maybe it'll save him."

Sam nodded. "Do it, Cindy. Take him out to the storehouse. I'll call you soon with further instructions."

"Listen." June scrabbled at her arm. "Don't stay. Put him in the storehouse and leave, get away from him. Drive away and wait for Sam to call. Please, Cindy. We'll explain later. I promise."

Cindy chewed her bottom lip. "Okay. I'm so confused, but okay."

June looked at Jason. "Help her get him out and into the car."

Jason let go of her and Diego took over. Cindy and Jason climbed into the helicopter. June couldn't let him die by his own mind, not after everything he'd done and everything they'd put him through.

Trina gently touched her arm, June's wounded wrist cradled against her stomach.

"We need to get you to a hospital," Trina said. "I know a broken wrist when I see one."

"No. I need you to take me to your lab."

"I'm not that kind of doctor. I can't set bones."

"Take me to your lab first. Can you run some tests on me?"

Trina frowned. "What kind of tests? I don't—"

"Can you test the paranormal hormones inside me, see how many there are?"

"I… Yes, it's a simple stick test, but I don't know why—"

"Take me there first." She lurched away from Diego and gripped Trina's arm. "Please. I need to know."

Micha still sat in the helicopter. He and Sam were both gazing at her. "Please, Trina," June said softly.

Trina sighed. "I'm not sure how I can deny someone who just put an end to the Institute."

June sagged. "Oh, that wasn't us. That was the bad guys. The only good they ever did."

* * * *

June sat on an exam table in Trina's office in a daze. She wasn't ready to process what she'd been through. She wasn't ready to think about how she'd escaped certain death not once, not twice, but three times tonight. She wasn't ready to think about killing a vampire with a screwdriver, or Robbie bleeding all over the table, or that one standing crag of the Institute as the rest fell into burning ruins.

Her mind was full of static. She was hungry, thirsty, tired, miserable.

And nauseated.

Trina supported June's arm in a makeshift sling so she didn't jostle her wrist too much, and a bag of ice was tucked in there to bring down the swelling. June refused the painkillers Trina offered for several reasons, one being that she would puke them back up without food in her stomach.

The clinic was quiet. Everyone else was out in the waiting room. Trina was able to enter the clinic and shut off the security system. She said she would probably get a reprimand when the clinic administrators found out, but she didn't seem to care too much.

"How the hell did you get Micha out of the hospital?" June asked.

Trina was looking at a chart in her hands. "It was easier than I expected. When you texted me to say it was going down, I went to his room and told him, and he told me what you were planning. We knew we couldn't let you do it on your own, so I called Aaron. I figured if anyone could save you guys, it was him."

"And he rented a helicopter."

"It was a long shot. He said maybe we could land on the roof and get inside, get you out of there, or help bring Robbie down. We were planning a rescue mission, but not the way it turned out. The building was already on fire when we got within sight of it."

"So again, how did you get Micha out?"

"I pretended to take him downstairs for some tests. And we just… left." She shrugged. "I know the security at that hospital. Micha being 'guarded' was a lot of smoke and mirrors. They were just trying to keep the press out."

"Aren't you going to be in trouble?"

"Maybe. Micha says he'll tell them he ran away on his own, but I don't think that's going to fly." She shrugged. "I'm working for the cause now. You guys are on the right side, and I want to be too. I'll take whatever I've got coming to me."

Another soldier for Sam. At least he had her vote.

Trina had a little monitor, like a glucose monitor. She stepped up next to June and showed her the screen. It said 108. She handed June the chart.

"These are paranormal hormone levels," Trina said. "A non-paranormal person is zero. One to sixty denotes weak or practically useless powers. But"—she tapped the chart—"sixty-one to one-ten are normal levels. You're on the high side, but you're in normal range."

June smiled.

"Of course, I don't know what your level was before. Since you wouldn't let me do any tests on you."

"One eighty-six," June said. "They tested me at the Institute."

One-eleven to one-sixty were considered "high." Anything above that was "abnormally high to rare."

"I guess that explains things," June said. "Why my eyes seem duller. I don't use my powers much so I haven't noticed a change in that. Why do I still have necromancy, though?"

"If you gain a power, you're not going to lose it." Trina set the chart and monitor aside on a table. "You'll have it forever. Even if your power weakens. It'll just be weaker."

"Great, so I get to see ghosts forever." She heaved a sigh. "That's probably why I haven't seen them much lately. I only saw Rose once, at the Institute. And Muse three times…four, if you count both times at the Institute. She had trouble manifesting to me, and it's probably because of my powers weakening, not because of anything on her part."

Trina folded her arms, her gaze sharp through her glasses. "Why are your powers weakening?"

June shifted her arm and winced. She rolled her head, trying to work the soreness out of her neck. "I need you to do another test. If you can do that here. I'll pee in a cup for you."

Trina had the means. Peeing in a cup with only one good arm, while every inch of her body hurt, was a feat to rival anything else she'd pulled off tonight. She returned to the table to wait, lying down and staring at the ceiling.

About five minutes later, Trina showed her a stick with two blue lines.

June took it with a sigh. "Goddamn it. What was I expecting, though? I was stupid so many times."

"The baby changed your chemistry." Trina sounded awed. "It's been known to happen, women completely losing their powers, or having them reduced when they get pregnant. A fetus alters your DNA in certain ways. This baby is saving your life."

June turned the stick over in her fingers. "Will I resume dying when it's born?"

"In the cases I've read about, the mother remains altered even after the birth. You can't exactly put your DNA back the way it was." She scrunched up her nose. "Congratulations?"

June set the stick aside and drummed her fingers on her chest. "I have a little problem…."

"I'm sure this wasn't planned, but what a blessing in disguise. There's always abortion or adoption, if you and Sam aren't ready."

June rubbed her face. "That's the problem. I don't know if it's Sam's."

Trina didn't seem shocked or offended. She simply nodded. "Oh."

June flopped her arm at her side. "It's too close to say. I know. I'm dumb. We should have been using protection, given our situation. Sam and I were, but not at first. And Micha and I kinda screwed up one night. Here, actually. The night Occam brought us here so you could test him."

Trina shook her head. "Romance."

"I know, right?" June sagged. "Unless I'm only a few weeks along, there's no way to say for certain it's Sam's. My periods have always been erratic because of my weight issues, so they're not a good indicator. Hell, I'm not even sure how I managed to ovulate. And Occam's vampire pregnancy test didn't tell me anything except I am."

"Occam knew you were pregnant?" Trina grimaced.

"He was going to turn me. But when he tasted my blood, he knew I was pregnant. That's why he was going to kill me, and I had to kill him first." She looked down at her sling. "He only wanted me if I was powerful."

"I didn't know vampires could taste pregnancy hormones. Of course, vampires don't like being studied."

"If you can find his charred corpse, you can study him." She paused. "Is it kind of weird I'm gonna miss him a little? He pulled my ass—all our asses—out of the fire multiple times. For his own selfish reasons, but still."

Trina patted her shoulder. "That's the Stockholm Syndrome talking, honey."

June shook her head. "God. I'm the most pragmatic person on earth. I don't deal in irresponsibility. How the hell do I have baby daddy drama? How the hell do I even have a baby?"

"I'd say it's a good thing you do."

"If I'd known, maybe all this could have been avoided." She touched her stomach.

"You have a lot to think about. Go to the hospital, get your wrist fixed. Get an appointment set up for prenatal care, or alternately, an abortion. But don't make any decisions right now. You've been through a lot. You need to decompress before you can even begin to think straight."

"You said a mouthful."

While Trina shut down her lab, June went out to the waiting room.

They had the TV on, and of course, the coverage was all about the Institute. On the screen was footage of the flaming wreckage with firefighters in the foreground. At the bottom of the screen it said, "Massive Explosion at the Institute For Supernatural Research: Thirteen Confirmed Dead."

Jason and Diego sat on a couch together, Sam on the arm of it. Sam watched her as she walked into the room, his eyes questioning.

Micha sat in a chair adjacent to the couch. He was hunched over, his head in his hands. Rose's notebook lay open across his knees.

June went to him and touched his shoulder. He was trembling. He lifted his head and tears streaked down his face.

"I'm glad I could get that to you." She stroked his hair, mostly dark now, the blond faded. "It was what she wanted."

Micha shook his head. He dropped it back in his hands, choking out a sob. "How could I be so stupid? How could I think she would do that to me?"

"Because you were a victim, and it's hard to think straight when you're being victimized, trust me." She bent over and slid her good arm around him, resting her chin on the back of his head. She focused on Sam. "It's all right," she said softly. "Now you can go through the process of mourning her."

Maybe her words weren't a consolation, but it was the first step to moving on—if he was around long enough to move on.

Sam stood up. "Can I talk to you for a moment, June?"

She let go of Micha.

They walked to a hallway off the waiting room. Sam stood across from her, hands on his hips.

"Is it true?" he asked.

"Yes. I just had Trina do a test. It's saving my life. Changing my DNA and reducing my powers. I'd be jumping up and down right now if I had the energy." She took a breath. "The Institute is gone. Robbie is gone. Occam's gone. We're safe, for the first time ever, and yet... I just want to sleep."

"I know the feeling."

They were silent. Soft sounds drifted from the waiting room—the TV, Micha's sniffling.

"Is it mine?" Sam asked.

She pressed her arm to her stomach and winced.

"I don't know. If it is, what do you think about it?"

His posture was stiff. She couldn't deal with the deluge of drastic changes in their lives right now. This wasn't the time.

"What do you think about it?" he asked.

"I think I can't make any choices right now. I think it's a blessing of sorts, if it's going to keep me from dying. Beyond that—I don't want to think about it right now."

"Micha is dying too. He can't be saved the same way, obviously."

"I guess the result of his situation remains to be seen. I didn't think there was any hope for me, either. We tend to get lucky."

He walked over to her and touched her cheek.

"I do love you, June."

She gazed up at him. "I know. And I love you, too, whatever happens."

"Are you going to tell Micha?"

She shook her head. "Not right now. I'm not telling anyone but you and Trina."

He nodded.

"I need to go to the hospital." She lifted her arm. "And make up a story about how this happened, not to mention my other bumps and bruises."

"Yes, we don't want to place ourselves anywhere near the Institute tonight."

"I hope no one tracked Aaron's helicopter."

"Speaking of which." He ran a hand through his hair. "I have a check to write...."

She'd send him a thank you card too.

Epilogue

The burly bald guy lay face down on the table. He had tattoos down both arms, around his neck, across his back. June gripped the tattoo gun in her left hand, filling in the design on his meaty side, right below his ribs.

Diego walked into the room. "Anything yet?" He grabbed a chair and rolled it over next to hers.

June turned the gun off and looked up at the TV on the wall. Snow fluttered in the darkness outside the windows.

"No." She resumed filling in the design. "Shouldn't be long, though."

The bells jingled over the door in the outer room.

Diego sprang to his feet. "Food!" He streaked out.

The man on the table grunted. "He'll get it. Everybody loves him."

June stopped again and lowered the gun, watching the TV. The scene was live from Jackson Park. Sam had chosen to have his watch party near the Jackson Park Massacre memorial. People in the crowd shouted and waved and held up supportive signs.

"It's a close race." June swiveled around to her inks on the table next to her. "You think Chicago is ready for their first paranormal mayor?"

"Lots of changes in this city. I think we're ready for a lot of things. They're even talking about building that supernatural institute back up again. You see that?"

"I read about it." June turned back to him.

Jason's voice drifted from the outer room. A moment later, he and Diego walked in. Diego carried a plastic bag full of food containers.

Jason wore a wooly winter coat, snow in his hair. He shook it out. "Hard at work, I see. You know, you own the place. You're allowed to go home when you want."

"Yeah." She resumed working. "My boss is a bitch, though."

Diego sat down next to her and started rooting through the bag. "You're a life saver, Jason. How'd your audition go?"

"Awesome." Jason twirled his knit hat on his finger. "I know it's just a bit part, but I'd love to get it. I was thinking about theater too. There's a huge theater scene in Chicago."

June snorted. "You can't sing."

"Not all theater is singing." He looked at the TV. "Cindy thinks I would do great in theater."

June rolled her eyes and sat back. "Cindy would tell you anything to blow your head up."

"Thanks for your support, Sis. When are the results in?"

"Soon." June looked at the boxes Diego was sorting through. "Did you bring me manicotti? I love manicotti."

Since she now had no restrictions on her diet, she'd spent the past eight months exploring food. She didn't like pastries and junk food, much to her disappointment. Everyone else in the world seemed to be having so much fun eating that stuff. She did enjoy carbs, though, and she'd done what Jason and Diego deemed "gross experimenting," mixing all kinds of foods together to see how they tasted.

Diego handed her a box. "Here you go."

"You mind if we take a break?" she asked the guy on the table. "We got about another hour of work here."

He lifted his head. "Nah, I could use a breather, anyway."

"Grab him a beer, Diego." She sat back in her chair.

Diego got up and walked to the mini fridge in the corner of the room. June focused on the TV and plopped the box on her protruding belly—nature's table.

She was slender, so she'd started showing early, but now, with just a month to go, she was massive. She had her own gravity well at this point.

It was a girl. She was going to name her Antigone, much to everyone's bafflement. She liked it. Greek drama and all that. At least Jason thought it was cool.

Diego handed their guest a beer, the man now sitting up, and they all watched TV.

"Are you going to the party?" Jason asked her. "I know you were invited."

Win or lose, Sam would have an after party.

"I don't have anything to wear. I can't fit in normal human clothes."

Jason sighed. "You can't miss it, especially if he wins. He wants you there."

Diego side-eyed her. "It's a plus one. Party like that, they'll have an open bar."

June stuffed a forkful of food in her mouth.

The man on the table looked at her. "You're invited?" He gestured at the TV with his bottle.

Most people didn't remember who she was, and that was okay. The Paranormal Alliance members who frequented her shop did, at least. She was grateful for their business, despite her celebrity status among them.

She finished chewing and swallowed. "Yeah. Us types, we gotta stick together, you know."

Jason hung out for a while, which meant Cindy was working tonight. They'd moved in together a few months ago, a cute little place near Wicker Park, and Cindy had taken up bartending in that area. Kevin, of all people, pulled a few strings for her. Jason didn't seem to know what to do with himself when she wasn't around. They were cute—also, kind of gross.

By the time she finished the man's tattoo, the results were in. Celebration erupted on the screen and in the shop.

"We have a new mayor!" Jason shook his fists. He'd quickly adopted Chicago as his city. "This is awesome!"

Diego hugged June. "Chicago has its first paranormal mayor. I'm so happy for you guys." He kissed her temple. "You have to go to the party."

Sam stood on a stage, surrounded by people patting his shoulders, shaking his hands, hugging him. He was practically glowing, full of his own power. His presence reminded her of the day she'd met him on Navy Pier.

"That's awesome," the dude on the table said. He was sitting up, checking out his side in the mirror.

She wasn't sure if he was referring to Sam or the tattoo.

"Come on." Diego gripped her shoulder. "We'll squeeze you in a dress. It'll be a good time. You've been working too much lately."

Jason's phone rang. He answered. "Cindy! Yeah, I saw!"

June hauled herself to her feet. "I need to go somewhere first. Go home and take a shower and change. Biggest party in town, right? Can't miss it."

Diego shrieked like a little girl. He hurried out. June started cleaning up.

She turned down the TV when Sam stepped up to give his victory speech. She'd heard his speeches, even helped write a few. He appeared proud, intense, the man she'd come to know and love all those long months in seclusion.

Her client left. Diego left. Jason was the last to go, giving her a kiss on top the head first.

"Mom is flying in this weekend," he reminded her. "I keep telling her she should just move here."

June stood behind the counter, flipping through her appointment book. "Maybe we can convince her to spend the summer here and spoil her grandchild. She was so happy during the holidays, getting to see me eat Thanksgiving dinner."

Jason rubbed her back. "Today is an awesome day. I knew he could do it, and he deserves it. He's what Chicago needs."

"Yeah, I guess."

"This is all going to work out, the baby thing, you know? You've got me and Mom and Diego. And Sam. You have Sam, June. I know things have been strained, and he's been really busy, but you'll work this out."

She smiled tightly. "I'll see even less of him now."

He kissed the top of her head again. "I'm gonna go to Cindy's bar and celebrate. Have fun at the party. If Diego gets too sloppy, call me."

"Oh, I think he'd love to have you come collect his sloppy drunk ass." She pinched his side. "Be careful in Wicker Park. You know they still discriminate there. The normals are going to be particularly riled up tonight."

"The city is ours."

He left the shop. She stood in the silence, staring at her appointment book. She had a full day tomorrow, and the next day, and for weeks. Sam wasn't the only one keeping busy.

The day he brought her to the shop and told her it was hers, she'd thought he was kidding at first. Her wrist was still in a cast, and she couldn't even think about tattooing yet, but they had to get the place up and running, anyway. June wasn't even sure she wanted to stay in Chicago.

Yet here she was, eight months later. The shop had been officially open for six. She'd already made Sam's purchase money back, thanks to the Paranormal Alliance. Diego had relocated to Chicago. He said he couldn't be without his partner in crime, and he liked Chicago, anyway.

She didn't hate the city as much as she used to. Yet part of her still felt like she was being kept here against her will.

She closed down the shop, bundled up, and stepped out into the snowy night. Down the street, voices and celebration issued from one of the bars. She hurried to her car at the curb and got in.

She drove through the slushy nighttime streets and out into the sprawling empty darkness of the industrial areas beyond the boundaries of the city. She drove until she reached the storehouse.

As she parked next to the building, the door opened, spilling yellow light into the night. She got out of the car and waved. Anthony stood in the doorway.

She crunched through the snow toward him. "Hey. We have a new mayor."
He stepped back to let her inside. "Yeah, I saw on the Internet." His
eyes flashed. "I never thought I'd see the day."

She stepped into the warmth of the building. Anthony had made a cozy
home for himself. The place had both electricity and running water in the
form of a sink and toilet, but Anthony had built the rest on his own.

The main room was his living and sleeping area, warmed with space
heaters, packed with furniture and decorated so one almost didn't notice
the place was a sagging old shack. He'd also made himself a kitchen with
electric burners, a toaster oven, and a microwave, and additionally rigged
up a shower with a hose from the sink. He had Internet through his phone.
A nifty hermit cave. June wouldn't have minded living there.

Sam's party in Jackson Park was streaming on Anthony's laptop.

"I'm happy for him," Anthony said. "He deserves this."

She peeled off her gloves. "It'll go down in history; that's for sure."

"You want something to drink?" He walked over to a cooler in the
corner. "I haven't seen you in a while. I'm glad you stopped by."

"Water is fine." She looked at the laptop. "I guess there really hasn't
been much news, until now."

He returned with a bottle of water. She took it.

"How's Micha?" He opened his own bottle.

"He says he feels fine, but I don't believe him. It's been a good solid
two months without him needing to go back to the hospital. They have
him on so many drugs."

"Is he still being hounded by reporters?"

She nodded. "Every day. He can't even walk outside without someone
snapping his picture. I feel awful for him."

"He's a strong guy. I think if he keeps a positive mindset, he'll be okay."

"I don't know how he can stay positive." She leaned against the back
of Anthony's couch. "He's trying to work again, trying to get back to
some kind of normal life, but it's hard. The way people treat him…" She
shook her head. "I wish he had some of my anonymity."

Anthony looked down at her belly. "And how are you doing?"

She rubbed her stomach. "All right, I guess. I've been working a lot.
Keeping my head down. Enjoying food. Sometimes I wish I could just
hide out here with you."

He chuckled. "I've thought about going back a few times, but…" He
shrugged. "I know since they found Robbie's remains they want to talk to
me. I don't feel like being grilled by the FBI."

She took a drink and lowered her bottle. "At least they think your brother blew up the Institute—well, he did, in a way. Chicago's greatest monster is dead."

He gazed at the laptop. "It's everywhere online, all the time. Reminding me I can hide, but I'll never escape it. I'll never really be free of him. And his followers are still out there. They won't stay in the shadows forever."

They fell into silence.

June glanced at the screen. "I gotta go to that party. I support Sam. I still love him, I just… I don't know how I fit in this world. His world."

"I know the feeling," Anthony said softly.

She looked at him. He stared back at her, his eyes flickering.

"Can I ask you a question?" she said.

"I already know what it is, of course." The corner of his mouth jerked. "And yes, I can. I didn't used to be able to see that far into the future, but now that there's no noise, now that I can focus with no interference—I can see so far ahead. It's amazing."

She touched her stomach. "So you see who the father is?"

"Do you want me to tell you?"

She could have an in vitro paternity test, and Sam had offered, on several occasions, to pay for it. Something kept stopping her. If she didn't know, maybe she could delay the inevitable fallout. Lately she'd been researching adoption, without mentioning it to anyone. She wanted to have choices, and she didn't want anyone trying to talk her out of those choices.

Knowing might take those choices from her.

She shook her head. "No. Not yet."

He nodded. "I understand. But if you ever decide you do want to know, I'm here."

She almost asked him if things would be bad, if there would be drama and heartbreak. But she didn't want to know that, either.

She looked back at the screen and sighed. "I suppose I should go get ready. I just wanted to stop by and say hello, see if you'd heard."

"It was good to see you again." He stepped over to her. "You're a good friend, despite our rocky start." He hugged her, her belly keeping them awkwardly far apart.

"Maybe I'll come hide out with you for a while one of these days."

He showed her out. As she walked to the car in the gently falling snow, he called out to her. "Hey, June?"

She turned. He leaned out the door, snowflakes catching in his curls.

"It's all gonna be okay," he said. "You're gonna be okay. Wear your black dress tonight. You'll look good, and you'll have more fun than you expect."

She smiled. "Thanks, Anthony."

She got in the car and drove off into the wintry darkness, back toward the city, back toward life as she knew it, at least for right now.

Meet the Author

Megan Morgan is an urban fantasy, paranormal romance, and erotica author from Cleveland, Ohio. Otherwise, she is a bartender by day and purveyor of things that go bump at night.

For more info please visit meganmorganauthor.com.

Twitter @morgan_romance
www.facebook.com/megan.morgan.author

Keep reading for a peek at the second book in Megan Morgan Siren Song series

The Burning City

On the run . . .

It's been four months since the head of the Institute of Supernatural Research was murdered. But that doesn't mean June Coffin is out of hiding yet. In a world where being different can get you killed, it's best to keep a low profile. Especially for a Siren who can control other people with the call of her voice. That goes double if your powers might be inexplicably growing...

On the hunt . . .

But June isn't the only one trying to clear her name. There's Sam, the charismatic paranormal rights leader, and Micha, the first human on record to go paranormal. All of them must bargain with a mysterious vampire named Occam Reed if they want to stay alive.

Out of time . . .

As tensions increase between humans and paranormals, June must decide who to trust. If only she could hear the song inside her heart...

On sale now!
http://www.kensingtonbooks.com/book.aspx/31861

Chapter 1

Vampires made a badass gluten free blackened chicken dish; however, their interior decorating skills were woefully lacking. June Coffin didn't need to be an artist to realize this. A colorblind hillbilly would attest the diner was the tackiest thing on the planet, and June had seen drag shows in San Francisco.

The diner, on Chicago's North Cleveland Avenue, was called Zing's and had a campy fifties feel crossed with Steampunk, which went together about as well as the concept sounded. The fixtures were bulbous and metal and the walls decorated to look like the interior of some retro spaceship that also served hamburgers and Coke. She sat in a black leather booth with a brass frame, the seat cracked and dingy from previous occupants. The scuffed black Formica table held her empty plate.

A sketchpad lay open in front of her. She drew in it with one of the few luxuries she'd been afforded in the past four months: a set of colored pencils. They weren't quite a tattoo gun, but her fingers itched to make art. All the other things she'd lost she'd been able to get used to—a cell phone was useless when she couldn't contact anybody, she'd forgotten how to put makeup on, and entertainment felt hollow and pointless. The outside world in general remained easy to access, though. They had laptops and cable at the house. Unfortunately, the news was always bad.

"How was everything?" a lilting female voice asked. A tall, curvy blond waitress stood over her. The woman had fangs.

"Great." June slid the empty plate toward her. "Can I get a refill?" She tapped her pencil against her coffee cup.

If she had to sit around, she might as well work up a good caffeine buzz. The restaurant didn't serve alcohol, though they should have, if they were going to torture patrons with the décor.

"Certainly." The waitress smiled unnecessarily wide.

Yes, I've seen your friggin' fangs. She wore a fifties style waitress outfit, but black—the only thing in the place not completely ridiculous.

June had learned a great deal about vampires. Sam Haain, erstwhile—if currently sequestered—leader of the Paranormal Alliance, had insisted she get a thorough education, and June didn't argue. She needed to know what she was up against, after all.

Vampires didn't naturally grow fangs. Those who had them either had veneers or had their natural teeth filed down. As Sam had explained, normal human teeth could bite through flesh. It was no more difficult than biting through an orange skin. He demonstrated this with an orange, which squirted her, prompting her to swear and throw a cup at him.

Biting proved much easier with fangs, though. Fangs were a sure sign of a militant vampire. The pussy ones went to the transfusion clinics to cleanse their blood.

She paused drawing and nibbled on the end of her pencil. She hadn't smoked since a certain incident in which a bullet went into her lung, but the compulsion to stick something in her mouth remained. She'd already endured the jokes.

The diner wasn't crowded—a few people sat at tables and several at the long curving black lunch counter. No one paid attention to her, though she was probably one of the few non-vampires in the place. Most of the other patrons were young and hip, with stylish haircuts and way too many vintage accessories. She didn't understand why more vampires weren't punks.

A girl sat a few booths away, alone, facing June. She had long dark hair and wore a halter top and a short jean skirt, her legs crossed beneath the table. She sipped from a coffee cup while reading a magazine, but occasionally, she glanced up at June.

The waitress returned with a silver carafe and refilled June's coffee cup.

"Thanks."

"Nice drawing. You an artist?"

June only had an outline at the moment, a skull with a cat winding luxuriously around it, the cat's eyes narrowed viciously at the viewer.

"Yep," June said.

"That's a badass little kitty."

"She certainly is."

"Looks like a tattoo or something." The waitress tilted her head to the side, exposing her neck. A faint pink scar traversed the tendon there.

"I'm a tattoo artist," June said.

"Oh, yeah? Where do you work?"

Steam rolled off the black surface of June's coffee cup. "Nowhere close."

The waitress smirked. "Didn't think you were from around here."

June took a sip of the coffee as the waitress sauntered off. The liquid burned her tongue. Hot coffee was one of the best things on earth, right up there with a clean shot of whiskey, a smooth red wine, and getting finger-banged in a stolen Porsche.

As June set her cup down, someone at the counter turned on his stool: a young sinewy black man. A mass of red-tinted dreadlocks peeked out from under the slanted baseball cap he wore.

She pulled the menu over and eyed the dessert page. This was her first night outside the safety of the house in weeks. Vampires were alive and physiologically human and so had all the old human needs, including the need to consume food. The myths were wrong. They didn't drink blood for sustenance, but to battle the bacteria that infected them.

While June pondered if there was anything on the dessert menu that wouldn't give her hives or death, a shadow fell across the table. She looked up. The young black man stood over her. He had starter gauges in his ears and snakebite piercings in his lower lip. He was cute.

"This seat taken?" He gestured to the booth across from her.

"You've been sitting at that counter as long as I've been here," she replied. "Do you think it's taken?"

The guy grinned, showing brilliant white, slightly crooked teeth and fangs bigger than the waitress's fangs, narrow and curving. How could he even eat with those things? He slid into the seat, dark eyes glittering. June closed the menu.

"I'm Zack." He leaned on the table, arms folded. He had tattoos winding down both arms, black on his shiny brown skin. His nails were pale and manicured. A scent like patchouli wafted across the table.

"Hi, Zack." June picked up her pencil. She started sketching again, adding detail to the cat's fur. She would have a hell of a time tattooing an image of a Tortie, with all the different shades and patterns.

"You ain't a vampire, are you?" Zack said.

"How'd you guess?"

"The clinic dogs don't come around here much." He leaned closer. "And you don't have fangs. But it's pretty obvious even without that."

"Are you looking to bite me or pick me up? Just so I'm clear."

He sat up, his fang-baring grin coming back. "Which are you hoping for?"

She put her pencil down. "Well, I'm not letting your mouth anywhere near my sensitive parts, that's for sure."

Zack laughed, a nice masculine soothing sound. June tilted her head. Vampires didn't have any sort of glamour, but Zack seemed to glow with attractiveness. Maybe he was just naturally hot. He leaned forward again.

"You're June, aren't you?"

She reared back and arched her eyebrows. "Finally! Jesus."

"Sorry to keep you waiting. You seemed to be enjoying your food. Didn't want to interrupt."

She slapped the sketchbook shut. "I haven't been enjoying sitting around here while the waitress tries to figure out which part of me is the most tender." She paused. "You said your name is Zack...."

"I'm not Occam. But I can take you to him."

"Good." June stuffed her pencils back in their pouch. "I'd like to get this over with."

"It's not that simple." Zack placed a dark hand on hers, stilling her.

A tingle shot up her arm.

He patted her hand. "I need to make sure you are who you say you are. Who we've been told you are."

"And how are you going to do that? I don't exactly have an ID. They took that at the Institute along with everything else."

"You do have a special power." He slid his hand off her. "Siren."

"Which I can't use on you," she pointed out. "Vampire." Vampires were immune to supernatural influences. No one knew why.

Zack sat back. "That girl over there." He nodded at the girl absorbed in her magazine. "She's not a vampire, either. Tell her to show you her panties."

The girl had her head ducked, her hair swooped forward.

"Are you serious?"

"Quite. She's been checking you out."

"Maybe. But that's not exactly my...thing."

Her savior-turned-friend, Cindy, had mistaken her for a lesbian once too. Why was that a thing with her? Was it her gruff exterior? Her lack of makeup? Her thick fingers?

"You want to meet Occam or not?" Zack said.

June finished jamming her pencils in the pouch. "I already hate vampires."

Zack smiled widely, showing his fangs.

June tossed some money on the table for the bill, gathered up her sketchbook and pencils, stuffed them angrily into her bag, and slid out of the booth. After a moment's hesitation, she strode toward the girl. Zack remained in the booth.

June stopped next to the girl's table. She looked up at June, her brown eyes questioning.

June cleared her throat and said softly, "Show me your panties."

June held her breath. A moment passed. Then slowly, the girl turned in her seat and unfolded her legs. June backed up but tried to shield her from view of the other patrons.

The girl gripped the edge of her jean skirt and slid it up. Her thighs were unusually thick for a woman. She hiked the skirt up until she exposed the triangle of her white silk panties.

A low laugh drifted over from June's former booth.

"Thank you," June said. "Go back to your magazine and forget about me." She turned and marched back to Zack, who was still laughing.

"Can we go now?" she said. "Take me to your freakin' leader."

"Occam is no leader." Zack slid out of the seat and rose to his feet. He stood a few inches taller than she, but then, everyone did. "Occam is a visionary."

"Yes, he's certainly got some clever disciples." The girl had slid back into the booth and returned to her magazine. "That's the first time I've used a junior high parlor trick since I made my brother's friend show me his dick."

"Now that's enchantment." He led the way out.

Despite the late hour, the streets were crowded. They were in the Nocturnal District, the main hangout for vampires in Chicago. Every vampire that passed eyed her, their leers more unnerving than the usual ones she got out on the streets, as if they wanted to eat her.

"Slow the hell down," she eventually huffed, a few paces behind Zack.

Zack slowed. The night was warm and humid, typical mid-May weather in Chicago, unlike Sacramento where it was dry and cool at night in the summer. June had discovered humidity was not her friend.

"I got shot in the lung." She struggled for breath as she fell in step beside him. "I smoked like a chimney every day until it happened, so it's taken a long time to heal. I don't have any lung capacity anymore." She also had limited use of her right arm, the muscles connecting it to her torso having hardened with scar tissue.

"You were shot at the Institute?"

"Escaping the Institute." June cringed as a tall Latino man looked her up and down with slow deliberateness.

"I don't know much about you." Zack slowed his pace more. "They don't talk about you anymore. Every once in a while someone will say, 'I wonder what happened to the Coffin twins?' but the papers and the news have bigger fish to fry these days."

"Yeah, Chicago seems to have forgotten we were ever here." Had they forgotten about them in California, where they were from, too?

"Most people believe you're dead," Zack said. "Normals think you were killed by the SNC or the Paranormal Alliance, and paranormals think you were killed by the Institute. It's convenient. A dead woman no one cares about. Best subterfuge you could ask for."

They stopped at a street corner, vampires sliding past them. Music thumped, muffled and distant, from nearby clubs. Neon seared the darkness. The smell of smoke, booze, perfume, and car exhaust hung thick in the air, making it even harder to breathe.

"Yeah, being dead is great."

Did their mother think they were dead too? Had she accepted the idea? When June closed her eyes at night, it wasn't thoughts of the Institute that plagued her, or the war that was slowly building, or what they'd do if the police—or worse, Eric Greerson's supporters—finally found them. Her mother's face loomed in the darkness. Her friends back home in Sacramento, uninformed and uncertain, haunted her thoughts. She was a spectator at her own funeral and she couldn't get her balance.

They crossed the street. On the other side, Zack slowed again.

"Not far now," he said.

Fewer people walked this side of the street. Shadows crawled across the pavement and cloistered them. She raked a hand through her hair—her right one, because Aaron's doctor told her the more she used her arm the better it would get, which so far had proved to be bullshit. Her arm fell limply to her side again when she lowered it. Her long hair was badly in need of a cut and shaping, not to mention her roots were showing like a bitch. Haircuts and shopping trips were infrequent while in hiding.

"Don't feel bad about being forgotten." They turned a corner onto a darker, quieter street with low-rise buildings and a few houses. "This whole city is about to collapse. It won't matter soon." He chuckled, an oddly tantalizing and companionable sound in the darkness.

"Sounds ominous."

"At the end of the coming clash, the vampires will be the only ones left standing. That's the beauty of neutrality. We'll be sifting through the ashes when the fight is over."

"Like scavengers. Picking the bones for treasure."

The media heralded the "coming clash" every day on TV and in the papers. The Paranormal Alliance grew more and more radical by the day.

Members of the SNC—Aaron's secular non-paranormal group—had either joined forces with Sam's group or splintered into rogue factions. All of them wanted the Institute closed down. Unrest swelled: violence, riots, even bomb threats and arson attempts on the Institute.

"The scavengers will inherit the earth," Zack said. "When the rest of you get done killing each other, we'll gather up what's left and rebuild this city in our image."

They stopped outside a brick building four stories tall, a small porch attached to the front. Lights were on in many of the windows. Music drifted out.

"How's your lung feel about climbing stairs?" Zack asked. "Because we're going to the top floor, and the elevator's been out of service for months."

June groaned.

www.ingramcontent.com/pod-product-compliance
Lightning Source LLC
Chambersburg PA
CBHW020747250626
47155CB00003B/956